"Actions speak louder than words."

Tears trickled down Abigail's cheek. The ice in her eyes frightened Gray. "I'm going back to Savannah. I'm going home."

"Abby." This couldn't be happening. Not when he was in love with her. "Stay. Please."

"We're done." She wheeled her bag around him.

Desperate, he blurted out, "I think I'm in love with you."

She stopped. Her shoulders shook. She turned around, pity filled her face. "You can't buy my love, Gray. That's not how it works. It's something I would have given freely."

Panic bubbled inside his chest like lava in a volcano ready to blow. "I'm not trying to buy your love."

She didn't even stop.

He ripped a hand through his hair. He'd been trying to help her, for God's sake, and she'd thrown everything back in his face. He told her he loved her. He had the money. He could fix her problems. Make her life easier. Why wouldn't the stubborn woman let him help?

Dear Reader,

Thank you for purchasing my debut Harlequin Superromance novel.

Southern Comforts is about sisters—a subject I know well. I have three of my own. And they are the reason this story came to life.

My sisters and I visited Savannah and I fell in love with this lush, quirky, vibrant city. In the magical historic district, oak trees drip with Spanish moss and squares are filled with fountains, statues and flowers. Ghost stories abound. The city made me wonder.

What if a group of sisters were struggling to run a bed-and-breakfast in their family's old mansion? Maybe the oldest sister, a chef, has big dreams but every dollar is poured into the business? Why not force her to feed a cynical, rich developer for six months? Will her lack of money and his wealth put barriers on their developing relationship?

Settle back with a glass of sweet tea and one of Abby's brandy pecan bars and find out if Abby and Gray can find their happily-ever-after.

I'd love to hear what you think. Please contact me through my website—nandixon.com. Or stop on over if you want some of Abby's recipes.

Happy reading,

Nan Dixon

NAN
DIXON

—

Southern Comforts

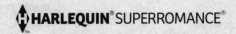

HARLEQUIN® SUPERROMANCE®

ISBN-13: 978-0-373-60891-1

Southern Comforts

Copyright © 2014 by Nan Dixon

Printed in U.S.A.

™ www.Harlequin.com

Nan Dixon spent her formative years as an actress, singer, dancer and competitive golfer. But the need to eat had her studying accounting in college. Unfortunately, being a successful financial executive didn't feed her passion to perform. When the pharmaceutical company she worked for was purchased, Nan got the chance of a lifetime—the opportunity to pursue a writing career. She's a five-time Golden Heart finalist and lives in the Midwest where she is active in her local RWA chapter and on the board of a dance company. She has five children, two sons-in-law, one grandchild, a husband and one neurotic cat.

To Mom and Dad—you taught me to work hard to make my dreams come true. I wish you were here to celebrate with me.

To my family—no one can top your enthusiasm, support and laughter. Don, Nicholas, Meghan, Dan, Allison, Joe, Anne, Matthew, little Lily, Dad E and Diana. My characters would be lucky to be blessed with loud, crazy, loving families just like ours.

Special thanks go out to my writing community. First, my critique groups—Ann Hinnenkamp, Ann Holliday, Neroli Lacey, Greta MacEachern, Leanne Farrell and Kathryn Kohorst. You've put up with my messy drafts, lack of conflict, lack of scene goals and pushed me to become a better writer. Second, my Golden Heart sisters: the Unsinkables, Starcatchers, Lucky13s and Dreamweavers. When I've stumbled, you picked me up, dusted me off and pushed me back into the fight. Even better, you're there to celebrate my successes—Prosecco for all! And I can't forget my RWA chapter, Midwest Fiction Writers. Our authors are gracious and willing to share their knowledge. They know how to pay it forward. Thank you.

I also want to thank the people who took a chance on me—Laura Bradford and Megan Long. I appreciate your confidence and advice.

And finally, this book is for my sisters—Mo, Sue and Trish. Without our weekend, I never would have written *Southern Comforts*. (Where are we going this year and will I get another series idea?)

CHAPTER ONE

Rule #1—The guests are always right, even when they're wrong.

Mamie Fitzgerald

"SCORE ONE FOR Team Fitzgerald." Abby tapped the occupancy permit against the porch railing and waved to her contractor as he headed for his truck. The final room on the second floor could be used.

She propped open the bed-and-breakfast's bright blue doors. For February 1, the day was gorgeous, with temperatures hitting the mid 70s. Sunlight streamed through the leaded-glass side windows and sparkled on the foyer's crystal chandelier. The gold streaks in the green-marble entry floor gleamed.

Abby wanted *all* of Fitzgerald House to sparkle like the entry.

That meant renovating the rest of the third floor, and finally the carriage house. They just needed a reasonable bid, money and a whole lot of luck.

Her hand brushed the brass plaque set inside the door.

Fitzgerald House—1837

Savannah, Georgia

Bed & Breakfast opened

March 1, 1998—Mamie Fitzgerald

Owners—Abigail, Bess and Dolley Fitzgerald

As always, she made a wish. *Let the renovation costs be reasonable.*

A fresh floral arrangement graced the console table. The tang of lemon wax mingled with the warm scent of the foyer's sandalwood candles. While she'd been with her contractor, the cleaning crew had performed their magic.

With no one in the entry, she held out her arms and twirled, tipping her head up, grinning. The sparkling prisms were all she could see.

Dizzy, she stopped. Whoa. Hadn't done that since she'd been young.

She'd call Mamma and her sisters later. Let them know they were one room closer to finishing the main house restoration. And she was one room closer to opening her restaurant in the carriage house. She gave herself a hug. One step at a time.

Abby walked over to the Queen Anne secretary they used for a reception desk. The front door opened as she logged on to the computer, and she glanced up. "Welcome to Fitzgerald House. How can I help you?"

A man stalked toward her. Black brows framed laser-blue eyes. He was tall and lean. *My, my.* Some days God took pity on working women and gave them something to dream about. She indulged in a quick fantasy of running her fingers through his thick black hair. Too bad he had a frown on his face and a cell phone glued to his ear.

Mr. Fantasy dropped his bag, smiled and pointed to the phone, holding up one finger. He patted his pockets.

She handed him a pen and a piece of paper.

He mouthed a thank-you.

"Severn," he said. "What was the contracted completion date?"

He wrote down the date in bold slashes.

"What's the remaining payout?" Again the hand-scrawled numbers on the paper.

Abby tried not to look, but the number was big. With that kind of money, she and her sisters could finish off the third-floor rooms and still have enough left over for new linens.

"So what's the problem?" the man growled.

Abby stepped back, giving him privacy. She wouldn't want to be the person failing to meet this man's expectations.

"The only way I'll extend the deadline is if we re-contract," he stated. "You have options. Overtime, more crew. Think about it and get back to me." He switched off his phone without so much as a goodbye.

Apparently Mr. Fantasy hadn't gone to the same customer-service seminars Abby had.

She stepped back up to the desk. "May I help you?"

"Grayson Smythe. *S-m-y-t-h-e*." The man's voice was as rich and smooth as bourbon, and his smile was just as intoxicating.

Abby searched the reservation system. Nothing. She tried incorrect spellings of the man's name. Nada. She tried his first name as his last. Still nothing. Her fingers tapped the desktop in a staccato beat.

The man's intense gaze weakened her knees. His dark eyebrows came together over his bright blue eyes.

Had the system eaten another reservation? She forced a smile. "Do you have a confirmation number?"

"No, I don't. My assistant confirmed the details yesterday." He leaned over the desk, staring at the computer screen. The temperature in the room seemed to climb ten degrees.

Abby kept smiling, but her mouth wanted to droop into a frown. She couldn't. She had a guest in front of her.

A quick patter of feet turned her attention to the open door.

"I told you, Mama." A blond boy, maybe four or five years old, darted into the entry. "I'll catch you a rainbow."

Catch a rainbow?

Sure enough, the sunbeams were now hitting the chandelier, and rainbows danced over her head. She hadn't noticed, too caught up in their guest. But she really hadn't noticed the rainbows since she'd been young. Since her dad had died.

Mr. Smythe whipped around at the noise.

"Joshua!" A thin young woman entered behind the boy. "Come back."

The boy jumped up and down, his hand outstretched. His clothes were clean, but the knees were patched. "I can't reach them!"

Mr. Smythe knelt in front of the boy. The little boy's eyes widened and he stepped back.

Abby moved out from behind the desk. She didn't want her guest snarling at this cute kid the way he had on the phone.

Before she could rescue the child, Mr. Smythe said, "Would you like me to lift you up?"

The boy held up his arms. "Yes, please."

Abby's eyebrows popped up as Mr. Smythe held him in the air. Joshua's hands waved, trying to grab hold of the colors.

"Hold still and the rainbow will shine on your fingers," Mr. Smythe said.

"I'm sorry." The woman leaned a hand against the desk, catching her breath. "He's so fast."

"Are you looking for a room?" Abby shouldn't judge the woman, but her clothes were…worn.

"Oh, no." Color washed over the woman's pale face. "I'm here about the help-wanted ad."

Abby nodded. "The housekeeping position?"

Both the man and the boy had rainbows coloring their palms. Mr. Smythe whispered to the little boy and Joshua giggled.

Joshua's mother straightened. "I know the ad is a couple of weeks old, but is the position still open?"

"It is." Abby smiled, trying to put the woman at ease. "Marion, our head of housekeeping, has left for the day, but if you come back tomorrow morning around ten, I'll make sure she knows you're coming in."

"*Thank you,* thank you." The young woman's smile erased the furrows in her forehead. She turned.

"Oh, what's your name?" Abby asked.

"Cheryl."

"Nice to meet you, Cheryl. I'm Abby." She hoped Marion would hire the young mother.

Mr. Smythe set the boy down.

"Mommy, I held a rainbow." Joshua threw his arms around her legs. "But I let it go so other kids can see it."

Cheryl took her son's hand. Staring at Mr. Smythe, she whispered, "Thank you."

"No reason to thank me." He grinned, flashing a dimple. "I held a rainbow, too."

A flutter filled Abby's chest. She loved dimples. And her guest had been kind to the child.

Cheryl gave him a nervous smile. Joshua took a little bit of the sun with him as the two of them headed down the porch steps.

"That was nice," Abby said, starting to type again. Where was Mr. Grayson Smythe's registration information?

"I like kids. The world hasn't screwed them up yet." His shoulders rose and fell. "Are we done?" The don't-screw-with-me tone was back in his voice.

Sometimes Marion or her sisters left her notes about reservations, so she searched the desk. A piece of paper peeked out from underneath the keyboard. The breath she'd been holding whispered out.

Abs—The Kennedy Suite is booked for six months starting Feb 1! Guy named G Smythe booked it. Marion's aware—you were in wine tasting when I finished the deal. Until I move other reservations around, I can't get his info in the system. 10% discount for the long-term stay and charge by the week. Two-week trial. We have to replace the reservation system!!! This year—not next. It's…

Abby refolded the paper without finishing Dolley's message. Her techy sister always ranted about their software. The replacement reservation system had to wait at least one more year, possibly two. Dolley knew that.

"I'm sorry that took so long." She wanted this stern man to know the Fitzgerald House team weren't incompetents. "I've found your information."

Her professional smile was fixed in place, but her heart rate revved into overdrive. She wanted to twirl and hoot. A six-month booking in their biggest suite meant cash. It wouldn't refill the gap left by last year's emergency purchases, but even at a discount, this was fantastic. "You're staying with us for six months?"

"That's correct." The man's bourbon-infused voice came with a crisp Yankee accent. "I've agreed to a two-week trial."

Abby quickly made his key cards. They would show Mr. Smythe Southern hospitality—Fitzgerald style. After two weeks, he'd be begging to stay.

As his credit card processed, she gave him her spiel on breakfast, tea and appetizers. "And since we're Irish, there's always Jameson whiskey in the library."

The man took it all in without reaction. Usually a guest nodded or smiled.

"Your room is on the second floor and to the left. There's an elevator down this hall." She pointed. "If you have any other questions, please ask our staff. We at Fitzgerald House want you to have a pleasant stay."

"Thank you." He slung his briefcase over one shoulder. "I'd like dinner brought up at seven o'clock tonight."

"I'm sorry." Abby shook her head. "We don't offer dinner—just breakfast, tea and appetizers."

He raised an eyebrow. "My assistant negotiated dinner with my extended stay. Your chef's reputation is the reason I chose this establishment." He did a little finger wave. "Perhaps you should call someone."

She reopened Dolley's note.

We have to replace the reservation system!!! This year—not next. It's archaic. One more unusual request on this res—twenty-five dollars extra per day for providing box lunch and dinner. Agreement's in the mail.

Her stomach churned. Dolley hadn't just been ranting about the software glitches.

She blinked, hoping the message would change. No luck.

She'd already seen how Mr. Smythe reacted when people didn't live up to their commitments. As upsetting as it was to be blindsided like this, she couldn't violate Dolley's agreement.

She dug deep for the graciousness Mamma had drummed into her daughters. "You're correct. However, we don't have room service. May I invite you to eat in the kitchen?"

"I'd prefer eating in my room."

Panic bubbled up in her chest. His room wasn't an option, since there wasn't enough space. And the dining room was already set for breakfast. Swallowing, she said, "I know you'll be more comfortable in the kitchen."

His eyes narrowed. "How much will it cost me for room service?"

The B and B wasn't set up for room service. Mr. Smythe would end up hunched over his coffee table. "I'm afraid it's not a matter of money."

"It's always about money." He raised an eyebrow. "Why don't you get your manager?"

Didn't anyone ever say no to him? She stood a little taller. "I'm Abigail Fitzgerald, owner, manager and your chef. This is an unusual request, and I apologize that Fitzgerald House can't accommodate room service. I would be pleased to serve your dinner *in the kitchen* at seven o'clock. Your dining experience will be more pleasant there."

He took a long, slow scan from her head down to her sneakers. She refused to squirm under his scrutiny.

"Fine."

He turned toward the stairway, his long legs taking the steps two at a time.

She headed down the hall. What was she going to cook? Catching a glimpse of her reflection in the mirror, she saw a streak of dirt on her face and dust all over her shirt.

What must he have thought? Now his dinner would have to be even more amazing.

THE ROOM WAS SPOTLESS. Gray wondered what the "owner, manager and chef" had been doing to get so dirty. Well, he had two weeks to decide if this arrangement would work.

Two people had recommended staying at Fitzgerald House. Derrick, the man who'd needed to liquidate his Savannah warehouse, had raved about the food, and his attorney. Gray hadn't planned to acquire property in Savannah, but his frat brother, Derrick, had been desperate.

And Gray had needed a break from Boston. Drawing in a deep breath, he pressed the aching sinuses between his eyes. God, he'd had this headache for what seemed like months.

Maybe Savannah would bring him peace. Maybe his mother and sister would leave him alone. Maybe he'd figure out what was wrong with his life. He rolled his shoulders. Right now, all he wanted was to get settled in his room.

While he unpacked, he listened to the CNBC newscasters dissecting the financial markets. He rolled his shoulders. The past two weeks in Boston had been a work marathon. Standing in the entry while trying to register, all he'd wanted to do was get into his room.

But helping the kid catch rainbows had been fun. He used to do the same thing with his little sister. He hadn't thought about that in years.

He set his laptop on the small desk. It barely fit. Now he understood why Ms. Fitzgerald had asked him to eat elsewhere, but, damn—the kitchen?

He was in the Jacqueline Kennedy room. Her biography on the coffee table had him smiling. His face ached a little, as though he hadn't smiled much lately.

He opened the French doors to his private porch overlooking a courtyard garden. Leaning on the railing, he took a deep breath. The air smelled green. New. Nothing like the snow he'd left this morning.

There was a tiny table and a couple of chairs on the porch. He could imagine having a beer or a glass of wine or even a shot of whiskey in the evening. But dinner? No way. At least the sofa in front of the flat-screen television looked comfortable.

His cell phone rang. Reluctantly he moved back into the room and answered it. "Smythe."

"Adam Severn." Severn's frustration vibrated through the phone. "We'll meet your deadline. Everything will be demolished and drywall installed and taped on time."

"Good." Severn didn't respond. Gray's eyebrows shot up. Did Severn expect gratitude for meeting his contractual obligations? "Anything else?"

"You're all business, aren't you, Smythe?"

Should Gray tell him he'd helped a little boy catch rainbows? Nope. Wouldn't want to ruin his image. "When I grant bids, I expect the work to be done as agreed."

"Well, the plumbers and electricians better not hold us up."

"Phillips will coordinate the other subs." His manager would monitor the timelines. "Make sure you keep him informed."

"I won't be held accountable for other people's screwups," Severn growled.

"Get your own work done in a professional manner, and we won't have any problems." Gray shook his head. Severn's company would never work on another one of his projects.

Severn grunted an acknowledgment and hung up.

If his time in Savannah was going to reduce the pressure he'd been under, he needed to turf problems like Severn to his project managers. Next time.

He opened one of the complimentary bottles of water and booted up his laptop. He rolled the cold bottle across his forehead.

Gray quickly worked through his emails. He hesitated, staring at Gwen's familiar address. He paused with the cursor hovering over the open-mail icon.

He shook his head and deleted the message. Why was Gwen still emailing him? He'd broken up with her. Just last week he'd asked her to stop contacting him. One of the bonuses about being in Savannah was that he wouldn't constantly run into her.

He worked through the rest of his mail. Nothing he couldn't handle from here. Pushing away from the desk, he checked his watch—almost five-thirty. The B and B's wireless connection had worked flawlessly. Excellent.

He had time to kill before dinner. He could walk around town or have a glass of wine. What quality of wines would a B and B serve?

The floor plan showed him a route to the library

via a back stairway. As he emerged on the first floor, Abigail Fitzgerald's voice filled the hallway.

"Damnation, Dolley," she said. "Why didn't you warn me about Mr. Smythe?"

He jerked to a stop before she could see him.

"I should have known about his meals before he checked in," Abigail said.

He shouldn't eavesdrop from the hallway, but his feet wouldn't move. He leaned his shoulder against the wall.

"The money is great. But—six months. Why didn't you tell me?"

There was a pause.

"Whoops?" Pause. "We have to communicate or we'll look like amateurs."

Not amateurs—just inept, Gray thought.

Another pause.

"Dolley, you owe me, big-time. The dining room's already set for breakfast. The desk in his room is too small for meals. For pity's sake, I was so stunned, I invited him to eat in the kitchen."

Invited? She'd insisted.

"I don't have time to Google guests."

Okay, that was enough. He would not listen to them discuss him like some sort of…object.

"I will not dig into his background." She hummed, "Na, na, na," just like a kid. "Stop. I don't want… He's worth *how much?*"

Enough. He moved to the doorway.

"Dolley Madison Fitzgerald, what would Mamma say?" Abigail scolded.

He rapped on the door frame. Loudly.

She turned. Her mouth dropped open and then snapped shut. "I have to go."

Gray crossed his arms.

"Could you schedule a family meeting?" Her hand shook, mussing her hair. "Samuel did the walk-through with me this afternoon."

She swiveled away from him, but he heard her say, "The third-floor remodel is going to be expensive."

Maybe that explained the dust on her cheek when she'd checked him in.

Again she paused. "Next time, baby sister, talk to me." Her low voice caressed the air, heating his body. She glanced over her shoulder.

Yup, still here.

"He's eating lamb chops tonight, and no, I don't have enough to feed you. I'm mad at you. I have to get to the wine tasting. Love you."

Gray waited.

Abigail stood and turned; her fluid movements reminded him of a ballerina he'd dated several years ago. She walked around the small desk and stopped in front of him.

"Can I help you, Mr. Smythe?" Her tone was cool, but her gaze was fixed on the wall over his shoulder.

She couldn't look him the eye. Interesting. His jaw unclenched. She didn't look like the same woman who'd checked him in. Her golden red hair fell to her shoulders. The brows above her bewitching green eyes were furrowed.

His gaze slid from the top of her head to her high

heels. From what he could tell, she had a killer body. Her silky top and skirt exploded with color. Pity, the skirt reached her knees.

"May I help you, Mr. Smythe?" Her brisk tone didn't match her blushing cheeks.

He waited, letting her guilt hang between them. "I guess I got turned around looking for the library."

"Please, follow me." She brushed past him, and her perfume, a dark, spicy scent, curled through the hallway. His attention gravitated to the sway of her hips. A man could lose himself in those hips.

He jerked his eyes up. He wasn't in a position to act on any chemistry with his innkeeper. He was here to do a job. He was here to clear his head.

"Is your room comfortable?" she asked as they entered the lobby.

"More than adequate." Charming, even. "If the service lives up to the room, I won't have any problem staying here for the duration." Some demon in him had him adding, "And I'm looking forward to lamb chops tonight."

Abigail's cheeks turned an even deeper shade of red at the reminder that he'd overheard her gossiping. "I know the service will exceed your expectations. Please notify the staff if there's anything you need."

He followed her through carved-oak pocket doors that she glided open. Five middle-aged women milled around the library.

Mahogany bookshelves and paneling gleamed. The cherrywood floor included a central mosaic that echoed the stained glass above it.

"Good evening. I'm Abigail Fitzgerald," she announced to the other guests. "I hope you enjoyed Savannah today."

Gray stepped farther into the room. The curved walls ran up two stories and were topped by a stunning stained glass dome.

As the women greeted Abigail, Gray moved next to the fireplace. He stroked a finger over the feminine lines of the white marble mantelpiece.

Abigail turned to him. "Ladies, may I present another guest, Mr. Smythe."

The women waved, and a couple of them asked, "Where are you from?"

"Are you on vacation?"

"How long are you staying?"

"I…I… Boston. Working. Six months." He escaped over to the table of appetizers.

Abigail grinned as she opened bottles of wine.

"Ladies—" she nodded to him "—and gentleman. Tonight, you'll taste Argentinean wines. They're from the Mendoza region. The first is Malambo Chenin chardonnay. See if you can note the citrus and spice tones." The cork made a hollow sound as she freed it from the bottle. She continued describing the wines and popping corks. "Enjoy."

Abigail knew more about wines than he did. He edged closer to the table, gesturing to the food. "What's all this?"

"Chimichurri. Try it on the toast points." She handed him a plate. "Next to it are vegetable empanadas with a dipping sauce. And that's a shrimp and scallop ceviche."

He blinked. "You made Argentinean appetizers?"

Abigail flashed him a chilly smile. "Of course. They match the wine."

She aligned a serving platter and adjusted the flame under a warming dish. Once everything met her standards, Ms. Fitzgerald glided out of the room. How did she move in those heels?

He frowned. Not a complication he needed. He was here to build condos.

GRAY TRIED TO enjoy the excellent wine and appetizers alone, but the women drew him into their conversation. By seven, he longed for solitude. Instead, he needed to endure eating in the kitchen.

Maybe he should have offered an additional twenty bucks to eat in his room. The B and B had to have a table they could set up. He just hadn't quantified his request properly. Everyone had their price.

Gray touched the kitchen's swinging door, but didn't push it open. Would Ms. Fitzgerald watch him eat? Talk his ear off?

The past two weeks, he'd worked like a Tasmanian devil. And he'd avoided Gwen and her endless calls and emails. Even before he'd broken it off with her, he'd been exhausted from her constant demands to attend parties where he'd have the same conversation night after night with people who lived off their trust funds.

For the past year, he'd felt like a piece of laminate

in the middle of a tiled floor. He was functional, but out of place. Something had to change. Maybe here in Savannah he'd get some perspective. And when he returned to Boston he'd find…peace?

He shivered. Crap, was this him getting in touch with his feelings?

Gray shoved that thought away and pushed open the door. He walked into a symphony of scents. Lamb, onions and an herb he couldn't identify. Abigail stood in front of a mammoth range with a monster stainless steel hood.

The walls were a warm yellow, and the granite counters were golden brown offset by white cabinetry.

She'd changed into a T-shirt and tight jeans. Oh, yeah, her body was as beautiful as he'd imagined. "You changed again."

She jumped at the sound of his voice. "Oh, I can't cook in silk—oil splatters. Have a seat, Mr. Smythe."

With a nod, she indicated a table in an alcove off the main room.

"Please stop calling me Mr. Smythe. It makes me feel old. People call me Gray."

The single place setting looked…lonely. A folded napkin sat beside a salad plate filled with field greens and red peppers. He frowned. He'd never noticed so much color in his life. He waved a hand at the table. "What about your dinner?"

Why had he asked? He'd wanted room service. Would have worked while he ate or watched the news. Now he didn't like the idea of sitting here and having her serve him.

"I'll eat after you're finished." She turned back to the stove.

"Eat with me." It sounded a little harsh, so he added, "Please."

Abigail raised one eyebrow. "It's not…appropriate."

She made the idea sound as if he'd suggested torture.

"I'd feel uncomfortable having you watch me eat, especially since I've interrupted your normal routine."

"But you're a…guest."

"One that's made an unusual request, right?"

"Yes." She gnawed on her lower lip.

He shrugged, not understanding why convincing her to join him seemed so important. "Eating together would be the most efficient way to handle this situation, Abigail."

"Efficient? I can see that." She stirred whatever was in the pan and then turned back to him. "I'll eat with you, but only if you call me Abby. Six months of being called Abigail and I'd feel like I was back in grade school."

"Done—Abby." The name didn't quite fit, but he'd already acknowledged that there were many sides to her. Maybe it fit one of them.

A bottle of Malbec, one of the wines he'd sampled earlier, sat breathing on the table. He poured a glass and then looked around for another glass for her. "Where are your wineglasses?"

"I can get everything set in a minute."

"I'll help."

"Umm." She chewed on her lip again. He assumed

that was her sign of nervousness. "Wineglasses are in the butler's pantry." She pointed across the hall.

He found a glass and figured he might as well grab dishes for her, as well. There were a bunch of flowery china dishes in the cabinets. No doubt she'd want them to match. He grabbed a plate in the same pattern from the shelf. If he guessed right about the meticulous *Miss Abby,* she wouldn't want him to use the wrong one.

He carried her glass to the stove. "Wine for the chef."

The space between the island and the stove was barely big enough for the two of them. He held the glass over her shoulder. The stainless steel vent reflected her frown as he crowded into her space.

"Thank you." She scooped the glass out of his hand. "But you didn't have to."

"I don't mind." A hint of Abby's perfume mixed with the great smells emanating from the pot on the stove. After all the appetizers, he hadn't expected to be this hungry, but his stomach growled. "Smells great."

Abby turned with a pan of potatoes and set it on the island, creating a barrier between them. She mashed the potatoes by hand, adding butter and sour cream.

He added another mile to his morning run.

"Please, sit," she said. "What kind of salad dressing do you like?"

"A vinaigrette if you have it, otherwise Italian."

"I've got balsamic vinaigrette." She pulled a bottle out of the refrigerator.

Gray eyed the commercial-size appliances. The Fitzgerald family had invested in quality goods. This was a working chef's kitchen.

Abby carried their plates to the table. The food looked as appealing as any meal he'd enjoyed in a fine-dining restaurant.

As Gray started to cut his lamb chop, she bowed her head and whispered a prayer. Hell. Christmas was the last time he'd heard grace at a table.

She grinned at him. "Please, eat."

Gray sampled a piece of lamb and then a forkful of potatoes. He followed up with crisp green beans. The flavors melted in his mouth. Closing his eyes, he moaned. "I've died and gone to heaven."

She laughed. A deep, mellow sound that vibrated through his body.

"How many marriage proposals do you get after people sample your cooking?" he asked.

"Not that many. Single men don't usually stay with us. We get a lot of Moons, Repeaters and sister groups."

"What?"

"Oh, sorry. Moons are honeymooners and Repeaters are anniversary couples. Bess came up with the idea of advertising for sister groups." She took a sip of her wine. "We use our own shorthand."

He frowned. "Are there really that many sisters around?"

"They don't have to be related. It's basically a weekend for women with a common interest—most of the time they know each other already, but some come for the theme and make new friends while they're here. We organize their activities during their stay. For the Scrapbooking Sisters, we reserve a parlor for them to work in. And Nigel, our driver, will take them to a supply store where we've arranged a discount." Her grin spread across her face. "Scary Sisters visit haunted houses and attend a Ghost Pub Crawl. But my favorite is the Sommelier Sisters weekend. It doesn't get better than tasting wines."

"Interesting marketing angle," he said.

She waved her hand. "It fits our brand. My sisters and I run the place, so we do what we can to play that up."

Gray took a few more bites of the best meal he'd had in months. Abby was a fantastic cook. At least Derrick hadn't steered him wrong when he'd recommended Fitzgerald House.

"It sounds like you're planning some renovations," he said.

Her expression fell away like dirt being stripped by a power washer. "We're hoping to work on the third floor."

"Hoping?"

"There's a lot of water damage up there." She absently shook her head, the ends of her hair brushing the tops of her breasts.

"You had roof problems?" He forced his gaze back up to her face.

"In the fifties." She nodded. "They repaired the roof but didn't fix the damage. I guess they weren't using those rooms at the time."

When she'd talked to her sister, she'd said it was *bad*. Had she meant the damage or the cost?

And why should he care? The sections of Fitzgerald House he'd seen were clean and well maintained. That was all that should concern him.

But renovations were his business. His parents' library restoration had gotten him hooked on rehab and real estate. "So what are your plans for the third floor?"

"More guest rooms." She leaned forward, propping her elbows on the table.

He ate while she talked. He plied her with questions because it was fun to see her eyes sparkle. Not that it took much prodding. It was easy to see that Abby really loved this old mansion. Loved what she and her sisters were creating.

Strange to think of working with your family.

"When do you start?" he asked.

She took a deep breath and exhaled. "Right now we're exploring the costs."

She nibbled on her lip again.

Gray looked down at his plate, unwilling to watch her teeth work over that pink lip. He blinked in surprise. His plate was empty, though he didn't remember finishing.

Abby noticed and brought over a tray of bars.

"Coffee?" she asked.

"Decaf, if you have it."

Abby ground beans and set an industrial-size coffeemaker to brewing. She gathered up a notepad and a pen before sitting back down.

"I need to get an idea of your likes and dislikes," she said. "Any allergies?"

"None. If tonight is an example, anything you fix will be better than what I normally eat." He'd have to look at pushing his housekeeper to be a little more adventurous.

"Beef, chicken, fish or pasta?" she asked.

"All of the above. I'll eat anything." He bit into a bar and groaned. "This is incredible."

"Brandy-pecan bars." She made a note.

His cell phone rang. His sister.

"Excuse me." He paced to the back of the kitchen and a small sitting area. The space overlooked a patio and garden lit with decorative lights.

"Hey, gorgeous, what's up?" he asked, finishing his bar.

"How could you?" Courtney blasted his eardrums without saying hello.

"How could I what?" Gray knew why she was calling. He forced his fingers to relax. He should never have dated his sister's best friend.

"You sent Gwen a breakup bracelet," she whispered.

How did his sister know that was his trick for getting out of relationships? "Stay out of this."

"Hang on," his sister said.

"Courtney, I'm—"

"Gray?" Gwen's voice was so soft he almost couldn't hear it over his pulse pounding in his ear.

He closed his eyes. "Yes?"

"Did you mean the bracelet to be a…a parting gift?"

It had worked before. "We broke up."

"But Mark and Liz invited us to the vineyard next weekend."

"Gwen." He closed his eyes. "I won't be home. I'm working in Savannah. Even if I was back in Boston, we wouldn't be together."

"But they—" She hesitated. "They expect us."

His headache was back, the pressure building behind his eyes. He should have read her emails. Then he could have avoided this phone call. "I'm not coming home for a damn party."

In the beginning of their relationship, going to parties every weekend had been exciting. Gwen's energy had been thrilling. Now she exhausted him.

"When will you be home?" Her voice was quiet and low. "I think we should talk."

He took a deep breath. "No, Gwen."

"Oh."

He rubbed the cords at the back of his neck. What a disaster. There were too many connections between his family and Gwen's. Their mothers had been best friends since college. Gwen and his sister had been best friends forever. It had been a mistake to date someone so entrenched in his family.

He glanced over at Abby as she filled a coffeepot. "I have to go. Say goodbye to Courtney for me."

He shut his phone off, but the call had soured his night. Back at the table, Abby poured his coffee. He tried to neutralize his expression, but he could feel himself frowning.

"I need to ask about lunch," Abby said. "Are sandwiches okay?"

He added cream to his cup and sipped. Great coffee. "Sandwiches are fine."

"Tomorrow," she said, "I'll serve your dinner in the dining room."

Listening to Abby describe the B and B's renovations had been the most relaxing dinner he'd had in months. He didn't want to eat alone in the dining room. "I'm good with the kitchen."

"Really?" She blinked her green eyes.

He wanted to relax. And she was calm personified. "The kitchen's fine."

CHAPTER TWO

Rule #11—If cleanliness is next to godliness, then Fitzgerald House must be heaven.

Mamie Fitzgerald

GRAY CHECKED THE time again. The contractor was late. He glanced at his checklist. It was already early February, and he expected to complete the bulk of the work by July.

He shoved at a stack of cardboard piled in the middle of the warehouse floor. He couldn't wait to get the renovations started, but he needed a contractor that matched his work ethic.

He'd never planned to work anywhere but New England. He had no contacts in Georgia. He shook his head. He hadn't been able to refuse Derrick's offer, even though he was sure his frat brother had remembered his phone number only because he'd needed financial help.

Gray slapped his hand on his thigh. Was Gwen any different? If he hadn't been rich, would she have ever been interested in him? Maybe their similar backgrounds and mutual friends had made their relationship too easy.

Maybe that was why he couldn't commit. His family wanted him to settle down with Gwen. But he wasn't convinced a relationship with her would make him happy.

Relationships were a mystery to him, but he trusted his construction knowledge. He knocked on the sturdy interior wall. This place could withstand hurricanes. It had been built on the Savannah River for commercial reasons, but the view would guarantee a good price for the condos.

The sun struggled to shine through grimy windows. He poured coffee from the thermos the B and B staff had sent with him this morning. He took a moment and sipped the strong brew laced with a hint of cinnamon.

At least here in Savannah, he wouldn't have to attend parties and benefits for causes he didn't believe in. He could avoid making small talk with people who didn't share his interests.

His dinner conversation with Abby hadn't been small talk. They'd talked about creating legacies and restoring a building that would last generations. There'd been reverence in her voice when she'd talked about her family's B and B.

His phone buzzed. Gray looked at the call display and smiled. "Hello, Mother."

"Grayson, how are you, dear? How's Savannah?" Her voice was so Bostonian. So different from the warm drawls he'd heard all morning at Fitzgerald House.

"I'm in hog heaven."

She groaned. "Gray."

"Georgia's great." He nodded. "The bed-and-breakfast I'm staying at is fascinating. Built in the early 1800s, so you'd feel right at home."

"I hope you're not implying anything about my age, dear."

His laugh echoed in the cavernous room. It sounded—rusty. "Never."

"Well, no matter how lovely Savannah is, I could never live there. Boston has always been home."

His mother had grown up in Maine, but he let it go.

"How's your warehouse?" she asked.

"A disaster."

"I hear that glee in your voice. You can't wait to get started."

"You know me too well."

"Well, don't be too much of a perfectionist. I would like to see you sometime. I know you said you'd be there for six months, but you will come home, won't you? It is possible I might miss my only son."

And he would miss her. If he was here long enough, he might even miss his sister, Courtney, but not if she kept pushing Gwen his way.

"I'm sure I'll come home, but why don't you and Dad come down for a long weekend? I can work something out with the B and B. If my breakfast today was an example, you won't push away from the table unhappy. Pick a weekend."

"Your father and I will discuss it."

"Savannah is amazing," he said, trying to entice her.

Yesterday, he'd driven through tree-lined streets around squares filled with statues, fountains and people. "I walked to work this morning." He sighed. "February, and I wore a light jacket."

The city had sparkled. The air had been cool but springlike. The stress had sluiced off him like paint peeling off a roller. "Come down. Bring Dad and that little pest, Courtney, too."

"She's the reason I called."

"What's she done now?" He watched a container ship chug up the river.

"Rather, it's what she says *you've* done. Did you really leave town without telling Gwendolyn?"

"We broke up." He turned away from the window, fingers choking the phone. "We haven't seen each other for over two weeks."

If what he and Gwen had had was special, he should miss her by now. All he felt was relief.

"Gwen's from such a good family," his mother said. "I'd hoped you'd suit. She's lovely and her manners are impeccable."

Gwen was his match, born of the right people, as his mother would say. She'd forced him to think about more than work. Forced him to get out and *do* things. She loved parties, loved having throngs of people around her. And she rarely took no for an answer.

Her constant need to be with people, to party, had worn him down. That wasn't how he wanted to spend his life. He wasn't sure what he wanted, but it wasn't crowds of people. Peace seemed too nebulous a desire.

"We don't fit together." Gray rolled his shoulders, trying to ease the itch that ran up his spine. Why couldn't he commit? "I'm not ready to settle down."

"Perhaps absence will make the heart grow fonder. Her mother and I would love to plan a wedding."

Her words were like the plop of slushy Boston snow invading the collar of his coat.

"I'm not ready to get married," he said. "My life's exactly the way I want it."

"If your life was perfect, I'd have grandchildren."

"So talk to Courtney."

The picture of Gwen as a mother didn't materialize. Abby's colorful skirt floating around dynamite legs flashed through his mind. He shook his head, but the image stayed.

"You're thirty-three," his mother began. It was a familiar refrain and not one he wanted to listen to again.

A door banged, rescuing him.

"The contractor is here." Finally. "I'll call when I can."

No time to argue grandkids with his mother. He had a building to finish.

CHERYL CLOSED THE back door of her car with her hip. "Here's your backpack," she said, handing Joshua the Spider-Man bag filled with his few toys.

They walked through a garden leading from the B and B's small parking lot. God, her car looked out of place among the guests' late-model SUVs and luxury sedans.

Her car was more rust than metal. The gray hood didn't match the green paint on the rest of the body. And it sucked gas and oil like a drunk with a bottle of hooch. But it ran.

They passed a small table in a secluded section of the courtyard. The table was all but hidden from the house and the rest of the grounds. This would work.

She swallowed. "Okay. Wait here for me." She pulled out Josh's crayons and a pad of paper. "Draw a picture. I won't be long."

Josh looked up at her, his big brown eyes so like Brad's her heart ached. "Can't I come with you?"

"I wish you could, but I have to talk to a woman about working here." She had to get this job. To keep Josh safe, she had to earn a living. She couldn't go back.

"The rainbow house?"

"Yes, the rainbow house." She knelt and cupped his cheeks. "Don't talk to anyone. If you get scared, run to the car and lock yourself in."

"Like you taught me when Uncle Levi smelled funny and got mean." He looked solemn and older than a five-year-old ever should. "I run fast, jump in the car and slam down the lock."

"Yup." She was a terrible mother, leaving her son alone in a strange place like this. She brushed a kiss on the top of his head. "I'll be right back."

She hurried around the corner of the house and up the stairs.

The entry was empty. She pushed the buzzer on the desk.

The house was big. She hadn't really noticed the day before. When they'd walked up the steps, Joshua had spotted the rainbows and taken off before she could get much sense of their surroundings.

"Can I help you?" An older woman came down the hall.

"I'm here to see…" Her mind went blank.

"Are you Cheryl? No last name?" the woman filled in.

"Yes."

"Then you're here to see me. I'm Marion. Last name Winters."

"Cheryl Henshaw." After running from Atlanta, she'd decided to use her mother's maiden name. Levi shouldn't be able to find them, since he'd never heard the name before.

Marion pointed to a small parlor. "We can talk in here."

"This house is beautiful." The words rushed out.

"That it is. And it takes dedication and elbow grease to keep it that way."

The rich smell of coffee mingled with the scent of lemon wood polish. Cheryl stared at a tray with two coffee mugs and a plate of banana bread. The aromas intensified her light-headedness, and she sank onto the sofa.

"Take a sip." Marion pointed. "You won't find coffee this good at any of those chain places."

"Thank you."

Marion picked up a second mug. "Are you from around here?"

"Atlanta most recently. Before that, Fort McPherson, though I grew up in Richmond." Cheryl took a sip. "Oh, this is good."

"How many years have you been cleaning?" Marion asked her.

Cheryl took another sip and then set her mug down. "I've cleaned all my life, but I've never…been paid to clean."

"Oh." Marion frowned.

"I know how to work hard. I won't let you down." *Please, please, please.*

Marion watched her, not saying a word.

Cheryl figured the interview was over. Sighing, she grabbed her wallet. Her Coach purse, a gift from Brad, had been hocked along with her wedding ring. She knew Brad would have understood; she needed to keep Josh safe.

She stood.

Where are you going?" Marion asked.

"I…assumed…" She pointed out of the room.

"Sit on down. Have a piece of that banana bread."

Cheryl sank into her chair. She couldn't swallow much more than the coffee.

"Here's what we're going to do." Marion tapped her finger on her nose. "We'll try you out for a couple of days."

"You will?" Had she really heard Marion right?

"Sure. Miss Abby says you've got a little boy."

"I do." She wanted to tell this woman with the warm brown eyes that her son was waiting in the garden for her. If she did, would Marion rescind the offer? "He's an angel."

"I'm sure he is. Can you start today? That damn fool, Kikki, took off for California with her boyfriend.

Going to be movie stars or some such nonsense. Put me in a bind leaving without notice."

Today? "I… I'd love to. But my son. He's here, outside, waiting for me in the courtyard." Her words ran together.

Marion tilted her head. "He's here?"

"I don't…" She took a deep breath, her face burning with embarrassment. "Miss Winters, I don't have money for day care." Without money for rent, how could she pay someone to watch her child?

"Is he in school yet?"

Cheryl shook her head. "He just turned five. He won't start kindergarten until September." If they were here that long. Staying away from Levi was more important than staying in one place.

"I'll bet he would love some of this banana bread." A grin spread across the older woman's face. "It'll keep him busy while I show you the ropes."

As the meaning of Marion's words sank in, Cheryl burst into tears. "Thank you!"

Marion moved over and laid a gentle hand on Cheryl's arm. "Now, now. No need for all that. Let's see how your boy is doing."

ABBY PUSHED THE remnants of lunch to the end of the kitchen table and convened the weekly Fitzgerald House staff meeting.

Dolley checked her laptop. "This week we have three sets of Moons checking in—two today, one on Wednesday. There's a Scrapbooking Sister group coming in today, thanks to Bess's efforts—two rooms and one of the parlors for their work."

"There's a group coming for the Scary Sister weekend—three rooms. They're staying Friday through Monday." Dolley tucked her bright red curls behind her ears. "Another Repeater couple, oh…it's their fortieth anniversary. Neat. They'll be here Saturday and Sunday."

"So I need three honeymoons and one anniversary basket. Got it," said Marion.

"Ten out of twelve rooms occupied." Abby grinned. "Nigel, keep the vacancy sign up. I'd love to fill up this weekend."

If they could keep up this pace *and* open more rooms, they would easily make their balloon payment. Assuming nothing else broke down.

"That's better than last year at this time." Dolley tipped her chair back on two legs. "We need to firm up Fitzgerald House's St. Paddy's Day plans."

"Give me a couple of days." Abby took a deep breath. The celebration, parade and bedlam would be here before they knew it.

"I can pull together the packages." There was an unexpected sharpness to Dolley's tone.

The group around the table went quiet. Abby pushed her hair back and looked at her sister. "You already do so much."

"So do you," Dolley replied.

"But I don't have to hold down an outside job," Abby explained.

"That doesn't mean you have to do everything around here." Dolley pointed a finger at her.

Marion patted Abby's arm. "If she's volunteering, let her do the work." She leaned in. "You need to learn to take help when it's offered."

"I do," Abby said defensively.

Marion raised her eyebrows. "And be gracious when you do."

Abby huffed out a breath. "Thanks, Dolley."

Her sister rolled her eyes.

Abby looked at her to-do list without seeing it. She *did* let people help her.

"Nigel," she said. "The hallway near Eleanor Roosevelt needs touching up—again."

He nodded, running his fingers through his white hair. How much longer would they have him to rely on? They'd celebrated his sixty-fifth birthday last month.

He'd been driver, handyman, assistant gardener and jack-of-all-trades since Mamma had first turned their home into a B and B.

"I think we should add wainscoting in the hall," he suggested. "It's too narrow. People bump the walls with their luggage. It would take a little more of a beating and we wouldn't have to paint the whole wall."

The group discussed the hallway and the following weekend's catering event.

Abby checked her notes. "Nigel, Bess would like the tables set up by four-thirty, so she can bring in the flower arrangements."

Bess was part owner and operator of Fitzgerald

House, but she also worked at a local florist and landscaping business, which was why she rarely attended the staff meetings.

"I'll shoot you copies of the St. Paddy's Day info before I post it." Dolley closed her laptop. "I've got to get back. My client is howling for his website redesign. Can I help it if he's changed his mind—three times?"

Abby couldn't wait for the day that her sisters didn't have to work second jobs. Someday the B and B would support them all. She would make it happen.

Nigel picked up his notebook. "I'll paint the hallway tomorrow and get those bids on wainscoting. Got to get to it." He ambled out the door.

"Hey, Abs, it's karaoke night at McMillian's." Dolley slipped her computer into a messenger bag. "Want to go?"

"I'll pass. I barely wake up with two alarms now. If I gallivanted with a night owl like you, our guests wouldn't get breakfast tomorrow. Plus, I have an association meeting tonight."

"Your loss." Dolley shrugged on her jacket.

"Any more surprises coming this week?" Abby asked. Although having dinner with Gray hadn't been a hardship.

"I'm sorry about the Smythe mix-up, really, I am." Dolley tucked her phone into her pocket. "I was working on the arrangements but didn't want to get your hopes up. The assistant was talking to two other places at the same time. Originally, he'd asked for a twenty-percent discount."

"I'm glad you talked him down to ten percent." She touched her sister's hand. "You're our best negotiator."

"Yeah, yeah." But her sister grinned. "We need new registration software. After I shifted the other bookings, I had to wait for a system backup before locking in Smythe's reservation."

"We need a lot of things. We need to fix the third-floor water damage. We need to open more rooms. But foremost, we need to make the loan payment."

Personally, Abby would like to replace her eight-year-old car, but that wouldn't get her any closer to restoring the main house and opening Southern Comforts. Hard work, frugality and dedication were the only ways she would open her own restaurant.

"You're right. Loan payment first." Dolley sighed and headed out the door.

Marion pushed her wiry body away from the table. "You know you can't live and breathe the B and B. A young, pretty thing like you should be out enjoying yourself."

Enjoying herself? "I've got a business to run."

"And you do it well." Marion wrapped her arm around Abby's shoulders. "Just don't be afraid to accept help when it's offered and to have a little fun."

"I feel guilty." Abby leaned her head on Marion's shoulder. "Both Dolley and Bess work so hard."

"And so do you." Marion gave her a quick, tight hug. "But there's more to life than Fitzgerald House. If your mamma wasn't taking care of your aunt in Atlanta, she'd say the same thing. Live a little."

Abby didn't think so. When Papa had died, Mamma

had worked 24/7 to make their home into a B and B. Enjoying life would come after Abby had opened her restaurant. "I'll think about it."

She had goals to achieve. She didn't have time for fun.

Marion gathered up her notebook. "By the way, I hired Cheryl, trial run."

"Good."

"Her boy is here with her. I said it would be okay until she got her feet under her. Don't be surprised if he's in the garden or near his mom."

"Of course." Marion had a big heart. "Do you think they want some sandwiches?"

Marion grinned and then piled the uneaten sandwiches on a plate. "I'll check how she's doing. I'm thinking these will be appreciated. She 'bout fainted at the sight of your banana bread."

GRAY WALKED INTO the sunroom, and Abby almost dropped the food and tea description cards she'd been setting out for teatime. No man should look that good in jeans and a chambray shirt.

Her face warmed. At dinner last night, he'd encouraged her to tell him about Fitzgerald House. He'd been easy to talk to. Had she talked too much?

No. If she had, he wouldn't have insisted on eating in the kitchen from now on. Right?

Mamma always advised her daughters not to get involved with guests. So Abby would stay professional if it killed her.

"Hi," she said. "Are you done working for the day?"

"I just met with a contractor," he said. "Now I need other options. I hope you can help or point me in the right direction."

"I'll try." Why was Gray in Savannah for six months? She should have asked when he'd registered, but yesterday had been…awkward.

She set the cards by the teapots and straightened the napkins. Still not quite looking at him, she asked, "What are you doing in Savannah?"

"Rehabbing a warehouse on River Street."

"The one that the work started and stopped on last year? I remember the man who owned it, but he hasn't been around for a while." He'd stayed at Fitzgerald House several times.

"That's the one. Derrick ran out of money and needed to liquidate fast." Gray had a gleam in his blue eyes. "I helped him out."

It sounded more as if Gray had gotten a great bargain. "Will you still develop it as condominiums?"

He nodded. "Great location. Very marketable."

Abby's shoulders tightened. How many times had her daddy used the same phrase about the Tybee Island condos he'd started to develop? *Great location.* Those condos had sat for years half built, looking sad and lonely. Actually, the previous owner of Gray's River Street warehouse reminded her of her father. Smiling, charming and unable to finish what he started.

Because of her father, her mother's family mansion was now a B and B. Because of her father, she and her sisters' college funds had disappeared. Instead of going to football or basketball games, they'd learned how to make beds and clean rooms.

Marion came in, wheeling the loaded tea trolley and distracting Abby from her thoughts.

"Marion, this is Mr. Smythe," Abby said.

"We met this morning." Marion maneuvered the trolley across the room. "How was your warehouse?"

"A mess." Gray eyed the food on the trolley as though he hadn't eaten in months.

"You'll soon set it to rights." Marion moved to the fireplace and turned on the gas flames. "There. That'll take the chill off the room."

"Thanks, Marion," Abby said, amused by the way Gray gaped at the food.

"My mother would kill for that trolley."

Abby could believe it. The silver four-tiered trolley was an heirloom that her own mother had always loved. She set the description cards next to each platter.

"It's been in the family for generations. Did you have enough to eat for lunch?" Abby had made two sandwiches, but she didn't know how big an appetite her guest had.

"Lunch was great." Gray headed over to the trolley. "But I've got room for one of those bars."

If the way to a man's heart was through his stomach, all she had to do to win Gray's was make him her brandy-pecan bars.

"Coffee or tea?" she asked.

"Coffee." He demolished one bar. "I'll have to run

to Atlanta and back each day if I keep eating this way," he mumbled around a second bar.

She poured his coffee and set the cup and saucer next to his chair.

As she left, she whispered to Marion, "Let me know if I need to bring up more bars."

She was almost out the door when he called, "Wait, Abby, I have a question."

She paused. He waved her over to a chair, before taking another bar.

"Can you recommend any contractors?" he asked. "I'm putting the work out for bids."

Settling into the chair, she tried to remember who'd worked on the warehouse before Gray took over. "Did you talk to Jeb Haskins?"

"Just met with him." He frowned. "Not letting that guy back on the project. I have a couple of other names, but I like the work you've done on your B and B. I wondered who you'd used."

"I can give you the names, but our focus has always been on restoration. I'm not sure this would be the same kind of job."

"You're right—I'm not looking for restoration, but I need a contractor who's experienced with old buildings."

Abby's heart warmed at his respectful tone. "I use Sam Forester. He's done all the work here since we started. He and his son, Daniel, run a local construction company. I'll call and see who he'd recommend."

"Thanks. Add this Forester to the list, too, would you? They've done a nice job here."

She froze. Gray wanted to talk to the Foresters? Samuel fit their work in between his other projects to help keep her costs low. Gray's work might slow down her own restoration.

But she couldn't keep business from Sam and Daniel. They were practically family.

Hoping he hadn't noticed her delay, she said, "I can do that."

Abby tapped her lip, thinking of other contractors she could direct him to.

Gray stared at her mouth, making Abby's heart beat a little faster. What was it the magazines said? If a man stared at your mouth, he was thinking of kissing you?

"I'll be back with those phone numbers." She scrambled out of the chair. "Have another bar."

He could have a bar, not her.

In the hallway, she leaned against the wall and inhaled. A man had stared at her mouth and stolen her breath.

AFTER ABBY LEFT, ten older women swooped into the sunroom. Half of them had the soft drawl Gray associated with Savannah and wore outrageous red hats. The other group was on one of those sisters things, like the ladies in the library last night.

Gray made polite chitchat for a few minutes. Then he guarded the pecan bars and let the women have the sandwiches. Their conversations churned around him.

His thoughts drifted to Abby. Today she wore a khaki skirt and sleeveless white blouse, and he'd wondered if she lifted weights to keep her arms so trim. As he'd been pondering what those plump pink lips would taste like, she'd taken off.

Abby came back into the parlor, giving no sign that she'd felt even slightly uncomfortable. She worked the room, setting a hand to a shoulder or giving a quick buss on the cheek to the red-hat women. She sat on an ottoman next to the ladies from the sister outing and asked about their day. Her smile wasn't the practiced one she'd given him earlier. This smile shone like a beacon.

Once she'd made her rounds, she stepped toward him. "I've talked to Samuel. He's come up with two contractors he feels are qualified."

She handed him a note written in clear, precise script.

"Thanks. I appreciate the help," he said.

"No problem." Glancing over at the trolley, she added, "I can bring out more pecan bars if you want."

He shook his head. "You're a witch, aren't you?"

She laughed. "Only in the kitchen."

Gray watched her walk away, appreciating her fine ass.

He grabbed another bar and cup of coffee and carried it into the courtyard garden to make his calls. He sat at a cast-iron table tucked under a green umbrella on the patio.

He set up appointments with contractors for that afternoon. When he phoned the Foresters he got the son, Daniel.

"Fitzgerald House still serves wine at five-thirty?" Daniel asked.

"They did last night, Argentinean wines." And damn fine appetizers.

"I'll just invite myself to happy hour. Then we can walk over to your building after a glass of wine."

"I'll see you then."

Pleased with his progress, Gray propped his feet on another chair and took a sip of coffee. He smiled at the fountain, a huge frog spewing water over copper lily pads. He could even swear he saw a bronze troll wink from where it was half-hidden under a palm tree.

The gardens were an intense green loaded with splashes of color. If his mother could see the landscaping, she'd probably try to lure their gardener back to Boston with her. He inhaled a lungful of flowery scents. The sun warmed his shoulders and eased the tension in his muscles.

There was something about this place. He could almost close his eyes and take a nap. For the first time he could remember, he noticed birds singing.

His phone buzzed. "Smythe."

"Gray, my friend. How's business?"

"Good." He didn't recognize the voice, and the number had come up as private.

"Just wondering if you've considered my proposition."

He still didn't know who he was talking to. "Who is this?"

"Jeremy Atwater. I ran into you at the opera opener last month. Intermission."

Gray frowned, trying to picture the guy.

"We talked about a great biotech investment opportunity," Atwater said. "You wanted to think about investing in the company."

Ding. Gwen had dragged him to the opening. This yahoo had caught him while he'd waited in the drink line.

"We're putting together a ten-million-dollar tranche. I'd love to get together and talk about how much of the tranche you'd like to take, unless you and your dad want to take the whole thing." Atwater laughed.

Gray gripped the table's edge. "I'm out of town. I'll have to forgo this opportunity."

"Oh." Atwater's tone dripped with disappointment. "I could talk to your father."

"You could."

"Umm. I can't get past his assistant."

Gray shook his head. "I'll mention you called." It was as much as he would commit.

"Great, great." Atwater rattled off his phone numbers, though Gray was barely listening.

Even from a thousand miles away, the vultures found him and tapped him for money. He closed his eyes and rubbed at the headache now pounding in his temples.

"Hey, mister, can we catch rainbows again?" a small voice asked.

Gray looked up into a face dominated by a pair of brown eyes. How had the kid snuck up on him? "Joshua, right?"

"Yup." The boy scratched at an ugly-looking scab on his hand. "Can we go catch rainbows?"

Gray checked his watch. "Sorry, kid, it's too early."

The boy's shoulders slumped. "Oh."

"Are you staying here?" Gray asked. He'd thought he'd heard Abby and Joshua's mom talking about a job, but maybe he'd been mistaken.

"Mommy's working." Josh kept rubbing at the small circular scab.

"You shouldn't pick at that," Gray warned.

"It itches."

"That's your skin healing. But you don't want to rip it off too soon, or it might get infected."

"I had infected before." The boy started to pull up his sleeve.

"Joshua!" His mother came out through a side door. She was twisting a cloth in her hand. Her face was as torqued as the cloth.

The boy turned and ran to her. "The rainbows aren't here yet. I have to wait."

His mom knelt. "I said you could sit at one of the tables, but you can't bother the guests."

"But he's at the frog table." Joshua pointed.

"You can sit here," Gray said. "I have…things to do."

Joshua's mom grabbed his hand and took a quick step back. "I'm sorry he disturbed you."

"No problem." The young woman was as skittish as the feral cat he'd brought home when he was ten. "So you got the job."

She inched away, glancing at the door she'd just come through. "I did. But it's on a trial basis."

"Well, good luck." Gray stood and started gathering his things. "Joshua can sit at the table."

The little boy snatched up a well-used backpack. It flopped on the chair.

"You're a guest." The woman was twisting her hands again.

"No problem. I'm Gray."

"Umm, Cheryl."

"Nice to meet you." He nodded to Joshua. "Be good for your mother."

The little boy took out a pack of crayons and a well-filled tablet of paper. He waved without looking up from his scribbling. "Bye."

Gray shouldn't be lounging in a garden anyway. People who wanted to succeed didn't sit around drinking coffee in the middle of the day.

ABBY SMOOTHED THE cranberry pencil skirt that ended a couple of inches above her knees and did a little spin. The matching jacket floated away from a white shell that showed a hint of cleavage.

"Looking good, Abs. Who are you trying to drive crazy with that suit?" Bess leaned against the kitchen table, snacking on a carrot stick.

"Jacob Tinsley."

"Do tell," her sister encouraged.

"I want to show him what he can't have." Abby tugged her jacket back into place. "He's asked me out at every meeting for the past three months. Then

I discovered he's living with one woman and dating another."

Was there something about her that attracted cheaters? First Maurice and now Jacob. Unfortunately, she'd been engaged to Maurice.

"I never liked Jacob," Bess said.

Abby could always count on her sister's support.

"Mr. Smythe's dinner is in the warming drawer. He likes vinaigrette on his salad. It's in the fridge on the middle shelf."

She walked Bess through the to-do list, even though she'd left instructions pinned to the kitchen bulletin board. "Serve the Petite Sirah with his stew."

"Trust me, I can handle this. I've hosted tastings for years." Bess looked at her watch and pointed to the doorway. "Out. No one will walk off in a huff because you miss an evening."

Abby kissed her sister and inhaled Bess's scent of earth and flowers. "Sorry to obsess. It's been a crazy start to the week."

Crazy because of their long-term guest, but she wasn't going to tell her sister about this weird attraction she was feeling. She could barely admit it to herself.

GRAY HAD TIMED his arrival in the library perfectly. Abby's back was to him as she uncorked a wine bottle. He was the first guest to arrive.

"What's the theme tonight?" he asked.

She turned and his smile dimmed. This woman's hair was almost the same color, but she wasn't Abby.

"Hello," she said with a warm smile.

"I'm sorry, I thought you were Abby."

"Thank you. My sister is lovely, so I'll take that as a compliment." The woman's smile filled her face. "I'm Bess."

"Nice to meet you. You and your sister look alike."

But the two sisters were different, too. Bess's nose was splattered with freckles. Her eyes had more gold in them than Abby's emerald ones. Abby's hair was an intriguing shade of strawberry blonde, while Bess's was redder. And when Bess smiled, his body didn't come to attention.

"What are the appetizers tonight?" he asked, trying to focus.

"Your theme is California Dreams. Artichoke dip, grilled tomatoes, olive tapenade, carrots, celery and other nibblers. California wines, of course."

Setting down the wine bottle, Bess extended her hand. He shook it, surprised at both the strength and calluses. She smelled like flowers with an earthiness he couldn't identify.

"I'm Gray Smythe."

She laughed, making him frown.

"Sorry," she said. "It's just that Abs was so mad. She didn't know about your arrangements before you arrived. Dolley wasn't able to get your information into the reservation system." She leaned over and whispered, "Our sister wants new software."

"There's three of you, right?" He'd read that tidbit in the B and B's pamphlet.

"Three girls. Our poor mother." She opened another

bottle and spoke over her shoulder. "Dolley's the baby. She's our computer expert and bookkeeper."

"What can I pour for you?" Bess asked.

He looked at the offerings. "The cabernet, please."

Bess poured a glass for him and then a small amount into another, swirling it around. She stuck her nose into the bowl and then sipped. "Nice."

She leaned against the closest armchair, seeming more relaxed than Abby's mysterious professional persona. "Is this your first visit to Savannah?"

"My second," he replied. "Is February always this warm?"

"You Northerners," she laughed, sinking into the chair. "This is cold."

"When I left Boston, it was snowing."

"If it ever snowed here, I'd lose half my gardens." She frowned. "Of course, the blasted kudzu would survive."

"I sat in the garden today. Your landscaper did a wonderful job."

She blushed, a pink that highlighted her pale skin. "Thank you. I manage the gardens."

"This really is a family operation." And an impressive one. "You work in the garden—Abby in the kitchen."

Without trying to show any interest, he sipped his wine and asked, "Where is Abby?" That sounded strange, so he added, "I wanted to thank her for getting the contractor names for me."

"She's at a Hospitality and Resort Association meeting." A smile played across her lips. "Abs went dressed to kill just to mess with some guy who thought he could date three women at one time."

"And he's in the association?" He could understand any man being fascinated by Abby. She'd been popping into his head throughout the day. Probably because last night had been the nicest conversation he'd had in months.

"The jerk's a manager at one of the area inns. He should know, no one treats a Fitzgerald like that and survives." She stood and helped herself to a carrot stick. Crossing her ankles, she leaned against the table.

"Where are the rest of the guests?" he asked.

"Tuesday is our lowest census day. I like to chat with the guests, if that's what they want, so I take the Tuesday wine tastings. Today, a couple of Moons checked in and there's a group of ladies and two couples who leave tomorrow."

"Moons? Honeymooners, right?" He moved over and loaded a plate with appetizers, chips and dip.

"Yeah. We get quite a few of them."

A tall man walked in the room and Bess's head jerked up, a frown creasing her forehead. "Forester, what are you doing here?"

Forester walked over and kissed her cheek. "Good to see you, babe."

Her frown deepened. "Don't call me that."

Forester winked and then poured himself a glass of wine.

"Are you taking a room?" She crossed her arms, scowling.

Gray hid his grin by sipping his wine.

"I'm meeting one of your guests." Forester chucked her under the chin. "Let me get some business done, and then you and I can catch up."

Gray walked over to him. The man looked around his age, early thirties. "Daniel Forester, I presume."

"Got me in one. Nice to meet you, Grayson Smythe from Boston."

"Gray works best."

"Gray it is," Daniel said. "Whenever you're ready, we can stroll over to your warehouse."

"Finish your wine. I'll have a little more of this dip." Gray patted his stomach. "I need to start swinging a hammer, or they'll have to roll me back to Boston."

"Our Abby is a dream in the kitchen," Daniel said.

Were he and Abby involved? Gray's shoulders tightened. The answer shouldn't matter. He'd left Boston to get off that particular merry-go-round.

"Do you know the previous warehouse owner?" asked Daniel.

"He's more than an acquaintance, but not quite a friend."

Daniel nodded. "He rarely came down to see the project. The rehab should be done by now."

"I'd agree with you on that. If we end up working together, I should tell you that I'm a hands-on manager," warned Gray.

"I can live with that."

As Gray finished his wine, one of the honeymoon couples he'd met this morning entered the library. How did they know they could spend a lifetime together? He'd never come close to feeling that about anyone.

As they left the room, Forester said, "How the hell do they know they're making the right choice?"

"I'm with you there. At least we know buildings can weather the storms. Let's go look at mine."

ABBY PARKED HER car next to the carriage house. The kitchen lights were on; Bess must be cleaning up. Maybe they could have a cup of chamomile tea before she headed to bed. Bess had added an herbal garden a couple of years ago and now made teas for the B and B. Abby loved having fresh herbs on hand for cooking.

She sighed as she got closer to the kitchen door. The cat had been hunting again and had left his prey on the step. Not the most appealing sight to come home to. Opening the door, she spotted Bess lounging in the alcove. "Reggie's left us a gift. I'd rather not clean it up dressed like this. I can't even bend over in this skirt. Will you get it, please?"

"Sure," Bess said. "How was the meeting?"

"The association contracted with a new food distributor. I'll check out their products and pricing. And the board is talking about raising the dues." Abby filled the kettle before turning to the table.

"Gray," she exclaimed. She hadn't expected to find him there. Darn it, her face had to match her raspberry suit. And her other sister was at the table, too. "Dolley?"

"Love the suit, Abs." Dolley pushed herself to her feet. "Thanks for the ideas, Gray."

"Anything I need to know about?" Abby asked as Dolley slipped by her.

"Gray and I were talking about the third floor. He had some ideas on how to make sure the rooms are soundproofed." Dolley gave her a hug. "I'll see you tomorrow."

"Watch out for Reggie's gifts," Abby said as Dolley headed out the door. How had their remodel come up?

Bess rocked to her feet. "What did Reggie leave?"

Abby shivered. "Rabbits. Two of them."

"That's two bunnies who won't be dining in my garden." Bess moved toward the door. "You've got to love a serial-killer cat."

"You may love him, but I don't like finding his gifts by the door."

Bess gave her a quick hug on her way out. "See you tomorrow."

The screen door slapped closed as her sisters left.

Without Dolley's and Bess's presence, Gray seemed to dominate the room.

Abby poured boiling water over the leaves, tapping her fingers as the tea brewed. She couldn't just stand here for three minutes. She gathered up the pot and her mug and moved over to the table, hoping her face had returned to its normal color.

"So did you drive him crazy?" he asked.

"What?"

"The jerk that suit was meant for?"

Embarrassed, she swore under her breath. She brushed nonexistent lint off her sleeve. "He drooled—

blubbered actually. I was cold and professional. I ground him under my heel."

"I'll bet you did." Gray toasted her with his wineglass. She froze as his gaze trailed slowly down her body. It was almost as if his fingers followed the same path. Suddenly the room felt like a sauna.

Swallowing, she picked up his plate. "Dessert?"

"No. In the past two days I've had a year's worth of sweets."

"Port, then?"

"I'd prefer cognac, if you have it. Otherwise port is fine."

She moved across the hall to the butler's pantry and took a deep breath. When that didn't calm her, she took another before retrieving a bottle and glasses.

"Say when," she said, pouring.

Instead of telling her, he cupped her hand, lifting the bottle. A zing shot through her arm. The bottle chattered against the rim of the crystal tumbler.

Gray didn't seem affected by their touch.

"Thanks again for the contractor leads," he said. "I'll get their bids, but I have a feeling I'll pick Forester."

Abby blinked, sinking into a chair. Her contractors? She'd screwed up her own restoration by being nice. "You've met with everyone already?"

"Can't stand to have the place looking like a bombed-out ruin."

"You're showing your Yankee." And the fact that he didn't have to worry about cash flow. What would that be like? "The summer heat will knock that impatience right out of you. Eventually you'll slow down."

"Like you?" He shook his head. "You're everywhere. When do you take time off?"

She frowned. "Never."

What a timely reminder. She needed to ignore any zings flying around her kitchen. Fitzgerald House was the most important thing in her life, and it deserved her full attention.

ABBY ADDED OLIVE oil and a dab of butter to her sauté pan.

"I hate to repeat myself—" Gray moved into the kitchen carrying an open bottle of cabernet "—but it smells incredible in here."

His smile had Abby melting like sorbet on a summer day. Earlier, she'd caught herself fantasizing about touching the dimple that appeared on his left cheek whenever he grinned.

Absolutely never get involved with a guest. She'd been repeating Mamma's rule often. Mamma had once dated a guest who'd stayed at Fitzgerald House for an extended visit. He'd later turned out to be married.

Abby was pretty sure Gray was single, but she didn't dare ask such a personal question. After nearly two weeks of dinners, she and Gray had yet to run out of topics to discuss, often talking well into the evening. She hadn't laughed this much since her childhood.

She could look but not touch. Their agreement with Gray was profitable and she didn't want to upset anything that helped Fitzgerald House.

Gray grabbed dishes from the pantry. He was a guest, but insisted on setting the table.

"Stop. You don't have to help." Abby waved her hand. She'd planned to get it done before he came in.

He swung by the range, dropping off a glass of wine for her. "I told you, I don't mind."

But she did. He was a guest. She took a deep breath.

"I haven't seen you around today." She'd wandered into the rooms where guests gathered on the off chance that he might be there. She hadn't been so foolish since her days of high school crushes.

"I spent the morning at the warehouse and then drove to Hilton Head to visit friends."

"How lovely." Abby hadn't been to Hilton Head in too long.

"It should have been nice."

His tone of voice, so stern, made her turn toward him. "It wasn't?"

"No." His lips formed a straight line.

"Why not?" She tried to sound casual as she sliced mushrooms for dinner.

"The wife was looking for funding for a summer camp." He took a sip of his wine. "She invited me to lunch to tap me for a donation."

That didn't sound so bad. "Good cause?"

He snorted. "Cheerleading camp."

"For underprivileged children?"

"Not in her world. I should have known she'd try something."

The mushrooms sizzled as they hit the sauté pan. "Why would you think that?"

"Everyone wants something—usually it's money."

What kind of world did he live in? "That can't always be true."

"Always."

"Do people ask you for money often?" she asked.

He pulled salad dressing from the fridge and set it on the table. "All the time. When I first got here, it was an investment banker and a biotech opportunity."

She chuckled. "That's sounds like a joke."

"Not when he was looking for ten million dollars."

Her spoon clanged in her saucepan. "Holy cow. You have that kind of money?" she blurted out.

He shrugged. "Yeah."

"Throw some of it my way," she said under her breath. They could finish off Fitzgerald House and put in gold-plated faucets.

His back stiffened.

She hadn't meant for him to hear her.

"Does this happen to your whole family?"

"Mostly to me and my dad, but my mother has her own charities."

Abby asked about his family, and they sipped wine as she finished preparing dinner.

"You've seen me with my family. How is yours different?" she asked, wondering whether money changed things there, too.

He didn't answer. Maybe she'd overstepped the boundaries of their relationship. "Forget I asked."

He held up a hand. "No, I was thinking about your question."

She flipped the mushrooms while waiting for his response.

"You and your sisters are close." He nodded. "You have each other's backs."

"Of course."

"There's no 'of course' about that kind of loyalty. You have something special. Something I admire."

"And your family isn't like that?" How sad.

He lifted his glass for another sip of wine, but the glass was empty, and he set it down. "No. Maybe it's because I only have a younger sister, but she's not someone I would trust with anything important. I keep waiting for her to grow up but it hasn't happened yet. I love them, but family for family's sake isn't that important to me."

"I'm sorry." Family was everything to her.

"I don't know any different." He rubbed his face, looking more tired than when he'd come in. "From what I've seen, you and your sisters are very lucky. It's nice to see your family working together."

She wanted to see him smile again and didn't know how to make that happen. Eating seemed to make him happy. "Dinner's ready."

He leaned down to the beef tenderloin resting on the counter and inhaled. "My mouth is watering."

She sliced the beef and added the mushrooms to the plates. Then she drizzled them both with the sauce she'd thickened. Roasted potatoes and green beans flanked the meat.

Gray waited through her prayer, his knife and fork already in hand.

"When I went to New York, this used to be my favorite meal," Gray said. He took a bite. "Wow, it tastes just like it."

"Maurice's, right?" *Maurice. The man who used me, made me believe I would be his partner in both the restaurant and his life, and then cheated on me.*

"How did you know?"

"I was his sous chef." She twisted her bare ring finger on her left hand.

"You lived in New York?"

"That's where I went to culinary school." Where she'd fallen in love. Where she'd been betrayed. "I worked at a couple of different restaurants before Maurice hired me."

"I remember reading something in the menu." She could almost see him processing the information. "They were rated, right?"

"Rising star the first year I was there." Her work, her food, her cooking.

"What's the scale?"

"Michelin ranks restaurants on a one to three scale. There aren't a lot of three-star ratings. Rising star means that the restaurant has potential for a star in the future." Would Gray laugh if she told him she wanted to run her own restaurant and earn a rating higher than that snake, Maurice?

"You're an incredible chef. Why did you leave?"

Abby had crawled back home to lick her wounds after Maurice's betrayal, but she couldn't tell Gray that. "My great aunt has rheumatoid arthritis. About three years ago, Aunt CeCe needed more help. We're the only family she has. Mamma's in Atlanta with her now. My sisters and I took over running Fitzgerald House."

Her vision of becoming the next Cat Cora on *Iron Chef* had evaporated. All her energy was focused on the B and B. She would bring Fitzgerald House back to its former glory and fix the financial problems Papa had landed them in. Then she would build Southern Comforts, her own restaurant.

"Well, I'm certainly benefiting from your expertise," Gray said. "You're an artist."

"Thank you." The man made her blush at least once a meal.

They talked about New York, places they'd eaten, shows they'd both seen. When she'd lived there, she'd actually had some free time—the good old days.

No pity party. She and her sisters were building something special at Fitzgerald House. To do that, she needed to stay focused. She wasn't quite the Food Network star she'd imagined being while in culinary school, but she'd given up on pipe dreams long ago.

"What did you do at the warehouse today?" she asked, clearing their empty plates.

"I cleaned up garbage and ripped out some walls. Felt good. Now I'm waiting on bids." He patted his flat stomach. "Another incredible dinner."

Abby brought over the cognac decanter and Gray's glass and then pulled out her pad of paper. "It's been two weeks. We need to talk about the meals. What's worked, what hasn't."

"You're probably feeding me too much," Gray said.

"It's those darn sweets, but I'm not going to tell you to stop sending the pecan bars in my lunch. If you stop, I'll end up coming back to the house for afternoon tea."

"I never realized my brandy-pecan bars had so much power. I'll keep sending them." She laughed. "Am I packing enough food for your lunch? Do you need another sandwich?" She tapped her pen on her chin.

Gray stared at her lips.

She pulled the pen away from her face. "Do I have something on my mouth?"

She reached up to check, but Gray beat her to it. His hand brushed against her cheek. She felt every callus on his palm.

Abby couldn't breathe. What would his hands feel like caressing her body? Heat shot through her like an induction oven.

"Gray?" she whispered.

It was wrong to want him to keep touching her. So why did she?

Dropping his hand, he slid his chair back with a screech. His blue eyes chilled, transforming from the heat of her gas range to the ice of a glacier.

He held up both hands. "My meals are fine. Everything's fine. Don't change a thing."

He stood so quickly that the chair rocked back and forth. "I need to make some calls. Good night."

He picked up his snifter and almost ran from the room.

She blinked. What had just happened?

She sank back into the chair like a fallen soufflé. One minute she'd sworn Gray was about to kiss her; the next, he'd treated her as though she had the plague.

Absolutely no guest involvement.

Mamma's rules made sense, but had she ever met a man like Gray?

CHAPTER THREE

Rule #5—Never yell at a guest. Not even under
your breath. (I've found the second-floor linen
closet is pretty soundproof.)

Mamie Fitzgerald

EVER SINCE GRAY had brushed Abby's cheek last Sunday, she'd vanished. Sure, her sisters had been around,
but it wasn't the same.

He hadn't seen Gwen for almost a month and
didn't miss her. But after five days, he missed Abigail Fitzgerald.

He poured another glass of wine and moved over to
the library window, staring out at the gardens.

He'd almost kissed Abby. Luckily, he'd caught
himself. His fantasy of pressing Abby up against the
counter and kissing her until those forest-glen eyes
blurred had to stop. No more wondering what kind
of underwear she hid under her clothes. Or how soft
her hair would feel if he released it from the clip she
wore when cooking.

It must be the wine and food—or the intimacy of
sitting in the alcove amid all those incredible smells
and the spicy scent that was pure Abby.

She fascinated him. He loved her different smiles—
the bright one she flashed at familiar guests and the

soft one she used to set strangers at ease. One minute she'd be checking people in and advising on Savannah sightseeing, and then she'd turn around and discuss wine characteristics.

Time to find her. Gray tapped his fingers on his jeans as he headed to the kitchen. He'd seen her handiwork all week, but no Abigail. People raved about the breakfasts, teas and appetizers, but every time he walked into a room expecting to find her, she'd just left.

What was it about Abby that he found so fascinating? Maybe it was that she was as goal-oriented as he was. He'd read her framed list hanging in the kitchen.

Complete restoration of Fitzgerald House
Open Southern Comforts
Get rated by international rating group—Zagat—Michelin (minimum 1 star)

Her list cost money. He had plenty of that. Was that why she was so nice?

She was like a sliver under his skin. He just couldn't pull her free. Maybe if he kissed her, his fascination would dissipate.

"Abby," he called, pushing the kitchen door open.

He jerked to a stop. He'd been looking for a confrontation, or at least an explanation for why she'd been avoiding him. Anything to help him resist this annoying attraction.

He shook his head. How could he argue with someone asleep at the table?

He stared at the counters. She'd been busy. The sinks overflowed with bowls and utensils. A rainbow of tarts covered every surface.

He headed to the table and stared down at her. Purple shadows under her eyes showed she hadn't been sleeping enough. And her neck was twisted. She couldn't possibly be comfortable. "Abby."

She didn't move.

He touched her arm, more a stroke than a touch. "You're going to hurt your neck."

She moaned and released a big sigh, but still didn't wake.

This time he shook her shoulder. "Abigail."

Nothing.

He tapped his foot on the floor. He couldn't leave her like this.

Gray hoisted her in his arms. Surely that would wake her. But she simply burrowed her face into his shirt, and his heart raced. She smelled of her baking—sweet and spicy.

Now what? He could lay her on the love seat near the fire—but it was way too short. She needed a bed.

"Oh, my." Marion entered the kitchen with a tray of empty wine bottles. "Is Abby okay?"

"Exhausted. She was asleep at the table. I tried to wake her." God, he sounded pathetic. "Can I carry her to her room or another room?" Did Abby live on-site?

Marion looked at the love seat and shook her head. "We don't have an open room tonight." She waved her hand at all of Abby's work on the counters. "The guests for tomorrow's engagement party filled all the vacancies."

"Why don't I take her up to my room and let her nap there? If anyone needs her, let them know."

"She sleeps harder than anyone I know. She needs at least three alarms to get her up every morning." Marion walked over and brushed a strand of hair off Abby's face. Then she stared into Gray's eyes. "You'll be a gentleman?"

"Absolutely." He might dream about stripping off her clothes, but he would never do anything without her active participation.

Up in his suite, he slipped off Abby's shoes and tucked her into his bed. She rolled over and curled into a ball. Her hair had come free from the clip and spread across the white pillow like a sunset. He wanted to lie down and hold her while she slept.

Instead, Gray went into the sitting area, leaving the bedroom door ajar. When Abby woke, he didn't want her to be confused.

Flipping open his phone, he called Daniel Forester.

"Thanks for getting your bid back early," Gray said.

"We really want to work on this project," Forester said.

"Well, it's yours if you bring over pizza and beer. I'm in the Jackie Kennedy room."

Forester didn't answer.

Okay, he knew his request had sounded strange.

"Abby fell asleep in the kitchen. She looked so uncomfortable, I couldn't leave her there," Gray explained. "I carried her up to my room, and she didn't even twitch. I want to be here when she wakes up."

What an idiot. He should have left her on the love seat next to the fireplace.

Honesty smacked him in the face. He'd wanted her in his bed, even if he couldn't be there with her.

"I'll be there after I pick up that pizza," Forester said. "Anything you don't like?"

"Anything goes."

ABBY ROLLED OVER and hugged her pillow. She'd been having such a lovely dream about the pine-and-sandalwood scent of Gray's cologne. She stretched and looked around.

No! Why was she in the Kennedy room? How had she ended up in Gray's bed?

The alarm clock next to her said nine o'clock. She'd lost three hours. Three hours! How would she get everything done?

Male voices filtered into the bedroom from the sitting room. She found her shoes and clutched them to her chest.

Abby tiptoed to the door but didn't have a clear line of sight. When she pushed the door a little wider, it squealed.

"Abby?" Gray called from the sofa.

She bit her lip. Trying to act nonchalant, she entered the room. Not only was Gray on the sofa, but Daniel Forester sat in the chair across from him. As if she weren't already embarrassed enough.

Gray stood and met her in the middle of the room. "Are you feeling better?"

He stood so close, she could whisper, "How did I get up here—in your bed?"

He stroked a finger under her eyes, down her cheek,

and tipped up her chin. "You were sound asleep at the table. I couldn't wake you, so I carried you upstairs where you could at least be comfortable."

He'd hauled her up to his room? She inhaled a sharp breath, trying not to scream. "How could you? I have things I have to do. What if someone needed me?"

"Marion knows where you are. Take a break—you're exhausted."

She pressed her lips together, but couldn't contain her anger. "I don't have time to sleep. That's why I was resting at the table." She jabbed a finger into his chest. "What gave you the right to interfere?"

She headed for the door.

He grabbed her arm. "I can help."

"You've done enough." She wrenched her arm free. "Your dinner will be ready in fifteen minutes."

"Forester brought pizza. I'm good."

Lord, now she wasn't living up to her commitments.

"Don't be mad. I was trying to help." He leaned down so only she could hear. "Have you been avoiding me?"

"Hey, Abby," Daniel called, looking away from the basketball game, concern creasing his face. "Everything all right? I heard you crashed and burned in the kitchen."

She straightened her shoulders. "I can't believe I slept that deeply."

"I can. Aren't you the sister that requires a dozen alarms to wake up?"

She mumbled a reply as she slipped her shoes on. Over the years, the Foresters and Fitzgeralds had become close, sharing meals and holidays. Apparently too close, if Daniel remembered her problem with waking up.

"We still have pizza." Daniel popped a beer. "A couple of beers left, too."

"I just lost three hours." She shot Gray an icy look. "I have to work."

GRAY SAID GOODBYE to Daniel and shut the B and B's front door. He checked his watch and saw that it was a little before ten o'clock. Would Abby still be in the kitchen?

He needed to apologize. He didn't feel guilty for letting her sleep. She had to have been beyond exhausted.

He would offer to help. Again. Maybe there was something he could do to help her catch up. Hopefully she wouldn't snap his head off this time.

His mother's voice rang inside his head. *You always assume you know how to run everyone else's lives.*

He straightened his shoulders and pushed through the kitchen's swinging doors. Incredible aromas greeted him. Whatever Abby was cooking made tonight's pizza, which had been a mighty fine pie, seem like cardboard.

All the tarts had disappeared. Now a massive pot bubbled on the stove. Piles of colorful sliced vegetables overflowed a cutting board.

"What do you need, Mr. Smythe?" Frost coated her Southern drawl.

He eyed the gigantic knife she was using. She waved it a little. He gritted his teeth—time to apologize.

"I'm sorry I messed up your schedule. I shouldn't have interfered." He couldn't remember the last time he'd apologized to anyone. It was hard to get the words out. "I should have worked harder to wake you up and find out what you needed. I shouldn't have hauled you upstairs."

She pointed her wicked knife at him. "No, you shouldn't have. That wasn't your decision to make."

"You were exhausted." He raised both hands in emphasis, which had to be better than shaking some sense into her. "And your neck was going to hurt."

She went back to mincing the mushrooms, the knife a blur. "You should have left me where I was. Don't overstep again, Mr. Smythe."

She turned, dismissing him. If he was going to grovel, the least she could do was forgive him.

He moved up behind her. "Abby."

She turned, her knife held out in front of her.

He jumped back. "I thought you'd only sleep an hour or so. The fact that you didn't means you were exhausted. Next time, I'll wake you after thirty minutes."

Her mouth dropped open, and the knife waved. "There *won't* be a next time."

His heart raced. Her damn foot-long knife was too close to his stomach. He caught her wrist, pulled the knife out of her hand and set it on the counter with a clang. "I don't feel like losing a body part."

"Get out of my kitchen." Her eyes reminded him of flashing northern lights.

He exhaled. Loudly. "Abby, I'm really sorry."

He set a hand on her shoulder, but she shrugged it off.

"Are you mad because I interfered with your schedule or because I let you sleep? Or because it was *me* taking care of *you?*"

"I don't need taking care of." She poked a finger at him.

"I know that." But he liked taking care of her. He stepped closer and captured her hand in his. He just couldn't stop touching her.

She looked up. There was more than anger simmering in her eyes. Desire?

He backed her into the counter. She smelled like herbs and flowers. The combination had him wavering between wanting to bite her or to carry her back upstairs.

"Gray…" She put her hands on his chest, and electricity shot through him.

Her pink bottom lip begged him to nibble it. Being this close to Abby was making him crazy. "Oh, hell."

Abby's fingers splayed across his chest, generating enough heat to brand his skin through his shirt.

He cupped her head between his hands.

Leaning in, he brushed his mouth against hers, just a feather's touch. They both inhaled, a sharp, sweet sound. Then he dived in for another kiss.

Abby sighed, a sexy moan that curled into his groin. She tasted of coffee and cinnamon. Her fists relaxed and then gripped his shirt as her body melted into his. Her breasts pressed against his chest.

"Abby." His tongue stroked hers, and heat flashed through his body.

Her fingers pushed into his hair, and he molded his body to her lush curves.

Her lips slid against his cheek. He ran his tongue along her jaw and nuzzled the frenzied pulse under her ear. Her arms tightened around his back.

"You taste so good." He dived back in for a kiss.

"Gray." She shook her head. "Stop."

He rested his forehead against her, gasping for breath. What the hell had just happened?

She pushed against his shoulders.

"That was better than I'd imagined," he whispered, drawing back.

Their kiss hadn't eased the tension from his body. Every muscle cried out to take this woman back to his bed.

"You…you…" Her eyes, once glazed with arousal, were now filled with anger.

For the second time that night, Gray apologized. "I'm sorry. I don't regret kissing you, but I was out of line."

"You idiot. You make me lose three hours of work, then interrupt me when I'm trying to catch up. You kiss me and then say *sorry?*" She was building up another head of steam. "Maybe we need to renegotiate your agreement. *I'm not* part of the Fitzgerald House services. If you can't keep your hands to yourself, you'll need to find other accommodations."

Gray backed away. An electrical charge still surged through him. "If you tell me you haven't thought about what we would be like together, I'll call you a liar."

Before she could take another swipe at him, he added, "I apologize—again. Let me help you catch up. Could I find someone to help you out? Maybe before the party. That would help, right?"

"No." She jerked away from him.

"There must be some sort of temp place. I could… find a kitchen assistant." He held up a hand. "Let me help you."

She glanced over at the unwashed pots and pans, and her eyes gleamed. "*You* want to help? *You?*"

He nodded.

"Soap's above the sink. Gloves are on the towel rack. Make sure the water is hot, very hot."

"Me?" This wasn't working out the way he'd planned. He'd figured he could pay someone to help her.

"You." Abby stalked away. "Keep to your side of the kitchen and stay away from me."

"SALAD'S UP." ABBY wiped one final drip of dressing off a plate. Perfect. The curls of beets, carrots and cilantro looked elegant next to the grilled white asparagus.

"They look too good to eat," Michael, her sous chef, said.

"The bride-to-be is beaming." Dolley stretched before she pushed out the cart. "The tables look spectacular."

"She liked the centerpieces so much, she's coming in for a flower consult." Bess hefted a tray of crudités. "Once they try your food, I'm sure they'll book the wedding reception here, too."

Her sisters followed the food up to the ballroom. Abby took a drink of water, kneading the small of her back.

Gray walked into the kitchen.

The muscles she'd just relaxed seized up again.

Abby snatched up the salad plate she'd set aside. She and Gray had to get back to normal.

She was upset with herself. When he'd kissed her last night, she'd wanted to lean into him and let him take her back up to his big bed.

She couldn't act on her attraction. He was a man who talked about ten-million-dollar deals. She worried about spending ten dollars on anything other than Fitzgerald House.

"Did you get everything done?" he asked, dodging a server carrying a tray of dirty glasses.

"Getting there." She couldn't stop her eyes from narrowing.

Gray held up his hands in surrender. "Do I have to apologize again?"

His last apology had led to a kiss that had almost consumed her. "No." God, no.

"Hey, Miss Abby."

Joshua stood next to Gray. How had she not noticed the little boy?

"Josh says his mom's working the party, so I told

him he could have dinner with me." Gray mouthed, "Put it on my bill."

She nodded, but she would do no such thing. Josh was a sweetie.

"You two men have a choice tonight. Do you want portabella lasagna or short ribs?"

Josh looked at Gray, his mouth scrunched up.

"My man will have lasagna, and I'll have the short ribs." Gray whispered to the little boy, "We can share."

Gray stepped out of Michael's path, taking Josh with him. "Busy in here," he commented.

"We're finishing up the party's entrées," she explained.

Gray helped Josh onto a chair.

She plated their meals and brought them to the table.

"Looks great," Gray said, digging into his salad.

Josh sucked in his lower lip as he stared at the lasagna. "Can you cut this for me?"

"Sure." Gray winked. "I used to do this for my sister."

Abby kept an eye on them as she pulled out the tart trays for Marion's staff to serve. The guests had their choice of raspberry, strawberry, kiwi or lemon curd tarts.

Seeing Gray's plate licked clean, she asked, "More ribs?"

"Yes, thanks. And maybe a helping for short stuff." He pointed at Josh.

The little boy's plate was clean except for a pile of mushrooms.

"Everything is delicious." Gray patted his stomach, and Josh mimicked him. "The people upstairs will be raving."

This was why Abby had learned how to cook. She loved seeing people smile after eating her food. And Gray's dimples were an even better reward. "Were you at the site today, on a Saturday?" she called over as she worked at the island.

"I wanted everything ready for Daniel's crew on Monday. I got involved, and before I knew it, I'd missed the wine tasting. What was today's theme?" Gray asked.

Abby placed the final tart on the tray. "Washington State. Smoked salmon, apple and bacon puffs with a pomegranate glaze and a cold curried apple soup."

He looked pained. "Do you ever do repeats?"

She chuckled. "I can."

With the tart trays loaded and on their way to the ballroom, Abby heaved a sigh. In spite of yesterday's unplanned nap, they'd finished. She could rest. At least until the dirty dishes came back down.

She joined Gray and Josh in the alcove, bringing a plate of tarts with her.

She propped her aching feet up on a chair. Oh, what she wouldn't give for a foot rub. "If you want more, you'll have to serve yourself. I'm too blessed tired."

"This was incredible." Gray had cleaned his plate—again. "Josh, do you want anything else?"

The little boy pointed to the tarts. "Red, please."

Gray passed one to him with a napkin.

Gray didn't bother with a napkin for himself. He

popped an entire tart in his mouth. "Okay, I may need more than one," he said as his eyes rolled back in pleasure.

The kitchen doors swung open and Cheryl stepped in. Her head jerked back and forth until she saw her son. "Josh!" Her relief was almost palpable. "What are you doing in here?"

"Gray askeded me to eat with him."

"Asked," Cheryl corrected. "And it's Mr. Smythe."

Cheryl shoved her pale hair back into her bun. She shot a guilty look at Abby before turning back to the boy. "You promised to stay put."

"It was my fault. Josh kept me company while I ate, but I should have made sure you knew where he was."

"I told you this afternoon, Josh is no problem," Abby added. She didn't mind the boy hanging around the B and B.

Cheryl twisted her hands together. "I don't..."

"He's okay with us." Abby glanced over at Gray. "I mean...me."

"Marion only needs me for another hour." The young woman covered her mouth with one hand. Her fingernails were chewed to the quick.

"I'm okay, Mommy. You want a picture?" Josh pulled out a sketch pad and a mammoth box of crayons.

"Where did you get those?" Cheryl's mouth fell open.

"I saw them at the store," Gray mumbled.

Abby was surprised to see color brightening Gray's

cheek. She hadn't thought anything could embarrass him.

"I remembered to say thank you," Josh piped in.

Why did Gray have to be so sweet? Abby was trying to resist the man. She moved over to Cheryl, catching her hands so she wouldn't twist them anymore.

"He's okay with me." Abby lowered her voice. "If he gets tired, I'll tuck him in on the sofa." She waved over to the sitting area.

"Thank you." Cheryl nodded to Gray and then touched Abby's arm. "For everything."

Abby squeezed Cheryl's fingers. "No problem."

After Cheryl went back up to the ballroom, the small group sat in a comfortable silence. Abby closed her eyes. Michael hummed as he cleaned. A dishwasher rattled. Josh's crayons scratched against the paper and then stopped. From across the table, she could smell Gray's cologne.

The table jostled, and Abby pried her eyes open.

Gray was lifting Josh up. "He fell asleep, like someone flipped a switch."

He settled the child on the sofa, tucking a throw around him. When he came back to the table, he asked, "Is Josh here whenever Cheryl works?"

"Mmm-hmm." She could barely keep her eyes open.

"Do something for me."

She tipped her face up. "What?"

"Make sure they're eating. Put it on my tab."

"I'm not charging you." Abby clenched her jaw. "Cheryl's my employee." She took care of her own.

"But…"

She waved a hand in the air, wanting him to stop talking and let her rest.

"I want you to let me pay."

"No," she mumbled.

He grunted. The table rocked as he sat back down.

She closed her eyes again. Bliss. A few minutes of rest and she'd be able to go a couple more hours.

Gray tapped her hand. "You need to tell me what I should do if you fall asleep. I don't want to get in trouble like yesterday."

The heat of his fingers warmed her whole body. She smiled without opening her eyes. "If my head drops to the table, kick me."

"Maybe what you need is to get out of the kitchen," he said. "When do you get a day off?"

"Tomorrow," she mumbled.

"Let's eat out tomorrow night."

Eat out? He was hitting on her. Again. "Gray, don't."

"We eat together all the time. Let me take you out for a change."

She sat up and pulled her hand away from his. "I don't date guests."

"Who said anything about dating? I said dinner. I'd like to thank you for the gourmet meals you've served me." His blue eyes held hers. "Think of it as an olive branch for the mess I made of your day yesterday. One more way to say *sorry*."

She frowned.

"It's just dinner," he coaxed.

"I guess." She nodded slowly. "Not a date."

His gaze stayed on her mouth.

The memory of his kiss made her breath catch in her chest.

"Great." He blinked, breaking the spell between them. "I'll come down later and grab a cognac. There's a basketball game I want to watch."

He headed out the swinging door, and the kitchen seemed empty without him.

Her breath came out in a whoosh. Why had she agreed to go to dinner? It had to be exhaustion and his darn blue eyes. And the sweet way he treated Josh. Even so, this dinner was bound to be a mistake.

The monotonous chore of loading dishes didn't take her mind off Gray. Saying good-night to Cheryl and Josh only made her remember how kind Gray had been to the little boy. He had such an easy way of chatting with guests. They had such lovely conversations, and he filled his jeans out… Whoops. Not going to think about that.

"Need anything else?" Michael asked, wiping down the stove.

"No. I think we're done. Thanks."

"See you in the morning." Michael left as she finished cleaning the counter. Abby would have liked to have gone to bed, but since the sisters were all together, she'd called a short meeting even though it was nearly midnight.

Dolley burst into the kitchen, a champagne bottle in her hand.

"Success," Bess called out as she followed, carrying three flutes. "They loved everything."

"How's Marion doing?" Abby asked.

"Everything's under control," Dolley said. "Let's pop this bad boy. We rocked."

The sisters gathered around the kitchen table. Golden liquid fizzed in their glasses.

"To the Fitzgerald ladies," Bess said, raising her glass.

The reasons Abby worked so hard to bring Fitzgerald House back to its glory were gathered round the table. She swallowed. Mamma had started the recovery. When Great-Aunt Cecelia had gotten sick, Mamma had asked Abby, Bess and Dolley to take over. But Abby had always been in charge. She had the relevant experience, and as the oldest, she'd always felt it was up to her to fix what her father had broken.

"Great party, ladies," Bess said.

"Did we have enough servers?" Abby asked.

"Amy and Cheryl did well for their first time. We could have used one more," Bess said.

Abby made a note on the tablet by her side. "I'll talk to Marion."

Bess yawned. "I've got to work tomorrow. Can we make this quick?"

"Sure. Samuel's given me his bid." Abby fanned the papers out in front of her.

"What's the bottom line?" Dolley filled her flute again.

"To finish the third floor, he's quoting a little over a hundred thousand dollars."

"Crap." Dolley ran a hand through her curls. "No wonder you keep pushing back the software upgrade."

"Samuel's also given us ballpark numbers for turning the carriage house into the restaurant. That's another three hundred thousand. If we add carriage house guest rooms, it's just under a hundred thousand."

Everyone groaned. The estimate might as well have been millions.

They talked through the possibilities and drank their champagne.

"The carriage house suites could be a little more modern. We could keep the furniture lighter and bring in the garden theme." Bess nibbled on her thumbnail until Dolley slapped her hand.

"Great idea, but the carriage house renovations will have to wait." Abby's chest ached. "Third floor first."

"I agree," Dolley added.

Bess covered Abby's hand. "When you moved back from New York, all you talked about was opening a restaurant."

Abby shrugged. Realism had set in the minute she'd sat with the B and B's accountant.

She was the reason Maurice had received the rising star designation. She wanted a real star rating to show him up. Without a restaurant, she would never be rated. She would just be...a B and B cook. Nothing special.

Dolley stuffed a tart in her mouth. "We have to finish the rooms in the main house first."

Bess shook her head. "Shoot, what if we can't get them booked?"

"We will." Abby swallowed the lump forming in her throat. They had to. "Samuel's bid has an option that allows us to finish one room at a time. If Nigel helps during the day, the short-term cost will be lower. In the long run, though, it will cost more, because the subcontractors would have to keep returning, rather than doing everything in one go."

Bess cradled her head in her hand. "Why can't this be easy? How about a loan?"

"Dolley?" Abby asked.

"I'll make some inquiries next week." Her sister grew thoughtful. "Maybe there's a development loan we can tap."

"We should extend that darn balloon," Bess complained. "It's hanging over our heads like a..."

"Noose?" Dolley filled in.

"That pendulum sword thing." Bess waved her hand back and forth.

"Wow, you guys are morbid." Abby figured she shouldn't have held this meeting after a long day of work for all of them.

The kitchen door creaked as someone pushed it open. The sisters turned in unison.

Gray's dark hair appeared in the doorway, and Abby's stomach fluttered as if the champagne bubbles were tickling her.

"Hi ladies, still—" Gray frowned and looked at the bottle, the flutes and papers covering the table "—working?"

"Yeah. All work and no play—that's us." Dolley waved him over. "Hey, you know about our renovations. Can you tell us if these bids are reasonable?"

What? Abby kicked Dolley's shoe.

Dolley glared. "What was that for?"

Abby tipped her head toward Gray and frowned.

He leaned against the dining alcove's half wall. Those steely blue eyes held hers as he took of sip of the cognac he'd carried in with him.

"He's a guest," Abby hissed. A guest she'd kissed. The best kiss of her life.

"I don't mind," he said.

But Abby did. This was Fitzgerald business.

Gray moved to the table. Dolley scooted over to make room for him as he took a seat. "What's going on?"

"Samuel's just finished the last second-floor room, but we want to open up the third floor," Dolley said.

He nodded.

Dolley shifted the papers in front of him. "We don't have the cash to do the whole floor, but can you tell us if the room-by-room costs look reasonable? Maybe you have some ideas."

Abby wanted to snatch the papers out of his hand. Guests shouldn't know about their financial situation.

"Abby mentioned something about water damage. And you talked about soundproofing." He scanned the documents. "Do you mind if I take a look upstairs?"

"I've got to get home. I have a landscaping install starting at seven tomorrow." Bess pushed away from the table. "That means I need to get to the shop by six."

Abby waved. "Get some rest."

"I should get some sleep, too. Worked most of last night." Dolley rubbed her face. "Abs, take Gray up to the third floor and let him poke around."

Before Abby could argue that was a terrible idea, her sisters had skedaddled like kids on the last day of school—the traitors.

"Shall we head up?" Gray's blue eyes twinkled as he looked at her.

Was he amused or did he pity her? How much easier would life be if she had his megabucks, the ones Dolley was always drooling over? And why had her sister invited Gray into their business?

"Let's go." Her tone was curt, her shoulders stiff. Maybe Gray would take the hint and head to his room.

She grabbed keys and pulled a flashlight off the wall charger.

He set down his glass and followed her out of the kitchen and to the locked door at the end of the hallway.

"I didn't know these stairs were here," he remarked as she unlocked it.

"We don't put them on the house map. We can't have guests up in this section of the third floor."

She climbed the narrow stairs. Even though he was behind her, she caught his scent. The higher they climbed the more intense the smell, until all she wanted to do was turn around and bury her nose in his neck.

Not going to happen.

She reached the top of the stairs and flipped on the

light. The bare bulb accentuated the stains, making the hallway look like a weird modern painting.

Gray moved closer, inspecting the walls. At the first doorway he grabbed the doorknob. "May I?"

At least he'd asked permission. She handed him the flashlight. "Be careful."

The room was a dark skeleton. It had sustained the worst of the water damage. Years ago, someone, probably her grandfather, had pulled up most of the floorboards. There were holes in the plaster walls. Half the ceiling had come down.

Ahead of her, Gray tested the plywood covering the floor joists and then stepped into the belly of the room.

Abby wrapped her arms around the ache in her stomach. The room looked...sad.

Gray tapped his knuckles on the dark wood studs. "They built these houses to last, didn't they?"

She leaned against the door frame. "Yes."

The house should have been cherished, but there were costs associated with that. Everything always came back to money.

The beam of light jumped as Gray looked around the room, first at the floor joists, then walls, windows and finally the ceiling—the half ceiling.

This was the room that would cost the most to restore. It would be last on the list. When she'd come through with Samuel, she'd seen the possibilities. What did Gray see?

He didn't speak as he studied the window framing, one of Mamma's first investments.

"Whoever put in the windows did a great job," he said.

"Samuel." Abby could hear the pride in her own voice.

"In that case, I'm glad I hired them." He moved toward her.

She backed into the hallway, not wanting to get too close.

He brushed past, and the chilly temperature seemed to jump about ten degrees.

He followed the same routine in each of the other rooms. These were less damaged, but still weren't ready for occupancy.

What's on the other side of this wall?" Gray asked.

"The ballroom."

He nodded. "Now I understand why Dolley was asking about soundproofing. It's pretty good right now."

She tipped her head, listening. Marion's cleaning crew must have finished the teardown. They'd earned their keep tonight and had a shot at catering the wedding reception. Score one for Team Fitzgerald.

Gray exited the last room, shutting off the flashlight. "I thought things would be dustier."

"Marion sends a crew up once a month." She frowned. "Why did you think they'd be dirty?"

He grinned, his dimple softening his face and making him look younger, less fierce. "Because when I checked in, you had a streak of dirt on your cheek."

"Oh." She grimaced. "That wasn't from up here."

"You take care of things." He didn't comment on

her admission. Instead, his gaze zeroed in on her lips. "If it's under your control, you care."

She crossed her arms. "What's wrong with cleaning a ripped-up section of the house?"

"I'm not making fun of it. I'm impressed."

"Umm. Thank you." Of course she took care of things. She had to. She was responsible. "I...I live here." Well, in the carriage house.

"Just because you live here doesn't mean you have to take care of everything." He waved down the hallway toward to the damaged room. "They didn't."

"No, they didn't." Her ancestors had made bad investments, suffered through the cotton blight and then the Depression. It took money to keep Fitzgerald House alive, something they hadn't always had.

He was still staring at her mouth. "Why did you have dirt on your face?"

She shrugged. "Samuel and I went through the carriage house. I don't have the cleaning crew in there."

He nodded, taking a step forward. She inched backward until the wall stopped her. His cologne was now the only thing she could smell.

She clenched her hands into fists, trying to keep herself from running her fingers through his hair. There were too many things keeping her from acting on this attraction, although she couldn't think of a single one right now as his blue eyes stared into hers.

"Are you afraid of me?" He rested his hand on the wall above her head.

"No." She was afraid she would give in to the urge to kiss him. There would be repercussions if she did.

She let one hand touch his chest to keep him from leaning down. "I think I was clear last night."

He leaned in anyway. "Two things were clear to me last night." He covered her hand with his. His heart raced under her fingers.

"Gray…"

He spoke over her. "One, there's an attraction, a chemistry between us."

She started to shake her head.

He touched her cheek and she stopped, then nodded.

"And two, you're afraid," he said.

"I'm running a business." She put both hands up. "Anything between us is inappropriate."

"Business. Right." He moved back and she took a deep breath, happy and disappointed at the same time.

Stepping into the center of the hall, she asked, "Have you seen enough?"

"For now."

She needed to watch her words around him. Needed to stay on her toes or she would give in to this need to stroke a finger over his dimple. "Then I think we're done."

His grin grew. "I'll grab your bids and we can talk about them tomorrow."

Tomorrow. They were going out to dinner. "Maybe we shouldn't…"

"Abby, you've had a long week. You're tired. We'll talk tomorrow."

CHAPTER FOUR

Rule #2—Absolutely never get involved with a guest. It's not well done.

Mamie Fitzgerald

ABBY ROLLED OVER and hugged her pillow to her chest. Eight o'clock and she didn't have to get out of bed.

Only one thing could make this better. A muscular man named Sven spending an hour massaging her feet and legs. But the image morphed into Gray running his hands up her legs.

She groaned. Would that be so wrong?

She lolled in bed for another heavenly hour, indulging herself with a good cookbook she hadn't had the chance to explore. Then, wearing sweatpants and a hoodie, she carried her coffee and a croissant into the courtyard. She planned to enjoy the early-March sunshine. She could read the Sunday paper and eat her breakfast. A small luxury.

Michael came to her table with a pot of coffee and topped off her cup.

"Thanks." She inhaled the sharp fragrance. "How was brunch?"

"Piece of cake. Well, really—French toast."

"Ha-ha."

"You're low on syrup," Michael added. "Plus, your long-term guest was looking for you."

A small shiver ran through her. "His name is Gray."

Saying his name made her stomach flop. Her body went on alert at the thought of seeing him.

Nothing existed between her and Gray, nothing but business. How could it? According to Dolley, Gray's family had enough money to buy and sell Fitzgerald House many times over. It was too bad her body heated up whenever he smiled. They were just too different.

"If you see Gray, tell him I'm in the garden."

Maybe he wanted to cancel their dinner. *She* should cancel dinner. Keep everything professional. Plus, staying in her sweats all day wouldn't be a hardship.

Michael left, and she worked on the Sunday crossword puzzle. Occasionally, she tilted her head, letting the sun warm her face.

Bess's gardens were alive with the twitter of birds and the rustle of leaves in the bamboo and live oak trees. The fountain splashed with a happy sound. Taking a deep breath, Abby filled her senses with the heady fragrance of the flowers Bess painstakingly nurtured. If she opened her eyes, the blooming azaleas would be nodding their bright pink heads.

She was as warm as when Gray's hand had covered hers last night—all mushy inside.

Gray was right. They had…chemistry. She couldn't let her focus slip from Fitzgerald House, but maybe they could act on their attraction. Anything between them wouldn't last. He was only here through July.

She took a shaky breath. Could she go into a relationship knowing there was a predetermined expiration date? Could she indulge herself that much?

Gray wouldn't pull her away from the B and B. Abby would make sure Fitzgerald House came first.

But she wanted Gray to kiss her again. Wanted to feel that sizzle flying through her body. Maybe dinner didn't have to be business. Maybe Gray would kiss her again.

GRAY NUDGED HIS empty plate to the center of the breakfast table. A man could get used to fine coffee and excellent food. Maybe too used to it.

Why the hell had he asked Abby out to dinner?

He pushed away from the table. Cheryl had let him know Abby was in the garden.

Time to find the woman who haunted his thoughts. He headed out the library's French doors into the courtyard.

He tapped the bid folder labeled with Abby's precise handwriting against his thigh. Why had Dolley asked for his help? Were they hoping for a loan?

He knew how to say no.

Abby's hair caught his eyes first. That red-gold color seemed to glow in the morning sunlight. He made his way over.

Abby sat with her head bent over a crossword puzzle. On the table, a cup of coffee sat next to a partially eaten croissant. With her sunset-colored hair, she looked like a flower blooming next to the bright green hedge.

He should stay away from her. He should ignore the way his body perked up whenever he saw her. But for some reason, the world was brighter when she was around.

He tapped the folder. Abby obviously needed money. Why else would they do the restoration piece-meal? Was that the only reason she was interested in him?

He would tell her the third-floor bids looked fine.

Then he would beg off their date. He rubbed his forehead. And this had been a date, no matter what lies they told themselves.

He and Gwen had broken up, but he wasn't in any position to start something with Abby. Even if they combusted whenever they were together.

"Hey, Gray." She smiled and the sun shone more brightly.

"I don't think I've ever seen you relax," he said. "What have you done today?"

"Slept in." She held up the paper. "Tried to work on the crossword puzzle and daydreamed. The perfect day."

He didn't care that he shouldn't start anything with her. He knelt beside her chair, stroking a finger down her translucent skin.

Reaching out, she ran her fingers down his cheek, mirroring what he'd done.

He shivered. She'd touched him before, but this felt different. More tender.

He stood, backed up and broke the spell she'd cast over him. "What were you daydreaming about?"

She blushed. Her gaze slid away and focused over his shoulder. "You."

His heart skipped a beat. He leaned a hip against the table and picked up her hand from her lap. "Want to be more specific?"

"Not on your life."

She sat up and looked at the folder in his hand. Another blush swept across her face. "You have our bids."

He nodded, fighting the impulse to move closer.

She winced, and he fought the impulse to move closer.

"I'm sorry Dolley coerced you into looking at them."

"Not a problem."

She shook her head. "It wasn't right."

"I don't mind."

"Thank you." She swung her legs down and reached for the folder. "It still wasn't right."

"The bids look good." Actually, based on the bid the Foresters had given him, it looked as though Abby and her sisters were getting a bargain.

"If you do the restoration room by room, it costs more," he said.

"We know. It's a cash-flow issue. We'll see if we can get a loan, but…" She shrugged with a tight smile. "I know how much you love my brandy-pecan bars. How much would you pay for a lifetime supply?"

A chill seemed to settle over his skin. Was she joking, flirting—or testing the waters?

He'd eaten in her intimate kitchen for the past three weeks. And they'd spent hours talking. He'd told her more about his life and his family than anyone back in Boston. They'd become friends. Why couldn't he tell what Abby wanted?

He was paying her for the room and the meals. And now Abby suggested he could buy a lifetime of her bars? Had to be a joke. He kept his own tone light in response. "It might be worth it."

He tugged her out of her chair, and when her body brushed his, it was as if he'd grabbed a live wire.

Did she feel this connection, too?

"Do you have a restaurant you've wanted to visit tonight?" He couldn't stop brushing her knuckles with his thumb.

He thought he saw confusion in her green eyes. At least he wasn't the only one.

"There's a little Italian place over on York Street called Amore. We can walk over if you want."

So they would go out to dinner. It didn't have to be a big deal; they'd had plenty of those already. Then they'd see what happened next. "I'll make a reservation."

ABBY SLIPPED INTO a soft green scoop-neck cashmere sweater dress she'd found on sale the year before. It clung in all the right places. She added a pale green shawl along with gold earrings and a necklace.

Was tonight more than an innocent dinner?

In the courtyard, she'd gazed into Gray's crystal-blue eyes and wanted more. The touch of his finger on her cheek had made her melt like a chocolate ganache.

But he hadn't kissed her. She huffed out a breath. She would enjoy a lovely dinner, one that someone else had cooked for a change, and appreciate having a conversation with an intriguing man.

That was all.

Unless *Gray* started something.

As she entered the courtyard, the quarter moon shone soft light on the quiet garden. Discreet solar lights lined the paths.

Gray met her in the center of Bess's gardens. The look of appreciation in his eyes stole her breath. He didn't even try to hide the way he cast his gaze over her body, from the tips of her toes to her head. She almost felt his fingers take that same slow journey. He captured her hands.

"You're lovely." His intoxicating voice warmed her more than her shawl.

"Thank you."

He tightened his grip on her hands and shook his head. "I keep telling myself I should stay away, that I'm not able to pursue…anything with you."

Abby's back straightened. His words were as bitter tasting as chicory on the tongue, but she knew it was the truth. First there was the money factor—her lack and his abundance. Those dynamics led to relationship imbalances. Then there was the fact that family wasn't important to him. Family was everything to her. "You're right. There shouldn't be anything between us."

But instead of backing up, he stepped closer. "I can't stay away."

"Gray…" She started to protest, but stopped. Inhaling, she took the final step and closed the gap between them.

"God, Abby." He cradled her face and brushed his lips against hers.

Abby would have plenty of time to regret her actions. Right now she wanted this kiss.

His hands stroked down her neck, down her spine and settled on her lower back, tugging her closer.

Her breath quickened, and his pine-and-sandalwood cologne swamped her senses. Gray surrounded her, overwhelmed her.

She slid her hands up his chest. Her thumbs brushed his nipples through his shirt.

"Abby," he groaned. They broke apart. "Come up to my room."

To his room. This was too fast, too…everything. Moments ago, he'd said he didn't want this attraction.

She shook her head. "I don't think that's wise."

He kissed the corner of her mouth. "But so much fun."

She moved away but left her hand in his. "I have to make sure whatever is going on here doesn't change your business relationship with the B and B." She pulled in a deep breath. "We need the money."

He stared at her so long, her hands started to shake. "Naturally."

Gray squeezed her hand and led her to the garden gate. "Let's eat."

GRAY STARED AT the menu without really seeing the words. What was he doing here?

Abby didn't want their personal relationship to affect their *business* relationship. Logically, he understood this. But as a man, he wanted to be more than cash flow to her.

The setting was perfect. Their booth in the back of the dimly lit room made it easy to touch her. Her skin glowed in the candlelight.

He pulled back and put a little more space between them. She was crack, and he was an addict begging for hit after hit.

His body didn't care about Abby's motives.

Money had soured too many friendships. Hadn't he learned that lesson in college? People had been attracted to his name and the connections they thought he could make for them. Hell, money was why he was working in Savannah. A frat brother had needed to liquidate and the first person he'd thought of had been Gray. Sometimes he wondered if people only saw his deep pockets and never him.

How would money affect what was going on between him and Abby?

"Why are you scowling?" Abby asked.

He forced his face to relax. "Nothing." He picked up the menu again. "What do you recommend?"

She smiled. "What if we each order something and then share?"

"Checking out your competition?" he asked.

"Of course." She tilted her head, and the gold in her hair caught the light.

What was it about her? Whenever he was with her, something drilled into his core. Even now, he couldn't quite trust her attention. She seemed to like being with him, but he paid her to house and feed him. Paid her to care.

They split a Caprese salad, shared her wild mushroom fettuccine and his veal scaloppini. They made easy conversation about St. Patrick's Day and how busy Fitzgerald House would be and the timeline of his warehouse restoration.

"Dessert?" he asked, pouring the last of a very nice Chianti into her glass.

"I don't think I should. I was a vegetable today. I don't want it to all go to my hips."

If she wanted to draw his attention to her body, he would oblige. His gaze lingered on her breasts before he brought it back to her eyes. "I'm looking at an incredible body and a beautiful woman."

The light was dim, but he could swear she was blushing. Could people fake that?

"You're too kind." She folded her napkin and set it on the table. "Thank you for my busman's holiday. It was wonderful having someone else cook for a change."

He signaled for the check. What should he do now?

He could walk her back to the B and B and say good-night. Or he could kiss her again.

She gathered her shawl around her shoulders and they walked down the quiet street. He took her hand, linking them together.

"What's happening here?" she whispered, leaning her head against his arm.

"Hell if I know, but there's something that keeps dragging us together."

"Chemistry?"

"Yeah." They stopped next to a fountain. "I need you to understand, I'm only here through the end of July."

Her green eyes looked huge. "July." She choked out a small laugh and looked away. "It sounds like it's just around the corner."

He tipped her head up, forcing her to meet his eyes again. "It's only March."

She paced to the fountain. Leaning on the edge of the basin, she stared back at him. "I want more joy in my life. I deserve a little joy."

"Joy." He'd never thought he could be capable of bringing joy to someone's life. It sounded like a burden.

Her heels clicked on the pavement as she moved back to him. She touched his face. "Until the end of July."

He cupped her face. "July."

The moonlight sparkled on her porcelain skin. He brushed kisses on her eyes and slid down her cheekbones until their lips joined.

"Thank you for a wonderful evening," she whispered as the kiss ended.

When they began walking again, Abby tucked her hand into the crook of his arm. She shivered in the chilly air.

He wrapped an arm around her shoulders. "Cold?"

She smiled up at him. "Not with your arm around me."

She fit. Perfectly. He could rest his cheek on her

hair and inhale that unique blend of spice and sweetness that was Abby.

At the garden gate, he hugged her. "If I asked you up to my room now, would you come with me?"

She traced his lips with a gentle touch. He couldn't hold back his groan.

"No." She stood on her toes and kissed him. "I had a wonderful night. It was magical, but this Cinderella needs to get to bed."

"I'm sorry to hear that." Had he read her wrong? Maybe she wasn't as interested as he'd thought. "Good night."

Abby climbed the steps to the carriage house's second floor. "Thank you," she called.

Inside the main house, he grabbed a shot of whiskey. It would be a long night.

CHAPTER FIVE

Rule #29—We're a founding family of Savannah. We will maintain our place in the city by cherishing our heritage.

Grandpapa Fitzgerald

ABBY PIPED *WELCOME BABY GRACE* on to the side of the cake. Rolling her shoulders, she eased away from her three-tiered masterpiece. If she didn't touch pink frosting for a month, it would be too soon.

The kitchen door creaked open behind her. "That's gorgeous," a familiar voice said.

"Mamma!"

Abby dropped the pastry bag on the counter and rushed to give her mother a hug. The familiar scent of her mother's perfume cut through the smell of buttercream.

"It's so good to be home," her mother said, giving her a final squeeze.

"Why didn't you let us know you were coming?" Abby asked.

Mamie Fitzgerald's golden-red hair hadn't changed since she'd found disgusting white and gray hairs intertwined with her original hair color. Abby could only hope that she and her sisters would age as gracefully.

"I called Dolley this morning to make sure there

was an empty room," Mamma explained. "Aunt Cecelia is taking a couple of days at a spa. She suggested I visit my beautiful daughters."

"I'm so glad." Abby checked the time. "Let me get this in the fridge."

"It's a beautiful cake, but very pink. What's it for?"

"Baby shower this afternoon." In two hours.

"Here?" Mamma filled the kettle, pulled out the teapot and looked through the teas.

The tension in Abby's shoulders eased. Mamma was home, and everything felt more under control. "In the ballroom. It's a little large, but the mother-to-be had her engagement party and her wedding reception here, so she wanted to come back for this."

"Repeat customers. That's wonderful."

Abby pulled out the bookings calendar. "We're getting more and more catering business."

Mamma took the calendar and flipped through the pages. She looked up, her green eyes shining. "You make me so proud."

That was what Abby wanted, what she needed. "I'm just continuing what you started. You showed me how to work hard. To set a goal and see it through."

"I would never have thought about restoring the ballroom and catering." Mamma tapped a finger on Abby's nose, just as she had when Abby had been a child. "That was all you and your white thumb."

She held up her thumb. "It's pink today."

The kettle boiled. Mamma warmed the pot and added tea leaves. "Don't forget to have fun every once in a while."

Abby thought about Gray. "I'm trying."

They sat in the sitting area, sipping their tea.

"How is Aunt CeCe?" Abby and her mother spoke on the phone fairly often, but it wasn't the same as catching up in person.

"About the same." Mamma rubbed her hands. "She's in so much pain. I wish I could do more."

Of course Mamma did. Aunt CeCe had come down and stayed with Mamma after Daddy had died. She'd helped with all the meetings with the attorneys and the banks. She'd even lent Mamma money. "It's nice she can have a bit of a vacation."

"The spa specializes in treating rheumatoid arthritis patients. They have nursing staff to do the things I've been doing for her, which is why I was able to come see you girls."

Her mother's eyes sparkled as they talked. Abby wished she could be just as capable as her mother, able to handle everything.

"I'm glad you're home." Abby squeezed her mother's hand. "I should finish the sandwiches."

"Show me what needs doing and I'll help."

That would be perfect. Then Abby could check on the ballroom preparations. The women throwing the shower should have arrived by now. "Do you want to host the tea?"

"Absolutely."

"You should also check on the room we just opened on the second floor." Abby tried to remember if it was booked for the weekend.

"The Barbara Bush room?"

Abby nodded.

"That's where I'm sleeping tonight."

"That's the best way to check it out." She got her mother set up with the sandwich makings and then headed upstairs.

Josh sat on the floor near the staircase, putting together a log structure. Wow, she hadn't seen Lincoln Logs in forever.

"That's neat." Abby knelt next to him.

"Gray saw them and thought of me." Josh's brown eyes gleamed.

Abby saw Gray and Josh talking together every few days. Sometimes Cheryl was talking to them, although she always looked ready to run.

"What are you building?" she asked.

He pulled out a picture that Gray had clearly drawn for him. "A house. 'Cuz we had to leave ours."

"I'm sure it will be wonderful." She ruffled his hair, wishing she could hug him. "Is your mom up here?"

He grimaced. "She's helping with baby stuff."

Laughter echoed in the hallway as Abby approached the ballroom. What a lovely sound.

"Abby!" Maddy, a friend of the mother-to-be, spun in a circle. "What do you think?"

The tablecloths, balloons and streamers were all different shades of pink. Small pink tutus were wrapped around pink flowerpots. At least there was green in the herb pots—Bess's work, of course. "Very pink."

"That's what we were going for." Maddy grinned. "I sure hope the ultrasound is correct."

Cheryl smoothed out a hot pink tablecloth. "Is this where you want the gift table?"

A second hostess came over. "Maybe we should move it to the wall."

Abby helped Cheryl shift the table. Cheryl had fit into the B and B rhythm perfectly. It seemed as if she'd been here for years instead of just over a month. "Thanks for helping them set up."

Cheryl looked around, her eyes a little wide. "It's fun. Pink, but fun."

"You should see the cake. It's a pink explosion."

Since there wasn't anything else to do but bring up their food, she, Cheryl and Josh headed back downstairs.

Marion and Mamma were loading up the tea trolley. Abby and Cheryl did the same with the shower food.

After being introduced to Cheryl and Josh, Mamma said, "I think I need a man's opinion on the sandwiches."

"I can help." Josh bounced up and down. He sampled each one, turning his face up at the cucumber sandwiches.

"I like this one best," he announced, helping himself to another ham sandwich.

"I can take the shower food up, Abby," Cheryl volunteered.

"Thanks."

"Josh, stay right here," Cheryl instructed as she pushed the cart out.

Marion tapped her finger on her forehead. "Oh,

Gray was looking for you," she said to Abby. "He's in the business center."

Heat rushed to Abby's cheeks. No one knew that she and Gray were…seeing each other. "I'll go check what he needs."

She hurried down the hall.

Gray was bent over the printer. His hair was mussed, while his jeans cupped him in luscious places.

"Hey," she said, hearing her own breathlessness.

"Hey back at you." He straightened and she saw ink on his fingers.

"Is the darn thing acting up again?" She frowned.

"Paper jam." He wiped his hands on a crumpled piece of paper. "I fixed it."

"Thanks."

He grinned and walked toward her, shutting the door. "Hey," he said again.

He was going to kiss her. The way he'd been doing for the past week. One of these days she was going to combust.

His dimple flashed, making her weak in the knees. She'd kissed his dimple just last night.

And her mother was just down the hall. Who'd told her she should have some fun.

He leaned over and pressed a kiss to her lips.

She wrapped her arms around him.

He kissed her again, teasing his tongue slowly against hers. Everything inside her lit up like an arcade game. She gripped his shoulders so she wouldn't shove him to the floor.

She wasn't ready for more intimacy, but the way he kissed...

He pulled away. His eyes were dark and dangerous. "You need a new printer."

"Hmm?"

"This thing is on its last legs. I've had trouble printing all week."

"Oh." After fogging her brain with lust, he was discussing the printer. "I'll...talk to Dolley."

He gave her one more kiss. "Good."

Her brain kicked into gear. "Gray?"

He stroked a finger down her cheek. "Mmm-hmm."

"My mother's here for a couple of days."

He grinned. "Can't wait to meet her."

Abby blew out a breath that made his hair dance. "I haven't told anyone about us."

His blue eyes seemed to chill at her words. "Okay."

"It's just...so soon."

"I see." He stepped away from her.

She didn't know what to do with her hands. "If we could..."

"It will be our secret." He grabbed the door handle. "See you later."

Abby felt as if she'd kicked a puppy. No, make that a panther. Not smart.

CHERYL LIT THE flame under the chafing dish for the chicken wings. Everything smelled great. But then Miss Abby was so talented. Wouldn't it be something to be able to cook like she did?

Cheryl needed to talk to her. She'd been trying to get up the nerve for the past two days.

She checked the lemonade and the ice bucket full of champagne bottles. The organizers had already gone through two bottles and the party hadn't even started yet.

"That's everything," Cheryl said to the shower hostesses.

"It looks wonderful," Maddy said.

It did. Cheryl touched her stomach, remembering the shower her friends had thrown before Josh was born. She and Brad had planned to have at least one more child, maybe two. She'd hoped for a girl.

But then Brad had died. She forced a smile on her face as she finished the final touches. What would Brad think of the life she and Josh were living now? Would he be disappointed in her?

"I'll check in periodically, but if you need anything, dial the kitchen." Cheryl showed them how to use the house phone. "I'll send the guests up the elevator as they arrive."

"Thank you!" Maddy called out as Cheryl left the ballroom.

Heading downstairs to the kitchen, she hoped to catch Abby alone. And she was in luck.

Abby was loading the dishwasher. Josh was asleep on the love seat.

"They loved everything," Cheryl said. "But I think they might need more champagne. They've already finished two bottles."

"Wow." Abby wiped her hair off her forehead with

the back of her hand. She had such pretty hair, all red and gold.

Nothing like Cheryl's pale blond.

"I let them know I'll be checking on them, but I also showed them how to call down here." She grabbed a glass of water, wishing it could give her courage.

Abby nodded. "If I'm not here, just leave me a note on how many additional bottles you take up."

"Will do."

Abby started to turn back to the dishwasher, but stopped. Her face was so serious that it made Cheryl nervous. "Cheryl?" Abby asked.

"Yes?" Oh, please don't be a problem with her working here. She'd thought she'd been doing okay.

"I just want you to know how much we appreciate all the hard work you put in."

"Really?" she squeaked.

"Really." Abby grinned. "When we were upstairs, I was thinking that it felt as if you've been here for years. In a good way."

Cheryl swallowed, releasing a shaky breath. "Thank you."

"No, thank you."

Now or never. "Abby, is there any chance… Could I use a washer and dryer at the B and B?"

Abby blinked. "Of course."

"I won't interfere with the B and B's laundry. It's just, the Laundromat near our place isn't safe. I got so scared a couple of nights ago." Her words rushed out. A man had been selling drugs right in front of her and Josh. It had been low-key, but she'd felt rattled and threatened all at the same time. Now she didn't think she could ever go back. "I'll bring my own soap."

"Don't worry." Abby came closer and touched her arm. "You use whatever you need to."

"Thank you. You and Marion have been so good to us. I don't know what I would do without your help."

"I want you and Josh to stay safe."

That was what she was trying to do. Her life had come down to one theme. Keep her son safe. That meant making sure her brother-in-law, Levi, never found them.

She just hadn't realized how hard surviving would be and how much she would miss her husband.

GRAY HEADED SOUTH to Oglethorpe Plaza and an electronics store he'd seen near the FedEx Office he'd used. He needed a phone charger for the warehouse. He was doing so much business on his phone that the darn thing wouldn't stay charged and he kept forgetting to grab the charger from his room. Too bad he couldn't use the surge he got from kissing Abby to charge his phone.

When he'd left her in the business center, she'd looked stunned. Off balance. Abby was rarely off balance.

He grinned. He liked her that way.

Abby wanted to keep this thing between them a secret. He rolled his shoulders, trying to relieve the tension between his shoulder blades. No one had ever asked him to do that before. It didn't feel right.

At the store, the clerk suggested, "You might want to invest in a portable battery charger."

"Maybe." He'd heard about them. "Will it get me through the day?"

"Absolutely."

They looked at options, and he picked one out.

As the clerk walked him to the register, they passed a printer display. "Let's look at these," Gray said.

The clerk's eyes lit up. *Guy must be on commission.* "What are you interested in?"

Normally he would buy jewelry for a woman he was dating. But Abby wasn't just any woman.

She'd love a new printer. Wi-Fi enabled and with all the bells and whistles. "Show me what you've got."

He couldn't stop smiling. He couldn't wait to see Abby's face.

He was still smiling as he pulled back into Fitzgerald House's parking lot. The wine tasting should have started by now. Dolley was scheduled for tonight, which meant Abby would be in the kitchen. He wanted to get everything configured.

He hauled the boxes into the business center and closed the door. Grinning, he set up the new machine. The extra ink cartridges went into the supply cabinet. The piece-of-crap printer went into the empty box.

In the library he grabbed a glass of wine before greeting any of the other guests, toasting his own efforts.

"Gray," Dolley called out from the other side of the room. "Come meet Mamma."

The woman standing next to one of the Moon cou-

ples waved. She was stunning. He could see all three
of her daughters in her. Abby had her hair. Dolley had
her eyes. And Bess had her height.

Mrs. Fitzgerald glided toward Gray, holding out
her hand. Abby moved like that, too.

"Mrs. Fitzgerald, it's very nice to meet you."

"Mamma," Dolley said, "this is Gray Smythe, our
long-term guest."

"Ah, the man from Boston. Please call me Mamie,
since I was really Mrs. Oliver."

He frowned.

"We have what people might consider strange cov-
enants in the transfer of Fitzgerald House." Mamie
grinned. "One caveat is that if there isn't a male heir,
the woman keeps her maiden name and passes it along
to her daughters."

Dolley leaned her head against Mamie's shoulder. "There will always be a Fitzgerald in Fitzgerald House. That's what our great-great-grandpappy
wanted."

"You sure do things differently down here," Gray
said.

"We like our eccentricities." Mamie's vowels
seemed to drip with Spanish moss and kudzu.

"How are your condominiums coming along?"

He talked freely. Maybe it was the fact that he'd
spent so much time with her daughters, but Mamie
made him feel comfortable. As if he was a cherished
guest. The Fitzgeralds had the gift of hospitality.

"I should mingle," Mamie said after several minutes of conversation. She moved over to talk to one of the Repeater couples.

Gray turned to Dolley. "Do you have a moment?"

Dolley set down the bottle she'd just opened. "Sure."

"Follow me."

He led her to the business center and showed her the new machine.

"Abby bought a new printer?" Dolley hurried over to it. "Wow, she went all out. Fax, scanning and wireless. I thought she wanted me to look at the old one tonight."

"I…picked this one up."

"You bought this?" She was already looking through the small manual. She frowned. "Why?"

Because the women he dated expected him to buy them gifts.

He couldn't say that to Dolley. Abby wanted to keep their relationship secret. That spot between his shoulders prickled again.

"I need a better printer while I'm here." He rolled his shoulders, but the itchy feeling didn't go away. "But I thought you'd like to set up the passwords."

"Would I ever." She looked at the directions and then got to work. She was already punching in numbers on the control pad. "Mmm-hmm."

"Don't tell Abby yet," he said, closing the door behind him as he left. He wanted to reap the benefits of his surprise.

ABBY SLID THE chile relleno and vegetarian stratas she'd pulled together for breakfast into the fridge. The chile relleno strata was a new recipe. She hoped her guests would like it.

Her wine supplier had found some nice Mexican wines. Tonight her guests were sampling quesadillas, cheese-stuffed jalapenos, dips and salsas, and taquitos. Since she'd been roasting chilies, she'd made enchiladas for dinner.

With Mamma home it would be a family dinner. Abby grinned. She loved having the whole family around the table.

She just needed to make sure Gray didn't expose their relationship. She'd ignored Mamma's warnings about not getting involved with guests. Now she worried she would disappoint her mother. If it came down to a choice between a relationship and her family, she would always choose her family.

Gray pushed through the door. "It smells great in here."

Her heart beat a little faster, and the kitchen seemed to warm up. "You say that every time you come in."

"Because it's true."

"My whole family is here for dinner tonight."

"Oh." His smile faltered. "Do you want me to eat someplace else?"

"No!" She shook her head. "I'm just warning you."

He grinned. "So it will be me and four beautiful Fitzgerald women. I like it."

She waited for him to come closer, but he stayed where he was by the door.

"I've got something to show you." He was smiling like a Cheshire cat. "Come with me."

She checked the oven and turned down the heat. "Sure. What's up?"

"I've got a surprise for you."

She pulled off her apron and hung it on the hook next to the door. "Surprise?"

"Yup."

What was he up to? "What did you think of the wines tonight?"

"Interesting. I don't think I've ever had Mexican wines before." He rested a hand on her back, guiding her down the hall. "They were good, but your guacamole was fantastic. And I may have eaten most of the chorizo-cheese quesadillas."

He stopped in front of the business center. The door was closed. Strange. They always left it open.

He pushed the door open. "Ta-da."

Boxes were scattered on the floor. She frowned. Why would Gray want to show her boxes? And why were they in here?

"Not the floor," he said, pointing. "There."

A mammoth printer filled the table. She gaped. They couldn't possibly afford this. "I'm going to kill Dolley."

Maybe they could take it back. She moved over to the machine and started to disconnect it.

"What are you doing?" Gray caught her hand and laced their fingers together.

"I'm returning it. Dolley better still have the receipt. She was supposed to *fix* the old printer. Not replace it." She tried to shake his hand away. But he didn't let go.

"Dolley didn't buy it." He grinned. "I did."

Gray wasn't making sense. "What?"

"Surprise." He pressed a kiss to her knuckles. "I bought you a gift."

She shook his hand away. "You *what?*"

"I bought you a printer." His grin faded a little. "Dolley's already set up the Wi-Fi."

"What? Why?"

"Because…" His smile dropped away entirely. "I didn't think you'd want jewelry."

Jewelry? He was talking gibberish. "No, I wouldn't."

"We're…involved." He shrugged. "You needed a new printer."

"I don't want you buying—gifts—for me, for Fitzgerald House." Her skin prickled as if ants were crawling inside her shirt. "It's not appropriate."

"But…" He waved his hand.

"Take it back."

"No." He crossed his arms. "I want a dependable printer to use while I'm here. You need one. Don't be so stubborn."

Stubborn? "Don't fling your money around to solve my problems," she snapped. "We can handle them ourselves."

He exhaled. Stepping closer, he touched her cheek. "I wanted to buy you something. Let's just leave it here for now. If you don't like it, I'll take it with me when I head back to Boston. Okay?"

He leaned in as though he were going to kiss her but stopped.

She should have pushed him away. Her stomach churned. Keeping the printer made her skin crawl.

He'd been trying to help. But his methods rubbed her the wrong way.

"Thank you," she said quietly. "I…I guess it's okay. For now. Just don't do it again."

He set his forehead to hers. "Do what?"

"Buy me gifts."

"Okay," he said, frowning.

He grabbed the boxes as they headed to the kitchen. This frustrating man could be so thoughtful.

She'd have Dolley fix the old printer before Gray went back to Boston.

But she wished he hadn't bought her something so expensive—much less something she needed.

GRAY PULLED THE contract off the printer and slipped it in a folder. He'd review the agreement after dinner. It was a week after he'd bought the printer, and Abby's reaction still irked him. Any other woman he'd dated would have been incensed if he'd bought them something so—mundane.

And she hadn't said a word to her family about them dating. Not even to Mamie before she'd left. He didn't mean to be egotistical, but back in Boston, women bragged about dating him.

Not Abby.

What did she really expect from him?

Shaking his head, he headed to the library for appetizers.

"You must lead a charmed life," Dolley said, pulling a cork from a bottle of wine.

"Why? What's going on?"

"Two rooms freed up for St. Patrick's Day. If your family's still interested in visiting, I've held the rooms." Dolley handed him a glass of wine. "As Fitzgerald House's favorite guest, you get priority."

"We'll take them."

His mother had liked the idea of experiencing St. Paddy's Day in Savannah. And it would be great to see his family.

He shoved his hair off his forehead. He didn't know what to tell his family about Abby. If his mother knew he was dating, she might start more marriage manipulations. He didn't need his mother interfering with whatever this was between them.

And Abby wanted to keep their relationship secret. Apparently, he wasn't important enough to her to acknowledge to her family. That grated. But he would keep Abby's secret and not tell his family.

"Use my credit card to reserve the room," he said. "I appreciate you holding them. Let me know if there's some way I can repay you."

"What for?" She frowned.

"For...helping."

"Don't be silly." She shook her head at him.

Everyone expected something from him, money or influence. He rubbed at the ache in his neck. What was the Fitzgerald family's game?

He sipped his wine and wandered over to the three women who'd stayed at Fitzgerald House for the past two nights. "How was your day down on Tybee Island?"

The ladies rambled on about their tour of Fort

Pulaski, Tybee lighthouse and shopping. This was what Fitzgerald House had given him. The conversation didn't involve his money or his family. It was a relief, right? He'd always wanted to be more than his wealth. He could be just Gray here.

His fingers rattled on the side of his wineglass. It was more unsettling than he'd anticipated. What did it mean to be "just Gray"? Who was he without his money?

THE KITCHEN DOOR OPENED, and Abby turned. "Hey, Dolley."

Her smile fell away. She'd hoped it was Gray. She checked the rice, not wanting her sister to see her disappointment.

She enjoyed every minute she spent with Gray. Being with him made her believe she could achieve her goals. He really listened when she talked about the B and B or her dreams. She hadn't had that from anyone other than her sisters in so long.

There were so many reasons to stay away from him. Every man in her life had let her down. His visit was only that—a visit. Short-term.

But she couldn't stop thinking about him.

"Who's minding our guests?" Abby asked her sister.

"Gray's keeping the wine flowing. Amy's waiting on some Moons to check in. She'll clean up at seven." Dolley plucked a mushroom out of the salad. "I'm hoping to mooch dinner."

Abby smiled. Gray was taking his role as "senior

guest" seriously. When he'd arrived, she would never have guessed that he'd be interested in mingling so much and making small talk. "There's enough for three."

Dolley set another bowl on the table. "I've got a couple of things to tell you. Our bank meeting is confirmed for ten tomorrow."

"Good." Abby made a note on her to-do list.

"Second item. A group canceled during St. Paddy's Day, and I saved the rooms for Gray's family. They're coming for the holiday."

"Really?" The Smythes were coming to Savannah? Her stomach flip-flopped. How would Gray describe their relationship to his parents? She hadn't said anything to her sisters. She didn't know how to explain why she'd ignored Mamma's advice.

The man in question walked into the kitchen. "How was your day?" she asked with a smile.

"Great. Daniel's crew is making progress. We're already tearing down walls."

"Tell me about it while we eat." She set out chicken-and-sausage jambalaya.

Throughout dinner, she and Dolley plied Gray with questions about the condominiums. Though Dolley seemed genuinely interested, Abby was distracted by the feel of Gray's foot stroking her ankle.

Dolley pushed away from the table. "I've still got work to do, so I'm going to head out. Thanks for dinner."

Abby tucked leftovers into a container and handed them to Dolley as she left.

"You take care of your sisters," Gray commented, clearing his dishes.

"Dolley hates to cook."

He wrapped his arms around her waist and pulled her toward him. "I missed something earlier."

Her heartbeat accelerated. The kiss started out gentle but quickly became greedy.

He caged her between his body and the table. "When are you going to let me make love to you, Abs? You're killing me."

"My body wants to say yes." She arched her neck, and Gray ran his lips down to her collarbone. She dug her fingers into his arms.

"Then say yes." Their next kiss seared any thought but him from her mind. His tongue mated and dueled with hers. She wanted to agree more than she wanted to breathe.

His cell phone rang. "I'm ignoring that," he murmured against her lips.

Gray hoisted her onto the table. The phone rang again, and he pressed Ignore to send the call to his voice mail. He tossed the phone on the counter.

Abby pulled him close, running her fingers through his silky hair.

"Let's go to my room, or your room, I don't care." Desperation filled Gray's voice. "I want to be alone with you."

"Gray…" Before she could say yes, his phone blared again. This time she glanced at the screen.

"It's Daniel. You should answer." She leaned her head against his chest. His heart pounded like hers.

He cursed.

Gray answered the call and wrapped an arm around her waist. "What's up?"

As he listened, his blue eyes turned steely, and he clenched his jaw tight.

"I'll meet you there," he told Daniel.

Gray shut his phone off. "The security alarm went off at the warehouse. We'll finish this later."

"WHAT'D THEY GET?" Gray fingered the smashed padlock.

"Copper." Daniel held the door as they walked inside. "They got away with the pipe before the police arrived. Started ripping out the phone wires, but the sirens must have scared them off."

"At least the gas was shut off. Too bad they didn't steal the pipes we're replacing." Gray swatted at the anchors that had once held the pipes to the walls.

"The security company sent someone over," Daniel said. "The guy's walking through the top two floors right now."

"We need someone here overnight, permanently. I don't want more equipment disappearing."

Daniel slapped his cap on his thigh. "We could fix up a unit for someone."

"First floor?" Gray suggested.

Daniel nodded. "I know which one you're thinking about. I'll take a look in the morning."

Someone staying on-site. What about Josh and his mom? He wouldn't need to charge them rent—hell, he could pay her, help them out. He grinned. Maybe

Cheryl would take on some of the construction cleaning. Win, win, win. Just having the lights on and people in the space should keep Cheryl and Josh safe. And he would make sure there was a top-of-the-line security system for them. "I might know someone who could stay."

Daniel nodded. "I'll see what we have to do to get an occupancy clearance."

Gray locked the door as they went outside. The unusual bite in the air had him turning up his coat collar.

"I've already called the plumbing sub." Daniel leaned against his truck. "Unfortunately, until the price of copper drops, we're going to keep seeing thefts like this."

"It happened on a couple of my jobs up north, too. The cops caught one, meth users in that case. They hit a series of construction sites." He ran a hand through his hair. "I guess the Savannah setting lulled me into thinking those things wouldn't happen down here."

"We've got all the big-city vices, but they're wrapped up in Spanish moss and charm. Sorry you're not experiencing our Southern hospitality."

Gray sighed. "I think staying at Fitzgerald House has been worth it."

A small smile played across Daniel's face. "Yeah, those sisters are something else."

How well did Daniel know the Fitzgeralds? "Abby's the only sister who lives on-site, right?"

"Yes." Daniel jiggled his keys.

"Sure seems like she never takes any time off. Does the lady work 24/7?"

"She's pretty focused." Daniel's eyes narrowed. "Why?"

Gray wanted to ask about the last man she'd dated, but Daniel looked protective. "I never see her slow down."

"The whole family had a hard time after their dad died. He left them in debt up to their eyeballs, and they're still paying it off. A sweet-talkin' liar, that's what my mom called him."

"Sounds like there's a story there." So Abby had more problems than just restoring the third floor. One more reason to keep anything between them physical and short-term.

"We'll have to talk about that one over a beer—or two. See you in the morning."

Gray climbed the steps up from River Street. As he crossed Bay, a group of people called out, "Do you know where Kevin Barry's Pub is?"

"Take these stairs down and take a left when you hit the river." Abby would laugh at the notion that he'd given directions to tourists. "Have fun."

Abby. When he got back to the B and B, she'd be asleep.

Gray wanted to be in Abby's bed. Somehow it didn't matter to him that she was in debt or that those debts might complicate whatever they had together. He no longer cared why she was with him. All he knew was that he wanted her.

"I NEED YOU to stay here." Cheryl set Josh's backpack on the floor in the Fitzgerald House upstairs sitting area. "Right here."

Just yesterday Josh had wandered into the kitchen while she'd folded towels. Miss Abby had been great, entertaining and feeding him, but Cheryl didn't want to impose.

She needed this job. She would never go back to Levi.

That meant she had to earn enough to pay for rent and eventually day care. And she needed to keep her car running. The man at the shop said she needed a new muffler and an alternator—soon.

Food was more important. And new shoes for Josh. She wrung her hands. He was growing out of his clothes so fast.

"I won't go anywhere, Mamma." Josh gave her his sweetest smile.

She pushed her cart over to the Lucy Hayes room. "I'll be in here."

She knocked, even though Marion had said the couple had checked out. "Housekeeping."

As she waited, she looked back at Josh. When no one answered, she swiped her key card and opened the door. She used the cart to prop the door open. That way if Josh needed her, he'd be able to get to her.

The room wasn't too messy, thank goodness. She hated when people left their condom wrappers beside the bed.

Pulling open the drapes, she stared at Miss Bess's

beautiful gardens. She'd abandoned her African violet collection at Levi's. Some of the plants had been her grandmother's, others her mother's, and it still hurt to think of leaving them behind.

She ripped the covers off the bed, wishing she could curl up on the soft mattress. No time. Moving into the bathroom, she grabbed the towels and stuffed them into the laundry bag with the bedding. Then she emptied the wastebaskets and started putting the room to rights.

She spotted cash on the desk under her card. Twenty bucks. She tucked the money in her pocket. She couldn't remember what the couple looked like, but they'd just helped buy her son new shoes.

Cheryl peeked out the door. Josh had his blond head down, working furiously in his coloring book.

She hated that they lived this way. Her son should be outside playing, making friends. Instead, he had to stay with her all the time. She hadn't been able to survive Brad's death. Hadn't given her son a decent home.

She grabbed the bucket of cleaning products and headed to the bathroom.

She wanted more than a cleaning job. Maybe she could learn to cook. Miss Abby worked magic in the kitchen.

She grabbed the mop and went to work on the floor. She would make everything sparkle, because she couldn't lose this job.

Sweat poured down her back as she took one final swipe.

"Looks good," a deep voice said behind her.

She swung around, wielding the mop like a weapon.

"Whoa." Mr. Smythe jumped back, his hands in the air. "I didn't mean to startle you."

Her mouth dropped open. "I'm…"

"I should have known better," he said, backing into the main room. "Marion said I'd find you up here."

Why was he looking for her? Her heart beat harder. *Josh.*

She hurried out of the bathroom and moved to the hallway. He was still where she'd asked him to stay. The breath caught in her chest came out in a whoosh.

Josh looked up and waved. "Hi, Gray."

"Hey, Josh." Mr. Smythe joined her in the hall.

She turned to Mr. Smythe, shuffling back a step or two. He was just so big. "Is…is there something you need?"

He held up his hands, as if surrendering.

She took another step back, hating herself for being afraid.

"I don't know what your living situation is, but I've got a proposition."

Her body shook. She risked another glance at Josh. "No."

"What?" Mr. Smythe frowned. "But you haven't even heard—"

"I may be…struggling." She shook her head. "But I won't stoop that low."

His eyes went wide. "That's not what I meant. God, no."

Rushing down the hallway, she stopped in front of Josh. "Come and work in the room with me."

She pinched her lips together, trying to stop them from trembling.

"No. Wait." He held his hands out, palms up. "Someone broke into the warehouse I'm rehabbing. I was hoping you and Josh would consider living there to help with security."

She stopped stuffing Josh's things into his backpack.

"I don't understand." She set her hand on her son's shoulder.

"You'd be helping me."

She looked down at Josh, then back up at Mr. Smythe. "Why?"

"There's a unit that we can fix up pretty quickly." He rubbed his cheek, his whiskers rasping in the quiet. "But we have a ways to go before the rest of the building is ready. I don't want my equipment or supplies walking away in the meantime."

"What would I have to do?" She wouldn't be a very big deterrent. She'd barely been able to fight Levi off, and he'd been drunk.

"Nothing. I just want it to be clear that the building is occupied. And if you hear anything, I'd only want you to call me or the police. Both. If I'm not here, you'd call Daniel Forester. He's doing the construction."

"How much would the rent be?" This sounded too good to be true.

"Sorry, I should have said at the beginning. The

rent is free. I need you more than you need me." He smiled. "No strings."

"Free?" She suddenly felt light-headed. This couldn't be real. *Free?*

"Okay." Mr. Smythe grinned down at Josh. "Your mom's a tough negotiator."

"My mom's the best." Josh hugged her legs.

"How about if I pay you a couple hundred a month?" Mr. Smythe asked.

"That's ridiculous." But she swallowed. No rent and more money? Maybe she could look into day care for Josh and cooking classes for herself. Wouldn't that be something? "Let me…let me think about it."

"I hope you'll agree." He ruffled Josh's hair.

Could she do this? "Yes." Tears threatened to fall, but she held them back. "Thank you."

Mr. Smythe nodded. "Good. I'll get Daniel to get the place ready."

A weird feeling bubbled in her chest. Hope. It had been such a long time since she'd felt anything like it. Maybe she could finally make a better life for herself and Josh.

ABBY WORKED TO nail down menus for the next two weeks. She wanted items she could prepare in advance. Then she needed to place her food order.

A deep voice said, "Sounds delicious."

She jumped and clipped Gray in the chin with her shoulder.

"That's the menu for the garden-tour teas." She

stroked his face where she'd bumped him. "Did I hurt you?"

"No." He pointed back at the list. "I vote for pecan bars."

"Isn't that a surprise?" She added the bars to the list with a shake of her head. "I thought I saw you leave this morning."

"I came back to make some calls and talk to Cheryl about something." He poured a cup of coffee and sat at the table.

His marvelous scent wrapped around her. She fought to keep herself from leaning over and inhaling. It would make her jumpier than she already was. She needed to channel her sexual energy into work. She had hours of labor ahead of her today and no time for daydreaming.

"What happened last night at the warehouse?" she asked. Anything to keep her fingers away from that dark hair.

"Someone broke in and stole copper."

She put her hand on his arm. "I'm sorry."

He waved her sympathy away. "I asked Cheryl and Josh if she would live there." His fingers tapped the table. "I'm going to pay her. I want someone on-site." His words rushed out. "Just a presence."

He wouldn't look her in the eye.

"Are you stealing one of my best employees?" she teased.

His blue gaze snapped back to hers. "God, no."

She laughed at his shocked expression. "Did she say yes?"

He rolled his eyes. "With tears."

"You're a very nice man."

"Don't spread that around."

But she thought about his generosity after he left and as she walked to the bank for her meeting.

"We will get this loan," Abby muttered. The day was too gorgeous for anything to go wrong. "We will succeed."

Abby tugged on the skirt of her navy blue suit. She'd dressed conservatively to show that she was serious. Failure wasn't an option.

She walked through the branch and pulled open the doors to the administrative wing of the First Savannah Mercantile Bank. As the door swung shut, the clatter of tellers and bank customers faded.

Abby checked her watch—fifteen minutes early. She and Dolley had agreed to arrive early.

A young woman acted as sentry outside Wayne's office. Wayne had been their loan officer ever since Mamma had begun restoring Fitzgerald House. His assistant didn't look familiar, and Abby had been here just a few months ago. He seemed to go through a lot of assistants.

Abby glanced down at the woman's nameplate. "Hi, Libby, I'm Abigail Fitzgerald. My sister and I are meeting with Wayne."

The young woman's fingernails clattered against her keyboard. She didn't even look up. "Libby left. I'm a temp. Are you Mr. Lennertz's ten o'clock?" she asked.

"Yes. Abigail and Dolley Fitzgerald," Abby repeated.

The woman looked up, a frown creasing her forehead. "You're the only one here."

"My sister's on her way," Abby explained.

"Mr. Lennertz is still in a meeting." The temp waved her over to the guest chairs. "Please, take a seat."

Abby sank into the chair. Whenever she met with Wayne, she felt like a poor relation begging for a handout.

At one time, the Fitzgerald family had been part owners of the bank. Unfortunately, her father had used the bank stock to secure the failed Tybee land deal. After he'd died, the sale of the bank stock hadn't covered the debt he'd accumulated. Mamma had been forced to take out additional loans to survive.

Wayne had been more than willing to share those details with Abby at the first loan-review meeting she'd attended three years ago. Along with the fact that if Mamma had dated him, maybe the Fitzgerald family wouldn't always be asking the bank for money.

Thank goodness Mamma had had the sense not to go out with Wayne.

Abby crossed her legs and glanced at the magazines. If she leaned a little to the left, she could see inside Wayne's office.

He had his chair rocked back. He and the man sitting in his office seemed to be shooting the breeze. At least Wayne had a smile on his round face.

She consciously stopped her fingers from tapping on her thigh. *Think positive.* They would get the loan, finish off the room restorations and build Southern Comforts. Her restaurant.

And maybe they could win the lottery without buying a ticket, too.

Dolley had better get here soon. Abby pulled out the projections. If her sister didn't show up, Abby needed to speak coherently about the B and B's financial progress.

She studied the numbers, but her mind was like a Teflon pan—every statistic slipped away. Dolley was their numbers person.

She checked her watch. Ten o'clock.

Where R U? she texted. Her stomach churned like a mixer set on high.

No answer.

Laughter rolled out of Wayne's office. At least he didn't know Dolley was late.

Dolley finally breezed into the waiting area ten minutes late, a scarf streaming behind her. Her curly red hair was pinned up in a big clip. "Sorry, sorry."

Abby stared at Dolley's outfit—jeans and a T-shirt. "That's what you're wearing?" she groaned. This wasn't a good start. "We're asking for a lot of money. Why aren't you in a suit?"

"Don't start with me," Dolley growled. "At least I threw on a jacket. I've been up all night—server problems."

Releasing her clenched fists, Abby approached the temp's desk. "My sister's here."

The temp actually snapped her gum and slouched her way to Wayne's doorway. "Your ten o'clock is here."

"Tell the girls to wait," Wayne called out.

Abby took deep breaths as she went back to sit next to Dolley.

Dolley tapped away on her phone. "Did I give you an update on other loan or grant possibilities?"

"No."

"I haven't found anything. We'll need to ask Wayne for help." Dolley wrinkled her nose.

They stood as Wayne and his guest finally vacated the office.

"Abigail, Dolley, good to see you." Wayne's voice boomed in the small waiting area. "Ginny, did you offer them anything to drink?"

Ginny looked up. "Would you like something to drink?"

"Coffee, black." Dolley sounded desperate.

"Water, please," Abby said. She wanted to get this meeting started.

Wayne led them to a small table in his office. The paneling was so dark it sucked the light out of the room. As she and Dolley opened their files, Wayne's assistant brought in their drinks.

"Dolley tells me you girls want to expand," Wayne said.

Girls? Abby gritted her teeth. Dolley rolled her eyes.

"We have seven more rooms to complete on the third floor." Abby pulled out the floor plan. "Then we plan to remodel the carriage house into a restaurant—Southern Comforts—and add guest rooms above that."

Wayne nodded absently. "That's ambitious."

"We can handle it." Abby forced herself to relax. Confident people didn't grip the edge of the table as if it were a life raft.

Wayne riffled through the stack of papers in front of him. Probably the family's financial history back to the 1800s. "When did you last update rooms?"

"We brought the last room on the second floor online this month," Abby said.

Wayne frowned as he flipped through financial statements. "You're doing pretty well."

"We're making a profit." Dolley rapped her pen on the tabletop.

Abby laid a hand on top of her sister's.

"We'd like to restructure our current loan and turn it into long-term financing." Dolley pushed at her curls.

"That's a stretch," Wayne said. "And what about this restaurant? You're requesting another three hundred thousand. That's a lot, given how many new restaurants fail."

"We have a great location and reputation." Abby schooled the desperation out of her voice. "This isn't as if we're starting from scratch. We have a built-in customer base."

"Plus, Abby managed a successful restaurant in New York," Dolley added.

Wayne nodded but didn't comment.

Dolley pushed a printout toward him. "Here's a record of people who've tried to book rooms during the next few weeks. We've had to turn them away because we're at capacity. We could easily fill the seven rooms we're asking to remodel and another houseful."

"That's for St. Paddy's Day." Wayne tipped his head. "Can you sustain that occupancy rate through the rest of the year?"

"We believe we can." Dolley's voice cracked.

"And your father thought he could sell those condos." Wayne tapped his finger against the file.

"This is a B and B, not our father's condos." Abby's hands shook.

Wayne waved his hand over the file. "The mistakes your father made are part of your family's credit history."

"We've never been late on a payment." Dolley's face was so red, Abby worried she might erupt.

"Do you know of any economic-development loans we might qualify for?" Abby asked.

Wayne scrunched up his mouth. "You might check with the SBA, but I don't think they'll lend you this much money."

"Maybe we could get a portion from them and the remainder from the bank," Abby suggested.

Wayne tapped his fingers together. "The bank would insist on being the primary security holder."

"You've already asked that we collateralize our loan with a mortgage on the entire Fitzgerald House. The bank will have at least five times more collateral than you need." Dolley folded her files. "Abby, it's time we look for another bank."

"Dolley," Abby gasped. Had a grease fire blown through and sucked the oxygen out of the room?

"You think you can change banks in this economy?" Wayne snapped.

"We need a bank who wants to be our partner." Dolley slapped her cup down and it sloshed on the papers strewn across the table.

How had this conversation deteriorated so drastically? They couldn't handle the work of changing banks while heading into their busiest months.

She grabbed her sister's arm. "Let's step outside."

Wayne shoved his chair away from the table. "Good luck."

Abby pushed out of her chair. "Can we take a time-out here?"

Dolley and Wayne glared at each other.

"Our relationship goes back decades," Abby pleaded.

"And we're not getting credit for our years of business." Dolley planted her fists on the table.

"Let's not be hasty," Wayne said. "Taking changes in front of the loan committee isn't easy. With the terrible economy and tougher scrutiny of the bank's assets, we have to be careful."

"And will you fight for us?" Dolley asked, staring him in the eye.

He hesitated before giving a slow nod.

"We're wasting our time. Obviously, Wayne doesn't

really believe we can succeed." Dolley stuffed papers into her briefcase. "Maybe another bank will appreciate our business. We're leaving."

CHAPTER SIX

Rule #12—Once guests check in, they're our responsibility.

Mamie Fitzgerald

GRAY SLID HAMBURGER patties onto toasted buns and set one on each plate. Amazing how natural it felt, grilling dinner on the small private patio in the Fitzgerald House courtyard with Abby.

She wasn't in the best of moods. While they ate, he planned to find out why she kept scowling. Hopefully, he could cheer her up.

"I've made your family's dinner reservations." Abby set the plates on the table.

"Thanks. Can't wait to introduce you to them." He shut off the gas. "How do you want to describe us?"

Abby rubbed her forehead. "I—I don't know. Let me think about it."

"Okay." He gritted his teeth, wanting to push her to acknowledge their relationship. And that wasn't like him at all.

"No. Go ahead and tell your family whatever you want," she said, waving her hand.

As she headed back to the kitchen, he said, "I should warn you, my mother…" How should he describe her?

"Even though she didn't grow up super wealthy, she's kind of a…snob."

"Nice to know." Abby turned at the door. "But I'm pretty good at handling people."

The screen slapped shut behind her.

Yes, she was. But this was his mother.

When Abby came back out to the patio, he asked, "How did your bank meeting go this morning?"

Abby slammed down a bowl, and cottage fries spilled out. "Awful."

Gray jerked. He'd never seen Abby angry. "Did they turn you down?"

"We never even got to that point." Abby's hands fisted at her sides. "Wayne harassed us about the debt our father racked up. Dolley freaked out at Wayne's condescending attitude, and she threatened to pull our business from the bank. Then she walked out."

Abby took a gulp of her beer. She was so tense, he could see the bottle shaking in her hand.

The screen door banged, and Dolley stalked to the table. "Bess says you called that rat, Wayne."

"I had to fix the mess you made." Abby slapped her hands on the table. "He wouldn't talk to me."

Abby's posture mimicked her sister's, fists on the table, body leaning forward. The women glared at each other.

"I'm serious about finding another bank for this loan." Dolley punched her fist against the table, and the dishes rattled. "We don't have to take that crap from anyone."

"We can't!" Abby threw her hands up in the air, knocking her bottle over. Beer sprayed all over the table.

"Why not?" Dolley yelled back.

"You're supposed to be the numbers person. Read the damn loan. I did after the meeting imploded." Abby righted the bottle and futilely mopped up the spill with a napkin. "We're required to maintain all our accounts at Mercantile until the balloon is repaid."

Dolley's mouth dropped open. Her already pale skin turned a little gray.

Abby threw down the sopping napkin and paced the small patio. "If we pull our accounts, we're in default. I may not have gone to business school, but I can read a damn loan document."

Dolley slumped into an empty chair and dropped her head in her hand. "Oh, shit. I forgot. Must be sleep deprivation."

Gray caught Abby's shoulders on her next pass. "There's got to be an escape clause."

"Full repayment of the loan." Abby rolled her eyes.

Dolley's head jerked up. "We can refinance with another bank. The other bank could pay off Mercantile."

"We don't have months to find another bank, and then get through the appraisal and loan negotiations," Abby snapped. "Samuel's already started working on the first room."

"We can try," Dolley said, twisting her hands together.

Abby scowled at her sister. "I should have sent you home when you told me you'd been up all night. You can't work those hours and then meet with Wayne. Combining a sleep-deprived, espresso-fueled sister with an idiot loan officer is a recipe for disaster." She pointed a finger at Dolley. "No one has a temper like you."

Gray sat, hoping Abby would follow his lead. "Sometimes there are ways around the loan stipulations," he said.

"Really?" Dolley turned to him.

"I could take a look if you want," he suggested.

"You'd review the documents for us?" Dolley asked as if he'd thrown her a life preserver.

"Gray is our guest." Abby crossed her arms and frowned. "This is *our* problem."

Guest. A sharp pain twisted in his chest. "I thought I was more than a guest."

"You…are." Abby's hand covered her mouth. She shot a look at her sister and shook her head.

Yeah, couldn't let the sisters know they were dating. He exhaled. "Between my real estate background and watching how you run the B and B, maybe I can see something."

"He's seen our renovation plans," Dolley said. "What will it hurt if he sees the financial side of our business?" Dolley held out her hand.

"I'm willing to help," Gray said, patting Dolley's hand.

"My sisters and I will take care of this." Abby's lips formed a straight line.

"I know I screwed up, but damn it, we can't do everything by ourselves." Dolley's frustration came through loud and clear. "Gray knows about this stuff. Sometimes we need help."

He stood and touched Abby's shoulder. Her muscles were as hard as granite under his fingers. "I'd like to help."

Tears glittered in Abby's eyes. Were they from anger or embarrassment?

"Our meeting this morning reinforced every misconception Wayne has about the Fitzgeralds," Abby whispered. "We need this loan."

"Why don't you let me look things over?" he offered again.

"Come on." Dolley stood and wrapped one arm around her sister's waist. "Maybe Gray can see something that we can't."

Abby sank into the chair. "All afternoon I worried I'd be the person who lost Fitzgerald House." She clutched at the hand Dolley placed on her shoulder. "Mamma left me in charge. It would kill her if I let something happen to the house."

She was carrying that kind of burden around? He'd had no idea things were that bad.

Dolley slumped in the chair and laid her head on Abby's shoulder. "Please, let Gray help. Then if I have to grovel to Wayne, I promise I'll do it."

Gray hated the defeated look on Abby's face. "Let me take a look," he said softly.

Abby's shoulders slumped. "Sure."

"What do you need?" Dolley asked him.

"The current loan agreements, the application and

any financial information you provided to the bank. That should start me off."

He pictured reviewing everything tonight while Abby worked on the St. Paddy's Day preparations. He liked the idea of working together in the evening. That was a better date than any dinner or benefit he'd attended back in Boston.

"My file's in the kitchen." Dolley gave her sister a small squeeze. "Abs, everything will be fine." Her curls bounced as she glanced at him. "Thank you. Hell, maybe you'd want to invest in the old house."

"Dolley!" Abby's glare could have seared her sister.

Dolley shrugged. "Gray has a better idea of how we operate than Wayne does."

Gray covered Abby's cold hand with his. "Is this okay with you?"

She hesitated before nodding. Her face was passive, and she just looked beat. All because of some idiot loan officer.

AFTER REVIEWING THE Fitzgeralds' information the night before, Gray was impressed. The family was asset strong, but cash poor. If he were looking to get into the B and B business, they would be the perfect takeover candidate.

They'd had big cash outlays over the past twenty-four months, but the expenditures had improved the house and the services their guests received. The bank should be jumping at the chance to loan Abby money. She'd work herself to the bone before allowing Fitzgerald House to fail.

At this afternoon's meeting, he hoped to get Abby's loan process back on track. He'd called Lennertz this morning, and the man had suggested they meet at a café on Broughton Street.

"Thanks for agreeing to this, Mr. Lennertz." Gray shook the man's hand. Soft, just like everything else about him.

"Call me Wayne." The chair creaked as the banker settled his weight into it.

"And I'm Gray." He nodded to the waitress standing with a coffeepot in hand and she poured him a cup. He doctored the brew with cream, wishing it were Abby's coffee.

Wayne ordered coffee and pecan pie. "You're rehabbing a warehouse over on River Street, right?"

"That's right." Gray sized up his adversary. He'd done his research before coming here this afternoon. The Lennertz family had run the bank since Sherman had delivered Savannah to President Lincoln as a Christmas present. Wayne held his position because of family, not talent. Gray had run into his type too often. The best way to deal with a man like this was to play to his ego. No wonder the Fitzgeralds had problems. He couldn't picture Dolley kowtowing to this man.

"What can First Mercantile do for you?" Wayne added a serious dollop of cream to his coffee and then stirred in some sugar.

"I've been staying at Fitzgerald House while I'm in town."

"I didn't know that." Wayne took a bite of his pie and sat back and sighed.

"I've had the pleasure of living there since the beginning of February." Gray leaned his elbows on the table. "I've taken an interest in the sisters' plans."

"Those sisters are something else. I can't believe they're thinking about starting a restaurant."

Gray's shoulders tensed at Wayne's tone. "You don't think they can do it?"

"Sure, if they use someone else's money. I doubt they'll ever break even with a restaurant. I won't let my bank take the risk."

"I heard the meeting yesterday imploded."

"Sweet baby Jesus, you should have seen Dolley blowing her stack." Wayne leaned back in his chair, grinning.

"She's got a short fuse."

Wayne snorted. "Those Fitzgeralds have always been so uppity. They got their comeuppance after their daddy lost everything."

"Sounds like you've got history there." Was that the real problem?

"Yeah. I asked Mamie out too many times, but she only had eyes for Beau. Beau's loan was the first one I ever made." Wayne's eyes narrowed. "I had to go back to working as a teller for two years because of his mess."

"But these women aren't their father." Gray forced a neutral expression across his face. "Fitzgerald House is the best-run place I've ever stayed in."

Wayne swallowed a chunk of pie. "I really shouldn't be talking to you about their loan."

Now Lennertz discovered discretion? Gray wanted to roll his eyes. Instead, he tipped his head, trying for a buddy-buddy tone. "Well, you know women. They've asked me to straighten up the mess Dolley's mouth created," he lied.

"'Bout time they got a man involved in their business. Maybe if they had more male influence, the sisters wouldn't be looking at defaulting on the balloon. Too bad they didn't bring you to the meeting yesterday." The man leaned back in his chair. "I'm sure I could find a buyer for that prime piece of real estate."

"They aren't looking to sell. If they were, I'd make an offer." But only if Abby and her sisters ran the place.

"With the depressed real estate market, a buyer could get a real bargain," Lennertz said.

"True, but I'm here to help get the loan application back on track."

"Yesterday's meeting was supposed to be a quick review before I take the loan request to the committee," Wayne drawled. "Too bad Dolley stomped out of my office."

"Can I answer any questions you didn't get to ask?"

"I don't have any." Wayne leaned forward. "I'm willing to support the house expansion loan, but no changes to the balloon loan and no additional funds for a restaurant."

This guy lacked vision. Gray had run into too many bankers who wouldn't see a vision if the Angel

Gabriel descended on them. "Have you ever been in the B and B?"

"Sure. Years ago."

"I can't count the number of guests I've met who come back year after year. Those sisters have loyal customers recommending their business to friends all over the country, all over the world." Gray held up a hand. "You can't buy that kind of marketing."

Wayne crossed his arms. "Are you sure you don't want to buy Fitzgerald House?"

"No. As I said, I'm just here to talk about the loan." Abby would skin him with one of her knives if she knew he'd met with Lennertz. "I'll suggest Abby call you. I'd appreciate it if you kept this meeting between us. You can tell her the loan committee will be reviewing their application."

"Have Abby call me." Lennertz wiped his mouth. "But if you're looking to invest in Savannah, I'd love to work with you."

Gray sat back in his chair. Investing in real estate in historic Savannah might be an interesting addition to his portfolio. His dad might like the idea of a partial interest in property in the heart of Savannah. He tapped his chin. It was definitely something to think about.

ABBY WANTED EVERYTHING to be perfect for Gray's family. Nigel had just headed to the airport to pick them up. Her fingers drummed the kitchen counter. She checked her to-do list. Baskets for the Smythes—check. Smythe dinner reservations confirmed—

check. She'd already left their weekend events itineraries in their rooms.

Time was flying, but she was on schedule. She'd finish the trifle while her sponge cake cooled.

She poured whipping cream into her mixer. When peaks formed, she added sugar and then sherry. She spread the finished cream into the six bowls she'd worked on the day before and then garnished them with crystallized violets and pansies. "If that doesn't say spring, I don't know what else would."

When the front-desk buzzer sounded, she set the last trifle bowl in the fridge. Time to be Abigail the hotelier, instead of Abby the chef.

As she walked into the foyer, her stomach gave a tiny flutter. The man and woman standing by the registration desk had to be Gray's parents. "Mr. and Mrs. Smythe?"

"Yes." Gray had inherited his hair from his father. Only a few silver threads glimmered in the man's thick black hair.

"Welcome to Fitzgerald House."

Nigel pushed a loaded luggage trolley into the foyer.

"Nigel, the luggage can go up to the Martha rooms. Mr. and Mrs. Smythe are in Martha Washington and their daughter is in Jefferson."

Gray had inherited his mother's bright blue eyes. "I can see your son is a blend of the best of both his parents. I'm Abigail Fitzgerald."

Mrs. Smythe blinked. The edges of her lips turned up, but the smile didn't reach her eyes. "Thank you—" she glanced at her name tag "—Abigail."

Abby pasted a smile on her face. Apparently Gray hadn't mentioned her to his family. She shouldn't be disappointed. She hadn't told anyone about their relationship, either.

"Here are your room cards. If you need transportation, let me know and we can set it up." She looked around. "I thought there would be one more in your party—your daughter?"

"Courtney is stretching her legs with Gwendolyn. The weather's so lovely, they took a stroll around the square," Mrs. Smythe said.

Her eyes widened. "I'm sorry. Did you say there were four in your party?" All their dinner and sightseeing reservations were for four. Not five.

Mrs. Smythe nodded. "We brought a surprise for Gray. Don't worry. Just put her in with Courtney."

Abby added another key card to the folder. Her? What kind of parents brought their son a woman as a surprise?

She didn't have long to speculate. Two young women walked in the door. They both wore sweater sets, beautifully tailored pants and strands of pearls. Gray's sister was easy to spot. She had his eyes and curly black hair. Her friend had long blond hair and gray eyes.

"Welcome to Fitzgerald House. I'm Abby. Here are your room cards." Her fingers shook as she handed them a floor map and pointed out the elevator. "I hope you enjoy your stay. If there's anything you need, please let me know."

"Can I have a key card for Gray's room?" His sister grinned at the other woman.

"Oh." Abby blinked for a minute. Something was off here. "I wish I could." Not really. "But I'm afraid I'd need his permission to let you have access to his room."

His sister's black eyebrows snapped together. "We'll pick one up later."

The two women headed up the stairs, arms linked.

Abby reached for her cell phone. Her fingers rattled against the keys as she pushed Gray's speed dial number.

Before he could say more than hello, she said, "Your parents are here. Why didn't you tell me your sister was bringing a friend? I can't get another ticket for the parade."

In the background, a saw buzzed. "Hang on," Gray said. The noise grew more muffled. "What did you say?"

"Your parents are here." She spoke slowly. "And your sister brought a guest. I need to change all your reservations to five people. There's no way I can get another ticket for the parade." Abby could hear the panic in her voice. This was not the weekend to be adjusting things. Four hundred thousand people would fill Savannah to celebrate all things Irish.

"I'm not slow, Abs, I just couldn't hear you." He sounded testy. Well, too bad. His family was messing up her day.

"I called in favors to get you into some of these events." Abby rubbed her forehead.

"Don't worry about the parade," Gray said. "I won't go."

"I'll start calling the restaurants."

"Thanks. I'll make it up to you. Do you know who came with them?"

"I heard her name, but I was too flustered to remember."

"I guess I'll find out tonight. Say, did you call your loan officer?" Gray asked.

"Yes. You were right. Wayne had calmed down. He's taking the package to the loan committee. What a relief."

"Great." Someone called Gray's name in the background.

"I'll let you go." She had calls to make.

Abby spent the next half hour on the phone. One restaurant almost refused to change the reservation. They couldn't tie up a table for six. She sweet-talked and begged. All for Gray, his family—and Gray's gorgeous surprise.

GRAY TOOK A quick shower. If he hugged his mother while covered in sawdust and smelling like a laborer, she'd be outraged. She hated reminders that he enjoyed ripping things apart and then putting them back together.

He pushed around the clothes hanging in his closet. He had a jacket, and he would wear dress pants instead of his normal jeans, but he refused to wear a tie. Hell, he hadn't even brought one to Savannah.

He called his dad's cell phone. "I'm heading downstairs for wine. It's in the library. See you there."

Abby wasn't setting up the wine tasting, and his disappointment was bitter. He missed her smile. They'd barely seen each other this week. "Hey, Bess, what's the theme tonight?"

"French Country. You'll be drinking a Muscadet wine from the Loire region of France." She looked at a small card. "Please note the aromas of anise and citrus. There's also a lovely Burgundy and Champagne."

Gray spread a tapenade of olives and figs on toast. He added a little duck pâté and a couple of grilled-leek-and-garlic tarts to his plate. Abby's creativity should impress his parents.

When Bess handed him a glass of wine, he said, "I thought Abby normally hosted Friday night."

"She's swamped because of this weekend's garden tours. Plus, St. Paddy's Day puts more demands on her. She'll probably sleep in the kitchen. This is an all-hands-on-deck weekend."

Guilt ate a little hole in his chest. Abby had wasted time changing his family's dinner reservations. Why had Courtney brought a friend without warning him? Unfortunately, this inconsideration was typical of his sister.

"Abby needs help," he said. "Can't Michael put in more hours?"

"Abby ask for help?" Bess shook her head. "You're kidding, right?"

"She works too hard."

Bess rolled her eyes. "Don't you know she has superpowers? According to Abby, she'll sleep in two months. She wants every dime to go back into this money pit."

Money. Of course. What else could it be?

"Gray." His mother's low voice had him setting down his glass and hurrying to her side.

"Mother." Despite the tensions of the week, it was good to see her.

She didn't seem to age. Her sleek silver-blond hair was styled in a chin-length bob. She'd worn it that way for most of his life. He kissed her cheek, hugged her and smelled the gardenia fragrance of home. "You look lovely."

"I've missed you," she whispered.

His father walked in behind her.

"Dad." God, it was great to see his parents.

They settled in a seating area with a love seat and two wing-back chairs. Gray brought them wine and plates piled with appetizers.

His dad took a glass, but his mother held up her hand like a traffic cop.

"I can wait until we order wine with our dinner," she said. "I can't believe a B and B's wine would be anything special."

"I've been impressed with the tastings," Gray said, still holding out her wineglass.

He waited.

"Oh, fine." She took the glass. "Don't loom over me. Sit."

His mother took a sip of wine. Her eyebrows arched up and she took a bigger sip.

"I told you." He grinned.

Reggie the cat stalked over to Gray's chair. His tail twitched as he stared up at him. Gray uncrossed his legs and the cat hopped up.

His mother blinked, her mouth dropping open. "What is that?"

Gray stroked the cat's thick white fur. When Reggie twisted his head, he scratched behind the cat's ear. "This is Reggie, the B and B's mascot."

"But you don't like cats," his mother pointed out.

"Oh, Reggie and I have an understanding." He hadn't had a pet since old Fred, his golden retriever, had died back when he'd been in high school. He missed having a pet in his life.

"Very odd." His mother took a sip of her wine. "You wouldn't think a pet would be allowed."

"I've seen a lot stranger sights in Savannah," Gray said.

His dad put his nose in his glass and then sipped. "Not bad."

"She pairs the appetizers with the wines. The best thing I ever did was negotiate to have dinner included with my stay. She's a miracle in the kitchen. I've probably put on ten pounds."

"You look wonderful," his mother said. "Who is *she?*"

"Abby. Abigail. She's one of the sisters who own

Fitzgerald House. She might have checked you in. I can't wait to introduce you."

He mother waved her hand. "Tell us about your project."

"The warehouse is on River Street, so it's a great location. I'll take you over...."

"Gray." Courtney wrapped her arms around his back.

His sister's overpowering floral perfume had him holding his breath. "Courtney."

Placing Reggie on the floor, he stood to hug Courtney. Even with all her flaws, he'd missed her.

His sister wore some combination of gauzy top and sweater, looking like the gaggle of girls that always surrounded her. Young, well-educated women who'd dedicated their lives to shopping.

He wanted more than that for his sister.

"I've missed you," Courtney said, giving his shoulder a small punch.

"Me, too, brat."

"I have a surprise, big brother." She stepped away and gestured with one hand toward the hallway.

"Gwen?" He couldn't believe his eyes when his ex-girlfriend entered the library. "What the hell are you doing here?"

"I *had* to see you." Gwen's voice was soft, her eyes downcast. "I want to make this right between us."

She moved toward him, hands out, tears hanging on her long eyelashes.

He glared at his mother and then at Courtney. "What have you done?"

"I told you this was a bad idea, Olivia." His father shook his head.

"Gray." His mother held up her hands. "You and Gwen dated for almost a year. You need to talk, to communicate and get through this rough patch in your relationship."

His mother's words piled on him like bricks. He couldn't breathe. "We broke up."

Gwen gasped. Courtney, that little traitor, wrapped an arm around Gwen's waist. Half the guests in the room stared over at them.

"You wouldn't talk to me." Tears filled Gwen's eyes.

"There wasn't anything to discuss." He stalked out of the room, his movements jerky and abrupt.

Footsteps clicked behind him in a running staccato. "Wait, Gray. Please." Gwen caught his arm, dragging him to a stop.

"Let go," he snapped. "I was clear how I felt. It's over."

"Why?" Gwen's silvery eyes swam with tears. "We were having so much fun, and then all of a sudden you don't want to go to parties anymore and you're working all the time. I don't understand what happened. I don't understand why you broke things off."

What a mess. "It was never going to work out the way you wanted."

"We belong together." Her voice cracked. "We know all the same people, go to the same club. I thought we'd get married."

"That's not what I want." Her vision of marriage sounded more like a prison.

Gwen tugged him into the small parlor off the foyer. "I don't believe that. We're too much alike."

They weren't alike. Maybe he'd changed here in Savannah or maybe he'd never fit in at home, but he was finally realizing how out of place he'd felt back in Boston.

He shook her hand off his arm. "Gwen, don't. We're through."

She tipped her head back to look up at him. Her lips trembled. "I've missed you. I…I love you."

Gray closed his eyes. He'd never loved her, never intended to give her any false hope.

"I've had a crush on you since high school," she pleaded. "I've *always* loved you. God, all the times I made sure I ran into you. Begging Courtney for sleepovers when I knew you would be home from college. You don't know how much planning it took to make our paths cross."

Tears pooled in her eyes. Their pale color used to fascinate him. Now he preferred bewitching green ones.

Abby. Oh, hell. How was he going to explain Gwen's presence to Abby?

He shook his head. "It's over."

"But it's always been you."

"I don't…feel the same." He spaced the words slowly, trying to be kind.

Gwen closed the distance between them. She ran her hands up his chest and laced them behind his neck.

"Stop." He reached up to loosen her hands from around his neck. "Gwen."

ABBY STRIPPED OFF her apron and smoothed her hair in place. She couldn't resist checking on the wine tasting.

Okay, she wanted to check on Gray's family. She would just peek into the room. Her jeans and T-shirt said kitchen, not front of house, but she needed to tell Gray about the change in their dinner reservation.

Hurrying down the hallway, she rounded the stairs. She had a clear view of the front parlor and caught a glimpse of a couple in an embrace. Whoops. Abby slipped into the library, not wanting to interrupt them.

The library was full of guests. Full. She grinned. And they were all enjoying her food. Nothing made her happier.

She spotted the Smythes near the fireplace, but no Gray.

"Mr. and Mrs. Smythe," she said, wishing she could have worn her power clothes. "I just wanted you to know I've updated all your reservations for five people. The Pinke House, where you're eating tonight, asked that you be punctual." Abby checked her watch. "You should head over. They won't hold reservations long during the holiday."

"Thank you," Mrs. Smythe said. "I hope it wasn't any trouble."

"Of course not," she lied. "Has Gray come down yet?"

"He and Gwen are talking." Gray's sister nodded toward the door. Courtney. His sister's name was Courtney.

Wait. That had been Gray in the parlor? With a woman wrapped around him?

Courtney handed her wineglass and plate to Abby. "I'll warn them that we need to leave."

Mrs. Smythe added her plate to the stack, making Abby feel like a maid. She was here to make her guests comfortable, but she also wanted the Smythes to know she was more than that to their son. Which was messed up when she wouldn't even tell her own family.

Abby set the dishes on the tray and trailed after the Smythes. They hovered at the entrance to the small parlor.

"It looks like you've worked everything out," Courtney said to her brother.

Abby swallowed and started to sneak around the group.

"There wasn't anything to work out." Gray's deep voice had Abby grabbing the banister. "Gwen shouldn't be here. We broke up."

"Talk to me," the other woman said gently. "Give me a chance."

Abby's fingers clenched the wood. Gwen and Gray had dated? The Smythes had brought an ex-girlfriend to Savannah to see him?

"No." Gray's voice echoed in the foyer.

She slid around Mr. Smythe's back to escape to the kitchen. Escape and think.

"Abby," Gray called out. His footsteps echoed in the foyer.

He caught her around the corner in the hallway, out of sight of his family.

She let him turn her to face him, forcing a smile to her face. She couldn't look him in the eye. "I've just let your family know that tonight's reservation has been changed, but that the table won't be held long. You should get ready to go."

He tipped her face up. Concern filled his eyes. "This isn't what you think."

Oh, she thought it was. "What? That your family brought a former—" lover? "—girlfriend to see you?"

He rolled his eyes. "Okay, it is what you think. But I broke up with her."

"I got that." And half the guests had probably over-heard, too. But apparently the ex and Gray's family didn't think they were broken up. She touched his arm. "You really need to go."

"She's nothing to me." He brushed her hair back. "I'd rather stay with you."

"You should head out. They won't hold your res-ervation." She was repeating herself, but she didn't know what else to say.

"I'm—sorry." He brushed a kiss on her forehead. "I'll come find you after dinner."

She continued on her way to her kitchen, her pace slow and steady. Once there, she latched the swing-ing door closed and slid to the floor.

Gray's family had brought his ex-girlfriend to Savannah.

His parents and sister hadn't known about her. If

they had, she hoped Gwen wouldn't be here. And that they wouldn't have treated her like a maid.

Neither she nor Gray had told their families they were in a relationship. There was a message in their actions. Actions were more important than words. Maurice had spouted words of love and then broken her heart. Her father had been able to sweet-talk anyone, but he'd left misery in his wake.

Gray's actions said she wasn't important to him.

It was time to follow Mamma's rule. The weeks she'd spent with Gray had been amazing, but they didn't belong together. By breaking up with him, she'd make sure Gray couldn't disappoint her. He couldn't break her heart.

The next time she saw him, she'd tell him they were through. Besides, they'd never really been together— had they? Not enough to tell either of their families.

Work. If she kept her hands busy, she'd stop obsessing about Gray.

She had sandwiches to prepare and scones to bake. Then she would make pecan bars.

Abby rubbed the heel of her hand against her chest. She didn't want to make brandy-pecan bars. From now on, she would associate Gray with those stupid bars.

Unfortunately, Dolley had already printed the tea menus.

Abby turned on the CD player and booted up a Sarah McLachlan album. She would bake away her grief.

GRAY SQUEEZED THE arm of his chair. Why the hell had he agreed to have dinner with his family? Never mind Gwen?

Because Abby had done twice the work to get them their reservations. What was Abby thinking now? All he wanted to do was head home—well, to the B and B—and be with her.

Gray hated knowing that his family had tried to manipulate him into getting back together with Gwen. Hated sitting across from her. Hated the looks his sister shot at him like a Gatling gun.

He wasn't the bad guy here.

Catching the server's eye, he said, "Jameson, please." It would be the only way to get through this evening.

He shifted and kicked someone's foot. Gwen jerked. The table was too damn small.

Courtney whispered in Gwen's ear. His sister covered Gwen's hand, and she shot another venomous look at him from across the tiny table.

"Gray, you could at least…" his mother started to say.

"Don't," he warned.

"Olivia." His dad shook his head at his wife. "Gray, tell me more about your warehouse."

He and his father discussed the project. No one else contributed to the conversation.

"Another Jameson, please," he told a passing waiter. His mother raised an eyebrow but kept her mouth closed. Good.

When his dinner arrived, it tasted like sawdust. Nothing like the meals he ate with Abby.

"Gwen, you should go back to Boston," he blurted out.

"The plane isn't available." His father grimaced. "An engine was acting up on the flight down here. The maintenance crew has it torn apart. The earliest it will be ready is Monday morning."

"Then we can book a commercial flight," Gray suggested.

"I texted my assistant on the way here. Nothing's available." His dad shook his head.

What else could go wrong?

"If we could just talk." Gwen turned tear-reddened eyes to him.

"There's nothing more to say."

His mother started to speak and then closed her mouth.

His parents talked, Courtney murmured to Gwen and Gray gave up eating the tasteless food.

Happy freaking family get-together.

Why had he thought it would be any different? Because he'd watched the Fitzgeralds care for each other. He should have known—his family wasn't anything like the Fitzgerald sisters.

Finally, dinner ended. Even back on the street, he couldn't draw in a full breath. He needed to find Abby and explain.

He and his dad let the women walk ahead of them.

"Sorry for this mess," his father said, puffing on his cigar.

"Can't imagine you had anything to do with bringing Gwen down here."

"I've always liked Gwen. She and Courtney are inseparable." His dad shrugged. A ring of smoke circled his head. "I wouldn't have talked you out of an alliance with her family."

"Alliance? This isn't the Middle Ages." Gray's hands formed fists. Or maybe they'd been that way since Gwen had walked into the library.

His father turned to him. "Marriage can work on many levels. Gwen's family may not be as wealthy as ours, but her uncle's a senator."

"And you'd want me to get married to curry political favor? The senator's not even from our party."

His dad grimaced. "I never thought you were that naive."

"I just hate all the...games." Maybe that was what had bothered him in Boston. Everyone jockeyed for a favorable position. "It is too much to want to be myself?"

His dad's eyes narrowed. "Anyone you interact with will be aware of your net worth. We're Smythes."

Abby was aware, but he didn't yet know what effect that would have on their relationship. She'd made one joke about pecan bars for money. And one serious comment about not letting their personal involvement screw up their business relationship.

What did Abby want from him?

He climbed the steps of Fitzgerald House and swiped his key card.

The women had already gone upstairs. A small blessing in an otherwise awful night.

"I'm going to grab a soda." And talk to Abby. "Want anything?"

"I'd better check on your mother." His father hesitated and then said, "Don't be too hard on her. She thought…"

Gray shook his head. "I'll see you in the morning."

He headed down the hallway but turned back. "It would be best if Gwen and I didn't see each other again while she's here."

His father nodded.

Gray stopped in the dining room and grabbed a ginger ale from the fridge available for guests. Time to see what Abby was up to.

Pans rattled in the kitchen. He leaned his shoulder against the door to push it open. And stopped dead.

The damn door was locked.

What the hell?

He set his free hand against the wood. She was in there. Working, even though she'd been up before dawn fixing breakfast.

He could smell the buttery scent of her pecan bars even through the thick oak door.

"Abby," he whispered, knowing she couldn't hear him.

She'd locked him out. Hell, he hadn't even realized she could lock the swinging door.

This night just kept getting better.

CHAPTER SEVEN

Rule #16—Never let a guest see you sweat.

Mamie Fitzgerald

"MOMMY, THERE'S A bunk bed!"

Cheryl hurried down the short hall and peeked in her son's new bedroom.

Her eyes filled with tears. She'd planned on heading to Goodwill to buy furniture.

Instead, Mr. Smythe had already furnished the small two-bedroom apartment. Packets of new sheets and bedding sat on the mattresses. A new sofa and TV had been set up in the small living room. Cupboards were filled with dishes and silverware. It was too much.

Josh scurried up the ladder. The worn bottoms of his sneakers slipped on the rungs. They were going shoe shopping after the holiday.

"No shoes on the bed," she warned.

He flopped onto the mattress and tossed his shoes over the railing. "I want to sleep up here."

She wiggled the rail. "All right. But you'll have to help me make the bed."

He turned on his side, his brown eyes huge.

"I will," he promised.

She checked her watch. "Okay, we need to wash sheets."

His face crumpled. "Do we have to go to the Laundromat?"

"We're never going back there." She tapped him on the nose. "We talked about that before. We have our own washer and dryer. Come on, I'll show you. Bring your sheets."

He scrambled off the bunk.

The small stackable washer and dryer were next to the bathroom.

"Let's rip these open," she said.

Mr. Smythe had even supplied a bottle of detergent. A cold shiver ran down her back. *What did he expect in return?*

"Spider-Man! Like my backpack." Josh hugged the sheets to his skinny chest as if they were his favorite toy.

With help from Mr. Smythe, she was making a better life for her son.

When the laundry had been started, she said, "We need to unpack your clothes. Then I have to get to work."

His smile drooped a little. "Okay." Those heartbreaking brown eyes stared into hers. Brad's eyes. "Uncle Levi can't find us here, right?"

"No way." She grabbed her son in a bear hug. "We're way too smart for him."

He clung to her like a burr on a dog. "We *are* too smart for him."

GRAY PULLED HIS car up in front of Fitzgerald House. As he waited for his parents, Courtney and Gwen exited the B and B arm in arm. He drummed his fingers on the steering wheel in aggravation. His anger hadn't cooled from the day before.

He'd tried to change the dinner reservations—again. None of the restaurants would split their reservation for five into two tables, unless they wanted to sit down at eleven at night.

He still couldn't believe Gwen was here. And Abby wouldn't talk to him about it.

He'd sent Abby a text this morning asking when they could talk.

Her reply—Sorry, I'm busy.

She couldn't spare five minutes? She'd locked him out of the kitchen last night, and now she was avoiding him?

His parents climbed into the car. He glanced at his mother's silk pants. "Are you sure you want to wear that to a construction site?"

His father smiled. "I've never met a woman who can stay as clean as your mother."

"I thought I'd show you the Historic District first." They could have walked, but Gray took them on a driving tour of the city. Maybe Savannah's charm would work its magic and put him in a better mood.

Pink-and-white flowers exploded throughout the city. The colors sparkled against black wrought iron fences and vibrant green hedges. Because of the one-way signs around the many squares, they enjoyed a leisurely trip through the prettiest part of Savannah.

"Look at all the Irish flags." His dad pointed to the sights out the window.

"Everyone's Irish this weekend," Gray said.

"The city is lovely," his mother offered from the backseat.

Gray wound his way as close to the warehouse as possible and parked the car. They stopped in front of his building, looking from the street to the Savannah River.

"The view is wonderful," his dad commented. "I was surprised when you bought this place. Now I see your vision. Nice work."

His father's compliment burned a warm path to his heart. He was thirty-three, but parental approval still felt nice.

Gray gestured to the building facade. "We'll add wrought iron balconies and open up the windows with sliders. We'll have the requisite colorful awnings on street level. I might keep a unit for myself while we're selling the others."

That had been his plan when he'd first bought the building. Now the thought of not staying at Fitzgerald House had him rolling his shoulders.

His mother tripped on the uneven cobblestones, and he put a hand under her elbow to steady her.

"The stones you're stumbling on are from England," Gray said. "They were ballast and dumped when the ships picked up their loads of cotton and tobacco."

"Very clever of the colonists." His mother tilted her

face up and gave him a penetrating stare. "You're not getting attached to this town, are you?"

"There are great properties available at bargain prices." He pointed to the warehouse next to his. "I may make an offer on that space."

"No." Sadness crossed his mother's face. "I like having my children in Boston."

"I'm debating other opportunities, as well. Fitzgerald House would be a great investment," he blurted out.

What would Abby think if he offered her a loan? Maybe helping her out would get her talking to him again.

His father frowned slightly. "You've never taken on hospitality property."

Gray shrugged. "I've looked over the B and B's financials. They're strapped for cash, but the potential is there."

"But you live in Boston," his mother insisted.

Savannah fit him better. As though he'd been wearing shoes that were too small and he'd finally slipped on the correct size. "It was good for me to leave."

"Gray, I won't interfere. I want you to be happy." She touched his face. "I thought you were happy with Gwen."

"I wasn't."

He inhaled and took his mother's hand. He'd never thought about being happy, but Savannah was the closest he'd come to feeling content. What had Abby called it? Joy. She'd brought joy and peace to his life.

"Gray," a young voice called.

Joshua ran toward him from the building.

"Josh." Gray grinned.

The little boy jumped up and slapped his hand. Then he turned around and stuck his hand behind him.

Gray gave him a down-low. "How's my man?"

"I got a new bed. It has a ladder and everything. And Spider-Man sheets."

Cheryl hurried over and caught Josh's hand. "You can't run away like that."

The fear in her eyes never left. What made her so afraid?

"But Gray was here." Josh turned his sunny face up to his mother.

Gray's parents stared at the boy and his mother. He quickly made introductions.

"How's the apartment?" he asked.

"It's wonderful." Cheryl crossed her arms over her chest. "The furniture, the linens, the food..."

"I got a bunk bed!" Josh piped in.

"Cool." Furnishing the apartment had been a kick.

"It's too much." Cheryl's hand waved around and then covered her mouth.

"You're doing me a favor, remember? Hopefully, your presence will stop any more break-ins."

"Break-ins?" his mother exclaimed.

"Someone grabbed some copper pipe." Gray shrugged. "Cheryl and Josh are on-site as a deterrent."

His mother didn't look convinced.

"Did you find the phone I left for you?" Gray asked Cheryl.

Her eyes filled with tears. "Yes. Thanks."

"Good." He didn't want her crying. "I programmed in the numbers for Fitzgerald House, my cell and 911."

"I saw the note." Cheryl's hand waved like the fluttering of a wounded bird. "It's too much."

"You need a phone to call if there's any trouble." He knelt and stared Josh in the eye. "Remember what we talked about. No going in the main building. And stay with your mom," he added.

"I will." Josh nodded solemnly.

"Thank you, Mr. Smythe," Cheryl said. "And it's good to see you again, Mr. and Mrs. Smythe."

His mother stared at their backs as they climbed the stairs. "Again?"

"Cheryl works at the B and B."

"Really?" his dad said. "And for you?"

"She's had it rough." At least that was his impression. "I needed someone on-site—she needed…" He shrugged. He really didn't know what she needed.

"So she's the reason you're fixated on Savannah." His dad winked.

"No. It's Abby."

His parents both gave him blank looks.

"Abby Fitzgerald." He rubbed the back of his head. "Unfortunately, when Gwen came with you to Savannah—" he pointed a finger at his mother "—it screwed everything up."

ABBY TIED AN apron over her pale green shirt and moss-colored skirt. This St. Patrick's Day she would be wearing the green. She was a Fitzgerald after all.

For St. Patrick's Day, she was serving a hearty Irish breakfast. Her guests would start with bacon, sausage, eggs, mushrooms, fried tomatoes and, of course, oatmeal. She'd already brewed a pot of Irish breakfast tea. Her guests might not notice all the details, but she did.

She and Gray were done. No more letting him distract her from the really important things. Their attraction had been a nice blip, but from now on she'd devote her energy to her business.

The Smythes had done her a favor. Now she could concentrate on her true priorities—Fitzgerald House and the future. She and her sisters would get through this cash crisis and then she'd move on to planning her restaurant.

Abby took a deep breath, pushing at the sharp pain in her stomach. After the holiday, Gray could have his dinner in the dining room.

Michael dragged himself into the kitchen, and she forced a smile on her face. "Good morning."

"What's good about it?"

"Ah, Michael, and you being a good Irish boy. Happy St. Paddy's Day to you."

He snatched up a mug like it was a lifesaver and he was drowning. Pouring a cup of coffee, he inhaled half of it.

She winced. It was so hot he must have scalded his tongue.

"We were swamped at the restaurant last night. I didn't get home until two and got up at six." Michael whipped an apron around his waist and knotted it with sharp movements. "When will you open Southern Comforts? I want to work for you full-time."

"We'll get there." Unfortunately, the timing was out of her control.

Michael perused the menu she'd posted. She didn't have to tell him what to work on. He heated up the flattop and laid out bacon strips.

As she cracked eggs, Abby worked through her to-do lists. Samuel had left a voice mail message saying that they wouldn't be able to work on the third floor of Fitzgerald House for two weeks. What she wouldn't give to be Forester Construction Company's most important client. That would be Mr. Money, Gray.

"I don't know how much longer I can wait, Abs." Michael touched her shoulder, his eyes filled with concern. "I'm interviewing for a sous chef position in Atlanta next week."

Abby's stomach flopped. She'd always assumed Michael would work with her at her restaurant. Their personalities and passions meshed well in the kitchen.

"Good luck," she whispered. She couldn't catch a break.

GRAY PEEKED INTO the sunroom and swore. He'd given Abby a day to recover and calm down. But he wanted her to know that he wasn't at fault here.

Time to find her. He checked the kitchen. Not there. He checked the garden, her office, the library. Where in hell was she hiding?

"Why aren't you wearing green, Gray?"

He turned. Abby. Finally. She came down the stairs, and his tense fists relaxed. Weight lifted from his shoulders. "I don't do the green thing."

He wanted to touch her. No, he *had* to touch her. Her green shirt matched her eyes. That sunset hair floated down her back. All he wanted to do was tug her into his arms and breathe in the scent he'd been missing for a day and a half. Unfortunately, she was giving him her impersonal smile. He hated that smile.

He moved next to her, but she ducked behind the reception desk.

She pulled out green bead necklaces. "Here. For you and your family and…friend."

He tried to hand them back, but Abby was already hurrying down the hall to the kitchen.

Rushing to catch up, he called, "We need to talk."

He reached for her hand. She jerked away from him as if she'd been burned. "I have a lot to do today."

"You *have* been avoiding me." Pressure settled on his chest. "Why?"

"I'm busy." She pushed through the kitchen door. "I have a business to run."

"Abby."

Her shoulders stiffened. "This isn't working."

"I don't care about Gwen," Gray sputtered.

She whipped her hair back into a messy bun that he wanted to pull apart. "This isn't about your ex."

He threw his hands in the air. "Then, what is this about?"

She stared at him with pain-filled emerald eyes. "I wasn't important enough to mention to your family."

Her quiet words erected more barriers than any of his work crews ever had.

"That's not fair." Panic seemed to burst inside him. "You haven't told your family, either. You're the one who wanted to keep everything a secret."

"I know." Abby set a massive pot on the stove. "It's so sad. Neither of us cared enough about each other to tell our families. If we had, your family wouldn't have put your ex through this misery."

He wasn't so sure that Courtney and Gwen wouldn't have tried anyway.

She grabbed large packages of meat from the fridge, then pulled a knife from the drawer and started trimming the fat.

Abby kept working. She wouldn't even stop long enough to talk about what they'd meant to each other. Didn't what they'd had together mean more than her work?

Hell, no. Her number one priority was Fitzgerald House. Maybe his anger wasn't fair, but right now he was raw.

Somehow he had to make her understand they weren't done.

He pulled her away from the counter. "I didn't know how to describe what was happening between us. Just because I was stupid—*we* were stupid—doesn't mean we're through."

"Gray." She shook her head. "It's over."

"No."

"It doesn't matter now." She pushed away from him,

stepping back to her counter with a sad smile. "After the holiday, I'll serve your dinner in the dining room."

"No."

She sliced into the meat. "Yes."

He raised an eyebrow. "You're that afraid of me? You can't even eat in the same room with me?"

"It will make things easier." A quaver filled her voice.

Gray moved behind her, close enough that the warmth of her body linked them together.

She jerked away, but not quickly enough.

He set his hands on her rigid shoulders. "We screwed up. So we're not perfect."

He turned her around. A single tear slid down her cheek, and she ducked her head.

He tugged the knife out of her hand and laid it on the counter.

"It's better this way," she said. "We're not right for each other."

His shoulders stiffened. For once in his life he'd felt as if he'd fit. Didn't she see that? "I don't agree."

"This won't work." She shook her head. "It's time to give up."

Maybe she was right.

But knowing he should back away didn't make him drop his arms. Instead, he hugged her. "That would be the smart move."

And he was always smart. Except around Abby. He cradled her face.

"So we're agreed?" Her voice cracked. "We're through?"

He shook his head. "I…can't stay away from you."

"But…"

"Give us another chance," he said.

She rested her forehead against his chest. "I don't understand this."

"Neither do I. But here's what I know—I've missed you." Gray lifted her head with his finger and kissed away her tears.

"I've missed you, too." She sighed. "But I didn't *want* to miss you."

Ouch. "So we're good?"

She stared into his eyes.

He held his breath, afraid she would reject him. What else could he barter—something for Fitzgerald House? The printer hadn't gone over well.

"We're…" She closed her eyes. "We're good."

He exhaled.

Their kiss ignited like dry kindling on a hot summer day. He devoured her mouth. His hand brushed and cupped her full breast, and she moaned.

When he opened his eyes, everything looked brighter, more vivid.

"I missed your smile." He nestled her against him, relief washing through him. "This is better, much better."

She nodded.

Taking a deep breath, he said, "Tonight I'd like to introduce you to my family."

ABBY TESTED THE lamb stew and added a little more thyme. Her mamma had started serving St. Paddy's

Day dinner at Fitzgerald House, and Abby had continued her mother's tradition. The B and B guests wouldn't have to fight the throngs of people who'd invaded Savannah for spots in restaurants.

Once the entrees were being served, she went to her apartment and changed. If she was officially meeting Gray's family, she'd make sure they wouldn't mistake her for a maid. She changed into a pale green silk skirt and blouse and added thin silver bracelets and matching earrings.

By the time she entered the dining room, Amy and Bess were serving the Baileys chocolate-mousse pie. Abby grabbed a coffeepot and circled the room, topping up people's cups.

Gray and his parents sat at a table near the crackling fire. Gray's ex and his sister sat at another nearby. It was petty, but Abby was happy the ex and Gray weren't sitting together.

She topped off Gray's coffee with decaf, her fingers resting on his back. Her hand didn't shake, but inside she quivered like unmolded gelatin.

"Dinner was fantastic, as usual." Gray took Abby's hand and kissed it. "Mother, Dad, this is Abigail Fitzgerald, B and B owner and chef extraordinaire. And the woman I told you I've been seeing."

His dad smiled. Mrs. Smythe swallowed the pie she'd just put in her mouth.

From the other table, Gwen let out a weak sob.

The Jell-O in her stomach started to dance. Hadn't Gray warned his ex?

Abby stepped back, but Gray stood and laced their fingers firmly together.

"Gray hasn't stopped singing your praises." His mother's tone was cool.

Out of the corner of her eye, Abby saw Bess moving toward the group. Her sister's eyes were as big as winter pansies. Bess pointed between Abby and Gray, a questioning look in her eyes.

Abby shot her a weak smile. Luckily, most of the guests were focused on their own meals.

Bess grinned and gave her a thumbs-up. Then mouthed, *We'll talk*. The sister cell phone circuit would be sizzling tonight.

"Oh, Gray." Gwen stood. Her manicured hand covered her mouth. "Did you have to flaunt her in front of me?"

"Gwen, we talked about this earlier." Gray's mouth formed a straight line. "I didn't do this to hurt you."

Courtney jumped up from her table and wrapped an arm around Gwen's shoulders. She glared at her brother. "You can be such a jerk." The two women rushed out of the dining room.

Mrs. Smythe stood. "Since I agreed to bring Gwen down here, I'd better see what I can do."

All the women in Gray's life had run away the minute he'd told them they were together. Abby wanted to disappear, too.

"Dinner was delicious," Mr. Smythe told her. "Your B and B is delightful. Sorry we had to add drama to this weekend." Gray's dad bundled up his napkin and dropped it on the table. He smiled at Abby, a tired smile. "It was nice to meet you."

Gray pushed out a sigh and leaned his head against hers. "That went well."

"In what universe?" Abby let out a forced laugh. "Now your family hates me."

"I don't care."

Abby didn't believe him. Her family had her back— always. Family was everything.

CHAPTER EIGHT

Rule #21—Whenever possible meet the guests'
needs and wants before they can voice them.

Abby Fitzgerald

"THAT WAS MESSIER than it should have been." Gray
held open the kitchen door. "I warned Gwen. I think
she just wanted sympathy."

Abby shook her head. "I don't want you at odds
with your family because of me."

Their footsteps echoed in the courtyard. The fountain sparkled in the moonlight, the water splashing in
a gentle song. The garden's flowery perfume wrapped
around them.

He tightened his arm around her shoulder and felt
her muscles relax. "They'll get over it."

"Family is everything."

"My family's…not quite like yours." Hadn't his
dad all but suggested he marry Gwen because of her
connections? "They shouldn't have pulled this stunt
and ruined the weekend for everyone."

He stopped at the edge of the garden. "My mother
will come around. She doesn't control who I date." If
she did, he'd be married to Gwendolyn by now.

She sighed. "I feel sorry for Gwen."

"Don't. She should never have come." He looked

at the carriage house. "Why haven't you invited me into your place?"

She caught her lower lip between her teeth. "You're too tempting."

"Tempting?" He pulled her into a kiss. Abby's spicy scent washed over him, and his body came to attention. His teeth nibbled on the lip she always chewed.

Her tongue brushed his and stoked flames through his body.

He cupped her face. "I really missed you."

"I was too busy to miss you," she whispered.

"Liar." Gray brushed his lips against her cheek, her throat, and nuzzled his way to the sensitive skin where her neck and shoulders met.

She shivered.

He pulled her hips tight against him. "Are you going to invite me in?"

Gray kissed her, not waiting for an answer. She tasted of chocolate and spice and that unique flavor that was all Abby.

"Abby." He gasped. "Invite me up."

Her head dropped to his chest. "I want to…"

"Wanting is enough for now."

Gray threaded their fingers together and tugged. They raced up the carriage house stairs.

"We haven't made too many improvements to this building. Just some work on this apartment."

Was she telling him the place wasn't furnished? He wanted to get her into a bed, any bed. He didn't care what it looked like.

"I needed to live nearby." Her teeth chattered as if she was cold.

"Are you nervous?" he asked.

Abby pulled a key from her pocket, but her hands shook too much to unlock the door.

He took her key and had the door open before she could ask for help.

She put a hand on his shoulder and looked up at him. Her green eyes were too solemn. "I… It's been a long time since I've been with someone."

"I'm feeling the pressure to make this memorable." He kissed her. Poured all his need into the kiss, and her knees gave way.

With a grin, he swung her up into his arms and kicked the door closed. "Which way?"

"I can walk." She tossed back her head and laughed.

"Not tonight."

He ignored the dimly lit front room. At the end of a hallway he bumped open a door with his hip and found her bedroom.

Sheer white drapes hung from the frame of the four-poster bed. The drapes and a snowy white comforter glowed in the moonlight. The scent of the garden drifted in through the open window.

Gray laid her in the middle of the massive bed. Her red-gold hair glowed against the bedspread. He stood back and stared.

She sat up. "What?" Her voice shook.

"I like looking at you." He kicked his shoes off and knelt on the bed next to her. Slowly, he slipped off her sandals.

"I've been thinking about this for a while." His hands moved up her calves, and she jolted. "So if you don't mind, I'm going to take my time."

Abby leaned back on her elbows, those mysterious eyes wide-open. Her breath came in short bursts. She licked her lips, and his body pulsed.

He needed that mouth, but he wanted her naked. Dilemmas, dilemmas.

First things first. Get Abby naked.

He pulled her up until she was kneeling in front of him.

With that delicious mouth so close, he needed a taste, so he kissed her.

Abby's clever fingers were working on his shirt buttons. "I know it's been a while, but I remember it's a lot more fun without clothes."

"I keep getting distracted." While he pressed kisses to her collarbone, he found the buttons on her blouse. Under the silk was a white lace bra that barely concealed her breasts.

He lifted her so she straddled his legs. Then he ran his tongue under the lace. His hand tested and shaped her breasts. When her breath choked, he sucked her nipple into his mouth. "God, you taste good."

Their arms tangled as she tried to push off his shirt, and he wrestled with unfastening her bra.

Pants and skirt were scattered. He pushed her back and explored her hips and the tiny V of lace between her legs.

"Come back up here," she pleaded.

"Not yet." He wanted to drive her crazy before they made love.

He reached up and rolled her nipples, plucking and massaging until she moaned. Her hands fluttered as she tried to stroke him.

"No, no, no." Gray moved out of her reach. He tested the shape of her belly button with his tongue. He used his teeth on her hip bones and finally tore off her panties.

"I want to taste you." And he did, shooting her almost off the mattress.

HE WAS DRIVING her mad. Each touch, each kiss, each word. She trembled under his onslaught and moaned his name.

He spread her legs farther apart.

"I want you inside me," she gasped. "Now."

He swore. "Condom. Damn, I almost forgot." He bounced off the bed, and the jingle of coins filled the room.

"Where were we?" he asked.

"Right about here." She reached down, stroking and positioning him at the entrance to her body.

He kissed her, explored her mouth, but didn't push into her body.

"Gray. Please."

He slid in, just an inch, one marvelous inch.

"More." She grabbed his butt, trying to pull him deeper.

He barely moved. He held himself rigid above her.

She tried to adjust, to open herself, hoping he'd feel her need.

He inched in, the friction setting her body on fire. Slow, so damn slow. She rocked, helping him stretch her, join with her.

"Ah." Gray's grin gleamed in the moonlight. "You feel so good."

She ran her hands along the hard muscles of his back. "So do you, mercy, so do you."

She rolled her hips, trying to entice him to move. He stared down at her through dark blue eyes.

He slid slowly in and out like a taunt. Each stroke went deeper, stealing her breath. His thumbs circled and tormented her breasts.

She wrapped her legs around his hips, trying to gain control but failing. Gray owned her body. Her fingers dug into his butt, pulling him closer.

He paused, poised above her.

She ran her fingers up to his nipples, needing him to move. When all he did was close his eyes, she rolled her hips. "Please."

"Not yet." He rested his forehead on hers. "I don't want this to end."

Abby tightened her inner muscles and rocked him deep.

"Abby," he groaned, stroking in and out of her quicker, harder.

Explosions waited on the edge. If he didn't move faster and deeper, she would die.

"I can't breathe," she gasped. "Move. Harder."

"Stay with me," he groaned.

She disintegrated. Gray thrust and thrust, pushing her into insanity. Then he joined her in madness.

The fireworks burned away, leaving halos of light behind. Her muscles were mush. She couldn't move.

Gray's weight lifted, but her body was embedded in the mattress. She heard him walk to the bathroom. When he climbed back into bed, he rolled her into his arms and tucked the covers around her.

"How can you move?" she complained sleepily.

His chest vibrated under her cheek as he laughed. "I feel so damn good."

She found enough energy to reach over and set her alarm clock and her phone alarm. "Will you stay the night?"

He turned and kissed her, long and hard. "You couldn't make me leave."

THE SOUND OF Abby's shower filled Gray's dreams. He could taste her on his lips, feel the pounding water as he drove into her body.

Gray opened his eyes, reaching toward Abby's side of the bed. No warmth remained. Her day started with the dawn. Without her, he couldn't sleep.

What a couple of days they'd had. She'd broken up with him, though thankfully that hadn't lasted long. And introducing Abby to his family could have gone better. But last night had been incredible. To say that she had rocked his world would be an understatement.

Rolling over, he wished Abby was tucked next to him. Last night hadn't been enough. He would need to play out that shower dream soon. And he'd like to spend the day with her, in bed.

With her schedule, that wouldn't happen. Hopefully, her workload would lighten up before he returned to Boston. Before this ended.

Uneasy, Gray tossed off the covers. He should have made sure they were still on the same page. Sex changed things. He had to make sure that Abby wasn't thinking any further than summer's end.

She'd left a toothbrush on the sink and folded his wrinkled clothes. He didn't bother with a shower. He'd say good-morning to Abby and then clean up in his room.

In the garden, he plucked a pink flower from the bush next to the kitchen door. Through the screen door, he watched Abby working, her moves efficient and precise. No wonder her arms were so shapely. She whisked batter in a stainless-steel bowl large enough to hold a small toddler.

At the slap of the kitchen door, Abby looked up and then stared back down at her bowl. The woman who'd begged him to thrust harder and faster wouldn't look him the eye.

"I didn't mean to wake you," she said.

He handed her the flower and then kissed her gently, tasting coffee. "I couldn't sleep without you."

That brief touch of their lips wasn't enough. He pulled the bowl out of her arms, cupped her face and kissed her more thoroughly, drawing out the pleasure. She swayed toward him, her body flush against his.

"Good morning," he whispered.

"Oh, yeah." She grinned. "This is a really great morning."

He loved that he could blur her eyes with a kiss. "What's for breakfast?"

"Vegetable frittata and apple-cinnamon or oatmeal-raisin muffins." She eased away from him. "I have to get the muffins in the oven or there won't be any. Go away. You're distracting."

He kissed her nose. "Last night was unforgettable."

"For me, too." She clasped her cheeks and laughed a little. "I'm getting red. I'm not good at this."

He brushed another kiss on her lips. It was going to be really hard to leave her at the end of July, but short-term was all they could have.

"I know," she murmured.

He jerked. He hadn't meant to say that aloud.

"Let's have some fun before you have to leave." She stared at the floor. "That's all I expect. I like the idea of this being...fun."

When she looked up, her smile lit the room.

Was it true? He hugged her, hoping it was.

He hoped that was all she expected. But would the fact that she had financial problems interfere with the temporary nature of their *fun* relationship?

"What time is your family's flight today?" she asked.

"I think they want to leave midmorning. The Lear is picking them up."

"They have a plane?" Her eyes grew wide. "Your family owns a plane?"

"Yeah." He didn't want her focusing on his family's money. Moving closer, he distracted her with a kiss.

She moaned. "Go away. I need to get breakfast ready."

After one more kiss, he let her push him out of the kitchen. He took the back stairs two at a time.

That hadn't gone badly. They were both in this for the sex. Nothing more. They would have fun and part as friends.

If he could dance, he imagined sliding down the polished wood floors like Fred Astaire. He started to whistle, needing an outlet for all this energy, and then stopped. Abby would have his head if he woke the other guests.

As he turned the corner and headed to his suite, his bubble of goodwill burst.

"Good morning, Mother."

"May I come in?" his mother asked, a cup of coffee in her hand.

He opened his door and held it for her. Funny how a night spent in Abby's room made this one seem empty.

"Your…relationship with the woman I met last night is serious?" she asked. His mother wasn't stupid. She knew he hadn't spent the night here.

"Her name is Abigail. Abby," he said, tossing his key card on the desk.

"I'm sorry. Yes, I mean Abby." His mother sat on the sofa. "So you're serious?"

Gray didn't follow his mother to the sofa. He needed space. "Abby knows I'm heading back to Boston when the condos are done."

"I thought Courtney and Gwen's plan was in your best interest." Her elegant hand smoothed the fabric of her trousers over her knees. For once, her clothes were rumpled and her hairstyle didn't look perfect. Strands of silver-blond hair floated around her head like dandelion fluff. "In Boston, everything made sense."

"If anyone had bothered to ask, I would have told them how stupid this idea was. Instead, you ruined the time we had to spend together. And you ruined Abby's weekend. She broke up with me after you arrived. Luckily, I was able to change her mind yesterday."

"I didn't know." She raised her hands in supplication. "You didn't tell anyone about—Abby."

Because he hadn't known what to say. "Gwen walked into the room and everything went to hell." His angry words rattled through the room like hammer strikes.

His mother shook her head. "I thought I was helping you. I thought you and Gwen just needed time together."

"We don't."

"But you didn't warn me. How important is this Abby to you if you didn't tell anyone?"

The same question Abby had asked. He flexed his fingers, trying to keep them from making fists. How important was she? They'd just started to date. "When have I ever talked about who I'm dating with my family?"

"Never." His mother sighed. "It's… Gwen is like

another daughter to me. When you started dating..." She shrugged. "Forgive me?"

"Sure." He tugged her off the sofa and gave her a hug.

His mom kissed his cheek. "Are we good?"

"We're good." But the conversation had taken the glow off his morning.

ABBY TAPPED THE edges of Gray's parents' bill and stapled the pages. Outside, Nigel loaded the Smythes' luggage in the van.

She should have let Marion or Amy check them out. She didn't need any more embarrassment. Although Gray's reminder about the short-term nature of the affair had been embarrassing, too. Did he think she wanted to sink her claws into him?

She sighed. Probably. That was the world he lived in.

The elevator dinged. Gray grinned as he came around the corner tugging two wheeled bags. "Hey, Abby."

Every sound and image faded away. He was all she saw. Her breath puffed out at the memory of their lovemaking last night. She wanted his lips on hers again.

She shouldn't have thought about last night. Now her cheeks were probably bright pink.

Mr. Smythe stood in front of the desk. How long had he been waiting?

"Thank you for choosing Fitzgerald House," she said, her voice formal as she handed him the bill.

"After this weekend, I understand why Gray is enjoying his stay." Mr. Smythe winked as he handed her his credit card.

Mrs. Smythe and her daughter came down the central stairs, each trailing their fingers on one of the banisters. They both wore tailored pants, silky scarves and simple blouses that likely cost more than Abby's annual clothing budget. They looked as if they belonged in Fitzgerald House.

Abby turned her attention to the credit-card machine. Before looking back up, she forced a professional smile across her face for the Smythe women. They would not intimidate her. She may not have their resources, but she was still their equal.

"Abigail." Mrs. Smythe's tone was solemn. "I'm sorry for the mess we made this weekend. Please, forgive me."

Abby blinked and glanced over at Gray. Had he orchestrated this?

Mrs. Smythe gently tapped her daughter's hand.

"Yes, I'm sorry, too," mumbled Courtney, her voice almost inaudible. She shot a venomous look at Gray. "We didn't know about you."

The credit-card machine began spitting and clicking.

"Thank you for the apology." Abby ripped out the charge slip. "I hope you enjoyed some of your time in Savannah."

She handed the receipt and a pen to Mr. Smythe.

"I hope you can understand." Mrs. Smythe looked

over as Gray brought more luggage out to Nigel. "I miss my son and I don't want to lose him."

"You won't." She reached out and clasped Mrs. Smythe's hand. Abby missed her mother every day. "I understand."

More footsteps sounded on the stairs, making the group look up. Gwen's eyes widened at the sight of Abby and Mrs. Smythe together.

Courtney moved to Gwen's side. "Are you ready to go?"

"Yes." Gwen stared at Gray as he came back into the foyer. "I'd...I'd just hoped. I'm so embarrassed." She buried her head in Courtney's shoulder.

"Let's get you to the car." Courtney linked their arms, and they went out the door without another word.

"Again, I'm sorry for the embarrassment we've caused you." Mrs. Smythe patted Abby's hand.

Gray leaned on the desk. "I'm riding to the airport with my family and Nigel. When I come back, can we have lunch?"

She thought about her long list of to-dos in the kitchen. "I'd like that."

"We'd better get going," Gray's dad said. "It was really a pleasure. I enjoyed myself."

"Please come back," Abby said, and this time she meant it.

His dad laughed. "I think that can be arranged, especially if Gray invests in your B and B."

"Invests in Fitzgerald House? There must be some mistake." She shook her head.

His dad nodded. "He mentioned you were having some cash-flow problems."

She looked at Gray, sure her confusion was clear on her face. What was his dad talking about? Fitzgerald House wasn't an investment opportunity. Had Gray discussed their financial problems with his father?

Gray's inhaled. "You're mixing things up, Dad. I'm thinking about bidding on a warehouse next to the one I own."

"Oh? I thought you mentioned…" Something in the look Gray shot him had Mr. Smythe not finishing his thought. "My mistake. We'll recommend your lovely B and B to our friends."

She walked them to the door, her head still spinning. In the kitchen, Gray had said their relationship was short-term. And she could live with that. Because she wanted some fun in her life. Fun without the possibility of Gray breaking her heart.

What if he bought another warehouse? If Gray stayed, what would happen to their relationship? How did it affect Fitzgerald House?

She stroked the plaque next to the door and made a wish. For the first time she didn't wish for Fitzgerald House's prosperity.

Please let Gray stay a little longer.

CHAPTER NINE

Rule #17—Hard work makes dreams come true.

Mamie Fitzgerald

CHERYL CLEARED THE last of the breakfast dishes from the dining room. It was always nice to see the guests talking to each other. In fact, the two Moon couples who'd lingered over coffee were driving to Bonaventure Cemetery together. Not what she and Brad would have done on their honeymoon, but it was a highlight for so many of their guests.

Someday she planned to take Josh there to see what all the fuss was about.

She rolled the cart into the kitchen. The scent of warm melted butter and sugar had her closing her eyes. It always smelled fantastic in here. This was the heart of the B and B. Here was where Abby made her magic.

Miss Abby was alone. Cheryl tapped her fingers against her leg. Now was the time to ask for help.

"Hey, Cheryl." Abby looked up from the cake she was frosting.

"That looks gorgeous." Cheryl spotted more red-and-orange frosting between the layers of yellow cake. Abby was covering everything with thick caramel-colored icing.

"I decided to try some new flavors in the tort fillings." Her hand was steady as she worked. She wiggled her eyebrows. "I'll test it on our teatime guests."

"It's amazing what you can do with just a few ingredients." The dishes clanged and chimed as Cheryl loaded the dishwasher.

"You're right. Sometimes I forget how simple baking really is when I get caught up in the techniques." Abby finished the frosting and wiped the plate. "Done."

"How did you learn all this?"

Abby moved the cake in the cooler. "I went to culinary school in New York. But I learned the most from working under some great chefs."

Culinary school. It sounded like a dream. "Sometimes you have your friend helping in the kitchen. Did he go to school like you did?"

"Yes, but he trained here in Savannah." Abby started tidying up her dishes.

"Oh." How could Cheryl ever afford training when she had to work to feed her son?

Abby brought a load of pots to the dishwasher. "Are you interested in learning the culinary arts?"

"I'd like to do what you do. People love your food." Cheryl puffed out a deep breath.

Abby grimaced. "Darn. All our good employees move on."

"I don't want to leave." Cheryl's words rattled out. "You and Marion took a chance on hiring me. I would never leave you in the lurch."

"I'd say we were the lucky ones."

"But I want to provide a good life for Josh." She sighed. "I was hoping there'd be some sort of on-the-job training."

Abby tapped her finger on the counter. "I have a Sauté Sisters group coming in next week."

Cheryl hadn't figured out all these sister events. "What will they do?"

"I'm giving them cooking lessons."

"Wow." That sounded incredible.

"Why don't you join us?" Abby suggested.

"Me?" Cheryl's heart beat a little faster. But then reality hit. "I have to work."

"The classes are short. We start at ten and run until twelve-thirty for two days." Abby grinned. "We can figure it out."

"That would be… Yes. Yes!"

"I like this idea." Abby gave Cheryl a reassuring smile. "We're going to have a blast."

Cheryl grinned back. She was going to have fun and start learning a marketable skill. Life was looking up.

DOLLEY PLOPPED A loan packet on the library coffee table in front of each of her sisters. "Happy April Fool's Day. Here's where we stand. The bank's not doing us any kind of favor. We can remodel the seven rooms—big whoop—but they won't extend the balloon or lend us the money to remodel the carriage house. The new loan is paid back over ten years, which is doable."

Abby closed her eyes. She'd known the terms. She'd

even reviewed the first version of the documents, but Dolley's words fell like lead weights on her shoulders.

"The attorney and accountant have reviewed the documents," Dolley added. "Everything's as tight as we can make it. Unfortunately, we're negotiating from a weak position. We actually need the money."

"Well, it's a start." Abby slapped her leg. "This gives us a fighting chance to meet the balloon payment next year. We can do this."

"Our attorney is surprised the bank's so tight-fisted." Dolley's fingers tapped against the arm of her chair. "We need to look for another bank. We'd have to have the next bank pay off all the loans and pay another set of loan fees, but First Mercantile is holding us back. Gray agrees with me."

"Let's get through busy season," Abby insisted. "I can't take on anything else right now. And I hate paying for something twice."

Bess spoke up. "I could take on more of your work, Abby. King's Garden isn't very busy right now."

"Thanks, but you both have to earn your keep from your jobs."

"Yeah," Dolley said. "The accountant suggested we cut back or eliminate our draws for a couple of months. Just to ensure we have the cash for the balloon."

"Whatever we need to do." Abby swallowed. She didn't have to pay rent, and all her meals were charged to the B and B, but cutting her draw would still hurt.

"God, is this all worth it?" Bess pushed off the sofa

and stalked to the fireplace. "Should we sell this pile of bricks?"

"How can you say that?" A lump formed in Abby's throat. She was responsible. "Fitzgeralds have owned this house for generations."

"One-hundred-and-seventy-plus years," Dolley added.

"Maybe we don't all want to be shackled to this money pit." Bess crossed her arms and leaned against the mantel. "Maybe we should sell."

Abby's mouth dropped open. "This is our home."

"Home?" Bess snorted. "We don't live here. I hardly remember living in the house as a family. I was barely eight when Daddy died."

How long had Bess felt like this? How had Abby missed her unhappiness? Dolley slid back in her chair, staring at the papers on the coffee table.

"But Fitzgerald House is ours," Abby implored. She couldn't fail Mamma. She wouldn't.

Bess picked at a scab on her hand. "All we do is work. Sometimes I swear the house is sucking out my soul."

Abby's heart sank to the pit of her stomach. She looked at Dolley. "Do you feel this way, too?"

"It's like we're always chasing something." Dolley grimaced. "I love seeing the guests happy, I love making sure the website reflects our personality as a B and B, but, Abby, even you have to admit—we don't have a life."

Sighing, Bess walked back to the sofa and sat next

to Abby. "Oh, ignore me. As Mamma would say—I've got a mood on. Bad day at the office."

"Do you want to talk about it?" Abby asked, touching her arm.

"No." Bess rubbed her hands over her face. "Let's finish. Is there anything else we need to know about this blasted loan?"

Abby barely heard Dolley describe the rest of the terms for Bess. How had she missed the fact that her sisters viewed the B and B as a burden and not a joy?

Even though she didn't have the restaurant of her dreams, she still cooked every day. She made people happy. And she had Gray. Every minute she spent with him was a little gift. Maybe she was taking more than her share of joy.

"Okay, if the creek doesn't rise, we'll meet the balloon with a cushion." Dolley straightened up her stack of papers. "A small cushion."

Abby signed five copies of the documents. With a deep breath, she pushed everything over to Bess. Then Dolley added her signature.

"Done." Dolley set the pen down.

"Hang on." Abby ran out of the room. She wheeled in a cart with flutes and a bottle of champagne along with a tray of cheese and crackers.

"Champagne." Bess smiled. "And Great Grandmother's crystal glasses."

"And snacks," Dolley added. "Good, I didn't eat supper."

"I don't care if we didn't get everything we wanted." Abby twisted the cork from the bottle and tipped the sparkling wine into the three flutes. "Now we've got a fighting chance."

The crystal glasses chimed a clear, sweet tone as they touched them together. "To the Fitzgerald ladies," Bess called out. "We rock."

"Wait," Dolley called, digging in her purse. "We need a picture."

She stacked books under her camera and set the timer. "Glasses up, everyone. Someone grab a damn loan document."

Abby forced a smile on her face.

"Say cheers," Dolley called.

They held up their glasses. "Cheers!"

Dolley checked the picture. "One more." This time she had them call out, "Go, Fitzgeralds."

When Dolley was satisfied with the pictures, they slipped back onto the sofa and chairs. Bess topped off everyone's glass. "We've got takers on our Sporty Sisters weekend. They're coming in May."

Dolley kicked out her legs from where she'd draped them over the settee arm. "What's the sports part of their weekend?"

"They'll kayak off Tybee Island," Bess explained. "I've scheduled a walking tour of Savannah and then an evening hike in Skidaway Island State Park."

"Good plan." Abby nodded her head. "We must have Sister bookings every weekend for the next two months."

"The website hits are racking up," Dolley muttered, staring into her glass.

"Thank you, computer geek," Bess razzed her.

"We each play to our strengths." Dolley tipped back her flute and drained it. "Mine happens to be cerebral."

Bess turned on some bluesy jazz music. Abby inhaled, forcing her shoulders to relax.

"Hey," Dolley said. "Mamma's coming home in a couple of weeks. She was happy the B and B's so full she has to stay at my apartment."

Bess emptied the bottle of champagne into her glass. "That's wonderful. Any particular reason?"

"Just her normal every couple of months visit."

Dolley leaned back. "I want to hear about Abby and Mr. Richie Rich."

"Stop that." Abby slid back into the sofa. "It's rude."

"Do you know how much he's worth? Megabucks. Mega, megabucks." Dolley slanted a sideways look at her. "Do you think he'll propose?"

"Dolley!"

"It would solve our problems." Dolley shrugged.

Abby shook her head. "We've already agreed—this will end when he goes back to Boston."

Bess squeezed her shoulder. "Are you okay with that?"

"I'm fine." She forced a smile. "I have my sisters, our mother and Fitzgerald House. What more do I need?"

ABBY WASN'T WAITING up for Gray. Her wine distributor had found some unusual options, and she wanted to create interesting hors d'oeuvres to match. She looked at the kitchen clock. Just because they hadn't spent a night apart since St. Paddy's Day didn't mean she couldn't sleep alone.

Liar. Abby dropped her head onto the table. She was waiting for Gray. He and Daniel had gone to the pub.

Straightening her cookbooks, she shut down her computer. Time for bed.

"Ah, Abby. Sweet Abigail." Gray stumbled into the kitchen. He wrapped his arms around her. "You waited for me."

"Gray." She pulled her head back at a whiff of his breath. "Did you have a good time?"

"Oh, yeah. It would have been more fun if you'd been there. Then women wouldn't have tried to pick me up." He held her face in his hands and said seriously, "I told them no."

She wasn't sure if that comment deserved a compliment. "Hmm."

"We went on a ghost pub crawl." He rambled on about Greg, one of Daniel's employees, who'd wanted to pick up a particular blonde.

"You don't have to buy a drink at every pub," she said. "As matter of fact, you don't have to buy any drinks."

He grinned. "But the blonde kept offering." He shook his head, frowning. "But I said no. The storyteller was good. You should have them add your house. You've got a ghost, right?"

"Every Savannah B and B has one." There was no way was she having inebriated tourists tromping on Bess's flowers.

Abby propped Gray against the table and retrieved aspirin and water. "Take these."

"You're good to me. And so pretty." He tried to kiss her but caught her ear instead.

She wrapped an arm around his waist, guiding him down the hallway.

"Hey, the stairs are thataway." Gray waved an arm and almost clipped her nose.

"Let's try the elevator tonight." Abby rolled her eyes. The doors closed, and Gray pinned her against the wall. "Greg thinks you're hot."

His tender kiss surprised her.

"Daniel thinks you're hot, too." He frowned. "No, he thinks you and your sisters are witches."

The elevator opened, and she guided him down the hallway. "Witches, huh?"

"Oh, Abby," Gray crooned.

"Shush. Guests are sleeping."

At the door, she dug into his pockets to find his key card.

"Farther left, babe." Gray actually giggled.

She helped him into the room and steered him back to the bed. At least he was a cooperative drunk.

"I told them you were mine," Gray solemnly intoned.

She pushed him onto the bed and pulled off his shoes. "Who did you tell?"

His arms waved in great big circles. "Everyone. And Greg and Daniel. And the big-breasted blonde." He frowned. "I told you I said no to her—right?"

"Yup." She tugged his shirt off.

"You can have your way with me." Gray wiggled his hips. "I won't stop you."

"Let's get these clothes off and we'll see what happens." She tugged off his jeans, fairly sure he was going to pass out the minute his head hit the pillow.

When she bent over him, he pulled her onto the bed. "Pretty Abby, kiss me."

She bounced a kiss off his nose and eased away.

He grabbed for her hand. "Stay with me. Don't leave. I don't want you to leave."

He sounded more clearheaded than before.

"I'm going to fold your clothes."

She worked from the bathroom light. By the time she'd set his jeans on the chair, Gray was snoring.

She sat next to him. He'd sprawled across the entire bed. There wouldn't be a place for her to sleep even if she stayed.

"You're not going to feel too well tomorrow." Abby brushed back his black hair.

Leaning forward, she kissed his forehead. He'd asked her to stay, and she wanted to. Unfortunately, they meant two different things. What would happen if she asked him to stay in Savannah?

Nothing. Gray lived in Boston. His life was there. End of story.

She swallowed the lump in her throat. Right now Gray couldn't disappoint her, couldn't let her down.

That was the way things had to stay.

CHAPTER TEN

Rule #40—Dream big, dream often, but don't
let it keep you from your work.

Mamie Fitzgerald

"THAT WAS FUN." Cheryl loaded another bowl into
the dishwasher. "Thank you for letting me help and
learn."

Laughter rang out from the kitchen table.

Abby bumped her shoulder. "They're enjoying what
they made."

The sister group—and Cheryl—had made lobster
bisque and a seafood salad along with fruit tarts.

She really wanted to learn how to cook. She had
no idea, as a single mom, how to make that happen.

"Why don't you grab another bottle of champagne
for them?" Abby said.

Cheryl hurried across the hall and into the butler's
pantry. She picked the brand the ladies had been sipping during their cooking lesson. It was still hard for
her to see normal people drinking at eleven o'clock
in the morning. The only person she'd known who
did that had been Levi. He'd drunk beer, lots of beer.

She never should have accepted Levi's offer to live
in his house after Brad died. The house had been her

in-law's and really was half Brad's, but she, Brad and Josh had always lived on base.

Living with Levi had been fine—at first. But he'd lost his job, and then all he seemed to do was drink. And he was a mean drunk.

God, she missed her husband. They'd met in high school, and nothing could have kept them apart. High school graduation, his enlistment, marriage, Josh and eight years of heaven and worry.

Then a month before he was supposed to come home from Afghanistan, his patrol had come under fire. Everyone had been killed.

She hugged the cold bottle to her chest. She was having trouble remembering Brad's face. But she could never forget his smiling eyes. Josh had Brad's incredible eyes. And his heart.

Plastering a smile on her face, she headed back into the kitchen. Since the guests' bottle was empty, she popped the cork and nestled the new one into the ice bucket.

"Thanks, Cheryl," one of the ladies called out.

Abby had gotten most of the pots and pans cleaned up. "I've got some sweet tea. Let's sit," she said to Cheryl.

Shoot, she'd been fretting about what was past when she should have been helping Miss Abby. "Let me get it."

She dished ice into glasses before pouring the tea. Abby was resting in the lovely sitting area that overlooked Miss Bess's gardens.

"What did you think?" Abby asked.

"About the class?"

"About cooking," Abby clarified.

Cheryl cupped her face with her hands. "I loved it."

"I could tell." Abby leaned closer. "Marion and I talked about it. If you're interested, we'll work something out so you can start helping in the kitchen. Probably mostly during catering events. We'll see what you can do."

Cheryl's mouth fell open. "You'd..." Her voice cracked. "You'd help me?"

"In the beginning you'll peel a lot of potatoes and chop a lot of onions." Abby smiled. "But I'll work with you."

Her whole body shook. "I...I don't know how to thank you."

"You just did." Abby patted her knee. "We don't want to lose you. You and Josh are part of the Fitzgerald House family."

Abby went over and checked on the sister group.

Cheryl sank back into the love seat. For the first time since Brad had died, she and Josh were part of something special.

ABBY SLICED AN apple and handed most of it to Gray. "What's going on?"

He sat at the table he'd pulled together with plywood and sawhorses. "What?"

"You've been distracted since I brought your lunch over." All weekend, really. "Are there problems with your remodel?"

A saw screeched a floor above them. Frowning, he

waited until it stopped before answering. "Nothing that can't be handled."

"Good."

But he was still frowning.

"Something else bothering you?" she asked.

He touched her cheek, his eyes never leaving hers. "I need to head back to Boston for a few days."

The news hurt more than it should have. "When do you leave?"

"Next Wednesday. I'll be back on Sunday evening, I think. I'm still working out the details."

She rose from the empty spool that was serving as a chair. Moving over to Gray, she cupped his face and gave him a gentle kiss. He tasted of salt and lemonade. "I'll miss you."

He stood and pulled her into a big hug. Tipping up her chin, he kissed her. His lips opened hers, and his tongue began a familiar and erotic dance. He took the kiss deep into the dark of night.

A saw screeched and Gray jerked away.

His gaze locked on hers. "Wish we were near a bed, or a room with a lock."

"Me, too." Her laugh was a little shaky, charged with sexual tension. "I'd better head home."

After leaving Gray, she walked slowly back to Fitzgerald House. April flowers bloomed in every garden. Their perfume saturated the entire city, but she couldn't seem to smile.

She'd gone into this relationship with her eyes wide-open. Gray was more than halfway through his stay; a little more than three months remained before he left.

Abby brushed her hair off her face. For the next three months, she would store up every minute of happiness.

A couple crowded her on the narrow sidewalk. She stepped closer to the wall, and her shoulder brushed against a for-sale sign. Her eyes widened.

The house next to the B and B was for sale. Carleton House was for sale.

This was kismet. She'd always wanted to buy it. She nibbled her thumbnail. The location was perfect.

She could picture guests filling Fitzgerald and Carleton Houses. They would all want to eat at Southern Comforts. Lines would form because tourists and locals alike would clamor for a table.

As long as she was dreaming, they'd buy a third property, the one catty-corner from Fitzgerald House, and open up more rooms there.

Why couldn't Carleton House have been put on the market two years from now? Once she and her sisters had paid off the balloon, they'd be on stronger financial footing.

She pulled the flyer out of the Realtor box with a shaky hand. She scanned the missive, looking for the price.

"Ouch." They were asking for the moon on a home that needed massive renovations.

Abby speed-dialed Bess. "You won't believe it— Mrs. Carleton's selling. We need to buy the house." She sounded like a crazy woman.

"Did Mrs. Carleton call you?" Bess asked.

"I was walking home and saw the sign." Her voice squeaked. "Sister meeting. Tonight."

"Okay, take a breath before you hyperventilate. In this economy, the property won't move fast."

"I have to get tea set up. Can you call Dolley? I know we're meant to get this house." Her heart pounded. "I can feel it."

Hope bubbled inside her as bright as the shine of her copper pans. This time she would be steps closer to opening her restaurant.

"WE'D HAVE TO finance the entire purchase and renovation," Dolley cautioned.

"That's what Mamma had to do when she started." Abby paced over to the library window and peered out at Carleton House. Dolley's warning didn't faze her. All afternoon she'd daydreamed about this expansion. They would make this work.

"Does anyone remember how many bedrooms Carleton House has?" Abby asked.

Bess joined her at the window. "Six? Maybe eight? But I remember parlors, lots of parlors. Samuel could convert some of those."

"It's the perfect opportunity." Abby stood on her toes trying to get a better view. They should have met in the ballroom. The balcony there overlooked the courtyard and the wall dividing the two properties. "We should craft an offer and make it contingent on financing."

From her reclined position on one of the sofas, Dolley grumbled, "It's a long shot that our bank will lend us money on this venture."

"I have an idea." Abby had been thinking about this all afternoon.

Bess looked at her. "Do tell."

"We'll use the money we've saved for the balloon payment for a down payment and to start the renovations."

"But we have to pay off the loan," Dolley said.

Abby slapped her hand on her thigh. "We'd ask them to roll that loan into the mortgage on Carleton House."

"It might work." Dolley nodded. "It just might work."

"That's what I thought." Abby stared over at Carleton House.

Dolley swung her legs off the sofa. "We'd better have Samuel do a walk-through and give us an estimate. Mrs. Carleton hasn't had the money for repairs. If she had, the asking price would be a lot higher."

Bess ripped a page from Abby's notebook and started to sketch. "We could tear down the wall between the properties. It's crumbling anyway. I could create some sort of enclosed garden." She added detail to her drawings. "We'd carry our flagstone paths over to their back door. That's how guests would move between the two houses."

"We should do family suites over there." Abby nearly danced back to the sofa. "Not having rooms with two double beds has been a limitation. That's the request I've been seeing from the Sister Weekend side of the business. If four women are traveling together, they don't mind sharing beds or they want adjoining rooms. Dolley, what do you see from the website stats?"

"We're getting more family hits. They want to keep the family all in one space."

Abby barreled ahead. "We should have Samuel assess the house for adjoining rooms. They would add flexibility."

Bess nodded, but Dolley didn't.

Abby rocked on the balls of her feet, as if that would speed up the preliminary work. "Maybe we could have some rooms open by December. You know how many guests we had to turn away last year."

"Better if we could open in November." Bess bounced up and down. "Pick up all the shoppers. Maybe push a Sister Weekend with a holiday theme—Seasonal Sisters."

"Great idea. We'll need to know how much the mortgage would cost and how many beds we need to fill to meet the payment."

"I'll go over the books with our accountant." Dolley ran her fingers through her short red curls. "Abs, I like your plan, but that doesn't mean the bank will lend us the money. Maybe Gray…"

Abby cut her off. The idea of asking the man she was sleeping with to lend them money was a nonstarter. "Don't say that. He's only here through July. I would never, *never* ask him for money."

Any time she'd allowed a man into her dreams, they crumbled. Her father and the family's security. Maurice and the restaurant that was supposed to have been theirs. Gray needed to stay far, far away from her dreams.

"But..." Dolley started.

"This is family business," Abby interrupted.

"You're right." Dolley sighed.

Abby linked her hands with her sisters. "We can do this on our own."

GRAY WASN'T WAITING for Abby in the kitchen— exactly. He'd lingered over some pecan bars and sipped his cognac, hoping she'd stop in.

What was going on behind the library's closed doors? Abby had been almost manic when she'd called him after their lunch.

He didn't want to go to sleep without seeing her smile. Gray might not understand what was happening between them, but watching her face brought him more peace than the endorphins from a five-mile run.

Abby came through the swinging door, and her wonderful smile lit up. "Gray." Then she frowned as though remembering something. "Did you eat?"

"Yup." Gray grinned. He couldn't seem to stop himself. "Just wanted to pick up where we left off at lunch today."

He caught her in the middle of the kitchen and pulled her into his arms. When she wrapped her arms around his waist, his world brightened. One inhale of the spicy scent of her hair and his body went into full alert.

What pulled him to this woman? Was it her smile? The tilt of her head when she listened to him talk about his day? Or was it the way she refused to lean on anyone—even him? What the hell did she want from him? Every other woman he'd dated wanted his money or his family connections. What about Abby?

Was he only a minor blip in her life? Sex, fun and short-term. That was their agreement.

But shouldn't she want more?

Even this tight embrace wasn't close enough. Gray crushed his mouth to hers. Only her taste could quell this rush of panic.

They should be talking. He should be asking what happened today.

He took their kiss deeper.

She ignited in his arms. Their body heat welded them together. Her hands clutched at him, her breath coming in short, sweet gasps. Under her flimsy shirt and tank top, her nipples hardened against his chest.

"Come upstairs with me," he groaned.

She didn't hesitate, just took his hand. They made it to the foot of the stairs before he caged her against the wall for another kiss. She stood on her toes, never backing away as his lips bruised hers.

Gray broke the kiss, cursing. What was wrong with him? He had a perfectly good bed where guests couldn't trip over them.

After almost running Abby up the stairs, the locked door slowed him down. He slid his key card, and then slid it again. "Damn it."

He made the mistake of looking over at Abby. She was leaning against the wall, her hair mussed from his hands and her green eyes cloudy with desire. She'd already unbuttoned her shirt. Her nipples budded under the pale blue tank top she wore beneath it.

The lock flashed green. Yanking open the door, he pulled her into the room. Even as the door closed, he backed Abby against the wood.

She moaned as he ripped off her top. Then he buried his face in those breasts that called to him day and night. "This is madness."

Her hands stroked him through his jeans, and he wanted those fingers wrapped around him. Now.

He tried to do too many things at once. Kiss her, unbutton her pants and toe off his shoes.

Abby had a lot more dexterity. His jeans were already unbuttoned and unzipped. Her laugh filled the room. "Happy to see me?"

He growled in frustration, until she pushed his jeans down and dropped to her knees. Her hot breath brushed his thighs. The first touch of her tongue almost set him off like a rocket. When she took him in her mouth, he groaned her name.

Pain and pleasure battered him like an ocean wave crashing against cliffs. "Stop," he cried between clenched teeth.

Gray tugged her up. His hands were rough as he pushed off her jeans and underwear.

She stepped out of them and kicked everything away.

When he picked her up, she wrapped her legs around his waist. He plunged into her with a groan.

He pinned her to the door, controlling every move, every delicious slide into her body.

Abby fought his shirt up his arms. His arms briefly caught high above his head until he shook the shirt away.

Then he took control once more. Every stroke, every slide of his body into hers took a century. Her nails dug into his back as she clung to him. His panting breath feathered her hair.

She twisted against him, trying to bring him deeper, to grind herself against him, but he wouldn't give her any leverage.

"Abby." Beads of sweat dotted his furrowed forehead.

He stroked deep and stopped. He wanted to hold off the inevitable. Stop time. Stay inside Abby forever.

"Please, move," she groaned.

He couldn't stop the inevitable.

He rocked slowly, one roll of his hips.

Abby came apart. She tightened around him, wave after wave of intense pleasure.

He drove into her, drawing out her climax until he came inside her in a rush.

They slid to the floor, limbs entwined and boneless. Their rasping breaths filled the room.

Abby's cheek rested on Gray's stomach. He brushed her hair off her face with a shaking hand. "Are you okay?"

"I'm waiting for my body to reintegrate. Maybe by morning." Her voice was husky and half-muffled.

"Jesus. I'm sorry. I didn't mean to… I shouldn't have…" He'd been too rough.

Gray gathered her into his chest. They stood

together and walked into the bedroom. When she lay down on the bed, he tenderly covered her with the sheet. The mattress gave as he slipped in beside her. He tugged her so they were face-to-face. Their legs tangled together.

He buried his face in her hair. "Are you sure you're okay?"

She pulled away and touched his cheek. "I'm absolutely incredible."

He tucked her back into the crook of his shoulder. Where she belonged. "Yes, you are."

THE NEXT MORNING, Gray topped off Abby's coffee and poured himself a cup. By eating breakfast in the kitchen, they got a little more time together.

"Do you want strawberries with your French toast?" she asked.

"Sure. Smells great."

"Good morning, Gray," Cheryl called as she loaded a tray of French toast on a cart.

"Hey, Cheryl. How's the crowd today?" he asked.

"Hungry. Even the newlyweds have already come down."

"Fruit holding up?" Abby asked.

"Looks fine." Cheryl wheeled the cart through the swinging door.

Abby waved her hand at the mound of fruit she must have cut this morning. "I guess I'm making fruit tarts for tea this afternoon."

"She seems more relaxed, doesn't she?" Gray asked.

"Cheryl?"

"Yeah."

"I think so." Abby pushed a few wayward strands of sunset-colored hair off her cheek. "A couple of weeks ago Cheryl asked what it took to learn how to cook."

"She asked for help? That is progress."

"I'm going to start training her. When we have catering events."

Abby would be a great teacher. Patient but thorough.

She sat at the table next to him. Gray took her hands and stared into her bright green eyes. "You're okay, right? Last night…I don't know what got into me."

Her dazzling smile seemed to light up the room. "Last night was incredible."

"I was rougher than I meant to be." He stroked a finger along her arm. "I gave you bruises."

"Did you hear me complain?"

He shook his head. "No, but I probably should have."

Abby brushed a kiss on his lips. Heading over to the beverage station, she brought a coffee carafe back to the table. Leaning close, she whispered, "Last night you made me feel desired and beautiful. How can I complain about that?"

He kissed her hand, tasting the oranges she'd squeezed. "I never want to hurt you."

Abby's smile wilted. "It will hurt when you leave. We only have so much time together. I don't want to waste any of it worrying about things I can't control." She straightened her shoulders. "I plan to store up all this happiness."

Gray reached for her hand, but she hopped up from the table and hurried to the teapot. She stood at the counter with her back toward him, pouring a cup of tea, even though she already had coffee.

"Abby." He didn't know what else to say.

When she turned around, a smile creased her face. Her professional smile.

He kept his gaze on her as she ate. Something seemed different. *Abby* seemed different. "What was the big sister meeting last night, or is it a secret?"

A grin broke over Abby's face, a genuine one this time. "I forgot to tell you! The house next door is for sale—Carleton House. This is perfect for the B and B's expansion. We could get ten more bedrooms." Her hands waved above the table. "We could market Carleton House to families. Connecting bedrooms or two double beds in a room would meet requests we haven't been able to accommodate. God, isn't it fantastic?"

Gray had seen their financial position. The Fitzgeralds were asset rich and cash poor. How would they pull this off? Keeping his tone neutral, he said, "It sounds like a great opportunity."

"It is. We have to craft the right offer price." Her eyes glittered like emeralds. "I'm going to propose that we use the money we have for the balloon payment as the down payment. Then the bank can roll that loan into the mortgage of Carleton House."

"That might work." If they had a loan officer other than Wayne Lennertz. "What did your sisters think?"

Abby clasped his hand. He could feel her vibrating with excitement through their joined fingers. "Bess is sketching ideas for the gardens and talking about taking down the wall between the properties. Dolley's worried about the money." She frowned. "Our bank has to see what a great opportunity this is for Fitzgerald House."

Abby bounced out of her chair as if on springs. "I know this will work. If we can get the cash to renovate, we'll fill those rooms. How could the bank not understand that?"

Gray rubbed the back of his neck. Walking past Carleton house, he'd noticed cracked windows on the second floor. "What kind of shape is the place in?"

Abby paced alongside the counter. "I have a feeling there's quite a bit of work needed. Its carriage house is probably in worse shape than ours." She slapped her hand on the granite. "But Samuel will help. I'm going to ask him to walk through the house with me. We'll need a renovation estimate for the bank."

She plopped in the chair next to Gray, propping her chin on her hand. "It always comes back to money, doesn't it? I won't skimp on maintaining Fitzgerald House, and we're committed to finishing the third-floor rooms. We have to keep up our standards. Otherwise we'll lose our repeat business and the referrals."

She bumped an elbow to his arm and grinned. "Maybe this is where you want to shower me with millions of dollars because I keep making your pecan bars." Her eyebrows wiggled. "How does a lifetime supply sound?"

Something in his chest twisted. It was the second time she'd joked about him giving her money.

"That sounds delicious, but do you need to expand?" he asked. "You're already adding rooms on the third floor."

"This will help with Southern Comforts."

"What?"

"My restaurant." Her eyes glittered. "It would be connected to Fitzgerald House but open to the public."

Gray sank into his chair. He'd forgotten about this dream.

"Ever since I came back from New York," she said, taking a deep breath, "I've planned to open a restaurant. With a larger B and B, there'd be more guests, and we could serve both our guests and walk-ins."

A restaurant. Guests would rave about her food. Gray nodded, not sure what to say. He didn't want to burst Abby's bubble, but he doubted their bank would loan them the money. Lennertz didn't believe in the Fitzgeralds.

She grabbed her to-do list and jotted notes. Muttering, she said, "Dolley needs to show the bank how many people are being turned away because we're full. No, I'd better handle any meeting with Wayne. Dolley can give me the facts."

"I'd like to see this place." Gray brushed a kiss on her nose. "Would you let me go through the house with you and Samuel?"

Maybe if it was in terrible shape, he and Samuel could talk her out of this crazy idea. Or maybe he could help her. The idea sparkled like newly installed windows.

She frowned. "I don't want to take up your time."

"I'll make the time. I'd enjoy it."

Her smile was hesitant. "Are you sure?"

"Absolutely."

He rolled his shoulders. She'd had more enthusiasm when she'd offered to sell him a lifetime supply of pecan bars. For millions.

He pulled her out of her chair. His hands found their way into her back pockets, and he pulled her against him. "I've got to meet Daniel. Call me when you set up the walk-through."

"I'LL BE DOING paperwork and making calls for the rest of the afternoon," Gray said to Daniel. "See you tomorrow."

"I thought you were touring Carleton House with my dad and Abby," Daniel said.

"You sure have your finger on everything that goes on with the Fitzgeralds, don't you?" Gray frowned.

"I keep my ears open." Daniel shook his head. "Carleton House will need work and money. Too bad their banker is so tightfisted. Anyone who's ever worked with those sisters knows they accomplish what they set out to do."

"The Fitzgeralds should find another bank. Or at least a different loan officer." Lennertz was an ass. The idea of investing in Fitzgerald House—in Abby's dream—had haunted him all morning. How would she react if he announced he'd loan them the money for their expansion?

He struggled with the idea of expanding his business in Savannah. How much longer could he stay without jeopardizing his Boston operations? Sure, everything was running smoothly up north, but he'd always been a hands-on manager.

He locked the condo door and headed down the hallway with Daniel. Additional property in Savannah would mean delegating more of his Boston duties.

Besides, his roots were in Boston. His family, such as it was, was there. His fingers clenched into a fist. The rough-ins on the condos were almost done. There was no reason for him to stay in Savannah. He could spend more time in Boston and let the realty company handle the remaining details. Hell, right now he lived in a B and B, just a step up from living out of a suitcase. There was nothing to hold him to this city.

Except Abby. He sighed. What the hell should he do about Abby?

Well, he was heading back to Boston next week. He'd check in with his project managers. Check out a new site in Lexington. Maybe he should start spending weekends in Boston, put some distance between them. They'd lived in each other's pockets for almost three months.

"If you decide to acquire another property, keep Forester Construction in mind. You're a pleasure to work with." Daniel pushed the elevator button. "I heard Dolley's worried they won't get the money for Carleton House."

"I don't get it." Gray held the outside door for Daniel, and they merged into the busy River Street foot traffic. "Abby just told me about Carleton House this morning, yet you seem to know all about it. Do you have the library bugged?"

Daniel grinned. "Nope, just my dad. He's their honorary father and that makes them my sisters. The girls tell him everything." He looked at Gray and corrected himself. "Well, almost everything. It took a while to realize you and Abby were an item. Of course, if you hurt her, you'll deal with the Forester men."

Daniel's tone may have been nonchalant, but his words cut into Gray as cleanly as one of Abby's knives. "And what happens to Abby if she hurts me?"

"Not one damn thing." Daniel slapped his back. "See you tomorrow."

The two men headed in opposite directions. Gray worked his way through the tourists who crowded the sidewalks. He stopped in front of the house with the for-sale sign.

Carleton House. Although this place wasn't as massive as Fitzgerald House, the three-story home still dominated the corner. Black shutters framed the windows, and lacy wrought iron edged each porch.

From the sidewalk, he could see that the shutters were crooked and railings had rusted. The six chimneys looked as if they might collapse in a strong wind.

As he waited for Abby and Samuel, he walked the property line between the two houses. Deep vertical cracks exposed the brick under the stucco. Looking up, he noted a number of roof tiles broken or missing.

His lips pressed together.

When Abby and Samuel arrived, he and Samuel shook hands. Abby's eyes kept darting to the house.

Gray could almost feel her vibrating. She wanted her hands on this place.

"Mrs. Carleton's a dear," she whispered. "Her husband died almost twenty years ago. Her son moved to California a few years ago and doesn't get home very often. She hasn't been able to maintain the house."

Walking up the decayed but clean steps, Gray supported Abby's elbow. He smiled at the blast of color from the trellised roses blooming on either side of an impressive front entrance. The house might be crumbling, but he suspected the furniture and floors would be polished and shining.

The door was opened by a petite older woman. "Abigail, Samuel, come in, come in."

Gray let Abby handle the introductions, and they all moved into the front parlor.

The smell of lemon oil mingled with the fragrance of the roses displayed in a cut-glass bowl on the entry table. He'd been right about the floors and furniture; they shone.

"Thanks for showing us the house." Abby bent down and picked up a gigantic gray cat that wound around her ankles. "Hello, Mr. Phelps."

Mrs. Carleton's hair was the same color as her cat. "I'm glad you're interested."

Abby rubbed the cat's head. "I've always been interested."

"I made lemonade," Mrs. Carleton said, pouring glasses for everyone. She bustled around the group like a bee visiting an open flower. "I thought you might like something to drink as you toured the house."

She led them back into the entry hall. "Carleton House was built around 1880. George, my husband, was never able to discover the architect's name."

As they passed the curving staircase, Gray tugged on the wrought iron banister. It seemed secure enough.

"George's great-grandfather built the home." Mrs. Carleton's foot stroked the entry floor. "The marble's from Italy. The rest of the house has hardwood floors. They've never been covered by linoleum or carpet."

Abby barely stopped in the outdated kitchen. "We'd have the guests eat at Fitzgerald House until we get the restaurant up and running," she whispered.

The dining room had once been lovely. The bleached-oak paneling and woodwork kept the room light and airy. The twelve-foot-high coffered ceiling boasted intricate plaster medallions in need of repair.

In the second-floor hallway, Samuel leaned over to Gray and whispered, "Does Abby even see the cracks and water stains?"

"How can she miss them?"

"Blinded by love," Samuel quipped.

Gray twisted a bedroom light switch, but nothing happened. "She certainly won't be blinded by the lighting."

Abby ran back into the room and grabbed Gray's hand. "Come see the music room. Samuel, I think we can make it into a suite. That would be at least two suites. We can have nine—no, ten—possible bedrooms on the two main floors."

After being shown the music room, Gray and Samuel checked out the basement while the women talked about the chandeliers. This had to be the original foundation, with rocks jutting out of the wall. Sections of the floor were dirt, other sections sported uneven, cracked concrete.

"Did you notice the exterior cracks?" Gray asked.

"Yup," Samuel replied. "And the cracks between the ceiling and walls in the southeast corner of the house. Might require foundation work."

"Need a structural engineer's evaluation."

"That's my thought, too." Samuel dusted off his hands. "I know a good one."

"Why don't you set up a walk-through with him?"

Samuel's bushy white eyebrows leaped into his hairline. "You thinking of buying this place, or is this Abby's project?"

"I'm getting ahead of myself. Abby asked for my input." That wasn't quite true. He'd volunteered. Abby never asked for anything. Never confided, never solicited his opinion. "We should both mention the foundation to her."

Samuel rested a hand on the low ceiling and stared at him. What did the man think Gray planned to do—snatch this money pit out from under Abby's nose? The idea was preposterous.

Wasn't it?

But if he bought the house and took on the restoration, he could lease the place back to the Fitzgeralds. The idea spun through his head like a top.

They joined Abby and Mrs. Carleton in the backyard. The garden area wasn't fancy. Nothing compared to the whimsical setting Bess had created next door. There was a small terrace with a stone barbecue and a modest vegetable plot. A profusion of rosebushes saturated the space with color, but the wisteria vine covering the carriage house looked wild.

"Bess will have a field day," he whispered in Abby's ear.

She poked him in the ribs as they neared the carriage house. "The walls look solid." She turned to Samuel to see if he agreed with her assessment.

He wiggled a loose door. "Hmm?"

"Is the carriage house structurally sound?" she asked.

"Oh, yes. If you're going to use it as guest rooms, the challenge will be the plumbing. Brick needs tuckpointing, too."

"So have you seen what you need to, Abby?" Gray asked after they'd said goodbye to Mrs. Carleton.

"God, yes. It's enough to make me drool." She practically pulsed with excitement. "Do you know how many more rooms we could add?"

They walked through the garden and into the Fitzgerald House kitchen. Abby pulled out a tray of sandwiches and bars and put the kettle on for tea. "What do you think?" She looked expectantly from one man to the other.

Gray let Samuel take the lead. The older man sketched out possible ideas on Abby's tablet. "Assuming you decide to live in the smaller carriage house, here's what I think you could do."

As Samuel talked and drew, Gray couldn't help but be impressed by his vision.

"So you suggest keeping a kitchen over there?" Abby fingers constantly bounced on the table. Gray had never seen her so keyed up.

"I'd recommend you keep something. People will want tea or coffee in the morning, unless you include coffeemakers in each room."

"Absolutely not. I'd still want to brew our coffee, not those awful small coffeepots." She tapped her nose as she thought out loud. "The dining room has those lovely carved pocket doors. We could use that room for small dinner parties if guests wanted to. If we have an event in the ballroom here, we'd have a space for something intimate at Carleton House."

"That's something to think about." Samuel made a note. "Honey, there are a lot of other problems with the house. Second-floor wiring needs to be brought up to code."

"But you can fix it, right?" Abby leaned over the table. "There's nothing really glaring, right?"

Gray spoke up. "You may have foundation issues."

"Really?" Abby bit her lip.

"A structural engineer needs to evaluate why there are cracks in the exterior and interior walls. You may have to repair the foundation."

She looked at Samuel.

He nodded his head. "I'll contact Garretson and see if he'll do a walk-through. That's probably your biggest problem."

"Thanks." She stopped chewing her lip and went to work on her thumbnail. "The other problem is getting the bank to understand what an opportunity this is."

"I know you've always wanted Carleton House." Samuel squeezed Abby's hand.

"I never thought it would come on the market so soon." She sighed. "Can you run a ballpark cost? I won't hold you to anything, but the bank will need numbers."

Samuel stood and patted her shoulder. "You bet. I'll get something to you in a couple of days." He took a sandwich. "Best be getting back to work."

Before Samuel went upstairs to check on his crew, she gave him a hug.

"You want this, don't you, Abs?" Gray asked once the older man had gone.

"So bad I can taste it. Let's say we get another eight to ten rooms out of Carleton House. We'll be up to thirty rooms. Thirty. It'll change the whole dynamic of our B and B."

Just as she had that morning, she paced and talked. "More staff, full-time cooks and servers, expansion of the catering. My restaurant."

Abby held out her hands. "My sisters wouldn't have to hold down their other jobs. Since we can't afford to live in Fitzgerald House any longer, at least we'd work together—as a family. That's what I want."

Her face was flushed, and her green eyes shone. Curls escaped the clip she'd used to pull her hair off her shoulders.

She was so alive.

Gray didn't want to see Abby's smile fade. The Fitzgeralds deserved a break. Maybe he could help.

CHAPTER ELEVEN

Rule #36—Make sure you don't turn Mary and Joseph away. There should always be room at the inn.

Mamie Fitzgerald

"HERE ARE SAMUEL'S IDEAS." Abby spread his Carleton House sketches on the kitchen table in front of Bess and Dolley. They scooted their chairs closer. "He thinks we could get ten to twelve bedrooms, plus meeting rooms and a small kitchen without too much modification. The main food would still be prepped here, but we could cater meals there, too."

"What about the carriage houses?" Bess asked.

"When we have the money, we'll finish the Fitzgerald carriage house with a couple more rooms." She tapped her finger on the drawing. "And then the restaurant. The Carleton carriage house could be used for family living space. I asked Samuel to design apartments for us with some common areas."

"That might work. We'd be big, Abs." Bess raised an eyebrow. "Are we ready for such a change?"

Abby didn't answer. She looked at her sisters' bright faces.

"If we get the money, yes," Dolley qualified. She squeezed Bess's hand. "I think we'd be able to cut

back on our non-Fitzgerald House hours. Maybe eliminate them altogether."

Bess grinned. "That would be wonderful."

"I wouldn't mind running my own website building business from here," Dolley said.

Abby looked at them. They'd be able to work and
live together. "Absolutely."

"Okay. All for one and one for all and all that."
Bess waved her hand. "What's Samuel's estimate?"

Abby flipped the number up.

"Gwaaack!" Dolley wrapped her fingers around
her throat and pretended to choke herself.

They waded through blueprints, numbers and assumptions.

"It's a lot to take in." Bess pushed away from the
table. "Are we sure we want to take the risk?"

"Yes," Abby said.

"I'm a yes," Bess said.

Abby and Bess looked at Dolley.

"Of course I'm a yes. We're family." Dolley
looked each sister in the eye. "But we could over-
extend."

Abby's heart skipped a beat, then another. "But we
could gain more. We could work together, one hundred percent of the time."

Her sisters nodded.

"So—we go back to the bank?" Abby asked.

Dolley nodded, heaving a small sigh of resigna-
tion. "Don't get your hopes up, anyone. And don't
quit your day jobs."

CHERYL PUSHED THE day care door open.

"Hi, Ms. Henshaw," the receptionist said. "How are you?"

"Fine, thanks." She handed the receptionist a check for this week's tuition.

For the last three weeks of April, she hadn't needed to use her tip money to pay for Josh's care. With Gray's and Abby's help, she was getting her financial feet under her.

"Go in and get Josh. I'll have your receipt printed by the time you come out."

"Thanks."

Cheryl had been lucky to get a spot at this day care, and at a reduced cost. The center was clean, provided a healthy lunch and it was on her way to work.

She walked into the older kids' room. Josh was playing some sort of board game with his new best friend, Zach.

"Hi, Mom!" he yelled. "I'm almost finished."

The teacher waved, kneeling next to a table of three girls.

Cheryl looked at the wooden board. Josh and Zach had different colored and shaped blocks of wood. Zach handed Josh a tall round piece.

Josh held it in his hand, staring at the small board. He grinned and placed the piece on an open square. "Quarto!"

"What? No way!" Zach shook his head.

"Solids," Josh crowed, pointing at four pieces on the board.

"Shoot." Zach nodded, putting the pieces away. "I'll get you next time."

"'Kay." He gave Zach a high five. "See you tomorrow.

Standing, Josh threw his arms around her legs and gave her a big hug. "Hi, Mom," he repeated.

"Hi yourself." She hugged him back. "Get your backpack."

She checked out the name of the game. Quarto. She'd have to see if the thrift shop had it. The Chutes and Ladders set they'd bought last month was falling apart.

"Bye, Sarah." Josh waved as the receptionist handed Cheryl her receipt.

They turned right when they left the day care, and Josh rattled on about his day. He grew silent as they walked by the gelato store.

Her little boy had learned never to ask for anything. But he stared at a little girl licking a cone.

She had a ten-dollar bill in her pocket. Since she'd covered tuition for the week, she'd planned to add it to her tips and see if she could get herself some cheap jeans.

Jeans could wait. "Do you want a cone?"

His eyes grew big. Brad's eyes. "Really?" he asked.

"Really."

He rushed to the door. "Thanks!"

He stood at the counter, looking at the bounty of flavors. "What's that one?"

"Cherry."

"And that?"

"Lemon cheesecake."

Josh scrunched up his mouth. "Do I like that?"

"It's my favorite." The girl behind the counter dug out a small spoonful. "Here's a sample."

He tasted it. "I do! I like it!"

Cheryl bought him a small cone and watched as her son happily licked it up.

"Want some?" Josh held up the cone as they headed down the steps to River Street.

She took a little taste, not wanting to take too much from her son. "Mmm, delicious."

She kept her hand on Josh's shoulder as they joined the crowded sidewalk. Unlocking the apartment door, she let them in and took his backpack off his shoulder. "Go eat at the table."

He made sure not one drip went anywhere but his belly.

She carried his backpack into the kitchen, emptying the paper and pictures. He loved to color and draw. Maybe next year when Josh was in kindergarten and her day care tuition was less, she could afford to get him some art lessons.

She pulled a bright green flyer out of the bag.

Josh pointed to it. "This is really cool, Mom. Day care has a summer camp down on the island."

"Tybee?"

He nodded, crunching the last of his cone. "They told us about it today. We'd get to learn about birds and swimming and boats and stuff."

She flipped the tap on and held him up so he could wash his hands.

"Can I go?" he asked, drying his hands.

She read the flyer. Then came to the price. "Three hundred and fifty dollars," she whispered.

Josh's smile crashed and burned. "We don't have the money."

She pulled him close. Everything was getting better, and her son asked for so little.

"Let me see what I can do."

He nodded but still didn't smile.

There was one way. One she hadn't tried for fear Levi would find them.

She pulled the phone number she'd looked up a couple of weeks ago. It was only four-thirty. She should still be able to call. She waited through the automated routing, punching in the right buttons.

Finally a human voice answered, "Survivor benefits. How can I help you?"

Cheryl took a deep breath and gave her real name. "I've moved. Can I get my checks sent to my new address?"

"Sure." The woman promised to email her the proper form.

Cheryl would have to use the computer and printer at Fitzgerald House, but it was a start.

Levi would be furious.

Too bad. She set the phone down and opened the fridge to make dinner. It was *her* husband who'd been killed in Afghanistan. The money was for their son, not Levi's drinking.

They'd left her brother-in-law's house three months ago. Levi should have found a job by now.

She shivered, unable to forget the memory of his hands pawing her.

But it was time to start taking charge of her own life.

"THANKS FOR LETTING me walk through the house again, Mrs. Carleton." Gray stepped around the cat and took a chair in the front parlor. Roses perfumed the room, and the coffee table gleamed. Too bad the foundation hadn't been taken care of as well as the furniture.

Mrs. Carleton poured two glasses of lemonade, then settled across from him. "Did Abby ask you to take a look at something specific?"

This was the tough part of his visit. "Abby doesn't know I'm here."

Mrs. Carleton looked at him with clear gray eyes. "Then, why are you here? I thought you were her friend."

He answered the easy question first. "I am. A good friend."

She waited. He could have used her in a tough negotiation. Her cat jumped up on her lap, turned and glared at him, too. Talk about pressure.

"I want Abby to be able to buy Carleton House, but I'm pretty sure the bank won't lend them the money."

"How would you know that?"

"I've met with their loan officer." He shook his head. "He doesn't understand that the Fitzgeralds are a sure bet."

"What would you like me to do about that?" She took a slow sip of her drink.

"I want to purchase Carleton House."

"You say you want Abby to have my house, but then you buy it behind her back." Her voice oozed with disbelief.

"I plan on making all the changes Abby and her sisters want. Then I'll sell the house to the Fitzgeralds on terms they can actually afford." He leaned forward. "I don't want Abby's dreams to be crushed because they can't get the right kind of financing."

"You're going to pay for their restorations?" Her fingers dug into her cat's fur.

"That's my plan."

Mrs. Carleton set her glass on her coaster with a clank. "What's in it for you?"

"Excuse me?"

"What do you get out of this?" she asked.

"I…" He'd been gathering paperwork, pulling strings, getting his money lined up. He hadn't thought of what he got out of this. "I get to help a family that deserves a break."

She simply stared at him.

He shifted in his chair. What if she wouldn't sell him Carleton House? What would he do then? How would he help Abby? He didn't have anything else to offer.

"Great answer." She slapped her hands together, and the cat leaped off her lap. "What happens now?"

He exhaled and pulled out the purchase agreement

he and his attorney had constructed. "I'd like you to keep this confidential."

Her eyes narrowed. "You don't want the Fitzgeralds to know."

"Carleton House is one piece of a bigger puzzle." And he was still jamming some uncooperative pieces together. "I want them all assembled before I give Abby the happy news."

GRAY LET HIMSELF into Abby's apartment. She was in the bedroom. Her perfume drifted on the air, that fragrance of flowers and spice that made him want her instantly.

"Gray?" she called, sticking her head out of the doorway.

"Yup." He started toward her, needing to touch her.

Her head disappeared, but she called out, "I'll be ready in a minute. Are you sure you want to go out for dinner?"

"I want you to relax tonight."

Over the past two weeks, she'd been a whirlwind. Between the inn, catering and creating a business plan for the bank, she'd barely slept.

He'd been making plans, too. He couldn't wait to see Abby's face when he told her he'd solved all her financial problems. He was just waiting on Lennertz. The man moved as slow as tectonic plates.

"I'm ready." She paused in the bedroom doorway.

He looked up, and every thought but Abby evaporated.

She'd piled her hair on top of her head, curls spilling

around her face. Her eyelashes were darker, emphasizing the slight tilt to her lids. Her lips were glossy and wet.

He got his first glimpse of her dress and forgot to breathe. He might have mumbled something, he wasn't sure. He was used to Abby switching between her professional clothes, silk dresses and demure suits, and her cooking clothes, tank tops and jeans. But this. Wow.

She stood smiling in an almost nonexistent strapless black dress. The material crisscrossed and cupped her breasts. The dress ended a few inches above her knees. Silver threads shimmered in the black fabric of the skirt. His gaze traveled down her slim legs to spiky red heels.

Drool probably dripped from his chin. "You blow me away."

She twirled and the skirt flared, daring him to touch.

He couldn't keep away. He moved closer until her eyes were the only things he could see.

"Don't you look nice?" She ran her fingers up the lapel of his jacket and brushed her lips against his. When he kept the kiss light, she frowned.

If he kissed her the way he wanted, they'd never leave her apartment.

"We should…go." His voice was rough with need. But he would contain it, so they could have one special evening.

They walked down to his car, and as she slid into

the passenger seat, she said, "I was worried I would have to walk far in these shoes."

"I wouldn't make you do that. Nice shoes, by the way." They made him want to nibble her toes and work his way north. "You look gorgeous."

"Thank you." She seemed surprised. Hadn't he complimented her before?

"Since you told me to dress up, where are we going?" she asked.

He shot a sideways glance at her. "Someplace special. You don't get seasick, do you?"

"No." She grinned. "Are we taking a dinner cruise?"

He'd thought of booking one. Now he was happy he hadn't. Gray wanted her all to himself. "You'll see."

They headed toward the marina. She pointed to the road they'd passed. "You missed the turnoff."

"Another time. Sit back. You haven't relaxed in weeks." He linked their fingers together.

They crossed the bridge and followed I-80. He pulled into the parking lot and hurried around the car to open Abby's door.

Leading her down to the wharf, he searched the slips, finally identifying the boat he wanted.

"Isn't this Daniel's sailboat?" she asked as they boarded a nice-size sloop. Brass fittings gleamed against teak decking.

"I think you might be right."

She looked nervous. "Does Daniel know we're here?"

Gray plucked a key from his pocket. "Of course."

While a marina employee cast off the lines, Gray started the engines. It had been a while since he'd sailed, but that wasn't the point of this date. He wanted to watch the sun set over the water with Abby.

"I didn't know you knew how to sail," she said.

He slapped a hand to his chest. "I'm wounded. I'm from Boston. We were sailing before Savannah was even a port. I could hoist a sail before I could ride a bicycle."

She laughed, a seductive, carefree sound. "Right."

Standing at the bow with her back to the water, she laughed again as the breeze tore her hair from its pins.

Abby stole his breath.

His happiest memories were of eating and talking with Abby. By acquiring Carleton House, he could help Abby's dreams along. Then when he was back in Boston, he'd be able to picture her smiling.

He rubbed his head. Heading home, being so far from Abby, was going to be painful.

She made him smile, more than anyone he'd ever met. She was an island of calm, like an oasis in the desert. He wanted to be with her when she laughed, when she cried and when she created the perfect meal. Every day of his life.

His heart stuttered. Stuttered, slipped and plopped at her red high heels.

Gray swallowed hard. Shit.

No way. He was in love with her.

He was in love with all the facets of this complex woman. The one who cleaned ovens, dug through an-tiques, really listened when he talked, created heavenly food, took care of her family and was more knowledgeable about wines than anyone he knew.

He almost rammed the boat into another slip.

Gray jerked the steering wheel, avoiding a crash. Abby grabbed the railing, her eyes wide.

"Sorry, sorry." He tore his gaze from her. They weren't out of the marina yet. He'd better concentrate on the boat and not this new complication.

"Can I do anything?" she asked.

"There's champagne and glasses in the galley." His voice cracked. Adrenaline or this new realization? Damn. Love? Now? No way.

"I can handle champagne." She kicked off those heels made for sinning and headed down the steps.

"I'm impressed. Perrier-Jouët." She came up from the galley with a wine bucket and glasses in her hands. "So this is what life is like when money is no object."

Gray's back stiffened. "I just wanted to do something nice." And he wanted to impress her, too.

Abby took the helm as they aimed toward Sister Island. Standing at the wheel with her feet spread for balance, she amazed him. She looked competent in any setting.

He eased the cork out with a gentle pop. His hand shook as he poured, bouncing the bottle on the glass. Should love make him feel as if he'd been smacked by a wrecking ball?

He walked over to her with a glass of champagne, managing not to spill. "What should we drink to?"

A pensive smile crossed her face. "To good news on our bank application."

"To Carleton House." His attorney and Mrs. Carleton's were negotiating. And Lennertz still needed to get back to him. Until those pieces were in place, he'd wait to tell Abby that her problems were solved.

Their glasses chimed.

At her first sip, she sighed. "This won't ever be on our wine tasting, but it's lovely."

He took the wheel, and they drifted downriver. Gray anchored the boat off Sister Island. He set up a table and chairs and brought out the food he'd had catered.

"I hope dinner is up to snuff," he said, plating the cold lobster. "The city's best caterer couldn't help me with this meal."

"Who did you want to cater dinner?" she asked, her tone laced with frost.

"You."

Her smile lit up her face like dawn breaking across the bay. "Good answer."

She dipped the lobster in the sauce and put it up to her lips. "The Fisher House catered our dinner, right?"

He nodded. They ate their way through salads and pasta, and then fed each other chocolate mousse. When the sun had set, he lit candles and scattered them on the table. Moonlight danced through her hair. Everything seemed new. He picked up her hand and planted kisses on the inside of her wrist.

"You've been staring at me all night." She dabbed her napkin around her lips. "Do I have food somewhere?"

"Everything is perfect." He tugged her onto the

cushioned bench next to him. She stacked her legs on top of his. With his arms around her shoulder and their faces tipped to the stars, contentment washed over him.

Was this love, or was he blinded by Savannah's atmosphere? Would he feel differently if they were in Boston?

He needed to know.

ABBY DID UP her seat belt and turned in her seat. "Tell me what's going on."

Ever since they'd had dinner on the sailboat last week, Gray had changed. When they spent time together, she'd find him watching her and smiling.

He hadn't even told her where they were headed for lunch.

"I hope you'll like where we're going." He linked their hands together. "Trust me."

"I do." She sighed.

When Gray left Savannah, her heart would crack. Maybe if she and her sisters got Carleton House, the work would fill the hole Gray's departure was going to leave.

His condominium restoration was going *too* well. The rough-ins would be finished by the end of June. It was only mid-May, but the next six weeks would fly by. She wanted to tell Daniel to screw something up so Gray would have to stay longer. She wanted more.

Gray drove to the northwest.

She frowned. "Is there a new restaurant out this way?"

"You're impatient. I thought you'd do better with surprises. Where's your phenomenal control, Miss Fitzgerald?"

She muttered under her breath, "You destroyed it."

He chuckled.

They entered the airport, parking next to the private hangars. His fingers tightened around hers.

"We're here." Gray reached into the backseat and pulled a card from his briefcase. "Your sisters want you to read this first."

As she tore into the envelope, her eyes narrowed. What was going on?

Dear Abby,
Everything is under control! Yes, we have the food covered—don't worry. Have a wonderful time in Boston. If you don't like the clothes, blame Dolley. She packed. For the next three and a half days, you are not to call or worry about the B and B. Gray is a sweetheart. Enjoy!
Love, Bess and Dolley

Abby read the note twice, finally turning for an explanation.

His smile faltered. "I figured you wouldn't come with me unless I had cleared the runway, so to speak."

He took both of her hands in his warm and calloused ones. "Come to Boston with me. I want time alone with you."

"You set all this up? Cleared my schedule? Had my sister pack my clothes?"

"Yes." He clutched her hands more tightly.

Did he think she would try to escape?

"I couldn't have done any of this without your sisters. Please." Gray leaned over and pressed his mouth on hers.

When he pulled away, her toes were curling. "Gray, no—"

He cut her off before she could finish her sentence. "Take a frigging break. Come with—"

"Let me finish," she interrupted.

His eyes blazed, but he held his tongue.

"No one has ever done anything so nice for me. No one." Her heart beat as hard as the paddles on her industrial mixer. "I would love to go with you."

His eyes flared. Then he grinned. Gray leaned over and kissed her, stealing her breath. Her body trembled. Her mind spun.

This was so much more than the casual affair they were supposed to be having. Gray was changing the rules.

She couldn't let that happen. She couldn't let him break her heart.

CHAPTER TWELVE

Rule #18—Fitzgeralds hold their heads up high,
even through adversity.

Mamie Fitzgerald

ABBY ATTRIBUTED SOME of her disorientation to the
champagne Gray had poured for her after they
boarded the plane. The luscious leather seat on the
Smythes' private jet had also lulled her into a sense
of being cocooned.

Now, as the hired car pulled in front of Gray's
home, Abby wondered when this bewildered feeling
would go away. He overwhelmed her. She couldn't
deal with the emotions ricocheting around in her head.

"Ready?" he asked.

She took a deep breath and nodded.

They stepped out of the car. Gray lived in a quiet
neighborhood. Ivy climbed the corner of the three-
story brownstone. Black shutters framed windows
and complemented the tan brick. This neighborhood
wasn't like her eccentric Savannah, where it wasn't
unusual to find a mansion on one corner and a bunga-
low on another, but she liked the old-fashioned street
lamps.

"I've only read about Beacon Hill. I never thought
I would actually be here."

Gray unlocked the front door and held it open. Rooms branched off a wainscoted hallway. A wide archway led into a parlor. Farther down the hall was a narrow kitchen. She guessed one of the closed doors was a bathroom.

Deep greens and browns conveyed an air of masculinity. The parlor was so…Gray. The sofa and wingback chairs had clean crisp lines, but whimsical end tables boasted colorful mosaic maps of each hemisphere of the globe. Marble candlesticks dominated a carved mahogany mantel above the fireplace. Seascapes adorned the walls.

Gray dropped their bags at the bottom of the stairs. "Would you like something to drink?"

He led her into the kitchen and opened the fridge. He held up a bottle of water, and she shook her head. "I asked the housekeeper to stock that tea you drink," he said. "We can make a pot of that."

"I'd love some tea, thanks." She found a kettle buried in one of his cupboards. Adding water, she turned on the gas and searched for mugs. "You have a housekeeper?"

"Not a live-in." He shrugged. "Agnes cleans, shops and sometimes cooks for me. She used to work for my parents. Working for me is like retirement."

She nodded. Their lives were so different. "Do we have an agenda this weekend?"

He wrapped his arms around her, and she leaned against him.

"We have dinner reservations tonight. In the morning, you can sleep in while I meet with my project managers. Then, in the afternoon, I'll take you on a tour of my Boston. Tomorrow night, there's a party at my parents' home. We'll take in a Red Sox game on Sunday and head back Monday morning."

"Back up. Party at your parents'?" She swallowed. She hadn't recovered from their last encounter.

The kettle whistled. She left the warmth of Gray's arms to make her tea.

"My parents are throwing a benefit for some charity." He stroked her shoulder. "Please come with me."

She sluiced her tea bag back and forth in the hot water. "I'm…nervous."

Gray rubbed a hand up and down her arm. "I want to show off Boston to you—and you to Boston."

When he said sweet things like that, how could she refuse? "If it's important to you, of course I'll go."

"Thank you." He gently kissed the back of her neck.

"And my sisters packed my clothes." What clothes would her conspiring sisters think were appropriate for partying with Boston's elite?

"Not to worry," he said. "I asked them to pack the dress you wore on the boat."

"And you wonder why I'm nervous," she said. "Let me take my tea and suitcase upstairs. I need to know what Dolley packed."

GRAY STROKED ABBY'S BACK. That had been easy.

Abby had suggested coming up to his bedroom. The rest was natural.

"I'm as relaxed as I can be without being comatose." Her hand slid up and rested on his chest. "I hope we're not eating an early dinner."

He could hardly move. "We have time to take a nap and then clean up."

"I still need to unpack my clothes." Her voice slurred with exhaustion.

"After you rest." He kissed her hair and felt her body loosen.

Gray crossed his hands under his head and stared at the ceiling. Lying in his bed seemed strange. When had Savannah become more familiar than his home of five years?

This weekend he intended to test this infatuation with Abby. Was this love? Sometimes he wondered if his feelings were a result of Savannah's magic. In the cold reality of Boston, would he feel the same about Abby?

He closed his eyes and inhaled. Even the air tasted different. He missed the moist, rich fragrance of Savannah.

He'd set things in motion to help Abby, and he needed updates from his attorney. He had a company to run—in Boston. His time in Georgia was almost over.

If this was love, what the hell would he do?

IN LESS THAN an hour, Abby would see Gray's family again. Her hand shook as she dusted blush on her cheeks.

Gray came into the bedroom and whistled. "I do love that dress. Car's here."

"Almost ready." She slipped on her red shoes and wrapped a red pashmina around her shoulders in deference to the cool evening.

Abby longed to be home catering a two-hundred-person wedding reception with five different courses. Catering she could handle. Dealing with her lover's family? Not so easy.

Their driver held the car door for them as she and Gray slid into the backseat. She shouldn't get used to being chauffeured around, but, oh, the luxury.

Abby settled into the crook of Gray's arm for the short drive. This had been the most time they'd ever spent together. She wanted more.

The car pulled into a curved drive. The gray stone building loomed over a rolling tiered lawn. Grillwork windows let shards of diamond-shaped light scatter across the landscape. Abby gulped. The Smythes' mansion made Fitzgerald House look small.

"You grew up here?" she said in awe, as the driver stopped the car under a covered porte cochere.

Gray smiled at her tone. "It's not that different from your home."

"Except we turned our home into a B and B. My God, this place is huge." A butler opened the car door. A real-life butler.

"Marcus, how are you?" asked Gray.

"Excellent, sir. The guests have gathered in the blue parlor and library. Ma'am, may I take your wrap?"

"Thank you. Marcus, wasn't it?" At his nod, she handed the shawl to him.

Hand in hand, Abby and Gray crossed the large

entryway. The black-and-white tiles extended forever. Double staircases climbed from the entry to a second-floor gallery. Three stories overhead, a stunning crystal chandelier splashed light through the foyer.

Gray led her down a long hallway. Abby shivered. This space was designed to intimidate.

They stopped inside the library doors. A smaller replica of the entry chandelier hung from the ceiling. She loved the bleached-wood bookshelves and the brass ladder that reached the top shelves. A gorgeous black marble mantel spanned the oversize fireplace.

Pocket doors between the parlor and library were pushed open. It made the room large enough to handle the crowd. Ceilings soared above Abby's head. This was what a mouse would feel like trapped in an empty Olympic-size pool.

Abby knew how much money it required to keep Fitzgerald House open. She swallowed back the lump in her throat. As Dolley said, the Smythes weren't just rich—they were mega, mega rich. This night might be the only time in her life she would be invited to a party like this. She took a deep breath and straightened her shoulders. She would enjoy this evening even if it killed her.

"You look pale," Gray said. "Are you okay?"

"A little nervous." She didn't want to embarrass him.

"You're the most capable woman I've ever met."

Maybe if she pretended this was just a wine tasting, she could survive meeting all these wealthy strangers.

"Thank goodness no one will notice me next to you," she whispered.

"You're kidding. Half the people in the room have already asked the person they're with who you are."

Abby saw heads turning, but knew they were tracking Gray's movements. She tipped her head close to his. "Only because they're admiring you."

Women wore jewels worth more than her car. Probably worth more than both her sisters' cars combined. She couldn't breathe. It was as though someone had thrown a fifty-pound bag of flour on her chest. When Gray left Savannah, he'd return to this glamorous world.

He moved in front of her, lifting her chin with his finger. "Don't let this group of *Yankees* intimidate you. You're special."

She stared into the midnight-blue of his eyes.

A lump formed in her throat. She wanted to take a moment to find her composure, but Gray tucked her arm in his and they worked their way through the crowd. People nodded, waved or called his name.

Mr. and Mrs. Smythe held court in front of a fireplace in the blue parlor. As Gray and Abby approached, people parted, allowing them to infiltrate the tight knot of socialites. Conversations trailed off. Abby straightened her shoulders, feeling as though she was heading to her own execution.

Gray kissed his mother's cheek. "You look beautiful."

Diamonds flashed from his mother's neck and fingers. Mrs. Smythe's deep blue dress made her eyes sparkle as brilliantly as the stones.

"Gray." Love filled his mother's voice.

Gray hugged his father. "Dad, looking good."

Turning, Gray pulled her forward. "You remember Abby."

"How could we forget?" Gray's dad bussed her cheek.

"I'm glad you could join us," Gray's mother said.

Abby tried to interpret the nuances in Mrs. Smythe's voice. Her tone was cooler than her greeting to her son, but that was expected.

"Mr. and Mrs. Smythe, it's good to see you again," Abby said.

"Oh, please, it's Wallace and Olivia," Mr. Smythe insisted.

"Thank you." Abby smiled. "And thank you for inviting me into your beautiful home."

Gray's muscles relaxed under her hands. Had he been worried about how his parents would react?

"How's the warehouse progress?" Wallace asked.

"Ahead of schedule." Gray gave them an update.

"You're home for good next month, right?" Olivia asked.

Gray's gaze slid to Abby and then back to his mother. His glance had that fifty-pound bag of flour resting on her chest doubling in weight.

"August 1," Gray said.

Abby hadn't expected anything else, but the words hurt to hear. She'd hoped something would keep him in Savannah just a little longer.

Her gaze flicked around the room. These glittering people were Gray's friends. Once his condos were completed, there wasn't anything to hold him in Savannah.

"What charity is this dinner for?" asked Gray.

"The ballet, dear. I volunteered to sponsor a dinner." Olivia looked around the room. "At a thousand dollars a head, we're making progress."

Abby swallowed hard. There must have been at least ninety people in attendance. "Maybe I should ask your mother to do a fund-raiser for Fitzgerald House renovations," she whispered when Olivia turned to speak to a passing waiter. "She's more effective than our loan officer."

"If anyone could raise money for you, it would be my mother."

He snatched two champagne flutes from the waiter before he left. "Where's my no-good sister?" Gray asked.

Olivia waved a hand to the opposite side of the room. "She was talking with Harris last time I saw her. Why don't you introduce Abigail to people before dinner, Gray?"

"Of course."

As they walked away, Abby said, "I'd be more than happy to have you park me somewhere while you mingle."

"No way. If I have to smile and remember names, I want you by my side."

Gray worked the room. He shook hands, kissed ladies' cheeks and analyzed the odds of the Red Sox taking another pennant. She didn't know this smooth-talking man of privilege, but he belonged in this setting. Just like she belonged in Savannah.

Abby pushed away her insecurity. Like a squirrel, she was storing up all the minutes of happiness she could.

Gray made sure she was part of the conversations. By the time dinner was announced, she'd convinced half a dozen couples that they should visit Savannah.

"The Chamber of Commerce should hire you," Gray said as they sat down. "Everyone you talked to was enchanted."

Dinner was fantastic, and when it was over, she asked, "Can you point me toward the bathroom?"

"This way. I'll be on the terrace having a cognac with my father." Gray looked happy and at ease here in Boston.

The bathroom would have been suitable for a hotel. Along with the two stalls—which Abby had never seen in a private home before—there was also a sitting area complete with mirrors and vanities. Abby took advantage of the chair and touched up her lipstick.

When the door opened, she glanced up to see Courtney enter the sitting area. The temperature in the room seemed to plummet.

"What are you doing here?" Gray's sister frowned.

"It's good to see you again." Abby hated the ice in her voice, but Gray's sister hadn't shown her any warmth, either.

Courtney gave her a blatant once-over. Abby gritted her teeth. Didn't this woman have any manners?

"I'm surprised he brought you here," Courtney blurted out. "He won't stick, you know."

"Excuse me?" Abby stood, unwilling to let Courtney tower over her.

"Gray. He refuses to commit to any woman. He knows women are only interested in his money."

"You don't know your brother as well as you think." Abby dropped her lipstick back in her purse. "And you don't know me at all. I'm not interested in his money. He's so much more than that." She clenched her jaw, refusing to waste words on a woman who was this unkind. "Why don't you like me? You don't even know me."

Courtney's shoulders slumped. "Gwen is my best friend. I wanted her to be part of our family. You ruined that."

"You're assigning blame where there is none. I had nothing to do with Gray breaking up with Gwen."

As Abby pushed past, Courtney put up a hand to stop her. "What will happen when Gray moves back to Boston? What will you do then?"

Grieve. "That's between Gray and me."

"Maybe you need to worry about why Gray is interested in you." Courtney's eyes narrowed. "Last time he was home, I heard him talking to Dad about you wanting to expand and needing money. He mentioned acquiring Fitzgerald House. Maybe you need to think about his motives."

"How can you talk about your own brother that way?" Abby was appalled.

Courtney stood taller. "He didn't get ahead by being a nice guy."

The excellent dinner Abby had eaten threatened to come up. Why had Gray discussed her financial problems with his family? Courtney was the second Smythe to mention Gray's interest in Fitzgerald House.

They had to be wrong. Fitzgerald House wasn't for sale.

The door closed behind her, shutting Courtney and her accusations inside the bathroom. She leaned against the hallway wall, weariness pressing on her body.

She didn't want to smile or make small talk. To clear her head, she headed to the empty foyer.

Courtney couldn't be right about Gray. She was a friend of his ex. That had to be the problem. Courtney had hit Abby where she was most vulnerable— Fitzgerald House. But Gray wouldn't destroy her dreams the way her father and Maurice had done.

"There you are." Gray strode toward her.

She beamed at him, hoping he wouldn't see the insecurity beneath her smile. "How was your cognac?"

"Nonexistent. They were smoking cigars." He touched her cheek. "You look tired. Do you want to head home?"

"Yes." Back to Savannah. With Gray.

GRAY KNELT NEXT to the fireplace and lit the kindling. The temperature had dropped below fifty degrees and he was cold. Apparently, he missed Savannah's heat.

Something was bothering Abby. From the time they'd climbed in the car, she'd barely spoken.

Once the fire caught, he crossed the room and took Abby's hands. "What did you think of the party?"

"Your mother throws an impressive benefit, and the food was wonderful."

He loosened his tie and whipped it off. "It was nice of you to send your congratulations back to the kitchen." And so Abby.

"The caterers earned the praise." She tipped her head. The firelight added golden depths to her emerald eyes. "It was…interesting to see you with your friends, to see you in your element."

Gray frowned, not liking her diplomatic turn of phrase. "I'm acquainted with those people. I wouldn't call them my friends."

Abby looked around the room. "You paid two thousand dollars for the benefit, flew me up in a private plane and hired cars to drive us around the city. You're as wealthy as all those people we were with tonight, aren't you?"

"Does it matter?" Even with his back to the fire, a chill ran through him.

"I guess I didn't… You're normal in Savannah. More like Daniel and his dad than all this." She waved her hand around the room. "I know people in Savannah who are well off, but not like this." She shook her head. "I don't know people who live the way you do."

"You know me." He liked who he was in Savannah. He wasn't sure he liked the person he became back in Boston.

He hung up his jacket and tie and placed his shoes in the closet. Unbuttoning his shirt, he crossed to Abby. They might be acting like a couple, but every muscle in his body was strung out.

"Money has always been a burden." He kept his back to her and put his cuff links on the dresser.

She laughed. "I could lessen your burden. Send some of your excess cash my way. I'll put it to good use."

"I never know why people are friendly. Is it me or my money and my name?"

"I'm sorry." She moved over to stand in front of him and touched his face. "I never thought of it that way."

"It's hard. Never knowing. Never trusting why people are with you." *Like you. Like the jokes you've made about me giving you money.*

She turned her back and swept her hair forward, exposing her zipper. "You sound cynical."

"Probably." His lips caressed her neck as he unzipped her dress. "Does money matter that much to you?"

"It's always been a problem for us. I need more than we have to keep expanding Fitzgerald House, to achieve my goals." She sighed. "Your sister said something strange to me."

"That's Courtney for you." Gray trailed more kisses on her silky shoulder. "What did the brat say?"

Her back stiffened. "That you wanted to acquire Fitzgerald House."

Damn Courtney. "I don't want to acquire Fitzgerald House."

"It was just so strange." Abby turned, her face serious. "Why would she say something like that? Because of Gwen?"

"I can't even guess my sister's motives." Courtney was too close to the truth, but now wasn't the time to share that. He wanted to give Abby the good news all at once. "This trip was supposed to be fun. I don't want to talk about money or business."

He slipped his hands inside her dress and pushed it down. "Nice. Very nice."

She stepped out of the dress and bent to pick it up off the floor. A flash of cleavage from her white bustier had him almost swallowing his tongue. The dusky color of her nipples beckoned to him. More lace led down to a triangle of white that hid heaven.

She gave a little spin. "This is Dolley's idea of underwear, a gift to me. I've never worn a garter in my life. What do you think?"

He pulled her close and kissed her. Curls of desire seared through him, burning away his worry. "I love it."

Gray wanted this woman. Coming to Boston hadn't changed that. He stroked his tongue inside her mouth, craving her sweetness.

She pushed off his shirt. Her fingers kneaded his muscles, pulling him closer. "I need you."

Her words were like gasoline on the flames. The bustier pushed her breasts up so they crested over the top. He suckled them and then raked his teeth on her lace-covered nipples.

Abby's sharp breath sent those breasts pillowing around his lips. Her hands tugged at his belt and pants.

By the time their clothes disappeared, Gray could barely draw in a breath. He set her on the edge of the bed. Her legs wrapped around his waist, and he plunged.

Too much, too fast. "Oh, God, Abby."

He captured her thighs, trying to hold on. She lifted her hips, forcing him deeper.

"Damn it, move," she cried.

He rolled his hips, a small action. She moaned. He slid into her heat and then out. Her body arched off the bed on a whimper.

She bucked against him. "Faster."

Her climax squeezed around him, and still he controlled the pace and the pressure.

"Stay with me." He leaned over, rolling her nipples between his fingers. She squeezed him with her inner muscles, the exquisite force causing him to lunge more quickly.

With his teeth clenched, he locked his gaze on hers and shouted as he came.

His arms collapsed and his breath whooshed in and out.

Her fingers tangled in his hair as if she wouldn't let him go.

He wanted to be with Abby every night for the rest of his life. Boston hadn't changed his mind. It had opened his eyes. Savannah wasn't the draw. It was Abby.

"I…" He stopped.

"Mmm?" she murmured.

"Go to sleep." He wanted to tell Abby he loved her, but something held him back. Maybe once he'd confirmed all his plans. He'd help her with her mortgage and with Carleton House. He'd prove he was good enough for her.

She shivered and cuddled into his chest.

"Are you cold?" He rolled so they lay nose to nose.

"Aftershocks. That was some earthquake." She traced a finger down his cheek.

"Are you saying I rocked your world?"

She kissed his lips. "Oh, yeah, you rocked it all right."

Gray pulled her back against his chest. Abby's breathing slowed as she fell asleep. The fire crumbled into embers.

Only then did Gray whisper, so softly that even if she'd been awake she never would have heard him, "I love you, Abigail Adams Fitzgerald. What are we going to do about that?"

ABBY SLAPPED HER hand on her alarm, but it wasn't on the nightstand. She pushed her hair out of her eyes. Had she knocked it on the floor?

Confused, she sat up. Nothing was familiar.

Gray's bedroom. She pulled up the sheet to cover her nakedness. Wow. Last night had been...wow.

It wasn't an alarm, it was her phone ringing. She snatched it up, hoping Gray wouldn't wake. The screen read *Dolley*. And it wasn't even six. "Yes?"

"Can you talk?" Dolley's voice sounded...off.

Something had happened. Abby had left Fitzgerald House and something bad had happened. "Give me a minute."

She pulled open the bathroom door and grabbed Gray's robe. It dragged on the floor as she snatched her phone and hurried into Gray's office, closing both doors behind her.

"What happened?" Dread filled the pit of her stomach. "Why are you calling me so early? Is someone hurt?"

"No. I haven't been to bed yet—a client's website got hacked."

"Nothing's wrong with the B and B?"

"Nothing happened at the B and B, but Lennertz left me a voice mail on Friday. I just listened to it."

Today was Sunday. "Did they approve our loan?" She clutched the robe around her. "Can we make an offer on Carleton House?"

"This isn't about Carleton House." Dolley dragged out her words.

"Just tell me." Abby's hand squeezed into a fist.

"Has Gray said anything…" Dolley took a deep breath before continuing, "Did he tell you he was buying our mortgage?"

"What?"

"He bought our mortgage."

"Bought our mortgage?" Even when Abby repeated the words, they didn't make sense.

"He didn't say anything to you?" Dolley asked again.

"Not a word."

Last night he'd assured her he wasn't interested in acquiring Fitzgerald House. How could he have lied to her like that?

"Why would he buy our mortgage?" Dolley asked.

Abby's head spun. Courtney had warned her to question Gray's motives. His father had mentioned investing in Fitzgerald House. Did Gray plan to take them over? "I don't understand."

"I didn't want to ruin your vacation…." Dolley's voice trailed off.

"No! You were right to call. I'll take care of it." Somehow. "I'll be home today."

Dolley probably said goodbye, but Abby had clicked off her phone.

Gray owned their mortgage.

Why? Why would he do this behind her back? Why had he lied to her?

Her breath caught in her chest.

She'd been blinded by lust. Gray was just another man, like her father and Maurice, ruining her plans. How could she be so stupid?

And he'd done everything in secret. Her chest ached. Fitzgerald House was just one more business transaction to Gray.

Her hand shook as she covered her mouth, holding in a scream. He'd slipped so easily into her life. And she'd let him. She'd shared Fitzgerald House's financials and the projections, discussed her plans and hopes.

Black spots shimmered at the edge of her vision. She set her head down on the papers on his desk. This couldn't be happening. Not again. Every time she let a man into her life, he destroyed her. Her father had smashed their family under a mountain of debt. Maurice had sworn he would be her partner, in life and the restaurant, then had thrown away her love to sleep with another woman.

Now Gray. His betrayal was the worst. He threatened the very foundation of her life—Fitzgerald House.

Tears slid down her face and splashed on the papers under her cheek. She was an idiot.

She needed home. She sat up, but the paper she'd cried on stuck to her cheek. She peeled it away and set it back in the center of his desk.

As she pushed herself out of the chair, the name Carleton caught her eye.

No.

She scanned the document, her heart pounding in her ears. Purchase agreement. For Carleton House.

Gray had made an offer on Carleton House.

That goddamn two-faced conniving Yankee.

THERE WAS A bump and bang. Gray jerked and rolled over, searching for Abby.

Her side of the bed was empty. He opened his eyes. Why wasn't she in bed? She didn't have to get up and cook breakfast.

The bang came again. This time from the closet. "Abby?"

Another thud, but she didn't answer.

He scrubbed his hand on his face. What was up with her?

He pulled on sweatpants and headed to the closet. "What are you doing?"

She had her back turned to him, clothes balled in her hands. "Packing."

"We don't leave until tomorrow." He tried to grab her hand. "Come back to bed."

She wrenched away from him. "I'm leaving today."

Even with sleep crusting his thoughts, he took a step back. What the hell had happened? "What's wrong?"

Her head snapped around, and her green eyes shot kryptonite at him.

"When were you going to tell me?" she fired at him.

"Tell you what?"

"You bought our mortgage." She tossed a shoe in her bag.

How did she know? This wasn't how she was supposed to find out. He'd wanted to take her out for dinner with champagne and candlelight. Who had told her? "Did Lennertz talk to one of your sisters? Is that how you found out?"

He moved closer, but she shot a hand out like a stop sign.

"I planned to tell you." The words rushed out. "I planned to tell you once I had everything in place."

Her eyes seemed to burn holes into him. She swallowed and straightened her shoulders. "Everything," she choked out. "You mean taking over our mortgage *and* buying Carleton House."

His eyes flared open. "You're not supposed to know about that. Not yet."

"*Yet?* Is that why you lied last night?"

"I didn't lie. I'm not acquiring you."

"Semantics. Why should I believe anything you say?" She took in a deep breath. "Tell me, when is the best time to tell a takeover target *who you're sleeping with* that you've acquired their mortgage and the property they wanted?"

She didn't wait for his answer. The rasp of her suitcase's zipper filled the room.

"That's not how it was." Panic bucked like a bronco in his chest. "I wanted to have everything in place and then take you to dinner so we could celebrate."

"Celebrate?" She swore. "Why would I celebrate the mighty Grayson Smythe trying to take over the Fitzgeralds?"

She dropped her suitcase, and it smacked his leg.

"I was going to tell you. Later." How had he lost control of this situation? She was supposed to be thrilled.

"Are you taking over Fitzgerald House?" Her words seemed calm. Her eyes—not so calm.

"No. No!" He shook his head. "It's not like that."

He couldn't stand the chasm growing between them. He moved closer, but she jerked away.

"Goddamn Wayne. Did he call you? He wasn't supposed to tell anyone. This was a secret."

He wanted to wrap his hands around Lennertz's throat. Abby was looking at him as though she despised him. If he'd been a bug, she would've ground him under her heel.

"I did this for you, to make your life easier." He had to reach her, to explain. "Lennertz was holding you back. That's why I bought your mortgage."

"And Carleton House? How can you justify that?"

"I've only made an offer on Carleton House. It hasn't been accepted." He held out his hand, hoping she would take it. "I wanted to help you. You weren't ever going to get a loan. Not with Lennertz standing in your way."

"You're delusional if you think I'll believe you did any of this to help us. I'm not that naive." Her eyebrows formed a straight, fierce line. "Is this a cheap way to get your hand on more property?"

"No! Is that what you think of me? You think I'd do that to you?"

"I have no idea what you'd do to me. You bought our mortgage and made an offer on the house we planned to buy. *Behind my back*." Her green gaze drilled into his. "I asked you a direct question last night and you lied to me! Lied! I don't know who you are."

Gray cursed. How had everything gone to hell? He held his hand across the breach forming between them. "I did this to help you."

"I don't need your help. My family doesn't need your help." Her voice cracked. "We're fine on our own. Whatever we need to do, we'll do as a family."

He wanted to take her in his arms and kiss her until they were no longer fighting. "I've got money. And you need it. You're so stubborn, you can't even see I'm trying to help you."

"I don't *want* your help. Every time I've trusted a man with my dreams, they've failed me. I don't trust you."

He threw his hand up in the air. "You're barely hanging on. This is the first vacation you've taken in years. I know. I asked Bess."

"That's my business, not yours."

And that was the problem. She wouldn't let anyone help her. He pointed a finger in her face. "And your business is killing you. And it's your fault because you won't accept help."

"My sisters and I can solve our own problems. We don't need some rich man swooping in and saving us. We're fine. We're more than fine." A tear streaked down her cheek, and she swiped at it. "Fitzgerald House is my concern. My problem. I… We don't need your money."

"What if I want to help?" His gut twisted. "What if I want more?"

"More? Like not just the mortgage but *all* of Fitzgerald House? Never." Her sunset curls bounced as she shook her head. "You'll never take my home."

"I don't want your home."

"Actions speak louder than words." More tears trickled down her cheek. The devastation in her eyes frightened him. "I'm going back to Savannah. I'm going home."

"Abby." This couldn't be happening. "Stay. Please."

"We're done." She wheeled her bag around him.

Desperate, he blurted out, "I'm in love with you."

She stopped. Her shoulders shook. When she turned around, pity filled her face. "You can't buy my love, Gray. That's not how it works. It's something I would have given freely."

Panic bubbled inside his chest like lava in a volcano ready to blow. "I'm not trying to buy your love."

She didn't even stop on her way to the door.

He ripped a hand through his hair. He'd been trying to help her, for God's sake, and she'd thrown everything back in his face. He'd told her he loved her. He had the money. He could fix her problems. Why wouldn't the stubborn woman let him help?

"Abby." He hurried after her, grabbing the suitcase out of her hand. "Don't leave like this."

"I can't stay." Her quiet words cut as deadly as her chef knife into his heart.

Words wouldn't keep her here. He set her bag by the front door when he really wanted to toss the damn thing through a window. "I'll have the plane take you home."

She sat in his living room, her back stiff and straight. He made the calls, roused the pilot and lined up cars.

This couldn't be the end.

Abby would realize that he'd done all of this for her. She'd come around.

CHAPTER THIRTEEN

Rule #32—Smile until your cheeks hurt.

Abby Fitzgerald

GRAY CLOSED HIS LAPTOP. "That's everything I wanted to review."

It was good he'd stayed in Boston. After the past three days, his temper had cooled—a little. Problems with the Lexington strip mall had kept his mind off Abby—for a while. He might have been able to handle the Boston problems from Savannah, but the fewer phone calls the better. His subcontractors needed to know he still ran his business.

Abby. What was she doing? His chest ached. Did she wonder where he was? If he was coming back?

Nothing could stop him from returning. She would just have to deal.

Phillips, his senior project manager, set his heels on Gray's desk. "I've been saving some news."

Gray took a sip of his coffee and almost spit it back out. Damn, Abby's coffee had ruined him for all others. "What news?"

Phillips grinned. "It's a rumor."

Gray couldn't even smile. "Spill."

"The Whaler is finally hitting the auction block."

"No way. Old man Forenaught died?"

"No, but he's been unloading properties."

Gray pushed away from the desk and paced his office. He'd made an offer on the property three years ago and been snubbed. He wanted to take the Back Bay warehouse and turn it into high-end condos. He had the vision. He had the staying power. "Is he using a broker or doing a direct sale?"

"Do you really think Forenaught is going to let someone have a percentage of this sale?"

"So he'll use his grandson." Gray snapped his finger. "The attorney. The one who's such a golf fanatic. Nathan. No, Nathaniel. That's it. Nathaniel Forenaught."

And the guy had gone to Roxbury Latin with him. A couple of years ahead, but they'd played lacrosse together. "I think I'll dust off my golf clubs."

NATHANIEL WAS MORE than willing to hit the links the next day. On the third tee, a par three, they waited for the group in front of them to finish on the green.

"I heard your grandfather is getting rid of some of his holdings." Gray threw his ball to his caddy.

Nathaniel laughed. "I was wondering how long it would take for you to ask."

"I wanted to concentrate on the game. I haven't played this season." His caddy threw the clean ball back and handed him a tee. Gray selected a five iron from his bag. "If your grandfather is selling the Whaler, I'm interested."

"You and half the developers in Boston."

"It's a fine location." Gray took a practice swing

and then lined up his shot. He caught the edge of the green. It would be a long putt, but at least he'd made the green.

"I've been telling him to get rid of the property. The warehouse has been unoccupied for too long."

"I heard you succeeded in convincing him to sell."

"Sure would like to know the source of the rumors." Nathaniel lined up and hit his ball within fifteen feet of the pin.

"Nice shot."

"I've heard some rumors, too." Nathaniel handed his club to his caddy and took his putter. "Heard you were living in Georgia."

"I've got a warehouse I'm turning into condos." And soon he might own Carleton House.

What would he do with a crumbling Savannah mansion if Abby wouldn't let him finance the restoration? She'd just have to see things his way.

"So you're living there?" Nathaniel asked as they headed up the fairway.

"I'll be back midsummer." He exhaled. Abby couldn't evict him from Fitzgerald House; he had a contract. The Fitzgeralds needed the income off his suite. At least he hoped she wouldn't kick him out.

"When you called yesterday, I asked Granddad if I could talk to you."

"And…?"

"Line up your funding. Bids are due June 20 and we'll determine the best offer by the end of the month. We want the deal closed in thirty days."

"That's a quick closing." One month between receiving a bid and closing a multimillion-dollar deal. No wonder Nathaniel suggested he get his funding lined up. He'd just committed his liquidity and more to a Savannah mansion. Damn. He'd need investors on the Whaler.

Nathaniel shot him a quick grin. "I don't want Granddad to change his mind."

"Can we get in the building?" Gray asked, lining up his putt.

"I'll take you by tomorrow morning."

Gray was so far from the hole, his caddy had to hold the flag. He adjusted for the break and stroked the ball. It headed right where he wanted, caught the edge of the cup, circled and dropped with a hollow rattle.

"Great putt," Nathaniel called out.

"Lucky." Or a sign? It didn't matter. He was meant to get the Whaler.

What would he do with Carleton House, then?

BESS RUSHED INTO the kitchen. The screen door banged shut, and Abby winced at the noise. She'd been home for four days and still couldn't sleep.

At least Gray had stayed in Boston. Maybe he would ask them to send his things back. Maybe she'd never have to see him again. She rubbed at the ache in her chest, a pain that hadn't disappeared since Boston.

"You were right," Bess said, a little out of breath.

"About what?" It must have been something big; Bess never moved this fast.

Bess sucked in a deep breath. "Mrs. C. says Gray made an offer on Carleton House."

"Is she accepting?"

Bess shook her head. "She didn't say. Her attorney is helping with the negotiations."

Something inside Abby shriveled. She'd actually hoped Gray would rescind his offer. So much for wishing things could be different.

Bess paced along the counter. "Did you know he was going to do this?"

"I saw the offer by mistake while I was in Boston."

"I don't get it." Bess stopped next to her and rubbed Abby's shoulder. "Why would he do this?"

"Maybe he thought it was a good investment." Wasn't that what everything came down to for Gray? Dollars and cents? She shrugged, continuing to work on the teatime tarts. "We'll just have to focus on Fitzgerald House. We'll be fine."

What would Gray do with Carleton House? Would he restore it the way she'd imagined? Or would he modernize it and turn the beautiful old home into condos?

He could do anything he wanted. The place would be his.

Bess was already on the phone with Dolley. "Meeting tonight. Seven o'clock." She looked over at Abby, who nodded.

Abby got through the afternoon tea, survived the evening wine tasting. She moved through the day because she had no choice. All the joy she'd experienced over the past few months had evaporated. She should never have trusted Gray. She knew better.

She had another five minutes before her sisters

descended. She checked the mail and found an envelope from First Mercantile.

She ripped it open, skimming through the greetings. If they could get the loan, they could bid against Gray.

"At this time, the bank cannot lend the requested funds for the Carleton House project."

Her shoulders slumped. Had Gray had something to do with this rejection?

She went through the motions, set up cheese, smoked salmon, crackers and a seafood salad she'd made for dinner.

Her sisters wandered in, snacking and pouring glasses of wine. Abby could barely breathe.

Dolley put salmon on a cracker. "Where is that bastard hiding?"

"I assume in Boston," Abby said. She took a sip of her wine to hide the quiver of her lips.

"I can't believe he fooled us all." Dolley slapped her hand on the table. "And I insisted he look at our financial information. I'm to blame, Abby, not you."

Abby shook her head. It was her fault. She'd talked about her dreams endlessly.

"Do you think he planned this all along?" Bess frowned.

"I don't know." Abby bit her lip. Had he? "He asked to tour Carleton House with Samuel and me."

Bess clasped her hand. "Gray's pretty sophisticated."

Abby's actions had brought a viper into their midst. She took a swallow of her wine but hardly tasted the Shiraz.

Dolley leaned over the table, her hands clenched into fists. "The paperwork's pretty clear. Next month our mortgage payment goes to Gray's bank." She gritted her teeth. "We will never, *never* miss a payment." All the sisters nodded their heads. "If I have to sell my car, my cameras, my computers—we will not give the bastard the satisfaction."

"Is this a takeover? Is that why his parents were down for St. Patrick's Day?" Bess looked puzzled. "I find that hard to believe. Gray seemed...nice."

Abby swallowed. "I should never have gotten involved with a guest." She rubbed her arms, trying to wake up her body. The numbness wouldn't go away. "We'll have to make do."

"He may own the mortgage, but we're current. The bastard can't take us over," Dolley said.

"Is there any chance we can bid on Carleton House, too?" Bess asked.

Abby pulled out the letter from the bank. "They turned us down. We'd have to find another bank." They were out of time. They couldn't compete with Gray's offer.

"I'm shocked," Bess confessed. "He didn't seem like the kind of man who would do this. He didn't come across as that ruthless." She paused as if thinking. "I really thought he'd fallen in love with you, Abs. He watched out for you, tried to take care of you, to get you to rest. I thought he loved you." She shrugged. "I thought you loved him."

Abby closed her eyes. "I..." She laid her head on the table and Bess rubbed her shoulders. Was that why she hurt so much? Had she fallen in love? She pushed up from the table. Oh, God, she'd fallen in love with Gray. Her stomach turned. Stupid, stupid, stupid. "I can't love someone who would do this to us."

Thank goodness she'd never said anything to Gray. He'd never know what a fool she had been.

She rested her head against Bess's shoulder. "If Gray hadn't known our plans, he wouldn't have taken an interest in Carleton House."

"It wasn't your fault," Bess insisted.

"It was." Pain seared her chest as hot as splattering oil. "I'm sorry. I'll make things right."

"We should kick him out," Dolley said.

"We can't. We have a contract. And I don't want the staff to know there's any…problem." Abby took a deep breath. "We won't break our word. If he comes back, he's our guest."

Nothing more.

THE HEAT SLAPPED at Gray as he pulled his suitcase from the car. Two in the afternoon, and it must have been near a hundred degrees with almost that much humidity. He was definitely back in Georgia. The air carried the scent of the river and rotting vegetation.

He looked at Fitzgerald House. What kind of reception would he get? He thought about going through the kitchen, but was afraid Abby would come after him with one of her knives.

Tossing his laptop bag over his shoulder, he locked his car.

In the five days he'd stayed in Boston after she'd left, he'd gone from anger to worry and back to anger.

Abby should be ecstatic that he was helping her out. She had money problems, he had money. Most of his acquaintances would jump at the chance to use his money for their ventures. What was wrong with her?

And what about them? Their relationship? It couldn't be over. He'd told her he was in love with her. And she'd walked out on him.

Abby hadn't answered his phone calls or his texts. She'd made it back to Fitzgerald House, but he'd only known that because of the notification from the car he'd hired to pick her up.

He lifted his roller bag up the front steps. Taking a deep breath, he stepped into Fitzgerald House.

"Welcome back, Mr.—" Cheryl corrected herself "—Gray. How was Boston?"

"Okay." At least Abby hadn't poisoned the staff against him. "How's Josh?"

"He's great. Just started a nature day camp yesterday." She checked her watch. "Shoot. I need to get back to the apartment. The bus drops him off there." She looked around as though she had more to do and chewed her thumbnail.

"I can run down to the condo for you." Maybe he was being a coward, but he needed to catch his breath before he talked to Abby. "I'll bring Josh back here."

Cheryl's mouth dropped open. "I couldn't ask you to do that."

"Not a problem." He set his bags down by the reception desk. "Could you keep your eye on my bags?"

"Of course. I'll take them up to your room." Her hands twisted the dust mop handle. "I...I could do the same. Run down and then bring Josh here."

"No. I'm good." He checked his pocket for the condo keys. "What time does the bus drop him off?"

"Around three. I should go."

"Don't worry about it. We're good." He set his bags together. He was avoiding Abby. "Is it okay if we tour the workspace? I'll keep my eyes on Josh."

"Umm, sure." Cheryl looked a little lost.

He waved and headed outside. The heat met him at the door. He would have slowed down, but he didn't want the five-year-old to wait.

He hurried across the square and over to Bay, then took the stairs two at a time down to River Street. Even in the heat, people crowded the sidewalks.

Where did the bus drop off Josh? He waited right at the door. He didn't want the boy to be worried when he didn't see his mother.

Daniel's truck was parked in the lot with a couple of other trucks. While Gray had been away, bright red awnings had been added to the first-floor windows. They looked good.

People wandered the street, window-shopping, going in and out of the pub and the candy store. A paddleboat was docked upriver. The outdoor dining area next door was empty. The heat had probably driven any late lunchers into the air-conditioned restaurant. He wished he'd put on shorts, but it had been cool when he'd left Boston this morning.

He nodded at another man who was sweating worse than he was. "Hot one today."

The man nodded. Big circles of sweat stained under the man's armpits. The shirt clung to the guy's beer belly. He must be too hot to even speak.

Gray checked his phone. He watched more people. And he wondered what Abby was doing. When he closed his eyes, all he saw was her face.

A diesel engine rumbled nearby. Not many vehicles negotiated the narrow street, so he hoped this was Josh's bus.

Sure enough, it stopped across from him. The door gasped open, and he heard the clatter of footsteps. Josh came around the front of the bus, waving at the driver.

"Hey, Josh!" Gray called.

The kid's smile broke across his face. "Gray!"

Josh dropped his backpack on the sidewalk. He jumped up and smacked Gray's hand, then spun around and wiggled his hand behind him. Gray slapped his hand. They were both grinning by the time Josh turned around. Being around the kid made him forget his worries, at least for a moment.

"Your mom's still working, so I'm picking you up," Gray explained. "But first I want to check out the condos."

The kid nodded and picked up his bag.

Gray's neck itched. He glanced around. The sweaty man who'd been standing next to him had moved under the awning and was staring at Josh.

Gray set a hand on the boy's shoulder as he unlocked the condo door. Then he pulled it closed. The guy was creepy. He'd have to warn Cheryl to keep her eyes open.

In the week he'd been gone, the drywall crew had finished hanging the walls. Some of it was taped. But he wondered how long it would take the mud to dry in this humidity.

"What kind of camp are you going to?" he asked Josh.

"Nature camp. It's cool. We get to use kayaks and swim and learn about all the plants and birds. I spotted a great blue heron before anyone else."

The boy's chatter kept him company as he toured the building. Progress hadn't slowed just because he'd been in Boston.

Gray waved at Daniel but didn't stop. He didn't want to talk to his friend before he had a chance to talk to Abby.

The kid was dragging a little.

"Do you want me to carry your backpack?" Gray asked as they climbed the steps and moved away from River Street.

"Yeah."

Maybe they should have taken the elevator.

"Tell you what." Gray knelt down. "Why don't I give you a piggyback ride?"

"Really?" His eyes opened wide. "My daddy used to give me those before he went to heaven."

The words seemed to smack Gray upside the head.

Cheryl hadn't breathed a word about being a widow. He knelt, and Josh clambered on his back.

By the time he climbed the B and B's steps, sweat was running like a stream down his back. Josh didn't mind; he just chattered about his day.

Gray wanted a kid. He wanted a kid with Abby's eyes and hair. The longing drilled through his chest like a power tool.

"Here we are." Gray squeezed the words out.

He opened the door and Josh jumped over the threshold. Gray guessed he'd gotten his second wind.

"How was camp?" Abby asked as Josh ran in ahead. Gray lingered outside the door, not wanting to intrude just yet.

Her voice churned up another brand of longing. One that had him wanting to hug her until she gave up this foolish insistence on not letting him help her when she needed it.

"Camp was great. I saw gobs of birds and they let me paddle." He made a muscle with his arm. "'Cuz I'm strong."

"You sure are."

Gray stepped inside and let the door close behind him. "Abby."

ABBY FROZE. SHE looked up, looked into those blue eyes that haunted her nights. "Gray."

He walked toward her. "Can we talk?"

She shook her head. There was nothing more to say. "No."

The door opened again. She, Josh and Gray all

turned. A heavy man wearing a sweaty T-shirt pushed into the foyer. Gray frowned.

The man pointed a finger at Josh. "Where's your ma?"

Josh cowered behind Gray's legs, shaking. "Don't know."

Abby moved next to Gray. She didn't know why Josh was so scared, but she would protect him. She and Gray formed a wall between the man and Josh. "Can I help you?"

"Where's Cheryl?" the man asked. "We got some business, family business."

Family? She reached back, trying to soothe Josh. Gray was doing the same. "I don't know where she is," Abby said, her voice cold and formal. "If you leave me your name, I can tell her you stopped by."

"Levi. I want to see her right now." He lunged, grabbing Josh's arm and twisting it. "You come here to your uncle."

"Stop!" Abby clawed at the man's arms, pulling Josh away from him. "Leave him alone."

"Mommy. *Mommy!*" Josh wailed.

"Give me my nephew." The man grabbed for the boy.

"No," she screamed. She would not let this disgusting man take Cheryl's son.

"He's coming with me," the man growled.

Gray blocked his grab. Then he pushed Abby behind him. Thank God Gray was here. Levi was so big, and Abby wouldn't have been able to fight him off on her own.

Josh sobbed. "I don't have to go with you. Mommy said. You can't hurt me anymore."

Abby scooped Josh up. His little arms clung to her neck. "Levi, it's time you left."

"Now," Gray growled, getting in the guy's face.

Abby swallowed. The man outweighed Gray by fifty pounds. The guy shoved Gray's chest, but Gray didn't move. He was like a rock, protecting her and Josh.

Footsteps pounded down the hallway. Cheryl called out, "Josh?"

Josh launched himself out of Abby's arms and into his mother's. "I don't want to go with Uncle Levi. Don't make me," Josh sobbed.

Levi shifted, reaching for the mother and child.

Abby moved next to Gray. Shoulder to shoulder, they formed a barricade.

"Cheryl, it's time you came home." Levi's voice boomed in the foyer.

"How did you find me?" Cheryl's voice shook as she tried to shield her son.

"I want you off my property," Abby said, forcing her voice to be firm. "Now."

"Not until my sister-in-law comes with me," Levi rocked back and forth, eying Cheryl and Josh. "I want my money!"

"Cheryl, take Josh in the kitchen and call 911," Abby said. "Lock the door."

She heard their footsteps move away, heard Cheryl talking to the dispatcher. But Abby didn't take her eyes off the man glaring at her.

"Go help Cheryl." Gray's arm moved around her shoulder. "Please, love."

"This is my home. My business." She wasn't letting some bully threaten anyone in her home.

"I want to talk to Cheryl." Levi shuffled sideways, but she and Gray continued to bar the hallway. "She owes me."

Levi lowered his shoulder and rammed into Abby. She blocked him with her arms just as he hit her. She staggered and fell. Her head smashed the wall, black spots filling her vision.

Gray punched the man in the gut. The hit didn't even rock the man. Her heart thudded. Levi could kill Gray.

Abby used the wall to help her stand. She needed some sort of weapon. She couldn't let Gray be hurt.

Levi threw a punch. Gray ducked, danced back and jabbed again. This time Levi's breath whooshed out.

Abby grabbed the vase from the console table and moved closer to the wrestling men. She needed a clear shot at Levi's head.

Gray hit him again. Levi stumbled. Fell.

She raised the vase over her head, but Gray was right there, sitting on Levi's chest.

"Don't," Gray gasped. "Cops are coming."

Sirens wailed, growing louder. She moved around the two men and propped open the door, still holding the heavy vase. Two policemen hurried up the walk.

"In here," Abby called. "The man on the floor tried to take a little boy." That should hold Levi for a while.

Levi tried to buck Gray off. Gray rammed his knee in Levi's groin and Levi squealed.

Gray eased away. He was almost on his feet when Levi kicked him in the arm. Gray fell half on the floor and half on Levi.

"Gray," she called, her heart pounding. She knelt next to him.

Gray pushed up to sitting position. "I'm okay."

The police cuffed Levi and pulled him to the door. He glared at Gray and Abby. "I'll get my family back."

"You'll have to come through me," Gray said, standing and helping Abby up.

"And me," Abby added, stumbling a little.

Gray wrapped an arm around her, supporting her. "You're hurt."

She curled into his shoulder. Even with the hot air pouring in from the open door, she was shivering. "I hit my head."

He gently examined her head. "Abby, you've got a bump back here. You need to go to the hospital."

She shook her head and saw stars. "I'm fine."

"I'm getting you some ice."

She started to refuse again, but he was already explaining to the cop and heading down the hall.

Abby moved into the small parlor and sat on one of the sofas, wrapping her arms around her legs to get warm.

Gray returned with a baggie of ice and Cheryl and Josh. The little boy clung to his mother like a monkey.

Gray sat next to Abby and held the bag to her head.

"I can hold it," she said.

He touched his forehead to hers. "Let me help, please."

Abby caved. She should be pushing him away, but she couldn't. He wrapped his arm around her so she was almost sitting on his lap. Abby leaned back against his chest, and he held her tight.

Cheryl and Josh held on to each other on the love seat, talking to one of the cops.

"Levi was my brother-in-law," Cheryl said.

"Was?" the young cop asked.

Cheryl brushed her tears away. "My husband, Brad, was killed in Afghanistan."

Abby's heart ached for her.

"When we had to move off base, Levi invited us to move into his house." Cheryl pulled Josh closer to her. "It was okay for a while. But then he wanted my checks."

"Checks?"

"My dependency checks." Cheryl rested her head on Josh's. "He made me sign them over to him."

"He hurt me," Josh said, pointing to a scar on his arm. "I pulled him away from Mommy. He made her cry."

"You were so brave," Cheryl said, tucking him closer. "You saved me."

Abby squeezed Gray's arm. What had they gone through?

Tears dripped from Cheryl's eyes. She looked at the cop and then at Abby and Gray, her face so pale Abby worried she might pass out. "He said I needed to sleep…" She shook her head rather than finishing the sentence. "I couldn't. We ran."

Abby left the warmth of Gray's arms and hurried over to sit on the coffee table in front of Cheryl. She took the young woman's hands and warmed them with hers. "You could have told me. Maybe I could have helped in some way."

Cheryl squeezed her hands. "I thought I was safe. I don't know how he found us."

"He was waiting outside the condos," Gray said, a frown on his face. "I saw him there. He must have followed us."

"How would he…" Cheryl's eyes opened wide. "I changed the address with the military last month. I thought it would be confidential."

The cop asked a few more questions, took statements from both Abby and Gray. Finally he stood. "I think we can hold him for a while. We've got plenty of charges."

Abby helped Cheryl stand while Gray walked the cop to the door.

"You're staying here tonight," Abby said.

Cheryl shook her head. "I couldn't."

"This isn't an option, this is an order." She tried to remember what rooms were booked. "Lucy Hayes is open." And the room had a Wii in it if Josh needed a distraction. "Can I pick up clothes for you and Josh? Would you let me do that?"

Cheryl's lip was starting to quiver. "Yes. Thank you."

"You go rest now." Abby hugged her. "Does Gray have a key to your apartment?"

Cheryl nodded.

When Gray came back in, Abby gave him a quick update.

"Cheryl and Josh are spending the night here."

"Good." He watched them walk up the stairs. Rubbing his knuckles, he said, "I wished I'd gotten in a couple more shots at the guy."

"I'd like to give him a kick, too." They were alone in the foyer now. She had to fight the urge to brush back the hair that was falling on his forehead. "I told Cheryl I would pick up some clothes. If you trust me with the key, I can run over there."

He cupped her face. "Let's go together."

She wanted to argue, wanted to keep things strictly professional but couldn't. Gray had just saved Cheryl and Josh from someone terrible.

She called Marion and asked her to stay for the wine tasting. Then they headed out the door.

The heat took her breath away. Light-headed, she grabbed the rail to keep from falling.

"You should stay." Gray caught her shoulder. "I'll go."

"It's just the heat. I'll be fine." She forced a smile on her face but couldn't look him in the eye. He was confusing her again. She'd told him actions spoke louder than words. What were his actions with Cheryl telling her? "It will be easier for Cheryl if a woman goes through her things."

She saw him nod from the corner of her eye. "You're right."

He took her hand. She tried to pull away, but he

held on. "If you go down, at least I can keep you from cracking your head again."

They made the trip in silence. She should have been uncomfortable. She'd walked away from him. Walked away from the man she foolishly loved.

Instead of taking the steps, he guided her to the elevator. "Thanks," she said, her legs still wobbly.

He let her into the warehouse and then a small first-floor apartment.

The place wasn't spotless, but it was clean. Two pair of shoes sat on a mat, one for Cheryl and one for Josh. In the kitchen, Josh's pictures covered the fridge.

The kitchen table, the sofa and television in the living room, even the beds, were all new. "You furnished their apartment, didn't you?" she asked.

Gray shrugged.

She moved to the closet and the drawers. "Can you find a suitcase?"

He nodded and left the room while she pulled out underwear, shorts and a top for Cheryl. Then she moved on to Josh's room. Bunk beds with Spider-Man sheet sets. Had Gray bought those, too? Had he noticed that Josh loved Spider-Man? She grabbed the same array of clothes for him.

Gray came back with a duffel bag, pulling off the tags as he approached.

"You bought that for them?" She hadn't heard him leave the apartment.

He shrugged again. "They don't have any luggage. I found this down the street."

She packed everything away. "I think that's it."

He took the bag from her. There was blood on his knuckles, which were swollen and red.

"Your hand."

He started to shrug.

"Don't you dare shrug this off," she hissed. "You were holding ice on my head when you should have been taking care of your hand."

He grinned—and shrugged.

She shook her head and stomped out the door. Gray was so confusing. First acting like a hero and then an ass.

GRAY HELD BACK a wince as Abby held his hand on the walk back to the B and B. Both his hands ached, but he wasn't letting go. Maybe they could rebuild their relationship.

"Will Levi stay in jail?" she asked.

If Gray were in Boston, he'd be able to call a family friend in the district attorney's office. But this was Savannah. "I got the cop's card. I'll check with him later."

"I should have locked the front door." She looked sideways at him. "Just in case they let him go."

"He won't be out that quickly."

She nodded, releasing a big breath. "I knew Cheryl was afraid. I should have asked more questions."

"I could have, too." This wasn't Abby's fault—or her responsibility.

"She doesn't trust men." She bumped his shoulder, hitting a bruise. "She can barely look at you, even with everything you've done for her and Josh."

"That's true." Was that Abby's problem? No, Abby's problem was about letting other people help her. She wouldn't ask for help or accept it when offered.

Her fingers squeezed his and then relaxed.

When they came through the B and B's front door, Marion was waiting for them. "I can't believe it. Are you okay?"

"We're good," Abby said.

"I settled Cheryl into her room. The poor thing. She said you two are saviors."

Marion hugged Abby, then Gray, and hit a bruise. He couldn't hold in the groan.

"You're hurt." Abby lifted up his sleeve. "Why didn't you say something?"

There was a large patch of red that was starting to turn purple on his arm, probably where Levi had kicked him.

"We need to get ice on this." She tugged him back to the kitchen, Marion in the lead.

At least he knew he would get to see the inside of her kitchen again. Maybe not the invitation he wanted, but this worked.

Marion held open the door as though they were two wounded warriors.

"Abby needs ice for her head," he said. "You didn't pass out, did you, Abby?"

"No, I'm good."

"You almost fainted when you walked into the heat," he reminded her. "You could have a concussion."

"I don't. I'm fine."

"Both of you sit." Marion pointed them back to the sitting area.

Abby moved toward an armchair, but Gray took her hand and led her to the love seat. She didn't fight him. Maybe the five days she'd had to think about things since walking away had changed her mind.

Marion came over with two bags of ice, both wrapped in towels. "I need to get the wine opened. The two of you stay put. I'll come back and throw together soup for all of you."

Abby started to stand. "I can…"

Marion pointed a finger at her. "You will let me help you."

Abby sank back down in her seat. "Yes, ma'am."

Marion laughed as she left the kitchen.

Gray helped Abby adjust her ice and then held his bag against his arm. Was that what it took to get Abby to cooperate, a stern voice and a pointed finger?

If he tried, he'd probably lose his finger.

CHAPTER FOURTEEN

Rule #26—It's the small things: baskets for new-lyweds and anniversary couples, and wine—lots of wine.

Marion Winters

ABBY EASED HERSELF off the love seat, trying not to wake Gray. Marion might have ordered her to stay put, but she could cut vegetables. She grabbed a couple of aspirin to fight the headache.

"You should be sitting down," Marion said as she came into the kitchen. "Accept a little help, girl. And keep that ice on the lump on your head."

"I iced it when the police were here." Gray had in-sisted. She swallowed, remembering his kindness. "I thought I could cut up veggies. If I get tired, I'll sit."

"Fine. You'll be having chicken-noodle soup and you'll like it."

There was a loaf of homemade bread in the freezer that would go with soup. Abby set it on the counter to thaw. "Gray fell asleep," she whispered.

Marion nodded. "I'm glad he was here to help Cheryl and Josh. He's been a good friend to them."

He had been, coming up with a place for them to live, furnishing their apartment, buying Josh thought-ful gifts. All things money could buy. But he'd also fought to keep them safe. Actions that were more important than his words or money.

Abby cut up onions, celery and carrots, handing them over to Marion. "Handmade noodles?"

Marion studied her intently. She must have looked okay, because the older woman nodded.

Abby pulled out semolina flour, salt and eggs. She mixed the dry ingredients and dumped them on the counter, forming a well. Cracking the eggs, she whipped them with a fork, enjoying the mindless process of pulling the flour in from the side until she had a ball of dough.

She needed to stay away from Gray. Her body wanted to curl up right next to him, even though her head knew he was dangerous.

He'd bought their mortgage and made an offer on Carleton House when he knew how much she needed it. She couldn't forgive him for that.

She cleaned the counter and then dusted it with flour. She kneaded the dough, pounding, pushing. A little zing of pain ran from her shoulders to her head each time she worked the dough, but she ignored it. She pushed and pulled the soft ball, working out the bubbles, but couldn't seem to work out her own problems.

Cooking was so simple. Why couldn't life be that way? Why couldn't love be simple?

"I think that dough's 'bout ready," Marion said.

"Oh." It was already firm. How long had she been kneading it?

She set the dough in a clean bowl and covered it with a plate. "Do you want some sweet tea?"

"Sounds good," Marion answered.

Abby pulled out glasses and filled them with tea and ice. She glanced back to the sitting area. Gray still hadn't moved. She went back to check on him.

His ice pack had melted. She slipped it out from under his hand. Judging from the shadows under his eyes, he wasn't getting any more sleep than she was. She refused to feel sorry for him. He'd ruined everything.

Marion checked on the guests in the library, and then they worked together on the noodles and finishing dinner.

"You wake Gray," Marion said, "I'll get Cheryl and Josh."

Abby wanted to say she would run upstairs, but Marion had already gone.

Gray was a guest. A guest who'd fought for one of her employees.

"Gray," she said, standing next to the love seat.

He didn't move.

"Gray," she said, a little more loudly.

He stirred but didn't open his eyes.

She took a deep breath, leaned over and touched his shoulder. "Gray. Supper."

His eyes fluttered open. His hand tugged her forward. "Hi."

He kissed her. Heat pulsed through her body.

Kissing Gray wouldn't solve anything. "No."

He groaned, curling into his shoulder.

"I'm sorry." She didn't mean to hurt him, she just couldn't kiss him.

"It's fine." He reached up and brushed her hair off her face. "Abby…"

"No, Gray." She stepped back. "Nothing's changed."

CHERYL FOLLOWED MARION into the kitchen. Josh clung to her like lint on a black sweater.

Would Abby fire her? She should. Cheryl was the reason Levi had come here, the reason Abby and Gray had been hurt.

Cheryl still had some pride left. She'd resign. Tonight.

"Where's Uncle Levi?" Josh asked, his voice too quiet, too filled with fear.

"He's not here." She set her son down and knelt next to him. "The police took him away."

Marion set a warm hand on Cheryl's back. "Come, have some supper."

Marion called back to the sitting area where Abby stood in front of Gray. "Let's eat, you two."

Heat filled Cheryl's face. She couldn't face her saviors. "We should go home."

Oh, Lord, what if Mr. Smythe wanted them to move? What if he didn't want any trouble in his building? She clutched her churning stomach.

Abby gently touched Cheryl's arm. "How are you doing?"

"Ashamed." She shook her head. "I'm sorry I caused trouble."

Abby's eyes flashed. "Don't you dare feel guilty about what happened."

"This wasn't your fault." Gray came up behind Abby. "I saw him waiting near the condos. I talked to him. He followed Josh and me."

Gray set his arm around Abby's waist but she slipped away from him.

"Josh, why don't you sit here?" Abby helped Cheryl's son into a booster seat.

"Mommy, sit next to me."

"I will, sweetie."

Josh grabbed her hand. His lower lip trembled. "I don't want to go with Uncle Levi."

"And you'll never have to." Cheryl forced her voice to be strong and steady for him. Josh had regressed to where they'd been months ago, afraid to let her out of his sight. "I'll never let him near you again."

Abby crouched on the other side of Josh's chair. "I'll protect both you and your mamma."

"No one's getting through me, young man." Marion touched his hand.

"You've got your friends at Fitzgerald House taking care of both of you," Gray said. "And I'm here to help, too."

Cheryl covered her mouth, choking back a sob.

"None of that." Marion handed her a full bowl of soup. "You'll feel better with my chicken-noodle soup in your belly."

"Thank you." She looked around at the people surrounding her and her son. "Thank you all.

lon't know what would have happened if you hadn't
ielped us."

Marion served soup and cut the bread.

"Tell us more about your camp," Gray asked Josh.

And Josh was off and running, telling everyone
ibout swimming and watching birds. "We cooked hot
logs for lunch. On a stick and everything."

Abby winced.

Gray nudged her with his shoulder. "Kids love hot
logs."

"But they're so…"

"Delicious!" Josh finished.

Everyone laughed. Cheryl hadn't thought she'd ever
augh again. But they laughed and talked through the
est of the meal.

As they cleared the dishes, Josh moved to the sit-
ing area to watch television.

She had to apologize.

Cheryl stepped in front of Gray and Abby. "Thank
/ou both for stopping Levi. If I can ever do anything
'or you, please, ask."

"No need for that," Gray said. "Friends help each
ither."

She'd hoped to do this alone, but Mr. Smythe wasn't
eaving. She had to get this out.

"Miss Abby." She took a deep breath. "I'll be giv-
ng my two weeks' notice."

Abby frowned. "Why?"

Cheryl glanced over at Josh. "Because I…I brought
rouble to your home, your business."

"No. No way." Abby's green eyes flashed. "Lev brought the trouble, not you. Don't you abandon me."

"But I showed poor judgment when I let Levi take money from me. Money I could have used to take care of my son. You don't want someone like that working for you."

"You did what you needed to." Softly, Gray asked "He hurt Josh?"

She nodded.

"Then the money wasn't worth it," Gray said.

Abby was nodding with him. "You showed grea judgment in taking your son out of that situation and finding him a safe place to live. Money isn't every thing."

"Sometimes you need to trust that people are doing things to help you." Gray stared at Abby.

Cheryl looked between them, confused. She didn' think they were talking about her problems anymore

Gray and Abby looked at each other and then any where but each other.

"But…" Cheryl started to say. She didn't deserve to work here.

"There are no buts." Abby put her arm around Cheryl's shoulders. "I refuse your notice."

"You both…" She couldn't get the words out "Thank you."

"Enough. Friends help each other out." Gray shook his head. "I'm going to check with the police for an update."

"Thanks…" Cheryl started, but Gray shushed her and headed out the door, scrolling through his phone

She turned to Abby. "He's been so good to Josh
and me."

Abby nodded, loading the dishwasher.

"He's a nice person, and he cares about you two."
Abby gave Cheryl a small hug. "I'll finish up here.
You and Josh go relax."

Friends. She had friends who were looking out for
her.

She hugged Josh to her chest as she carried him upstairs. They had friends. They belonged. Hope bubbled up inside her like the garden fountain, sparkling
and happy.

"We're going to be okay."

ABBY TURNED TO MARION. "You should get home."

Marion checked the kitchen and then hung up her
towel. "Get some sleep. I'll see you in the morning."

Abby flipped on the radio and hummed as she
wiped down the table.

"They're holding Levi for the night," Gray said as
he pushed through the door. "He'll be arraigned tomorrow."

"I'll let Cheryl know."

"I caught her in the hall."

"Oh, good." She moved over to scrub the counter,
even though it was already clean. "Good night, then."

Abby didn't want to be alone with Gray. She was
too exhausted to fight with him.

She couldn't reconcile the man who'd fought for
Josh and Cheryl with the businessman who could
make heartbreaking decisions. Gray had told Cheryl

money wasn't everything. But every big gesture he made involved money. She rubbed her head. Except saving Cheryl and Josh.

"Your head still hurts." Footsteps sounded behind her. She inhaled and caught Gray's cologne. If she turned, she'd be in his arms.

"I'll be fine."

"We need to talk." He was so close that even without touching her, his heat suffused her body.

"There's nothing more to say."

"Why can't you understand I was trying to help you? Can't you trust me?"

"This isn't about trust." She spun around, pushing him back a step so she could breathe. "This is about you taking over my business."

"I was trying to help." His lips tightened. "But you won't take help from anyone, not even Marion. Cheryl is willing to take help, but not you."

"How does your making an offer on Carleton House help me?" She clenched her hands into fists.

"You were never going to get the financing. When I talked to Lennertz—"

"Wait." She threw her hands up. "When did you talk to our loan officer?"

His face went blank.

"When?" she whispered, knowing she wouldn't like the answer.

"After Dolley blew up at him." Gray reached for her.

She jerked away from his touch. Away from his piney scent that made her want to wrap her arms round him. That wouldn't solve their problem. You've been planning this since—March?"

"No, I—"

"You saw an opportunity and grabbed it." Abby pointed a finger at him. "Your sister said you were ruthless, and I defended you. I'm a fool."

"That's not true." He pounded on the counter. "You can't achieve your goals without cash. I'm trying to help by investing in your dreams."

All the air left her lungs. "We don't have investors in Fitzgerald House."

He tried to take her hands, but she shook him away. "I just want to help."

"This is a family business. If we can't make it on our own, we deserve to fold." Her voice cracked. "We deserve to lose Fitzgerald House."

She headed for the door to the backyard. She had her hand on the knob, but turned. Gray still stood in the middle of the kitchen.

"You told me money has always been your burden." She shook her head. "Look at what you're doing— buying your way through life. Maybe people only see your wealth because that's all you're willing to share. Maybe you hide behind your money."

She stepped out into the heat and let the door close between them.

ABBY WAS WRONG.

Gray took another sip of his cognac and stared at her apartment from where he sat on his balcony. She was wrong. He stacked his feet on the chair across from him. He didn't hide behind his money. What was so bad about helping Abby and her sisters?

So maybe talking about investors had drained the color from her face. He didn't want to take an ownership position in Fitzgerald House. He wanted…he wanted Abby to love him.

Lightning flashed. A storm was coming.

Abby's bedroom curtain shifted.

How could she kiss him like she had earlier and still not understand that he was doing what he could to help her out? How else could he show her he cared? Buy all the houses on the square and give them to her?

He took another sip of his drink. Let the fire burn its way to his stomach.

Then he stewed and waited for the storm.

GRAY RAN A hand along the varnish on the floor of the model suite in the warehouse. The finish was as smooth as Abby's skin—not that he'd been able to touch her since he'd returned from Boston. "With all the humidity, I worried nothing would dry."

"Last week's storm and cold front helped." Daniel made a note on his clipboard. "We got a good start on Friday and then finished on the weekend."

"Your idea of a cold front and mine are miles apart."

Had the storm only been four days ago? It was Monday, and Gray had barely said hello to Abby since their latest argument.

She hadn't kicked him out of Fitzgerald House. He was still eating dinner in the kitchen. But they were never alone together. Friday they'd eaten with Marion,

Cheryl and Josh, Saturday with Dolley. Her glares had burned holes in his skin. And Sunday Bess had joined them. Bess hadn't glared, she'd just seemed puzzled.

He hadn't had a chance to talk privately with Abby. To tell her she was wrong. He wasn't buying his way through life.

"The model looks great. And a week early." He pulled his focus back to the condos.

"I should have held out for a bigger completion bonus," Daniel joked.

"I probably would have agreed."

"Cheryl's been up here cleaning." Daniel made a note on his clipboard. The two men moved through the suite in tandem.

"It's great to have her back on-site." She'd insisted on heading back on Saturday.

"It is." Daniel raised an eyebrow. "Heard there was some excitement at Fitzgerald House the day you got back from Boston."

"Cheryl's scumbag brother-in-law was waiting here when the school bus dropped Josh off." Gray paused in front of the windows facing the river. To his left he could see the Talmadge Memorial Bridge traffic and to his right, the tourist riverboats. "Thank goodness I was there to pick him up and not Cheryl."

"Heard this guy was a big one. I'm surprised you were able to take him down."

"The guy is mostly fat, but he got in a few good hits." Gray rubbed the bruise on his arm. It still ached. "Can someone touch up the windowsill enamel and fix the closet door that isn't plumb?"

"Already on the punch list," Daniel said. "Why don't we wait until the furniture arrives and then re paint, just in case they bang up the walls?"

"Good idea," Gray said. "I'll let the decorator know she can schedule the furniture load-in."

Once they had furniture, the realty company would open up shop. They'd posted a sign outside the ware house a month ago and already had a list of inter ested parties.

"So what's happening with this guy?" Daniel asked

"He's still in jail. The scumbag couldn't make bail," Gray said.

"How long could he get?"

"If they can make a kidnapping charge stick, life imprisonment. But if they only charge him with stealing Cheryl's checks, it's one to ten years." Gray opened a kitchen cabinet. Cheryl must have cleaned in here, too.

Daniel nodded. "Let me know if he ever makes bail and my crew and I will keep our eyes open."

"Will do. I haven't seen your dad around Fitzger ald House since I got back," Gray said, leading Daniel out of the suite now that the inspection was complete. "How did you get all this info?"

"I'm not revealing my sources." Daniel held the door open for him and they stepped into the interior hall.

"How come there isn't any work happening on the third floor of the B and B?"

"We picked up a couple more jobs. Abby knows we

have to fit her in between other jobs. That's the only way we can bid so low."

That wouldn't help Abby meet her goals. "I noticed Abby's costs were a lot lower than mine. I might expect a lower bid next time."

Daniel shook his head. "Not going to happen. What's your next project?"

Apparently Daniel's spy hadn't told him about the offer on Carleton House. "Don't have one."

Daniel patted his stomach. "I'm starving. Lunch?"

"Not today. I need to take care of something back at Fitzgerald House."

Gray didn't hide behind his money. Abby wanted actions rather than words? He knew just how to prove her wrong.

CHERYL STUFFED THE trash into the bag. One last room to clean on the second floor and then she'd move to the library. There were so many wonderful books there. Abby had said she could borrow any she wanted. She'd already read the entire Tolkien collection. She thought she might tackle Jane Austen next. But there were also culinary books. Maybe she should borrow one of those.

"Just the person I was looking for." Gray filled the doorway.

She jumped, but not as much as she used to. "Hi, Gray."

"You promised you would help if there was anything I needed." Gray smiled and took a step closer to her.

No. He wasn't Levi. She forced herself to stay where she was. "What…what do you want?"

His smile disappeared. He shook his head. "I'm not Levi. I won't hurt you."

She swallowed. She must not have hidden her nerves as well as she'd hoped. "I know."

His mouth curled up a little at the corners, but it wasn't a real smile.

"I'm sorry." She rubbed her hands on her face. "You've only been kind to me. You don't deserve this. I don't know why you put up with me reacting this way."

"Because I want to help you." He waved a hand. "You're diligent and work hard. I appreciate that. And if I can help you and Josh…"

"Thank you." She relaxed. "It's been a long time since I've had someone do something nice without wanting something from me."

"I know what you mean." Now his smile was bigger. "I don't expect anything from you. But if you have trouble, I'm your friend. Let me know what I can do to help—as a friend."

"A friend." She tried out the word. Brad had been her last true friend.

"I would like your help," Gray said.

"What can I do?" She smiled.

"There's a door to the third floor by my room. It's locked."

She nodded.

"I'd like a key."

"It's supposed to stay locked." She rubbed her hands together. "They're working up there."

"Forester had to pull his team off." He rubbed his neck. "I'd like to work on the third floor without Abby knowing."

"A surprise?"

He nodded. "I promise you won't get in trouble."

Cheryl hesitated. He'd done so much for her and Josh, given her hope when her life had been so bleak. Now he was going to help Miss Abby.

She made her decision and sorted through the keys on her ring. "Sure."

GRAY CHANGED INTO a T-shirt and jeans. Grabbing his tool belt, he made sure the hall was empty before he slipped the key in the lock and headed up to the third floor.

He scouted the work Samuel had already completed. Signs written in Abby's bold print hung by each room. The work had started on the least-damaged room, the Lady Bird Johnson room. The holes in the plaster had been repaired, although the plaster medallions in the ceiling still needed replacing. Sheetrock needed to be hung on the new bathroom walls. The floor needed to be sanded and prepped for varnish, though Abby might catch wind if he brought up a sander.

The electrical and plumbing subs had been through the rooms, every room except the one with the most water damage, the Mary Todd Lincoln room. He leaned against a wall. If he brought tools in at night, she might not catch on.

Samuel's team had left a few things behind. Gray set a shovel and crowbar in a battered wheelbarrow and headed to the Lincoln room. He'd seen the plans. Everything should be demolished.

Smashing walls was mindless, satisfying work. He chose his first enemy—the wall with the least plaster remaining. He took a swing, and the thwack filled the room. Another and another until the plaster finally crumbled. Scooping up the debris, he tossed it into the wheelbarrow with a deep thud. He whacked and scooped. Twenty minutes later, he'd cleared the wall and filled the wheelbarrow. He was breathing a little hard and wishing he'd brought up a jug of water.

Could he chance dumping the garbage down the chute? It was on the opposite side of the house from the kitchen. But Abby was always wandering around.

He'd have to dump at night. Since Abby still refused to talk to him, it would give him something to do.

He should be lining up investors for the Whaler project. He'd hired an appraiser, but he needed to line up the financing.

Maybe his dad would want in on the fun. The Whaler project was big enough for even his father's eyes to light up. He grinned. Yeah, Gray would ask him to tap his cronies. Then he'd come in and close the deals, making sure he still retained control of the project.

Unlike Ms. Abigail Fitzgerald, *he* wasn't too proud to ask for help.

ABBY PULLED ANOTHER tray of bars from the oven. She'd been getting her baking done in the morning when the temps were a bit cooler. Thank goodness they'd had another storm last night. She'd been able to get both the bride's and groom's cakes baked and stored for Saturday's reception.

And she had to keep busy. If she wasn't working, she ended up thinking about Gray. Which was like grabbing a hot pan with her bare hand, over and over again.

The condos would be done soon and he'd head back to Boston. Maybe then her heartache would ease.

She swiped at a drip of sweat and checked her to-do list. She needed to keep moving, keep doing.

The door swung open, and Gray walked into the kitchen. His blue eyes searched the room and zeroed in on her.

Her heart reached for him even as she glued her arms to her sides to keep from holding out her hands. "Something you need?"

"Water." He moved through the kitchen as if he owned it and grabbed a glass from the family cupboard. Then he filled it from the filtered water spigot, drank deeply and filled the glass again.

She watched his throat move as he swallowed. Who would have guessed that watching Gray drink water could turn her body into a puddle?

He set the glass in the dishwasher. "Better."

Shouldn't he be at the warehouse? It was only midmorning.

"Something smells good in here. What have you been making?" Gray turned and leaned against the counter. Did he know that his chest muscles strained the fabric of his shirt when he did that?

He frowned. "Abby? Everything all right?"

"Sure." He'd asked a question. "I baked the wedding cakes for this weekend's reception. I've made bars and cookies to cover a month of teatimes." She shrugged. "I like getting the baking done while it's cool."

"Doesn't feel cool to me."

"Yankee." She tried to smile and couldn't.

"Anything I can do to help?" He stepped closer.

Even though the counter separated them, she caught the scent of Gray's cologne and the pure essence that was only his.

"Help?" She didn't want him in the kitchen, much less helping her out. Then she noticed his hair. "You're filthy."

"I can wash pots." He moved a little closer. "I've done that before."

Their first kiss. That couldn't happen again.

"Wait. I thought you'd finished all the condo demolition?" she asked.

He shifted, looked at the floor. "Just a little side project I'm working on."

Carleton House. Goosebumps formed on Abby's arms even in the heat of the kitchen. He was already pulling things apart over there and he didn't even own the building.

"I'm good, thanks." She moved to the fridge. She'd make lavender cakes. Keep her hands busy and her mind off Gray.

"I've got to go back to Boston tomorrow."

She turned back to him, her movements slow. This was what she wanted. "Thanks for letting me know."

"I'll only be gone until Thursday." He touched her cheek, and heat burst through her body. "I'll miss you."

She froze.

"You're wrong about me, Abby." He brushed a kiss on her cheek. "I don't hide behind my money."

She should move. Should turn away from his stare. Should push him away.

Her body refused.

Gray leaned in once more and brushed her lips with his. "I need to get back to work."

After he left, Abby slumped against the wall. What was wrong with her? She had to be strong enough to break away. Had to be.

Gray could destroy her more than her lying, cheating ex-fiancé ever had.

ON FRIDAY, ABBY ran a finger along the mantel in the ballroom.

"The staff will clean this afternoon," Marion said as she slid a table a couple of inches to the left.

"I don't understand why it's so dusty." Abby shook her head. "Samuel hasn't worked for almost two weeks."

"The dust's settlin', that's all." Marion was frowning, too. "This is good dust."

"Good dust?"

"It means you're expanding." Marion patted her

shoulder. "I'll add another cleaner tomorrow, just in case. Cheryl, if she's up to it."

"Don't push her." Cheryl had seemed fine, more animated in the past week. Maybe she was finally sleeping.

Abby wished she could rest. All she did was toss and turn and think about Gray. He'd gotten back from Boston last night, too late for dinner. At least he'd called to say his meetings had run long. The only reason she'd cared was she needed to know whether to make him dinner. And which sister to call so she and Gray were never alone.

He'd told her again that she was wrong about him.

She looked around the room one more time. "Make sure they check the bathrooms, especially the men's. Samuel's subs sometimes use them."

"Already on my list." Marion headed out of the room.

The scent of perfume hit Abby first. White Diamonds.

"Mamma," she whispered.

She heard heels clicking across the wooden floor, but before she could turn around, familiar arms enveloped her. "Mamma, you're early. I thought you wouldn't be here until tonight. What a treat."

She sank into her mother's embrace. For a few moments, she didn't have to make a decision, or worry about cash flow or grieve her losses—Gray, Carleton House, her restaurant… She could just be Mamie Fitzgerald's daughter.

"I hurried home." Her mother held her at arm's

length and then hugged her one more time. "Couldn't wait to see my girls." Her mother's cool fingers stroked her cheek. Her eyebrows knit together. "You're tired."

"Oh, well you know. The heat," she lied. "I'm so glad you're home."

"Abigail." Her mother cupped her chin and stared into her eyes. "I know you and Gray aren't seeing each other anymore."

Abby nodded. Her shoulders slumped.

Mamma hugged her. "I'm sorry."

Abby waved off her sympathy. "I knew it would never work."

"That doesn't make the pain any easier."

"Working helps. Catering is busy." Abby took a deep breath. "If I can't open my restaurant, at least I'm cooking."

"Oh, sweetie, I'm sorry I can't relieve the burdens I've left you holding."

"Don't ever feel that way," Abby assured her. "Aunt CeCe needs you. Family comes first."

Her mother hugged her tight. "I wish you'd grown up with a better example of love."

"You loved us."

"Your papa did, too." Mamie touched Abby's cheek. "He just…always took the easy path. I wish I'd been able to stop his scheming. Then you wouldn't have to work so hard."

Her mother had dealt with so much more pain than Abby was going through. She could survive her current heartbreak. "You taught us how to persevere."

"You make me burst with pride." Mamie touched

a hand to her heart. "Of course, you know what will make your dreams become reality?"

Together they said, "Hard work."

Abby had heard that phrase all her life. "You're right."

No one had worked harder than the woman standing in front of her. How could Abby do less? "How is Aunt CeCe?"

"Good. Better." Mamma's eyes sparkled. "Did you get her email?"

"Yes." Abby frowned. "But I thought she had trouble typing with her fingers."

"She does, but she just got voice recognition software. She's having a blast."

"Dolley promised to send her a ton of pictures," Abby grinned. "That should keep her busy."

Her mother looked around the room. "The ballroom looks great." Mamma did a perfect pirouette, in heels. "Come on, join me!"

Abby grinned, kicked off her shoes and came into fourth position. "I haven't done these for ages."

They spun, trying to outdo each other with double and triple pirouettes. Their laughter filled the room. Dizzy, they collapsed to the floor.

"I always loved to dance in here." Mamma patted Abby's knee. "Looks like there's an event this weekend."

"Wedding reception. They want appetizers with the champagne reception, full dinner—three courses plus the wedding cakes. Free bar all night long." She hugged herself. "One hundred and thirty head count."

"If you need a hand, I've got two." Her mother held up her hands.

"You know we can always use extra hands, but you don't have to work. It's your vacation."

"Piffle. I want to work with my girls. What would you like me to do?"

They linked arms and walked out of the room.

"I need to work on the reception prep," Abby admitted. "But our guests would love having you host teatime and wine tasting."

Her mother's laughter wrapped her in love. "You bet I will, honey. Let me at the tea trolley. And don't forget to include the famous wine and appetizer cards."

They worked together in the kitchen. As the day progressed, first Bess and then Dolley joined them.

Abby organized stations so her sisters and mother could prep the appetizers. With all this help, they'd already finished the seafood and broccoli-and-ham quiches. Now they were putting together the mushroom, shallot and Gruyère ones. She wished Gray could see. She was accepting help. Lots of it.

"I forgot my camera," Dolley complained. "I downloaded pictures for the website last night and it's still connected to my computer."

"Check my desk." Abby pulled her apartment keys out of her pocket. "You just want to get out of assembling quiches."

"What are you working on, Abs?" Bess asked.

"The vegetarian entrée for the wedding is lasagna. It's also our dinner tonight. I made the sauce this morning."

The conversation swirled around Abby as she layered ingredients into four lasagna pans. Dolley danced about the room, snapping pictures of their laughing group.

This was her family. All these incredible women and she was one of them. Gathered in her kitchen, the heart of Fitzgerald House, were the reasons she worked so hard—her family.

No more brooding over Gray or a nonexistent restaurant.

GRAY PAUSED IN the kitchen doorway. Conversation bounced and pinged around the room. The Fitzgerald women had their own language, and he didn't have an interpreter.

Wafts of Abby's pasta sauce curled around his nose and tried to wrench him into the room.

Abby and the others formed a fascinating tableau. Colors swirled. Purples, blues, greens, setting off the milky complexion the women shared and their magnificent fire-drenched hair. White teeth flashed as they smiled. When they laughed, green or blue eyes sparkled.

Dolley told some complicated joke, gesturing in her big, bold way. Mamie pulled trays of pastries out of the oven. Abby was elbow deep in sauce and cheese and Bess stuck meat on wooden skewers.

They were a team.

His family had never had the closeness of the Fitzgeralds. Gray couldn't imagine Courtney pitching in to make his company a success. The image of his sister taking a sledgehammer to a wall wouldn't materialize. Even cleaning a site would be beneath her. He gave a small shake of his head.

He couldn't picture his family preparing a meal together—and laughing about it. Adversity had not molded the Smythes. Money had. Could his family pull together if they had to? Did they love each other that much? Gray wasn't sure he wanted to answer his own question.

Reggie slammed into his legs and then shot into the kitchen.

Gray jerked, bumping into the door frame.

The cat slid on the polished kitchen floor and banged into the cabinet. His yowl had the women looking over to the door.

"Gray," Abby and Bess called out. Dolley glared and aimed the camera at him. The flash blinded him.

Abby looked over, her smile cool. "Mamma, you remember Gray."

Mamie spent a quiet minute looking at him, as if he were a juicy worm and she were the early bird.

"It's good to see you again," Mamie said.

"Mamma's hosting the wine tasting. Then we'll eat," Abby said. She turned back to her mother. "Gray will join us for dinner."

Mamie nodded. What had Abby told her mother? What had her sisters said?

"Let's head on up to the library," Mamie said.

He offered Mamie his arm.

In the hallway, she glanced over at him, her green eyes blazing. "Tell me why you've acquired the

Fitzgerald House mortgage and why you've broken my daughter's heart."

He took a deep breath. "I wanted to help. And it's the other way around. Abby broke up with me."

"Do tell," Mamie said.

He had a feeling he was in for a good old-fashioned Southern belle grilling.

ABBY HELD UP the pan of lasagna. "Another slice, Gray?"

The women and Gray filled the table in the kitchen alcove. He twitched in his chair. Talk about being a square peg in a round hole.

He indicated a small one. "This is fabulous." He held up his glass of Chianti. "To the chef and another delightful dinner."

Everyone raised their glasses. "Hear, hear."

Abby didn't even smile. "Thank you."

His foot brushed hers under the table. His body relaxed at her touch. When had a woman's nearness ever given him a sense of peace? And why did it have to be a woman who didn't believe in him?

Abby shifted her foot away.

Mamie glanced at him. Again.

During the wine tasting, she'd listened to his complaints about Abby not accepting any help. She hadn't said much, just nodded and asked more questions. Maybe she could talk some sense into her daughter.

He nodded at Mamie. "How long are you in town for?"

"A long weekend." Mamie brushed a curl off Dolley's forehead. "I get back home every couple of months. Aunt CeCe's best friend comes to stay with her. My aunt knows I need to see my family."

Bess squeezed her mother's hand. "We're so glad you're here."

The sisters asked questions about their aunt, and Gray finished his meal.

"There is one more thing." Mamie fidgeted in her chair. She looked into her daughters' eyes in turn. "I'm engaged."

Dolley jerked out of her slouch, almost knocking the wine bottle off the table. "What? Who?" Bess and Abby seemed too stunned to speak.

Mamie fussed with her napkin, pleating it into a fan before she answered. "Martin. Martin Robbins."

Bess's eyes were as big as a spool of cable. "Who is he?"

Mamie sat a little straighter. "Aunt CeCe's neighbor. He's a cardiologist. He's so very nice."

She pulled a necklace out of her shirt and detached a ring. She slipped it on her finger. The damn rock could have put someone's eye out. "I wanted to tell all of you together."

Abby and her sisters mobbed their mother. An explosion of hugs, tears and sighs over the ring made Gray feel as out of place as a Frank Lloyd Wright house surrounded by skyscrapers.

He squirmed in his chair, tapping his foot on the floor. Something seemed to squeeze in his chest.

Abby beamed, happiness radiating off her in waves for the first time since she'd left Boston.

What was he doing here? He was making Abby's life miserable. What kind of jerk did that to the woman he loved?

"We need champagne." Abby brushed his shoulder as she headed to the butler's pantry.

Gray pushed out of his chair. He kissed Mamie's cheek. "Congratulations. I'll leave you to celebrate with your family."

Abby's head popped up as she pulled a bottle of champagne from the wine cooler. "Isn't this exciting?" Even in the dim light, her eyes glittered like jewels. "Mamma's getting married."

"Yeah, great." What else could he say? "This is a family celebration. I'll head to my room."

Her smile dimmed. "Oh."

He couldn't win. Couldn't make Abby happy and couldn't stop hurting her.

He got to his room and changed into his work clothes.

The Fitzgeralds would be celebrating. They wouldn't hear him working on the third floor.

He could do this for Abby. Help her in secret.

Her happiness meant more to him than his own.

CHAPTER FIFTEEN

Rule #37—A weary traveler must rest his head.
It might as well be on our pillows.

Mamie Fitzgerald

ABBY ADDED A note to her to-do list. Was it only two weeks since her mother had announced her engagement?

Gray had been gone more than he'd been in Savannah. Absence didn't make the heart ache less. That lesson had been brutal to learn.

Stay busy. Even though she had months to create a menu for her mother's reception, Abby wanted to keep her mind off Gray.

She knew what cakes she would bake. Mamma wanted an almond-flavored white cake for herself and a chocolate cake for Martin. Appetizers were easy. What should she do for the entrée? She flipped through recipes. Prime rib might be nice. Or something lighter—lobster or fish?

Marion brought in the last of the breakfast dishes. "I didn't think the Shelbys would ever leave."

Abby smiled. The newlyweds were in their seventies. "They're a cute couple."

Marion started to scrape and load dishes into the dishwasher.

"I can get that." Abby waved her off.

"You look like a breeze would blow you over." Marion glared. "Sit. I'll do it. What are you working on?"

"Putting together ideas for Mamma's reception menu."

Marion's expression softened. "It'll be nice to see your mamma getting married again."

"I don't think I've ever seen her so happy."

"I wish some of you sisters would get off the starting line and get yourself husbands. I want grandbabies to play with."

"Check with Bess and Dolley." Abby closed the cookbook and opened another. Marion's words sliced little pieces off her heart. Abby was in no hurry to fall in love again. It hurt too much. She was still bleeding from Gray.

Marion closed the dishwasher and started it. "Haven't seen Gray around for a while."

"He's back in Boston." Abby didn't look up, just kept turning pages.

"The time sheets are on your desk." Marion set her hand on Abby's shoulder.

Abby wanted to lean into the older woman's strength, but she couldn't. If she started to lean on anyone, she would crack wide-open.

"I can enter the hours." Marion gave her shoulders a gentle massage.

"Oh, that feels good." She forced her muscles to relax under Marion's strong fingers. "I'll get the hours entered before the payroll deadline."

"You need to let up on yourself, girl." Marion pulled

away and bopped her on the head. "You need to take help when it's offered. How many times do I have to tell you? You're more stubborn than my husband was, and that man sure tried my soul."

Not this again. "Everyone works hard here. And I'm ahead on my baking."

Marion started to leave. "Why don't you get ahead on your sleep? That's what you need." She pushed open the door, but added, "If you need me, I'll be folding linens." She laughed. "Of course, that would entail asking for help."

Why was everyone accusing her of not taking their help? Abby flopped the book closed. If Marion didn't have so much to do herself, Abby would take her up on her offer.

In any case, it was easier to stay busy. Then maybe she wouldn't miss Gray so much. Her head knew that he'd destroyed her dreams, but her heart still ached for him. She'd lost both Gray and Carleton House at the same time.

She headed to her office to enter the payroll hours. Otherwise she just might curl into a ball and cry.

GRAY TAPPED THE appraisal packet on the conference table. He'd been back in Boston for most of the week. "That's a lot of zeros in the estimated value." He'd gone through the assumptions but hadn't found any flaws.

"Once we bring the condos on line, they'll be snatched up," Gray said.

"Absolutely." Phillips, his project manager, nodded "Forenaught will expect top dollar."

Gray paced his attorney's conference room. "I'l have to go after more investors."

He'd been stupid, making all those financial commitments in Savannah. All for a woman who didn' believe in him.

"My dad and I will keep a majority vote," he said "We've already got a lot of people interested."

"Will they understand they're silent partners?" Phillips asked.

"That's the problem with people and their money For some reason, they want to be in control." Tha was Gray's role. He controlled the Whaler. "They'l have to toe the line."

Jacob, his attorney, knocked. "We're closed or Carleton House."

Gray forced a smile on his face. "Thanks."

Carleton House. What the hell would he do with the old mansion?

He'd intended to help finance Abby's expansion. He was still a little fried that his big gesture had blown up in his face. Abby's banker wouldn't have lent them ice in a desert. With Abby refusing to take any help from him, what should he do with Carleton House?

GRAY STEPPED AROUND the scaffolding in one of the third-floor units in his Savannah warehouse. "They've hustled."

Daniel nodded. "Humidity dropped again, so the tapers finished this weekend."

"Doesn't feel like it dropped." Gray wiped the sweat off his brow.

"You'll only have to deal with it for a couple more weeks, right? Then you can head north. How many inches of snow do they still have up there?" Daniel held the door open for Gray as they left the condo.

"Ha-ha. Snow melted this morning." He headed for the stairs.

"How's the bid on the project up in the frozen north coming?" Daniel asked.

"Good. Wish you and your team could come up and do the work."

"It sounds like a peach of a project, but I'm not leaving Savannah."

Before falling in love with Abby, Gray had planned to leave as soon as the condos were roughed in. He would have come back to check on sales and additional work, but he wouldn't have been living here. Now he also owned Carleton House. He had no clue what to do with the property.

"You up for lunch?" Daniel asked.

"I'm meeting with Amanda from Fawcett Realty in the model downstairs." Gray glanced at his watch. "I can catch up with you after that."

"Works for me."

Gray took the stairs down to the model suite.

"We've had our first offer," Amanda called out as he came in the door. A smile filled her face. The older woman was the perfect choice for this office, knowledgeable but not pushy.

"Let's see it."

Gray and Amanda huddled around the small con
ference room table, reviewing the purchase agree
ment.

"It's ten thousand dollars lower than I'd hoped."
Gray poured a cup of coffee from the machine and
doctored the brew with powdered cream. Yuck.

Amanda tapped her manicured nail against the pa
pers. "I know this Realtor. He's aggressive. He wanted
to know if we'd had any bids yet."

"What's your recommendation?" Gray asked.

"The offer's low." Amanda tipped her head.
"There's a balancing act between getting someone
in the space and how much of a haircut you're will
ing to take."

Gray nodded.

"I recommend you counter," she said.

It was worth getting the first contract signed. One
sale could start an avalanche of others. Then he could
head back to Boston. And leave Abby.

If he got the Whaler, there was no question he'd be
hauling his ass home. But each time he went north, it
was as if he was walking into a foreign country. He
didn't know where he belonged anymore.

He and Amanda constructed a counteroffer.

She gathered the papers. "This is more than fair. I'll
present the terms tonight and let you know."

Gray could almost hear the strings connecting him
to this city and Abby snap.

Outside, he found Daniel checking the brick's tuck
pointing.

Daniel looked up. "Ready for lunch?"

"Good to go. Got the first offer on one of the top-floor units."

"You don't sound thrilled. Did you accept?"

"We're countering."

They turned in tandem and headed down River Street. The heat and humidity slowed their pace, as if they were pushing through warm syrup. They stepped into the dim pub, and he pulled in a breath of cool air.

The hostess showed them to a table, and they ordered sandwiches and beers.

The two men had settled into a comfortable friendship. Gray had known men longer, yet he felt closer to Daniel than anyone from Boston.

But it was the same old story. Gray had hired Daniel. Was Daniel a friend, or was he just protecting an income stream?

Right now, Gray needed a friend. He heeded to believe he'd found one in Daniel.

He shredded his paper napkin into small pieces. Looking up, he said, "I need to tell you something."

"'Bout time," Daniel said.

"What?"

"Are you finally going to confess that you made the offer on Carleton House?" Daniel stared at him.

Gray blew out a big breath. "It closed yesterday."

Daniel leaned across the table. "What the hell are you going to do with that old mansion? A house the Fitzgeralds want?"

Their beers arrived, thank goodness, giving Gray time to respond.

Daniel tipped back his glass. The good-old-boy look on his face had evaporated. "What's going on?"

"I bought the damn house for Abby. I knew the Fitzgeralds wouldn't get the loan. Lennertz has a vendetta against the family."

"Man." Daniel ran his hand through his hair, making it stand straight up.

"Stupid, right?"

"But Dad says you and Abby aren't speaking."

The damn Forester communication channels were good. Gray threw the napkin pieces in the center of the table. "Sucks to be me."

ABBY OPENED THE ladder and positioned it below the burned-out bulb. Why couldn't lights have a ten-year life? She loved the kitchen's high ceilings. She just didn't love changing the inset cams. Standing on her tiptoes was the only way she could even reach the bulb.

She tried to unscrew the bulb, but it was stuck in there as though it had been glued. She twisted harder.

The ladder rocked. "Whoa." She grabbed hold of the top step.

"What the hell are you doing?" Gray's voice echoed behind her. She hadn't heard him come in but couldn't let that distract her now.

Abby stretched. She needed just a little more leverage. If the wall was closer, she could use it for support, but there was nothing.

"Damn it, Abby." The ladder rocked beneath her. "Let me do this."

"I've almost got it." She stretched and twisted. The bulb gave a little. Off balance, she slipped down a step with a gasp.

Footsteps shook the ladder. Gray's arms appeared on each side of her body. "You're getting off this ladder before you kill yourself." He tugged at her waist. "Now."

"I can do this." She didn't need help.

"You're too short." He tugged again. "It's not safe to stand on the top. You know that."

"Fine," she spit out.

He moved, and she followed him down. Stepping back, she crossed her arms as he headed up. He didn't have to step on the top to reach the bulb. It just wasn't fair.

He twisted, and the lightbulb came out as though it was greased. She'd probably loosened the thing.

He waved the offending light down at her. "Do you have a new one?"

She grabbed it from the counter and moved up the ladder, exchanging the bad light for the good. "Here."

"Don't snap at me because you got caught doing something stupid." Blue fire seemed to erupt from his gaze, and she had to look away. "You're just too stubborn to ask for help."

Never yell at guests. But Gray had ceased to be a guest months ago. "I can change a light."

He gave the bulb one more twist. Light blazed down on his clenched jaw. His work boots thumped on the metal steps.

"You could also fall and break your neck." He

snapped the ladder closed and the sharp sound punctuated his words. "Does this go in the carriage house?"

"I'll put it away," she shot back.

He glared but set it by the door.

She should have been thanking him. But she couldn't choke the words out.

Abby didn't have time to fight with Gray. Three couples were coming in for a wedding tasting tonight. She checked her menu to see what needed to be prepped next.

He stomped over and leaned on the other side of the counter. "Would it hurt to ask for help? It doesn't even have to be me."

"I am sick of hearing that phrase." She stirred the glaze for the chicken and tasted it. *More ginger.* "You're a guest. And this is my business. I don't ask anyone...I mean, any guest, for help."

"You got it right the first time." He pointed a finger at her. "You don't ask *anyone* for help."

"I ask for help," she yelled. Gray was so irritating.

"Where's Nigel?" he shouted back. "He's tall enough to change the bulb without breaking his neck."

"I can change my own lights."

"Apparently you can't. Couldn't this have waited until I got home?"

"Home? You're a guest, remember?"

His teeth snapped shut.

She wouldn't dream of asking him to help with something like this. She grabbed a handful of crystallized ginger and began to mince. She wished it were Gray's words she was slicing through. A part of

er knew he was right. She just couldn't ask for help
rom…most anyone. She was responsible for Fitzger-
ld House.

She chopped more quickly. "Have you forgotten
ou live in Boston?"

"How can I when all you want is to get rid of me?"
Gray flung his arms wide. "Of course, you want the
money from our agreement. You just don't want me
with it."

"It's always you and money." She swept the ginger
nto the honey glaze and stirred. "Does your cash keep
ou warm at night?"

"Warmer than your independence. At least I know
now to ask for help."

"Right. You ask for bids—not help."

"I delegate. You should learn how to do it if you're
n charge of a B and B."

"It's so easy to delegate when you're rich. Espe-
ially when you let everyone know by flashing your
money around." She aimed the dripping spoon at him.
'Have you ever helped someone when it didn't involve
pending your money? Just your time?"

"You wouldn't believe the ways I've helped un-
grateful people." He winged the words at her.

"You mean me?" She pointed a finger at her chest.
'With your help, we'd end up being employees, not
owners."

He slammed his hand on the counter. "I am not in-
erested in acquiring you!"

"Your actions paint a totally different picture."

"Then you need glasses."

Without thinking, she yanked open the oven and grabbed the pot of short ribs.

Pain seared through her palms. She dropped the handles and stumbled back.

"Abby!"

She held out her hands. Her palms and fingers were bright red. Stabbing pain radiated up her arms. Her legs wobbled.

"Oh, Abby." Gray gently lifted her off the floor.

When had she sat down?

"We need to get these in water." He guided her to the sink. "How bad is the burn?"

"I don't know." Her voice shook. "Cool water, not cold."

The water deepened the ache, bringing tears to her eyes. She wiped her cheek with her shoulder.

"I'll take you to the doctor." Gray cupped her hand under the water.

"No." Her body was starting to shake.

"Then, do you have ointment?"

The shape of the handle was burned into her palms. How could she have forgotten to use a pot holder? The burn on her right, her dominant hand, was darker red. "No ointment. I have some honey I use. But I'll also need gauze and wrap."

"Where?"

The room started to spin. "I need to…"

Gray hugged her from behind, holding her up. "I've got you, Abby."

She rested against his chest. "Could you…put water in a bowl for my hands?"

"Sure. Sure." He helped her over to the love seat. "Put your head between your knees."

The movement of the air on the burns sent splinters of agony through her hands. She held them up but lowered her head. She took deep breaths, trying to relax. Nothing worked.

Gray came over with a large pot of water. "Okay. Set your hands in here."

The water eased the pain to a dull roar. "The first-aid supplies are in the cabinet above the phone."

Cupboards banged as Gray searched. Abby closed her eyes. How could she have been so stupid?

Arguing with Gray about their faults had made her careless—and crazy.

She hung her head, ashamed. She'd treated Gray—a guest, and a man she'd thought she'd loved—abominably.

"Here." Gray rushed back to the love seat.

Kneeling, he ripped open the gauze. "Now what?"

"Pat my palms dry."

He swallowed. "I don't want to hurt you."

It was too late to worry about that. And she wasn't thinking about her hands. She pulled her hands out of the water and held them, palms up, to him. Closing her eyes, she said, "I'm ready."

He was so very gentle as he dried her hands. "I shouldn't have been arguing with you."

"Neither should I. I'm…I'm sorry. I raised my voice to you. I screamed at you."

Gray held up the honey she used for meals. "Is this the right one?"

"No. It's Manaka. No, Mānuka honey. It should be in with the aspirin."

He dashed back to the cupboards.

She leaned against the love seat, biting her cheek to take her mind off the pain.

Gray stuck a jar in front of her face.

She nodded.

He dipped a spoon in and drizzled honey over both palms. "Hang on." He spread the mess out with the back of the spoon.

She took in shaky breaths, one after the other.

Finally, Gray placed gauze pads on each hand, and then held up a roll. "This was the wrap I found."

She nodded, barely able to speak as the agony gnawed into her hands. "Before you wrap them, could you get the ibuprofen?"

"Sorry, I should have thought of that." His boots pounded as he headed back to the cupboard.

She inhaled and exhaled. She'd been burned before. Tomorrow would be better. And the day after that.

And she had an hour before her wedding consult arrived.

Gray shoved pills into her mouth. Then he tipped a glass to her lips.

"Thanks."

He wrapped each hand as if it were a precious Ming vase. "Let's get you to the car."

"Car?"

"So a doctor can look at your hands."

"They're just burns." She shook her head. "They hurt but they'll heal."

"But they're your hands. This is how you make a living."

They hurt like the devil, but she hadn't seen a blister. "No. I just need to figure out..." She reached up and brushed her hair back. And hit her hand. Tears ran down her cheeks.

Gray brushed her hair away for her. "What do you need?"

"I need..." Help. "Could you close the oven door?"

She started to get up, and Gray was right there, cupping her elbow. Since her legs were a little wobbly, she let him.

"Before you close the door, could you check the liquid level in the pan?" She gave him a little smile. "I do own pot holders."

He pulled the pot out, and they checked the short ribs together. "Do you want to taste? You always taste when you cook."

She nodded.

He stirred and dipped a tasting spoon. Blew on the hot liquid. Then held the spoon to her lips.

She wrapped her lips around the spoon and stared into his eyes. And the memory slammed into her.

They'd eaten ice cream like this. Him feeding her while they were naked in bed.

"Good." She backed away and looked down. "No, wait. It needs more wine."

"I'm your hands. Where's the bottle?"

She pointed. "Give it a good slug."

He poured.

"More."

"No wonder they taste so good."

He grabbed her list. "What's next?"

She looked at the list. Then at Gray. "I need Marion and Cheryl." She swallowed. "And I need your help."

"SHE'S ROCKY RIGHT NOW," Gray said to Marion and Cheryl after explaining what had happened. Josh listened silently. "But she swears she can get through tonight's consults. She asked for our help."

"If that's the case, she must be hurting. Either that or a miracle's occurred," Marion said as they hurried to the kitchen. "Are you sure she shouldn't go to the doctor?"

"I told her I'd take her." Gray hands tightened into fists. Maybe he should have just bundled her into the car.

They stopped at the swinging doors. "Is there anything in housekeeping not done?" Marion asked Cheryl.

Cheryl nodded. "I haven't changed out Gray's towels. And I haven't cleaned the Bush room, but we don't have anyone coming in until Friday."

"My towels can wait." Gray could use the towels for one more day. Hell, for another week if it helped Abby.

"Okay. If we have a walk-in, the Jefferson room is open. If we have two, I'll clean during the wine tasting." Marion straightened her shoulders. "Let's do this."

Gray had the urge to salute.

The foursome entered the kitchen. Abby was sitting at the kitchen table, looking at her to-do list.

Marion hurried over and wrapped an arm around
her shoulders. "How are you?"

Abby leaned her head against Marion. "I'll be fine."

"I'll make you a picture, Miss Abby," Josh said. He
rubbed his arm. "I was burned once."

"Thank you, Josh," Abby said. "It was a stupid accident."

But Gray knew it hadn't really been an accident.
He'd been screaming at her to the point she'd forgotten what she was doing. Every time he tried to help,
she ended up getting hurt both physically and emo-
tionally. It was time to pull away. He couldn't keep
hurting her.

"Everything's ready for the wine tasting." Abby
lifted her hands and inhaled sharply.

"We're your hands," Cheryl said. "All you have to
do is sit."

"Okay. Yeah." She closed her eyes. Took a deep
breath. "Wine tasting first."

She rattled off the appetizers and the wines. Marion
took notes and then started to load up the cart.

Cheryl stood. "What can I do?"

"Test the potatoes gratin." Abby started to stand.
"Then we're going to prep the fish entrees."

Gray helped her out of the chair. "Let me get a
stool."

Abby frowned. "There's one in my apartment
kitchen."

"Be right back." He rushed across the courtyard.
He still had her key. He should give it back.

He'd hoped they could work things out. But it was

time to let Abby go. He had to leave before she for
got how to smile.

By the time he'd set the stool at the counter, Chery
was seasoning the fish. He helped Abby up. "Give m
something to do."

Her pain-filled eyes stared into his. She nodded
"You know where we store the catering dishes?"

"Yes."

She described the dishes she wanted. "We'll serv
family-style, so please grab serving forks and spoons.

He washed his hands and moved back and forth
confirming the selections.

Marion came back in and saw the dishes on a cart
"I'll get the place settings set up in the dining room
Dolley's coming for the wine tasting."

Gray helped Marion set the tables, then went back
into the kitchen. "Next?"

Abby started to push back her hair, but he beat he
to it. "The wine for the wedding consults, I guess."

"You're exhausted," he said. "I could call and cancel."

"They'll be here in fifteen minutes." She shook her
head. "I can get through this."

She winced.

He grabbed ginger ale. "Try this."

He startled her. "How did you know my stomach
was bothering me?"

Because he'd memorized all her facial expressions.
He couldn't tell her that. "I'll get the wines set up."

Somehow they made it through the evening. Cheryl
cooked. Gray and Marion served. While the couples

were sampling the cakes, Gray helped Abby don her chef's jacket and supported her into the dining room. He hung in the background as she talked about menu options and left the couples additional information.

"I forgot about your dinner," Abby said as they walked back to the kitchen.

"I can see what's left in the library." And he'd help Dolley clean up. Guilt was making him too nauseous to eat much.

In the kitchen, Marion and Cheryl were doing dishes while Josh colored.

"Thank you," Abby said. "I couldn't have gotten through tonight without all of you."

She set her head on Gray's shoulder.

"And, Cheryl, you were great," Abby said. "You have a gift for cooking. They raved about your fish. Awesome job."

"I just did what you've taught me." But Cheryl was smiling. "I'll be here in the morning to be your hands for breakfast."

"Oh. Oh. Thank you."

"Go rest," Marion called out. "We've got this covered."

Gray led her out of the kitchen. He would get her settled and then start figuring out how to extricate himself from her life.

ABBY LEANED ON Gray as he helped her back to the carriage house.

"I've got you," he said.

And he did. Gray had her, and she was letting him And her world wasn't crumbling.

He unlocked the door with the key she'd given him all those weeks ago. She'd never asked for it back. Why?

She headed to the bathroom. It was awkward having limited use of her hands. And they ached, really ached. She managed to drop her shorts on the floor.

Back in the bedroom, she asked, "Could you help me with my shirt and bra?"

A spark lit his eyes, and then disappeared. "Sure. Turn around."

He pulled her tank top over her head, then unsnapped her bra. His fingers stroked her shoulders and she shivered.

Not more than a couple of hours ago, they'd yelled hurtful words at each other. Why had they been so cruel?

Gray pulled a T-shirt carefully over her head. He gently tugged her hair out from under the collar and smoothed it down her back. He knelt at her feet and untied her sneakers. His shoulders slumped.

"Gray?"

He glanced up. "I'm so sorry. Sorry I was yelling and you were hurt."

"I'm sorry, too. I said terrible things, but this—" she held up her bandaged hands "—isn't your fault. I grabbed the pan."

He hugged her legs. "I wish I could take the pain away. I would do that for you. I could still take you to the hospital."

"I'll be better in the morning." But she still wouldn't be able to work. Panic bubbled up in her chest. She would have to rely on others. "Could you get me more ibuprofen?"

He swept the decorative pillows off her bed and pulled back the comforter and sheets. She slipped into bed and sank onto her mattress.

After giving her pills and a glass of water, he tucked the sheet around her chin. "Do you want a blanket?"

"No."

He stooped and brushed a kiss on her forehead. "I'll be back with ginger ale and crackers. Try to get some sleep."

He shut the curtains, blocking out the setting sun.

"And let me know about the wine tasting," she murmured, but he was already backing out of her room.

She shut her eyes and let go.

"How's our girl?" Marion asked as Gray entered the kitchen.

"Hurting." Because he'd been yelling at her.

"Cheryl and Josh have headed home." Marion gave the spotless counter one more swipe before hanging up the towel. "Dolley's just cleaning up in the library. I'll be heading home unless you need some dinner."

"I'll see what's left in the library." And hope he could choke it down. It would give him a chance to talk to Dolley.

Marion gave him a hug. "Thank you for taking care of Abby. You're a good man."

He froze. Marion would hate him when she found out he was the reason Abby was hurt.

Dragging his feet, he headed to the library.

Dolley was picking up dirty dishes. "How's Abby?" she called, setting the dishes on a tray.

"Resting." He went over and made himself a small plate of food. "She can't use her hands."

"Poor Abby." Dolley frowned. "Marion didn't ask me to help with breakfast."

"Cheryl's coming in. And I'll be there." He had to make this up to Abby. "It was my fault."

Dolley's frown deepened. "What do you mean—your fault? Marion told me she burned her hands on a pot."

"She did." Gray grimaced. "But it was because I was yelling at her."

Dolley frowned. "I don't think—"

He interrupted. "I need to talk to you about something else."

"What's up?"

He took a deep breath. "You know I bought Carleton House."

Her face went blank. "Yes."

"I'm going to follow the plans that Abby and Samuel drew up. You and your sisters will control the renovations. Then I'll sell you the place."

"What?" Dolley's mouth dropped open.

"We'll work out a contract for the deed, maybe based on your occupancy, something like that." Gray waved his hand. "That way you're not locked into a set payment you can't afford, and you won't have to

qualify for a loan. I know you'll make your payments.
I believe in you."

"Why would you do this?"

"It was always for Abby." He exhaled. Cutting his
ties to Savannah hurt. "I never wanted the property
for myself. Just for Abby."

"But…"

He'd never seen Dolley speechless. He would have
smiled if he had any joy left in him.

"Call your attorney," he said. "He can draft the contract. I'll pay the fee. I don't want you to ever think I
took advantage of your family."

She nodded, her mouth still hanging open. "Does
Abby know any of this?"

He shook his head. "Can we keep it that way?
Please?"

Dolley's eyebrows snapped together. "This isn't
some sort of joke, is it? You're not lulling us into a
stupor, and then you'll take us over?"

"No." The Fitzgeralds all thought he was taking
them over. A weight settled on his chest. "I won't do
anything underhanded."

"Okay." But Dolley still didn't seem entirely convinced.

What had Abby said back in Boston? Actions speak
louder than words. He would make his actions shout
that he cared. "I need to bring Abby some ginger ale
and crackers. Are we good here?"

"We're…good."

"I'll tell my attorney to expect a call. Then I'll get
out of your lives. I promise."

Abby didn't need the pain he'd caused her. It wasn't just her hands. It was the pain he saw in her eyes, the bleakness he'd put there. She was right. He hid behind what his money could do. And that had to change.

Whenever he was around, she didn't smile anymore. He loved her smile. Loved her. She was better off without him.

ABBY ROLLED OVER and pain shot through her right hand. "Oww," she whimpered.

"What happened?" Gray must have been nearby. He hovered over the bed, his hair hanging down on his forehead. "Is it your hand?"

"I rolled on it." She tried to push herself up and he was right there, pulling her gently into a sitting position. "Thanks."

She reached over to turn on the light, but he beat her to it.

"I'm an idiot." Gray grabbed throw pillows from the floor and stacked them up on both sides of her body. "I should have thought of this earlier."

"Thanks." She set her hands on the piles and wiggled into the cushions he'd stacked behind her back. "How are things going?"

"Smoothly." He handed her a glass. "Ginger ale."

She took a sip. Having Gray here felt both right and wrong. He was helping, but refused to look her in the eye. They'd lost their connection.

"Oh, your crackers."

He'd arranged them on a china plate. She'd have eaten them out of the sleeve. "Thanks."

"Dolley's cleaning up the library. Marion and Cheryl cleaned the kitchen." Gray sat next to her on the bed. "Tomorrow, if you let me, I'll be your hands."

"Really?" They would work together in the kitchen.

"Really." The solemn look wasn't leaving his eyes.

"Thank you." How many times could she say that?

"Good, then." He stood. "I'll be back at six."

She settled in, wishing Gray hadn't left her alone, but also glad he had. She was so confused.

"You do this every morning?" Gray asked. His arms were sore from beating muffin batter.

"You should know. You have two or three every day." She raised an eyebrow. "Cheryl, could you fill the muffin tins?"

"Sure." Cheryl took the bowl from Gray. "Bacon's done, too."

"Can I do somethin', Miss Abby?" Josh asked.

"You already did. You greased the muffin tins."

"I want to do more. Mommy said you're still hurt."

Abby grabbed her step stool. "I've got something for you."

Gray snatched the stool out of her hand. "I'm your hands, remember?"

Abby nodded. "Hop up here. Gray will put the coffee beans in the grinder and you can help him make the coffee."

Gray had seen Abby make coffee hundreds of time. He tried to remember the right quantities. Then he showed Josh which button to push.

"I did it." Josh hopped up and down on the stool Gray grabbed him before he got hurt, too.

"Holy cow." Bess walked through the courtyard door. "Nobody told me we were having a party at—" she checked her watch "—six-thirty in the morning."

"Everybody's here," Abby said.

Bess gave Abby a hug. "You okay?"

"Look at all my helpers." Abby set her head on her sister's shoulder. "I'm okay."

"You're actually letting other people cook?" Bess frowned. "In your kitchen?"

Apparently Gray wasn't the only one who knew he'd ruined Abby's week.

Abby elbowed her sister. "It's kind of…fun."

Just one more thing he loved about Abby. She could turn a disaster into a party.

"What can I do?" Bess asked.

Abby looked around. "Finish cutting fruit. Then we're done."

Bess washed up.

Abby came over to him. "Thank you for everything. I think I have enough help now."

"Will you be okay?" he asked. "Today?"

She held up her left hand. That burn wasn't as bad as the one on her right. "I'll be able to work with one hand with Cheryl's help."

He pulled her into a hug. He couldn't stop himself. "I need to get back to Boston."

She stood in his embrace. Finally, her arms wrapped around his waist.

Was this the last time he would hug her?

"When you get back, we should talk," she said.

He wasn't looking forward to that conversation. It was time to make a clean break. "Of course."

CHAPTER SIXTEEN

Rule #15—Fitzgerald House is important, but family is everything.

Abigail Fitzgerald

GRAY YANKED OFF his tie and threw it on his attorney's conference room table. He'd been back in Boston for two days. If he had to have another lunch with potential partners he would rip out his hair.

He'd rather be with Abby, but every time he called she sounded fine. Somehow she'd turned the corner on letting people help her. All it had taken was burning her hands.

Phillips looked up from the document he was reviewing. "Did Fredrick agree with the terms?"

"Finally." Gray moved to the coffeepot and poured a cup.

The project was coming together. He could almost taste success, so why did it taste so damn bitter?

Jacob, Gray's attorney, bustled into the room waving a sheath of paper. "We've got Fredrick's agreement."

"That was fast." Phillips tipped back in his chair.

"I told him the deadline was three o'clock." Gray leaned forward. "Let's get this bid finalized. I'm heading back to Savannah."

Back to tell Abby he would be returning to Boston for good.

The three-page document he signed didn't reflect the money and time he'd already poured into this project. He had to get the Whaler just to keep his mind off everything he'd be giving up when he left Savannah.

Jacob's assistant faxed the offer and handed everyone a copy of the confirmation.

They talked about next steps until Jacob's phone beeped. "The courier's delivered the originals."

Gray nodded.

"Now we wait," Jacob said.

Phillips slapped his hands on the tabletop. "Good luck." He shook Gray's hand. "Can't wait to start work on that warehouse."

"Thanks for everything." Gray started to gather up his files and stuff them into his briefcase.

"Got a minute?" Jacob asked.

Gray checked the time and sat back down at the table. He still needed to pack. "Fifteen."

"I got a call from the Fitzgeralds' attorney."

"Good."

"Are you sure this is what you want to do?" Jacob pinched his lips together, then blurted out, "Have you lost your mind?"

Gray gave a tiny smile. "I messed up her life. I need to make it up to her and her family."

"Her?"

"Abby." His throat tightened around her name, as if it wanted to hold her in.

"That's the oldest one, right?"

"Yeah."

"You could earn more on your investment if you put the money in Certificates of Deposits and they pay nothing." Jacob paced the conference room. "I'm not your accountant, but between this and that mortgage you took on, I have to say you're making terrible investment decisions."

"These are the best investments I've ever made." Gray believed that more strongly than he'd ever believed anything.

"You're earning next to nothing on these properties." Jacob held up his hand.

"It doesn't matter. I want to help the family succeed."

"I strongly advise against the contract for deed."

"I hear you." But Gray wasn't about to change his mind. He was finally doing something right. "Keep the terms as I dictated."

"You're crazy." Jacob shook his head. "You've changed since you were in Savannah."

"God, I hope so."

He hoped he was a better person for knowing Abby. He hoped he'd learned how to be a better son to his parents, a better brother to his sister. Hoped he'd learned that his money didn't solve problems. Then he might be a better person someday.

Those lessons had only cost him Abby.

ABBY ENTERED INVOICES one-handed. Slow, but over the past two days she'd almost caught up with all the data entry for the month. No one was letting her work in her own kitchen.

Footsteps in the hall had her looking toward the doorway.

"Samuel." It was good to see him back working on the third floor, at least for a few days.

"Hey, Abby. Sorry about your hands." He leaned against the door frame.

She flexed her left hand. "They're healing."

"Just be more careful. Who will cook my anniversary dinner if you're hurt?"

"I'd figure out a way." She leaned back in her chair. "Did you need something? Cheryl left sandwiches in the kitchen for you and the crew, right?"

"We polished those off, thanks." He shook his head. "I wanted to know who's been upstairs."

"On three?"

He nodded.

She shook her head. "No one."

Samuel scratched his chin. "You need to come and see this."

Abby didn't ask questions. She followed Samuel up the stairs, dreading what she would find. Did they have more water damage? Had some animal gotten in?

Samuel pointed into the Lady Bird Johnson room.

"It's almost done." She smiled at him. The last time she'd checked, the bathrooms had only been framed in. Now the drywall was hung.

He frowned. "My team didn't do this. I checked with Nigel. He hasn't been up here working."

He led her into every room, showing her more work that his team hadn't done.

"It has to be your crew." Abby tapped her fingernail against her lip. "No one else has a key."

He opened the door to the Lincoln room. All the plaster was off the ceiling and walls. New drywall had been hung on half the walls. The room had potential. "We didn't do any of this. And the Dumpster's full. Someone's put in a lot of hours up here."

"Was it Daniel?" She leaned against the hallway wall, a little light-headed.

"No. I checked with him."

Gray. She inhaled. How many nights had he come to dinner with dust in his hair? And then left without his normal cognac, saying he'd be down later. Her heart beat a little too fast. For weeks he'd been working on her B and B. He'd done this after she'd broken up with him. "I think I know who it was."

"We'll frame in the bathroom here and finish the drywall. But we can get the tapers in this week. I was worried we were behind schedule, but your guardian angel kept us on track."

Guardian angel. She headed back down the stairs. Was that what Gray was?

She leaned back in her desk chair. Gray had been working on Fitzgerald House—and never told her.

She pushed her hair off her face with the back of one hand. Why had he helped her? He'd put in hours of work. Why had he kept it a secret?

Because she would have thrown his help back in

his face. Made him stop. She dropped her head to the back of her chair.

Gray was right. She didn't know how to ask people for help. She couldn't even accept it when it was offered.

He'd been right about so many things. They were never going to get Carleton House. She'd used the offer he'd made on the property to push Gray away—because she'd fallen in love with him.

She stared at the ceiling. She'd pushed Gray away because she'd expected he'd hurt her.

And he'd been secretly working on Fitzgerald House.

Actions speak louder than words. How many times had she thrown that phrase in his face?

He really did love her. And she kept pushing him away, insisting he was hiding behind his money.

Her stomach twisted. She'd been awful to him, judging him based on her father and Maurice.

She'd thrown hateful words at him, but she'd been the one who'd been hiding. Hiding because she'd assumed he would hurt her.

Her lips trembled. She didn't want to lose Gray. She wanted to go back to the moment when he'd said he might be in love with her. She wanted to throw her arms around him and tell him she was absolutely in love with him.

Could they find their way back to each other?

"Hey, Abs." Bess and Dolley filled her office doorway.

She checked the time. Three o'clock. "Shouldn't you two be working?"

"We need to talk." Dolley's usually animated face was stern.

Since Abby's office didn't have guest chairs, they moved into the kitchen. Bess brewed a pot of tea, and Dolley piled a stack of pillows under her right hand.

"How are you?" Bess asked, sitting next to her on the love seat.

Abby flexed her fingers and winced. "Healing."

"Not quickly enough for you." Bess rubbed her back, her touch as soothing as the tea she'd brewed. "I looked for healing herbal teas I could make you, but couldn't find much. Everything was a topical application. I brought you some chamomile tea to help you sleep."

"Thanks."

Dolley turned away from the window. "Have you talked to Gray?"

Abby's body warmed at his name. "Last I knew, he was still in Boston." Her sisters stared at each other. Bess nodded to Dolley.

A chill zipped through Abby. "What?"

Bess touched her shoulder. "Has he talked to you about Carleton House?"

The chill settled like ice in her stomach. "No." She shook her head. "I must have been dreaming when I thought we could get the property."

"With Lennertz in charge, we didn't have a chance," Dolley said.

"Have you heard something about Gray's plans?" Abby asked.

Dolley nodded. Her uncharacteristic quiet made Abby lean into Bess's shoulder for support.

"He's going ahead with the renovations you and Samuel developed," Dolley said.

"He's going into the B and B business?" Dolley couldn't have heard this right. Gray wouldn't do this to them, to her. Not when she'd started to believe in him. "I don't believe you."

"He's not going to run a B and B." Dolley shook her head. "He's making all the investments, all the improvements. Then he's offered to sell us the house. On our terms. As a contract for deed."

"What?" She grinned. "He's a wonderful, foolish man."

Bess turned and looked Abby in the eyes. "There's more."

Abby looked between her two sisters. More? The only way she could be happier was if Gray planned to stay in Savannah. She couldn't picture living her days without Gray by her side.

"His car is out front. He's packing." Dolley's voice was too solemn. "A couple of days ago, he told me he has to leave so he'll never hurt you again."

"Leave?" Her hands started to shake.

Dolley nodded.

Abby sank into the love seat. He couldn't leave her. Not after letting her fall in love with him—forcing her to face her faults. Abby straightened her shoulders. She'd show her damn conniving Yankee he couldn't make her fall in love with him and then just walk away.

GRAY SEALED THE box he'd packed. How had h
acquired so much stuff in a few months?

He lined up the condo folders in another box an
then added the Carleton House files. He needed to tal
to the Foresters and have them develop official blue
prints and a bid. Then he'd have the Foresters mee
with the Fitzgeralds.

He could do all this remotely, because seeing Abb
and not being able to touch her would kill him.

He moved into the bedroom and emptied th
dresser, stuffing clothes into his open suitcase. H
needed to finish this and get out.

His fingers caught something stuffed in the bac
of the drawer. He pulled it out. Purple. Soft. Abby'
scarf. He sank to the bed and raised the cloth to hi
nose, wanting to capture Abby's scent one last time

He inhaled, drawing in her spicy, citrusy fragranc
He rubbed the silky fabric on his cheek. Then h
folded the scarf and tucked it carefully into his brie
case.

There was a pounding at his door. Five shar
smacks. Then five more.

He frowned. No one knew he was here.

The pounding started again, and he yanked ope
the door.

Abby. His chest ached at the sight of her, fist raisec
face stern in concentration.

She pushed past him. Stopping, she stared at th
boxes. He followed her gaze to the bedroom, wher
his suitcase was half filled.

Her shoulders straightened, and she spun arounc

etting her hands on her hips. The thick bandage on er right hand gleamed against her blue shirt. "Do ou think you can leave?"

"I…" What kind of question was that? "I need to eave."

"Oh, no, you don't." She stepped close and elbowed is side. "You have a contract until the end of July."

"I planned on paying in full." Her words hurt more han the little poke she'd given him.

"Oh, no, you don't, Yankee." Green flames sparked her eyes. "You are not just up and leaving me."

Leaving her? That didn't make any sense. "I can't tay. I can't keep hurting you."

"If you go north, who's going to supervise the reno-ations on Carleton House?" Her lips pressed together. I don't have time. My sisters don't have time."

Abby knew about Carleton House. Knew about the eal he planned to make. "Dolley wasn't supposed to ell you."

"Give me a break." She rolled her eyes. "She's my ister."

He raised and dropped his hands. "The Foresters vill make sure everything meets your specifications. ou'll get your expansion."

"I don't want it." She stepped in closer and tipped er face up to his. "Not without you."

His mouth dropped open. She didn't… She ouldn't…

She reached up and touched his cheek. "Not with-ut you," she repeated.

"What do you mean?" His voice cracked.

She walked away from him. "I always thought tha what I needed to feel whole, to be a success, was t open Southern Comforts. People would know hov great a chef I was. I'd be able to hold my head u high."

"You're a fantastic chef. You're better than far tastic."

She turned, a smile lighting her face. "Thank yo But you taught me something more important."

His heart thumped in his chest. "What on eart could I teach you?"

She moved back and touched his face with her goo hand. "That loving someone means more than an starred reviews or even the expansion of my busines Loving you is more…" Her eyes shimmered. "It just…more. More important, more fulfilling. *More*.

Was this real? "You love me?"

She nodded.

Gray pulled her into his arms. Hope fluttered lik a fire just starting to catch hold. "I love you, Abby.

Her arms squeezed him hard. "I was hoping you tell me again. Last time I was—rude." She looke into his eyes. "I love you so much."

He swept the sofa clear, pulling her onto his lap Hope blazed in a glorious flame now. "I never though I'd hear you say those words."

Gray captured her face and raised his mouth t hers. He brushed kisses on her eyes, her cheeks an the corners of her mouth.

"I've missed you, missed us." Abby twined he arms around his neck.

Her mouth was sweet as her tongue mated with his. The pressure of her breasts against him was heavenly. Nothing mattered more than this woman curled in his arms.

"I assumed I'd lost you forever," he breathed into her hair. "But you're wrong. You're the one who's taught me."

"What did I teach you?"

"How to share myself with the people I love." He pressed another kiss against her tempting lips. "You showed me how to be part of a family. How to love, truly love someone without expecting—payment. You were right. I was hiding behind my money."

"You're more than your money," she protested.

"I wasn't. Not before you."

"You're wrong." She pulled away and looked him in the eye. "Who did all the work on the third floor? Who helped get us out from under an oppressive mortgage?"

He started to shake his head.

She held up her injured hand. "Who taught me how to accept help and stop pushing people away? Who made sure Cheryl and Josh had a place to live? Who bought Carleton House when we couldn't?"

He grinned. "I guess—me?"

"Yes, you, you crazy Yankee."

He brushed his knuckles along her soft cheek. Then pressed his lips to the same spot. "I think you're going to have to marry me, Abby."

Her eyes sparkled. "I think I might just have to do that."

"Is that a yes?" His heart pounded like a drum. He'
started the day resigned to giving Abby up. Now h
might have a lifetime to prove how much he loved he

"That's a yes." Joy bubbled in Abby's voice.

He kissed her until they were both breathless. Pul
ing away, he cupped her face. "There's more that I'v
learned from you, Abby. You taught me that love i
unselfish. You taught me love is giving. And you an
your sisters taught me that a family works togethe
That's what I want. I want to be part of your family

She stroked his face. Her green eyes glowed. "The
we'll do this together, as a family."

EPILOGUE

Rule # 4—This is our guests' home away from home.

Abigail Fitzgerald

November

ABBY STEPPED INTO the foyer. The scent of pine and cinnamon saturated the air.

Cheryl nestled a poinsettia dusted with gold glitter into the mass of other poinsettias.

"It looks lovely," Abby said.

"It's fun setting up for Christmas." Cheryl brushed a petal. "I can't imagine how many hours Bess has put into decorating the house."

"She loves it." The sisters had spent the past couple of nights getting trees up and the decorations on. Then Bess had rearranged most of the ornaments to her specifications.

The door opened and Josh burst through. "Mom! Miss Abby!"

"Walk," Cheryl warned.

Josh slowed down and looked at the arrangement his mother had just finished. "That's pretty."

Abby smiled. Josh was so happy now. It was nice

that the bus could drop him off at Fitzgerald House.
"How was school?"

"My picture of Reggie is going to be in the Christmas art show!"

"That's wonderful. I think that deserves a cookie." She looked over at Cheryl. "If your mother approves."

"Mom?" Josh's big brown eyes took on a pleading look.

"One."

"I left a tin on the counter for you," Abby said.

"Thanks, Miss Abby." He ran over and hugged her around the legs.

"Grab your cookie and we'll go home." Cheryl ruffled her son's hair as they headed down the hall.

What a difference nine months had made. Abby smiled as she headed to the desk and opened the registration system.

The front door opened. "Welcome to Fitzgerald House. How can I…"

Gray walked in, a garment bag over his shoulder. His grin lit the room. "I'm looking for a room, innkeeper."

She grinned right back at him. "Do you have a reservation?"

"Check under Smythe." His bourbon-infused baritone no longer sounded quite so Yankee to her.

She pretended to search. "I'm sorry, sir, I don't have a reservation under that name."

He draped the bag over the desktop. "Try Gray or Grayson."

Her fingers clacked on the keyboard. "No. Nothing. Perhaps you have your confirmation number?"

He came behind the desk and pulled her into a hug. "Try fiancé."

"Aah, there it is." She stood on her toes and kissed him.

His scent of wood and pine was like coming home. Everything melted inside her.

"Hey, you two—get a room," Dolley called, walking in the front door.

Gray pulled away and brushed a kiss on Abby's nose. "I'm negotiating the rate right now."

"Gwaaack. Get out of here." Dolley pointed a finger at the two of them as she headed to the library. "Glad you made it home, Gray."

Home. Gray was home.

"How was Boston?" Abby asked.

"Lonely." He kissed her again.

Arm in arm, they walked back to the kitchen. "I was lonely, too," she confessed.

"What's with all the Christmas decorations? It's not even Thanksgiving."

"Be glad you didn't have to help decorate the fifteen trees we put up. How is the Whaler?" She'd been thrilled when he'd gotten the project.

"Not too many problems. I won't have to go back for two more weeks."

She squeezed his waist. "Thank goodness."

He'd been going back to Boston every other week. Then when he was in Savannah, he'd switch gears

and work on Carleton House. "Two weeks sounds li[k]
heaven. I have wedding tasks for you."

He groaned. "But you're the expert."

"Oh, no, you don't." She tried to tickle him, but [h]
wiggled away. "I'm not making every decision."

"But you're the best. Let me do what I do best–
planning the wedding night and honeymoon." H[e]
pushed open the kitchen door and caged her again[st]
the wall. "Did I tell you I missed you?"

He didn't let her answer. His body pressed again[st]
hers, her legs weakening as his kiss stole her breat[h]

He pulled away, resting his forehead on hers. "I'[m]
so happy."

She sighed. "Me, too."

He leaned back down, but then sniffed. A smi[le]
made his dimple shine. "Brandy-pecan bars. Yo[u]
made me bars."

She cupped his face. "I believe the offer I made w[as]
to make you bars for a lifetime."

He kissed her, deep and sweet. "A lifetime may n[ot]
be long enough."

* * * * *